Last Act
in
Urbino

Last Act in Urbino

Paolo Volponi

Translated from the Italian
with an Introduction by
Peter N. Pedroni

ITALICA PRESS
NEW YORK
1995

ITALICA PRESS, INC.
595 Main Street
New York, New York 10044

Acknowledgements: P: 77: *A Leopardi Reader,* trans. by Ottavio M. Casale (Urbana, Il: Univ. of Illinois Press, 1981), p. 173; P. 109: *The Divine Comedy – Purgatorio – A Verse Translation* by Allen Mandelbaum (New York: Bantam, 1984), V: 119–120, 128–129, p. 44.

Library of Congress Cataloging-in-Publication Data
Volponi, Paolo.
    [Sipario ducale. English]
    Last act in Urbino / Paolo Volponi ; translated from the
Italian with an introduction by Peter N. Pedroni.
        p. cm.
    ISBN 0-934977-33-X : $14.95
    I. Pedroni, Peter N., 1938- . II. Title.
PQ4882.O4S513 1994
853'.914—dc20   88-81096
                                                       CIP

Printed in the United States of America
5 4 3 2 1

Cover photo: Ronald G. Musto

ABOUT THE TRANSLATOR

Peter N. Pedroni, a native of New Haven, Connecticut, is a professor of Italian at Miami University in Oxford, Ohio, and director of the Miami University Summer Language Institute in Italy (Urbino). He has studied at the University of Florence and has academic degrees from Yale University, Middlebury College, and Rutgers University. He is the author of *Existence as Theme in Carlo Cassola's Fiction* (New York: Peter Lang, 1985) and *The Anti-Naturalist Experience: Federigo Tozzi* (Tallahassee: De Soto Press, 1989) as well as several articles on, interviews with, and translations of, Italian writers of the twentieth century.

Author's Dedication
to
Guido Piovene

INTRODUCTION

When Paolo Volponi (1924-1994) won the Premio Strega in 1991 for his novel, *La Strada per Roma* (the road to Rome), he distinguished himself as the first person ever to win Italy's most prestigious literary prize twice, having won it for the first time in 1965 for *La macchina mondiale* (*The Worldwide Machine*). In all he published eight novels and five volumes of poetry. His first poetry was published in 1946 and earned him the praise of Italy's most important poets such as Giuseppe Ungaretti and Nobel Prize winner Eugenio Montale, as well as the life-long friendship of the then up-and-coming poet, novelist, and movie director Pier Paolo Pasolini with whom he shared a poetry prize in 1955. He won critical acclaim and international recognition in 1962 with his first novel entitled *Memoriale (My Troubles Began),* inspired by the problems of disorientation experienced by country people who, during Italy's economic miracle period, were being attracted to work in the factories of the big cities.

But Volponi was certainly not a passive observer of society. On the contrary, for over twenty years, at the same time that he was writing poetry and novels, he was highly involved in the world of Italian industry. In 1950 he was hired by Adriano Olivetti of the well known office-machine company and by 1966 he had risen to the position of director of human resources for the entire Olivetti company. In this capacity he devoted his immense energy to improving working conditions in the factory and preserving the individual dignity and human spirit of workers required to spend their days on the assembly line. In 1971, under pressure because of his leftist political views and feeling that he had accomplished all that he could, he resigned from Olivetti, held another important position at Fiat for two years, and then withdrew altogether from industry to become an art consultant for a company in Milan. He was also active in journalism with Italy's leading newspapers and was among the founders of the literary journal *Alfabeta.*

Volponi was born in Urbino in 1924 and divided his time between Milan, Rome, and Urbino where he returned often to the house in which he was born. He completed his entire education in Urbino from kindergarten through his university degree in law which he received in 1947. He refused to fight on the Fascist side during World War II and was thus forced to live clandestinely for a period of time in the Apennine Mountains. He returned to Urbino on August 28, 1944 with the first Allied forces. In 1981 he decided to take a more active role in the political life of his country, and in 1983 he was elected to the Italian Senate. He was re-elected to the Senate in 1987 and in 1992 to the Chamber of Deputies, from which he resigned for health reasons in January 1993.

In one of his early poems Volponi, referring to the city of his birth, wrote:

> The hostile figure that remains for me,
> the image of Urbino
> that I cannot flee,
> her cruel celebration,
> tranquil amidst my anger.
>
> This I would have to leave
> if I had the courage
> to let my precious
> wounds heal.[1]

The abundant contradictions expressed in these verses (cruel – celebration, tranquil – anger, precious – wounds) are suggestive of the psychological conflict that characterizes Volponi's life and literature. Central to this poetic statement is the verb "flee" and the inability to flee from Urbino. But the obstacle to leaving is not external but rather internal. What is lacking is the courage to leave that which is familiar and secure albeit painful.

Fleeing from Urbino means fleeing to exile, but staying in Urbino means being exiled from the possibility of poetic self-fulfillment. So it is that Volponi's protagonists are typically drawn between the familiar and the secure on the one hand and the challenge of exile on the other. In *My Troubles Began,* the protagonist Albino Saluggia gives up his familiar rural life-style to seek the perceived advantages of work in a big-city factory, only to be bitterly disappointed by the highly efficient but dehumanizing structure of the factory, which, contrary to his expectations, does not provide a new kind of community atmosphere in which he can live, nor does it give him the opportunity for greater self-fulfillment.

Here the factory is a metaphor for today's highly efficient, capitalist, and centralized society to which, like Saluggia, the world's small-town and rural populations have been steadily migrating, with similar disillusioning consequences. The problem is paradoxical.

It is in the nature of human beings to struggle for the improvement of the conditions in which they live, and, given the necessity of coexistence, to struggle for a perfect organization of society. However, the closer society comes to perfection, the less individual initiative is tolerated and the less it is possible to satisfy the quest for self-fulfillment. Furthermore there appears to be a kind of unstated natural law expressed in Volponi's work that punishes those that abandon their Urbinos. In the final chapter of *Il sipario ducale* (*Last Act in Urbino*) when some shots are heard in the nearby hills, the protagonist Subissoni explains that they are "Old shots at those who want to go away, at those who pass by, at those who don't want to die with them, at those who are alive and that therefore are a threat against their lives."

One must be very courageous or perhaps a little crazy to leave. In fact, Saluggia is a neurasthenic and almost all of Volponi's protagonists are at least atypical and outside the mainstream of society. Thus Anteo Crocioni of *The Worldwide Machine* is a rebellious farmer-philosopher who is alienated from both traditional rural society and from bureaucratic Rome; and Gerolamo Aspri of *Corporale* (Corporal) is an ex-industrial manager who is alienated from bourgeois society. Volponi chose outsiders as protagonists because by nature they are social rebels; to use Volponi's own words, "because I consider them more suffering, and therefore more sensitive recorders of the burden of unhappiness that shakes the earth, more capable of inquiry, of reaction, of introspection, than normal people, a kind of magnifying glass for focusing on certain problems. The atypical is also a rebel, outside of the norm."[2] By extension, if "norm" is substituted for Urbino, then exile can also mean away from or outside of what is considered normal.

In this sense Anteo Crocioni is clearly an exile. Whether he goes to Rome or stays in the hills he is considered abnormal by those around him and thus he is effectively exiled from society. Like Saluggia, Crocioni is motivated by the quest for self-fulfillment, which he attempts to express through a treatise that theorizes that man as we know him today was generated by a less perfect machine and is thus capable of generating an infinitely better machine. Frustrated by his failure to find anyone who will take his treatise seriously, he chooses total exile through suicide.

Volponi's protagonists are autobiographical in the sense that he used them as vehicles to express objectively his own ideas. But in *La strada per Roma*, *Le mosche del capitale* (The Flies of Capital), and *Corporale* the protagonist's story is more closely identifiable with Volponi's life. Gerolomo Aspri of *Corporale* is effectively exiled from the society of upper level management. The various ills of the oppressive society from which he is fleeing are summed up in the atomic bomb and according to his calculations, the Urbino countryside is sufficiently distant from all industrial and strategic centers to be relatively safe from the immediate effects of an atomic explosion. In his effort to survive he intends to go further into exile by constructing a personal bomb shelter in the mountains. The atomic explosion seems to suggest a possible purification of society in which the exiled survivors could live in great hardship, but free to manifest their uniqueness.

Il Pianeta irritabile (The Irritable Planet) is, in this sense, a continuation of *Corporale*. The four protagonists, a baboon, a talking elephant, a trained goose, and a human dwarf, are survivors of an atomic explosion in the year 2293 that almost destroys the earth. All four belonged to a circus. The three animals were performers while the man had the job of cleaning up the animal excrements during the performances. This humiliating task is similar to that performed by Crocioni when he was employed by a circus in Rome. This and references in *Last Act in Urbino* to some circus animals that die in the cold of the Apennine and Pyrenean winters are reminders that for Volponi the circus was a symbol of captivity, humiliation, and degradation. The "universal circus" of *Last Act in Urbino* is a metaphor of Western society.

Like all of Volponi's protagonists, the human dwarf is driven by the quest for self-fulfillment, which is impossible within a self-satisfied society, but he is held back by his nostalgic attachment to the familiarity and security of that society. Exile, whether forced or voluntary, is not sufficient. Only complete freedom from society allows for complete self-fulfillment. Freedom from the norms of society can be expressed through abnormality. Intellectual freedom can be expressed through idiosyncrasies. For the writer, this freedom may be manifested through the freedom of verbal expression.

Volponi considered *Corporale* his maximum effort at the freedom of verbal expression and his most important novel. That is why he was disappointed, not to say embittered, by what he considered the rather cold reaction of most Italian critics who generally considered it too egocentric and inaccessible.

After taking nine years to write *Corporale*, Volponi followed in less than one year with *Last Act in Urbino*. In response to an interview question he said, "I wrote *Il sipario ducale* between '74 and '75, in less than a year, in reaction to the rather cold reception of *Corporale* on the part of the critics. I wrote it as if to say: You want a simple novel? a novel as novel? Well here it is all ready."[3] Clearly Volponi was influenced by his critical reading public and, taking him at his word, wrote *Last Act in Urbino* in reaction to it. But more important than the reason for doing so is the satirical tone in which he expressed himself. It is not difficult to understand the very human reaction of the author, who after pouring everything into what he considered his most important work, saw that work dismissed for inaccessibility. It is in this same satirical frame of mind that he wrote *Last Act in Urbino*. It was as though he were saying: "Well, if you literary critics are too dull and insensitive to understand and appreciate a really new and original work of art, I'll knock out something traditional and neat for you in very short order." In fact the author makes an occasional appearance in the novel seemingly to remind his critics that they are being led about by the hand. Here is an example that Enrico Baldise reprinted in his *Invito alla lettura di Volponi* (Invitation to a Reading of Volponi): "These pages, as the reader has probably noticed, reflect the admiration of the author for Prof. Subissoni and for his ideas...."[4] Here is an even better example of the author's satirical concern about his critics' ability to follow the story: "...during the trip home he designed another plan, the application of which we will see point by point further ahead." These direct communications between the writer and his readers are expressed either in the impersonal third person (the reader) or in the ironic unification of the first person plural, but also in the more direct and blunt second person (if you want, excuse me). And Volponi's satirical attitude is not limited to the occasional appearance of the author-narrator, but rather characterizes the entire novel, distinguishing it clearly from his previous novels and making it the delightful novel that it is.

Regardless of what Volponi's intentions might have been, *Last Act in Urbino* is neither simple nor traditional in any negative sense. Certainly it is relatively rich in plot development, pathos, suspense, cause and effect, and in the definition of time and place. But to read the novel only at that level is to miss its real artistic value. The novel's perfect chronological sequence during a very specific historical time period becomes obvious. At least a dozen times the author tells his readers the date and sometimes even the time of day. At first we find this gratifying, then annoying, and finally we sense the sarcasm of Volponi saying in effect, "Did you have trouble keeping track of time in *Corporale*? Well, we'll take care of that." Urbinoites and Urbinophiles cannot help but notice the precision of the abundant references to exact locations in Urbino where most of the novel takes place. One is tempted to follow Subissoni, with street map in hand, as he turns a corner or walks up a hill. But the author's irony is quickly apparent. Large parts of *The Worldwide Machine* and *Corporale* also took place in and around Urbino, but Urbino was depicted there with the eye of the artist rather than with the eye of the photographer. In those novels Volponi gave us paintings and sketches. In *Last Act in Urbino*, lest his critics should feel uneasy about where they are, he gave them photographs. The presence of the satirical author-narrator is so strong as to be at least as important as that of the characters whose lives he is describing. Even when he does not clearly announce his presence, as in the preceding examples, he is nevertheless always there at the edge of the scene, actively interpreting everything for us through his satirical point of view. For example, in the following paragraph the observation is not Oddo's; it is the narrator's: "Oddo remained in the piazza until two o'clock on that half workday, moving toward the confluence of the Monte, of Lavagine and of Valbona to see the arrival of undulating squadrons of country people and the very hurried faces of the more restless townspeople who had already consumed a meal with their families and who, having bid them good-bye with a grunt, were heading with their maximum sporting zeal toward the rummy and poker tables of the welcoming and charitable civic clubroom."

Oddo is the last male descendant of a local aristocratic family whose exploits the narrator describes in a mock heroic style reminiscent of the chivalric poems of the early Italian Renaissance. Speaking of a certain Oddantonio, lord of Urbino, he tells us that, "...he lost his dominion because the populace rose up against his taxes and his wastefulness and slew him, just an eighteen year old, in 1444, flushing him out and already mortally wounding him there, under his bed." The heroic dimension of our present day Oddo, or Oddino, is even more sarcastic, as in the following description: "Oddino came down in his bathrobe and put an end to those discussions. He sat at the head of the table and waited for his bowl of barley to be followed by his cup of hot chocolate."

When describing Giocondini, a rather slimy and devious taxi driver frequently employed by Oddo, the narrator uses a style more reminiscent of the long and intricate, yet rhythmic and symmetrical sentences of Giovanni Boccaccio's *Decameron*, as in this passage:

> Giocondini too, driven by the same power of suggestion that vividly captured the truth of his corporal condition and relative position on the seat, betraying the greatest degree of his incontinence, noted with relief those shrubs and directed himself toward them while saying that he would see what views might open up beyond there or find someone whom he might ask. He came back smiling and everyone understood what it was that he had found and how he had rapidly made arrangements inasmuch as he was bouncing along and rubbing the tips of the three fingers that are generally most used, and also most displayed and also imposed in benedictions and indeed in aspersions.

Even Subissoni, the elderly anarchist, federalist, unemployed professor, in whom Volponi portrayed some of his own idiosyncrasies and through whom he expressed some of his political ideology, is treated satirically, albeit with much empathy. The narrator refers to Don Quixote in connection with Subissoni, but in his contemporary and humble surroundings he is more of a Chaplinesque character. Here is an example: Realizing that Vivés is seriously ill:

> Subissoni was frightened; he got up so as not to show it too much and started dealing with the espresso maker: he unscrewed it and noticed that it was already prepared, at least its filter was filled with coffee; he shook it to hear if there was water in the bottom and let it slip out of his hand: the coffee fell on his shoes, the water that filled the bottom part to the proper level splashed on his shirt sleeves and his pants.
>
> "Look what I've become," he muttered, "I'm pissing on myself and my shoes."...
>
> He tried to gather up the coffee piled on his shoes, but in his anger ended up spreading it all over, puffing and shaking like a fan.

Of the principal characters only Vivés, the Spanish anarchist with whom Subissoni shares his life, is portrayed without satire, and it is through her that the author more seriously presented his political message, which is that Italy's problems are a result of having had a politically unified state forced upon it by the House of

Savoy, when a federation of republics would have been preferable. In Vivés' words: "The unification of any country under any external authoritarian or unreachable power – as in the democracies with a central parliament – is always an obstacle to the freedom of common people"; or in Subissoni's words: "Cultural unification, and then linguistic and then so many republics: that's the way the best ones thought about it, even Manzoni and Leopardi. A united nation is always the possession of somebody." But Subissoni's satirical attitude extends to heroes – he describes Cavour as "a small ignoramus with some French stuffing," Mazzini as "presumptuous," and the Carbonari as "that herd of rich kids and loafers" – and to cities – "The city of Fano has always been against the Duchy of Urbino and in more recent times always in favor of Italian unity, of the Savoyard monarchy... and is so miserable that every year it sets up a carnival celebration with a costume parade and with lots of throwing of chalk confetti: and then every summer it repeats the same celebration, with the same floats, with the same papier-mâché caricatures and with the same confetti."

This image of a staged carnival celebration relates to the metaphorical title of the novel, which in turn is an expression of the author's satirical attitude. *Sipario* in the original title is a theater curtain and *ducale* (ducal) refers to the ex-duchy of Urbino. Subissoni perceives Urbino as a theater; the theater in which he seems destined to play out the rest of his life. Theatrical terms in reference to Urbino occur throughout the novel, as in "the side-wing of the Ducal Palace." The piazza is referred to as "that wingless stage." When Subissoni is angry he refers to Urbino as "this miserable little theater of very bad actors." But the theater image is not necessarily a negative one. On the contrary, Subissoni expresses the concept of life as the opportunity to act, as in action. Each person must choose the stage, that is the place, on which to act and the scene, that is the situation, in which to act, as he explains to Vivés: "You shouldn't have left Mera, and I should have stayed in Urbino and blown up the Fascist headquarters. The hell with going to be actors on the stage of history. Every man carries his own scene with him."

There are worthy theaters and worthless theaters, as in the case of Oddo who enjoys the "freedom to stand over his little theater, always like the omnipotent one that pulls the strings and moves each scene and actor." But the real problem is that Urbino itself has become a worthless or non-functioning theater, as symbolized by the fact that its theater, in the literal sense, was closed and non-functioning. And this is a result of the centralization that comes from unification and more directly, it is a result of the centrally-controlled mass media. In a word, television, the theater of the unitarian state, has replaced the local theater. Urbino is connected to the real world by television. Urbinoites are no longer players in their own theater, but only distant spectators of a distorted representation of a centralized play. Oddo, who should be the protagonist of a local play, is instead a TV addict who can't miss *Carosello*. But even Subissoni and Vivés are reduced to viewing the world through a television screen supplemented by centrally produced newspapers. The bombing of a bank in Milan makes Vivés think that in order to participate in real life, to act in a worthy theater, she must leave Urbino and go to Milan.

Vivés was herself a translator and must have understood the awesome sense of responsibility inherent in the act of translation. Whoever reads *Last Act in Urbino* will be reading Volponi through my translation and therefore will be dependent on my reading of Volponi. It must be recognized that a dialogue exists between writer and reader, that a reader may not necessarily read the way a writer intends to be read, and that different readers may read the writer in different ways. In effect a translator must attempt to suppress his or her subjective readership and attempt to read as the writer wishes to be read, a difficult task at best, especially when the reader reads the writer with the enthusiasm that I have read Volponi.

My first recollection of Volponi is from 1975 when, in Piazza della Repubblica in Urbino, a colleague pointed him out to me as a successful local writer. He had the appearance of a very likable person who talked with everybody and who seemed completely immersed in his environment. His fourth novel, *Last Act in Urbino*, had just come out and so I hastened to read it. As a summer resident of Urbino and an Urbinophile, I quickly fell in love with this delightful book. Subsequently I went on to read all of Volponi, first his novels and then his poetry, to study them and to write about them. My reward has been my acquaintance with the man, first through his work and then personally. He was a man filled with humanity, energy, and the desire for the freedom that can lead to self-fulfillment.

INTRODUCTION

In the summer of 1989, in the same Piazza della Repubblica in Urbino, Volponi and his wife Giovina introduced me to their son Roberto, an intelligent, sensitive, and affable young man brimming with enthusiasm for life. I introduced him to my students and he quickly became part of the group. In this way we passed many pleasant hours together discussing among other things his father's works, of which he had a keen understanding. He also spoke with much enthusiasm about the vacation he was soon to take in Cuba. He was going to be among the first Europeans to take advantage of the recent opening of Cuba to tourism. As such it was to be a journey toward the extraordinary and the unknown; a manifestation of his desire for the freedom to explore the world and himself; a desire for self-fulfillment that we all share and that is fundamental in the work of Paolo Volponi.

And so, following the tragic airplane crash near Havana on September 4, 1989 that took his life, I decided to dedicate this translation to the memory of Roberto Volponi.

*

One of the pleasures of academia is the close association with students and colleagues with whom we can share and discuss our work. There are many whom I thank for their help and encouragement regarding this translation. I am especially fortunate to have as my colleague and friend Sante Matteo to whom I am grateful for the many valuable suggestions he has made. I am also grateful to all the teachers who, formally in the classroom or informally in the piazza, have taught me the Italian language and culture and thus contributed to this translation, for which I am nevertheless solely responsible.

Peter N. Pedroni
Oxford, Ohio
August 1994

NOTES

1. This is my translation, "Two Urbino Poems," *Italian Quarterly,* 29, 114 (Fall 1988: 81) of vv. 1–9 of "Le mura di Urbino" ("The Walls of Urbino") in Paolo Volponi, *Poesie e poemetti, 1946-66* (Turin: Einaudi, 1980), p. 105.
2. Peter Pedroni, "Interview with Paolo Volponi," *Italian Quarterly* 25, 96 (Spring 1984): 85.
3. Ibid., p. 83.
4. Enrico Baldise, *Invito alla lettura di Volponi* (Milan: Mursia, 1982), p. 61.

1

The iron flagpole fixed in the wall over the portal squeaked continuously, and from the roof garden across the way, piled up with snow, came the reply of some lost thrushes.

Prof. Gaspare Subissoni raised his collar and then also his eyes with angry patience toward those familiar confrontations, grumbling about the too narrow path through the snow and fearing that a threatening gust of wind, since it was whipping up again chasing roguishly around under his feet, might crash down on him. He was castigating himself with little punches for having left his umbrella at home, when he had thought that it would be better to keep his hands in his pockets. And that miserable path was so insecure that it forced him, even though he had on galoshes and felt pads, to hold his hands out like fins to negotiate its unpredictable twists and turns. His anger was growing because of that squeaking, because of the almost certain threat of a powdering of snow on the back of his neck, and the professor swore in Spanish with vigor, the same vigor with which he pointed his heels and dug in his felted soles. He was also getting mad because the path in front of the University was probably wider than the one he had to take, and probably already covered with wood shavings and ashes to permit the lofty procession of the figure of the "magnificent."

With that phony sense of balance... the cigar ashes... the hat, the words..." Hee! Hee! Hee!" Professor Subissoni simmered down. "...Weighty, pensive sense of balance...." But he quickly turned his attention to his feet by now at the edge of the shoveled and shiny area in front of the threshold of the Oddi-Sempronis; it was shining too much to not be the reflection of treacherous ice. He leaned on the door to get by and heard it run through with the sound of a television travelogue.

"Oh no! Oh no! Here too!" and he found the force to move on more quickly. At the end of Via Ca' Fante he reached the automobile route and could relax with a sigh, still in Spanish. He hadn't translated Garcia Lorca, no, but he really knew the language, with its accents and lisping s's, verbs and endings, and could still speak it like Italian, perhaps more affectedly.

The snow on the road, because of the traffic that had pounded it until just before then, was so soft that the professor thought about taking off his felt pads; in that moment the street lights came on, and he saw the white line of the wall under the Pincio swell up, as well as half of the Mercatale, and also the Vigne, that looked like a chalkboard half-way up, tilted forward by the darkness toward the interior as though ready to be used by a little schoolboy.

He began feeling emotional, without using Spanish expressions this time, and opened his arms with a deep breath.

"I was a man of action, I was!" and he banged the felt pads with determination unconcerned about the splashings. "And who says that I can't be one again! Even up here they saw what I could do... in March of '21, the eighth day, Sunday, at dawn: because my work had come out clearly. At half past nine under the sun, the first ones that went walking beyond the theater saw on the field of the Vigne a huge 'down with' symbol inscribed next to the letters 'Italy U.'"

"U" with a period. Hee! Hee! Hee! Every letter lasted for more than two days. I had done it with these feet, stamping the snow bit by bit from three in the morning until six."

Subissoni had come to a halt staring at the hill of the Vigne and his memory was overcoming the darkness. Snow had always stimulated him to speak, each time like running across old friends, but always new.

"It came out very well, with the staffs of the 'down with' symbol thirty-five paces long and the letters twenty four: twenty-six the capital I and the U; to make the period after the U, I sat down, because I was also dead tired. The evening before I had seen that beautiful untouched sheet – twenty centimeters of snow had fallen during the night between the sixth and seventh – that stood right before my fellow citizens. That night in bed it came back to mind and I understood what I could do with it. I was risking getting ill, susceptible as I was. But Cattaneo inflamed me; the nationalists disgusted me by that time like my mother's zabaglione. I trembled with joy thinking that it was not without reason that at the moment in which they had erected the platform of the unification of Italy my grandfather had renounced his title as count, which the Subissonis had since the twelfth century, already when Federigo II was a minor. A Gasparo like me was among the supporters of the unsuccessful expedition of Corradino of Swabia."

The professor's forehead was shining and one of his eyelids was dripping continuously. "I held open the book 'the city' until the moment I got up. While I was getting dressed, I repeated: 'The idea of equal rights among unequal forces, the idea of federal justice, was a ray of light reserved for illuminating very remote generations. The impending, inevitable, relentless destiny was one of unlimited emulation.'

Then I was ready and I put my plan into effect, when I wasn't quite twenty years old. On the threshold of unlimited emulation,... Hee! Hee! Hee! Unlimited all right, Hee! Hee!"

Gaspare Subissoni turned toward the Giocapallone and at the stronger lights that he encountered, "reserved for the University," he chewed bitterly: his face turned showing the crease of his left eye, blinded in a bayonet battle at Guadalajara and which since then had continued its shiny watering, still alive even if blind... outside of his head... inside and outside,... always... like that ray of light.

"So many people got themselves worked up over that writing in the snow! For one thing because they didn't understand the meaning of the 'U.' All the honorable gentlemen, the veterans, the loafers, the slobs... raised banners and shields from the wall across the way... with patriotic poems, damnation! shouting and jumping up and down, but nobody did anything about it... Hee! Hee! Hee! Nobody!"

At the edge of the piazza Subissoni had to turn his face to the left down toward the Ducal Palace and the Cathedral so

3

as not to be forced to see the Bonaventura Palace, seat of the University, at the risk of getting a stiff neck, and also because of the gust of wind that was usually waiting for him at that precise winter hour.

Meanwhile in the houses below, the television travelogue continued with its alarmed little bell and with views of fortresses and of provinces that disappeared one behind the other.

The largest and the newest of the city's televisions dominated the library of the Oddi-Sempronis, affirming its own superiority over the old gryphoned tables, over the credenza with lead-framed glass panes, over the faded gilded picture frames and over the leather covers, the parchment, the cloth, the silk, the handmade paper, the straw, the morocco leather of the innumerable books buried one next to the other, abandoned at the edge of the darkness: dilapidated walls, though solid, of a construction for decades mute and unattended.

The screen seemed indeed to expand in order to suddenly show, going beyond the central regions of the Tiber, of the Trasimeno and of the Abruzzi high plains, with strong contrasts between fortresses, passes, peaks, tunnels, arches, rhombuses, thrushes, the white and engineerish space of the swing bridge at Taranto, which seemed to open immediately for the running passage of a destroyer, bristling with radar, vibrant with antennae and cannons.

"This," murmured the acute and firm voice of a young man from the center of the long rectangular room, "This!" repeated the same voice more loudly to confirm with a command his decision. A complete silence followed, also because the television had stopped for the pause that precedes a change.

The silence concentrated around the figure of the young man who had spoken: it made the figure stand out clearly, with subdued tones, with the aphonia of lacteal surfaces that while changing were solidifying in the lines of his face and figure, so as not to disappear. There emerged his lips, cheeks, jaw, and then the line from his shoulders to his hands, white, on the table positioned as if to signal a time limit. This temporal space reverted back by cutting one of the hypotenuses to the forehead of the young man, ample and tense over his eyelids. From his eyelids it turned, who knows why, toward his sideburns and the down that descended from them very sparsely, but long and vortical, vivid like the perennial ray of Professor Subissoni's blind eye. Hair for hair it traveled, always in the lacteal light of the TV, to his chest, caved-in, hidden under a virginal undershirt, frightened of being there, alone, among the enormous collars of his dressing coat, relatives of the furnishings that shined through from their hiding places and certainly did not venture out of their order. The order came from his eyes, gilded, surrounded by pearl that lasted, shading his whiteness, up to the crimping above his lip. His cheeks were depressed toward his neck, in the opposite direction of the irregular path of his down.

The order was perfect and from his enormous eyes, staring right at the center of the oval, it went to his knees upon which it based itself.

To break it up, it was necessary to return to his face which expressed it; discover his entire mouth, half open, in balance over a possible wobbling, the movement of which however, would be noticeable in his dimples which were excavated between his mouth and his down, in two or three depressions down to the base of his jaw. These dimples rolled around restlessly, upsetting everything, toward the TV or the doors or the high window, toward the courtyard and the hanging garden. His aunts called his dimples "little birds," and they also called "Little Bird" their whole mysterious nephew inside his television-palpitating feathers.

"Are you laughing, little bird," shouted the noble Oddi-Semproni ladies. "Laugh, laugh. Here are the little birds flying away, indicating with their fingers, both of them, the dimples of their perennially-seated nephew, "Here they are coming to your aunts," they said looking at each other pleased by the linked plurals, "on our hands, on our lap. Not in our hair," they screamed, "don't mess up our hair, don't get us ruffled up, naughty little birds."

Thirty times out of a hundred, in three days, their nephew laughed; another thirty times he held back or forgot his little birds with indifference; the remaining forty times he tore them to pieces with a gesture of boredom and got rid of them, and threw them away with a gesture and with a mood, black and winged, scratching and scurvied like a big rook, that went about landing on and spreading its droppings on the china ornaments, upon which went unfailingly landing the eyes of his aunts, a little bit to protect them, a little bit to get support from their centuries-old presence, a comfort in their own childhood, and another little bit because in their internal parts were safeguarded the keys to their most precious desk drawers and the money for their everyday expenses.

The young man's down sparkled with satisfaction, dense like the subject of a Bronzino portrait: and also just as indulgent, in its ambiguity, on the face of that sacrament very close to the age at which the not-yet Professor Gaspare Subissoni had written with his feet on the untouched chalkboard of the field between the Albornoz fortress, the hill of the Vigne, the triumphal arch of Valbona, and the roofs of Mengacci, the Pla Madonna and of Pietrac above the Mercatale, by dint of stamping and of getting soaked... of getting chilled and moved to pity for unlimited emulation which really was being announced, real as the dawn that he saw spring forth low and tiny and true as a country milkmaid from the tower of San Polo, down with Italy U., which meant United or Unique or Unified or Umbertide or Unirailroaded, Unihighwayed, Unijudged, Uniguided, Unimortified.

Instead our little Count Oddino Oddi-Semproni called his aunts, distracting them from their evening pudding, and ordered clearly, so that his little birds, even though pressed here and there by the movement of his mouth, did not disturb him in the least: "Have Giocondo Giocondini come. Tomorrow morning at the time that will be considered suitable, rather early I believe, we will depart for Taranto, to go and see the swingable bridge." That "able" ending was very noble and stood peremptory like the arm of an executioner, like the princely threat of a torture as wise as it was hard, and already liberating just on the threshold of its journey.

The aunts looked at the majolicas and sighed meekly: "Another trip… fine, little bird, fine. But with this snow… Will the roads be open?"

The interrogative already committed them to his initiative "Oh! If they're open… it will be a beautiful trip, to Taranto, in Apulia. With our little bird! Call Giocondo Giocondini right away, he knows for sure if the roads are open and at what time we have to leave. Who knows where we can eat at noon… maybe in Bari!" and they went on getting curious with increasing felicity, having already recovered from the fatigue of the trip to Triest and Redipuglia of three days before. They instructed their part-time maid to go on with the pudding at the same temperature until half of the water had boiled out, and through the hallway on the ground floor, on the left side of the courtyard, they made their way toward their rooms.

Halfway down the hallway they glanced at the also satisfied Count Sempronio Semproni, portrayed by no less than Bronzino in his forumsemproniense armor. His thin beard glistened and his pride, rather silly at that, had not suffered insults in four-hundred years of ostentation, nor was it faded by the boredom of that location in the passageway at the bottom of the stairs. He seemed to be astonished every time the light reached him from the windowed arches of the courtyard and to become curious every time someone passed by and headed up the stairs. The constant humidity of the hallway, onto which opened the doors of the storerooms and the wine cellar, had maintained intact the oak board of the painting, just barely causing it to bend in the middle, as if to emphasize the sternum of the white armor. Since it was a three-quarter profile of Count Sempronio, from the left side, this part of the armor was wider, down to the groin and to the hilt, and reflected, always with the increasing pride of the gentleman who almost moved his glove so as not to upset that space-mirror, the passage of whoever was heading toward the stairway and also, and then with an enlargement, almost a sign of concern, for whoever turned toward the right to take the ramp down to the wine cellar.

The two sister countesses passed the side of their ancestor, holding hands, bearing down on their slippers like on skates, in a sign of conviction and of happiness and also of urgency for their impending duties and tasks: their bending accented their gestures of joy and got them already started on the trip.

Halfway up the stairway, by then past the mirror one said to the other: "Snow before Christmas lasts as long as a snowflake at Carnival time." They laughed again together, and then: "like a marengo....," added the first one.

"Or like a love affair... a falling in love... a burst of passion at Carnival...," continued the other, getting risqué because by then she had reached the door of her room inside of which she would hide and savor her daring and her blushing.

2

While the two sisters are meticulously preparing their luggage, choosing two of each item, but in different colors, and singing the same rhyme, it might be useful to take a look around the house and make some precise observations about the history of the family that inherited it and still lives here, after exactly four-hundred and thirty-nine years.

The palace was constructed between 1523 and 1530 by Count Oddo Oddi, who would die at the fine age of eighty-one years just when he was ready to move in. He had started the work right after redecorating the tomb of Duke Federico of Montefeltro, the greatest of the Urbino lords, with the addition of a canopy, two putti, and a heraldic oak tree. The same Oddo had opened the tomb at San Bernardino thirty-five years after his death, that is, in 1517, when the duke's corpse was found unspoiled. His amazement and commotion inspired him to write an epigram of seven distiches; *"... Incorrupta fides membra incorrupta meretur – servasse; hoc pietas religioque facit."*

In 1523, having finished the ducal tomb, he went on to start work on his own palace, apparently with the same enterprise, with the same architect, and with some residual funds from the ducal allocation. This inspired him to write, in that moment of fervor and gratitude, another epigram; three distiches followed by seven hexameters.

"Hunc ego iamdudum, fateor, Oddus adisse et meruisse manum stringere saepe suam;..." and then, in translation: "I came to know every angle of his agile body which nowhere was excessively pale. So if now he dwells among the heavenly, it is right that we keep our Duke in a monument of gilded marble.

"Just now I described him and I added a poem: If someone asks why under a canopy, let it be known that he often took his repose under the stars, that he endured the freezing cold and the burning sun, entirely taken up with his work," and continuing to the end: *"Pulvinar erat sibi targa* (his shield was his pillow), *ciboque parcus, aqua et pomis nimium contentus* (he was content with some water and an apple) *et istae delitiae victoris saepe fuere."*

Coming back to the house. From the main entrance one goes through a vault twelve paces long to a portico which opens onto the courtyard. The portico, with a width of four paces, extends to the left for twenty paces, alongside of two rooms for studying, astronomical and meteorological observations, geometry, calculus, herbalism, plumbing, mechanics, etc. and another little room with a loom, and finally, a modern opus, a little flush-type toilet bowl, but without the enclosed and compact water box and the pertinent floating ball and chain, perhaps for the lack of pipelines in the vicinity. The outer side is on the courtyard, paved with bricks and green from the mold: a sad and continuous presence of winter and of the most obstinate gloom of both the Oddis and the Sempronis. A sanctuary of cursing and head knocking. There was placed the gilded wooden eagle of the Urbino Guf – the Fascist University Youth – by authority entrusted to Count Oddo, a pharmacy student, father of our television spectator.

On the right side the portico was thirty paces long and ran in front of the library, by itself eighteen paces, a large store-room, with high shelves full of disheveled bottles and flasks, the sink, clenched and bristling with pipes and faucets, the kitchen, the scullery or little room for the infantile weeping of all the Oddinos, Gian Leoninos, Marzias, Battistas, Clelias, Cecilias, both the Oddis and the Oddi-Sempronis. A little warm aromatic room, with cooks' aprons and patient and indulgent maidservants, individuals capable of the redressing of wrongs, slaps, scrapes, wounds, stings, falls, sympathetic consolers, with vigorous contributions of inhalant and refreshing essence of garlic, celery, field balm, roman mint, fennel, vinegar, pepper, nutmeg, laurel, juniper, onion, cask herbs, rocket, almonds, violets... and also of their maternal, savory perspiration of bone menders, general healers, handy mistresses subject to the impromptu desires of the male family members of whatever generation: obliged by the master's haste, to hurry, while still perspiring, their amorous participation. With his cheeks hardly reddened the count man, father, uncle, son or nephew had already gone on to the drawing-room, or up the stairs, or in the attic to busily look for an old, important very urgent tool.

They took their revenge, even more sorrowful and clement, attending to them and even helping them to die, getting them through their ultimate fear with a sharp word, a shrug, a gulp, a candle...; and then by closing their eyes, washing them, dressing them in appropriate magnificence, combing them, crossing their arms on their chest, closing their mouth; checking them over once more, with one last aspersion of vinegar, by this time packaged away in the nobility of the coffin.

This scullery had a simple little iron grating up high, at the point where the portico became steps rising toward the upper floor, while back a few paces, it had turned in the other direction, like a loggia, to go on to enclose the courtyard, here too paved in brick, but less green, and inhabited by a large cheerful terracotta vase with a big satyr's face whose horns went backward to form two handles for its use which had already been obsolete for decades.

Facing the part of the portico that bordered the courtyard were the windows of the drawing room, the sitting room, the dining room, and the smoking room in a row and traversed by means of wide matching doors that began in fact with the one at the bottom of the stairs in front of the small and high grating of the scullery, the spy-hole of the good moods and the grievings of the entire household. Celebrations and expressions of happiness burst forth on the stairway and generally ran along through the doors that led through the sitting rooms and the dining room. Then the domestic staff could only listen through the usual grating or could go out to take a look and to congratulate each other without even really knowing for what, from the kitchen door.

Well let's go inside and beyond the entrance, which has along its flanks two little matching doors across from each other, on the right side for the library, the real entrance toward the Oddi-Sempronis, even more so after the advent of television; on the left side toward the science laboratories today used for washing, drying, and ironing the laundry; having reached the portico let's turn to the left, toward the main door of that side. Behind it and between the herbalist's area and the mechanic's area, among phials and pulleys, just to the left of the central world globe, stands a large 1920 motorcycle, Triumph, 500cc., double-shafted, four cylinders, four gears and a reducer, disk breaks, generator operated headlight, tail light, tires with inner tubes of two atmospheres of pressure, hand-operated accelerator, etc., etc.

Colored olive-green and black, sharply tapered with its chrome handlebars bristling with control levers, this mighty motorcycle, more dashing than a Leonardian war machine, stands tall with its front wheel inclined to one side, like the gesturing of a horse that impatiently awaits its triumphant master, right toward the door, toward us as if to look us over, select, recognize the courageous motorcyclist. Ready to hand him his helmet of yellow leather, his goggles with a fine plush around the lenses and with a potent rubber strap, calm and trustworthy leather gloves, with two snap buttons on the bottom capable of securing more than armor and any war or industrial machine, and better than any maternal fastener, mended or reinforced by a maidservant, nurse, and cook.

At the base of the globe there is a real map enclosed in leather and celluloid, within reach of the motorcyclist. The latter was the nobleman Gian Leone Oddi-Semproni, brother of the grandfather of our Oddino. The grandfather Oddo born in 1892 died in 1920 in Bologna, crashing with his airplane while attempting a figure eight on the fourth of November during some veterans' manifestation. Just in time he had given to his brother Gian Leone, fifteen years younger and not very adept at flying, a sort of degenerate mistake of his already old count father, the beautiful 500 cc. Triumph.

Young Gian Leone mounted this motorcycle regularly for four, six, eight hours a day every day of his life until 1933, the year in which around March he became mute, a prank of springtime; in July he got sclerosis, a result of that particularly stuffy summer; and then developed a paralysis that, lengthy as his journeys, accompanied him hour by hour to his death in 1935, that sixth of October in which his nephew Oddo was embarking in Naples with the rank of second lieutenant for Eritrea, inspired to relieve his boredom more than to serve the king or *il duce,* for both of whom, exactly because of that boredom, he bore more indolence than deference. The news of that embarkment stayed on the ground floor, and the sisters Marzia and Clelia learned about it down there, at the kitchen door, when they were sent to get some coffee and a breath of fresh air so that they would not be present at the conclusion of their uncle's untidy death throes.

There they stayed, without feeling the need to seek solace in the little room, even when the nurse came to say that their uncle had expired. Their motorcyclist uncle had traveled in thirteen years of motorcycling, a little more or a little less than thirty thousand hours, approximately a million and a half kilometers, without ever leaving the portico to the left side, in the winter, or the courtyard in the middle, directly toward the entrance, in all the other seasons.

Every morning and not always, but frequently in the afternoon too, he got all dressed up, he put on his helmet, his gloves, still unbuttoned, checked the map, decided his destination and his route, buttoned his gloves, arranged his goggles, and then got up on the cycle and started the motor while the rear wheel, the drive wheel, was mounted on a stand: and then he would switch gears according to the condition of the road and take the curves, beep his horn, look here and there, and read out loud the road signs; Furlo, Cagli, Pesaro, Fossombrone, Fano, Cattolica and so on. Some afternoons he would decide to go to Pesaro for coffee and, in the summer, even to Rimini. He was not allowed to go in the evening to see the variety show in Rimini or Bologna. At night he took only one trip, in the winter of 1932, to rush a lady to the hospital who was found injured at the side of the road. It was his nieces Marzia and Clelia, by that time women, who took her from his arms and assured him that they were taking her to the operating room, right to Dr. Beverandi, a friend of the family. The nieces even imitated his way of twisting his cigar while he was talking and his way of cursing because of the ashes that would fall on his beard running the risk of burning it.

When that night Uncle Gian Leone had left some of his cycling outfit for the first time in the doorway of his room, the two sisters went back down to the kitchen, which seemed very big, deserted as it was at that unusual hour, which the alarm clock was indicating noisily in the direction of the window and the cold. They looked around and then turning their backs to each other and talking simultaneously, they confided to each other that as yet no one had shown any romantic interest in them.

Three months later, the motorcycle took its place next to the globe, and did not lose, cared for on an equal basis with the other instruments of study and experimentation, any of the characteristics of its aggressive functionality.

The gasoline was taken from the tank and burned in the winter of '43.

That the destiny of the Oddi-Sempronis has always been on the road is demonstrated by the following excerpts from their and Urbino's history. A Count Oddo Oddi was run over in 1441 along the fortress road, the only level and well-beaten one in the whole city, by the racing horses of the lord of Urbino, the fifteen year old Oddantonio who raised and trained the fastest and most ferocious chargers in all of Europe. For this passion, which was in addition to a few others, he lost his dominion because the populace rose up against his taxes and his wastefulness and slew him, just an eighteen year old, in 1444, flushing him out from, and already mortally wounding him there, under his bed.

Another Count Oddi perished in 1473 crushed by the collapse, during a ferocious tempest, of the stone masonry bridge on the Molinelli Stream along the road to

Fossombrone. His body was fished out of the Metauro a few days later devoid of any clothing, arms and jewels, as it wandered along on the surface, dragged by the current still in the direction of Fossombrone.

Another Oddi was assaulted and assassinated by bandits just beyond the Montesoffio Pass on the road to Urbania: his quartered limbs were nailed to trees on the road in display, it was believed; or to indicate the route, others deduced, whether the correct one or a mistaken one was not known. In fact, some local pseudo-historians suggested the probability that rather than brigands the assassins were the count's own peasants, fed up with his pestering and his bristling about the fields, the city, the farms, homes, wells, courtyards, wine cellars to number, stamp, remove, check, weigh, and also to cudgel.

In 1548 the Oddo Oddi of the moment, successor to the Oddo embalmer and poet of Duke Federico – he too expired on the road while he was trying to reach, proud and happy, the new door of his new Palace in Via Ca' Fante – fell awkwardly on the pavement from his horse during a ducal party, perhaps weighed down by excessive libations. Even the falcon left entangled in his hand pecked furiously at his head as he expired in the arms of his squire who could not believe his own eyes.

Eventually a more noble end, but still on the road, in the open air, on a public street or piazza, was met, in 1573, by the last of the Oddis, the generous one that dared to oppose the abuses of power of the wicked "Pesarese" Guidobaldo II. This duke preferred Pesaro and almost always resided there with his court, pouring forth favors for both the city and the court. Urbino could not tolerate that affront and much less those expenditures, which it was supposed to support, in large part, and which yielded nothing in return. On the twenty-sixth of December in 1572, thinking that better celebrations were being enjoyed by the hated Pesareses, the populace rioted and forcefully assembled the general council against the will of the duke's lieutenant, who was Master Niccola Tenaglia – which means pincers or pliers, a beautiful name for an excise man – not even an Urbinoite, in addition to being a scoundrel. They all shouted that they did not want any more taxes and that the duke and his court should come back to Urbino as soon as possible, otherwise they would elect another lord, a noble and true Urbinoite, and they would follow the new lord against the Pesarese lord and against all the Pesareses. The Urbinoite populace elected thirty-five ambassadors from among the elders of the city and, as the first, Count Oddo Oddi. It is said that this Oddo was among the most hot-headed, certainly among the few of those elected to accept the responsibility voluntarily and with conviction. And then that he was the most ruthless against the duke's countermeasures and the first to take up arms in the name of Urbino and the Urbinoite duchy and also the first to spread the rumor that deep down and not so deep down those Della Roveres had come from Senigallia. There were diplomatic missions, skirmishes, clashes, incursions, betrayals, pacts until a papal brief ordered the Urbinoites to lay down their arms and to submit everything to the clemency of the duke, who, having retaken the upper hand, was so clement that he began by having the heads of fourteen of those thirty-five initial ambassadors cut off in the fortress at Pesaro, on June twenty-fifth, down there just so that those poor things couldn't even console themselves with a last glance at Urbino's walls and hills, and also by throwing into prison, also down there, another sixteen of them, who through various mishaps and illnesses, kicked the bucket there in the course of a couple of years. But the worst treatment he reserved for Oddi, whom he kept near himself, like a courtier of the first rank, during all those outrages, making him watch the torturing and calling him brother and, in the meantime, having him guarded night and day. They had been young together and good friends between '30 and '40, so much so that Guidobaldo had wanted a portrait made of Oddo too by the famous painter, Bronzino, whom he had brought from Florence for his own portrait.

Once the deaths, one after the other, of the poor prisoners had begun, on the first of August 1573 the Duke pretended to leave for Urbino, with a very restricted group, among them Oddi. When the convoy reached the banks of the Foglia, which crossed the road between the two cities, Guidobaldo got out of his carriage and invited the others to do the same in order to refresh themselves and also to urinate from the height of the bridge. After this, continuing to laugh, he gave an order for Count Oddi's throat to be slit and for the walls of the bridge to be instantly painted with his blood and for his bloodless corpse to be left to the dogs. In addition, he assigned the family name, title, and property of the Oddis, so that a house so illustrious in Urbino and in the whole duchy and also in Rome not perish, to one of his faithful henchmen, a half-noble from Fossombrone, Sempronio Semproni, who had distinguished himself in the war. He also gave him in matrimony the widow Oddi and ordered him to have children; but this new Count Oddi-Semproni only had children four years later and with his wife's daughter, Clelia, who at the moment of her father's death and of her mother's second wedding was nine years old. Thus were born the Oddi-Sempronis of whom many had a sad and meditative nature, so that one, Gian Leone, 1603-46, even got to be a poet.

And with inspiration in their eyes that night of the twelfth of December '69 the two Oddi-Semproni sisters, each from her own window, were looking at the shrubs, the potted plants, the flower beds neatly arranged in their garden; shadows going to brood over the ancient suffering of the bony depths of the courtyard.

The garden paths in the form of a cross reappeared as they did every evening, in every season, only to disappear in the morning in a frill of light in flight beyond the wall and the very walls of the city. It is right to travel, to go, to go far away to Taranto with that flower of a nephew whose aroma after a few hours would fill the automobile.

3

It was 8:05 PM when, like every other evening at that hour, Prof. Subissoni met his wife who had finished her work as a bookkeeper for the Cooperative Store. Usually they squeezed each other's hand while giving each other a smile and then went for supper at a little family-run restaurant, where they had been regulars for the evening meal for almost twenty years.

Some evenings they would take a little stroll as far as the theater before supper and then at the half-way point, beyond the Hotel Italia, the professor got the courage to take the woman's arm and turn his head toward her to just barely touch her hair with his chin. This gesture was as rapid as it was furtive and was carried out with wide-open eyes by the man who often ended up with her head bumping him under the tip of his chin. After turning around, on the way back, in the same place, he let go of her arm and moved decidedly to the right side of the street to proceed in a straight line that would bring him rapidly to the table, to the table cloth, that with its glasses and silverware was set just for two. They had been living together since 1939 without ever getting married; they had met each other in a prison camp in Spain at the end of the Civil War and never left each other again, not even inside the camp. He had gotten himself into the female section without anybody stopping him; in fact, the guards limited themselves to teasing him and to considering it an appropriate sign of degradation and cowardice that a half-crazy and nonbelieving red would want to stay among the women. This allowed Subissoni to not die, clinging to that woman's breast, stretched out beside her, to caress her hair, to hear her speak. They stayed in that camp until September 1940, when they were sent to Morocco, then to Algeria and from there to France, where they arrived in January '41, disembarking at Toulon. There they separated themselves from the group and went up as far as

Aix where Subissoni could work at cleaning, translating and looking after Latin tombstones in the local museum. At the beginning of '43 he was identified and was deported to Italy. The director of the museum was able to have the woman leave with him, indicating that she was a very good interpreter of German, in addition to Arabic and Spanish. They arrived in Urbino – from which the professor had departed for Paris seventeen years before – in May, with no luggage and with little money. They were put up in the guest room of the Zoccolanti monastery without the brothers even noticing that one of them was a woman. Although beautiful, she was not very feminine and what's more she had been wearing male clothes for twelve years by then.

Subissoni applied once again to the University but was again rejected. Neither of the two had work, money or friends: they went back and forth on the road from the cemetery to the crossroads, going up to the city, always speaking Spanish, once a week, to do a little shopping and to exchange books at the university library. During their long walks along that country road they often picked berries, clematis and a few broad beans or peas that stuck out between the fences. Until they were noticed and arrested again. This time they were separated, and Subissoni risked dying in the Urbino prison for lack of the will to live far from his woman.

It was she who freed him and sustained him the very evening of August 28, '44, the day of the liberation of the city. She had come up with the Englishmen of the Eighth Army and the Poles from Filottrano, where she had presented herself and had been taken on as a polyglot interpreter. Dressed once again as a man in an English uniform, Vivés Guardajal, Catalonian, with a degree in philosophy from Barcelona and in mathematics from Cologne.

This evening, even before squeezing his hand, the woman said something to Subissoni that agitated him to the point of slapping his hands noisily, even though they were at the edge of the central piazza, amidst other people.

Vivés had given her man the news, learned a few minutes before in the office of the Cooperative, of a terrorist attack in Milan, that had caused many victims.

"Who was it?" asked Subissoni.

"It's not known," replied the woman, "they're only making hypotheses. It seems to me always the same ones and in the same way."

In that instant the taxi of Giocondo Giocondini crossed the piazza headed toward the Giocapallone and Via Ca' Fante so rapidly that it sprayed the woman's trousers with slush.

The two of them decided not to go to supper, but to go to the Paci wineshop to watch the 8:30 news. The few groups in the piazza were talking about the same news, and their voices here and there were getting louder, more in the groups on the side toward Valbona, composed, according to the city's chess-board customs, of proletarians and artisans.

Subissoni and his wife were tempted to make some contacts but did not know how to begin and to whom to address themselves.

For years, they had been avoiding useless polemics, like lowly doctrines and stock phrases. They thought and lived in anarchy: she, more firm and serene, engaged for three hours a day and for almost all day Sundays writing an ideological treatise and translating some utopians into Russian; he, more uncertain and drawn between, on the one hand, his historical research projects, which he regularly abandoned at the point where the reasons for the event that he was studying started to seem banal and mechanical, and, on the other hand, his notes for a book of memoirs from the time of his examination for a university professorship, to his exile, to the war in Spain, to his liberation from the Urbino prison.

They stood still and undecided, turning their heads from one group to the other, each beginning to get smaller and to move because by then people were withdrawing toward home or directing themselves toward a television set.

Vivés, standing still in the same place, was twisting her hands in silence, with a grimace that was devouring both her lips. With that compunction she bent to the left and this gesture seemed to her companion the start of their displacement toward the wineshop so that he began walking. The woman brought a hand to her mouth and followed him, moving that hand still higher, her left one, to the nape of her neck as to arrange the knot of her hair.

In the wineshop Subissoni approached the bar with embarrassment and hastily ordered a glass of white wine; only afterward he turned toward Vivés and smiled at her, to excuse himself, and with a chivalric gesture he offered her the entire bar indicating to her the rows of bottles.

"No partying," she said, as if she needed to speak. "But I'll have a glass too, a small glass of grappa."

They drank together looking each other in the eye, to give each other support: she accompanied her own emotion with tiny sips and finally she was able to rest her entire gaze upon Subissoni. He was standing up straight and trying to look vigorous, even if he was wobbling a little, with the liquid of his blind eye that by changing light continuously emphasized his instability. Even as a young man, at least at thirty-six when she had met him, he swayed continuously, or else he tightened up and began inflating little by little until causing concern that something inside him might blow up: instead in the end he heaved a sigh and resumed oscillating. He played around a little at pretending to be a tree, at least after she had suggested it to him, discovering this image for him.

That evening he had on a nice-looking, honey-colored corduroy shirt and a short dark green wool tie: the wine went well because it livened up his pallor. Subissoni noticed, after a long moment of admiration in which he had indulged to alleviate at least a part of the anxiety and the wait for more precise news, that his woman looked painfully frazzled and showed a line of tension from under her ears up to the point of her neckline.

"What's the matter?" he asked and added other interrogatives in Spanish, undertone, getting closer to her, as well as away from the bar where they might have been overheard.

"Nothing," replied Vivés raising her arms again to show that she was throwing away something of no importance, "old fears." But he was grieved and angered, profoundly touched by the truth of those two words; he abandoned his glass and clenched his fists, swaying in a more emphasized way.

"No outbursts," she wanted to reassure him. But by then everyone was gathering around the television set, high up on an awkward tripod at the back of the room, on whose screen the fake world globe was already rotating among trumpets. An instant later the news was already funereal on the face of the announcer. Slowly, holding himself tall and rigid above his copy sheet, he confirmed the most ugly rumors and data, with a recitation that emphasized the empty spaces, as though keeping quiet even more dramatic events and consequences; "Twelve dead and one hundred injured in an attack on the branch office of the National Bank of Agriculture at Piazza Fontana, in Milan... the bombs exploded under the table in the middle of the lobby where transactions are negotiated, particularly intense today, like every Friday, market day....

The explosion stopped the clocks in the area at 4:37 PM... a second bomb on the premises of the Italian Commercial Bank did not explode.

Almost contemporaneously bombs exploded in Rome, the first at 4:45 PM in an underground hallway of the National Bank of Labor... thirteen injured among the employees, of whom one seriously; the second device exploded on a terrace of the Altar of the Fatherland, on the side toward the Imperial Fora...."

Subissoni flinched two or three times and said: "Fascists! They're the only ones that go up those stairs and can stand those fora...."

"Quiet," one of the spectators, who did not look like an Urbinoite, shouted angrily in his face.

"Eight minutes after the third explosion, again on the second terrace, but on the side toward the Ara Coeli."

No one said anything else; it seemed like the two comments, Subissoni's and the stranger's, had exhausted every reaction.

The crowd slowly started to break up, but with determination, as if everyone had gotten a share. There followed the commentary and speculations of the newscast and the announcement of inquiries and investigations. The latter sparked a little attention, and Vivés moved closer to the set so she could concentrate.

Subissoni was wobbling, partly because of the grave insult that he felt he had suffered. It appeared to him that everyone was avoiding him while secretly giving him dirty looks and whispering and that nobody had said anything to him as they went out.... He went closer to the bar to get himself out of the draft between the TV and the door; he ordered another glass and turned toward the bottles. They were lined up vulgarly and arrogantly, displayed pompously on three levels like another altar of the fatherland, and all of them together on the right – with regular glasses and small glasses in between – constituted another stairway toward the heavens. He swallowed a string of insults, chewing his gums and getting mad, as angry as if he were in front of the real monuments and with the possibility, given those proportions, to intervene and beat and kick them to pieces.

"It couldn't last," said the barkeeper. "Too many strikes! We were doing too well!" Subissoni tried to say something benevolent to him, something didactic, but before he could find a way Vivés's hand grasped his left arm.

"Can I drink?" he said holding his second glass ostentatiously as proof of his Pantagruelian capacity and of the vastness of his drama, "can I drink? can I drink...?"

"Yes," she answered him tenderly, "certainly," and added, seeing his need to get something out and to avenge himself: "Tell me, what would you like to say?"

"I don't believe any of it: not one word. The numbers, certainly, the facts,... but it's all false, the rest of it, the

23

mourning, the indignation. All an alchemy… of this herd of swindlers. The Altar of the Fatherland, the temple of the heavens, the banks… all stuff of theirs… since forever… and always used in the same way… like a bow! In reality as a knot… and what a knot!"

"It's clear that it's an intimidating maneuver against the unions, for the purpose of forcing them to give in… at least psychologically, with the usual fear of right-wing blackmail, of the leap into the dark," said the woman exhaustedly, trying to animate her words one by one, so that they might convince her man, who was so furious that he was shaking as though blown about by an ugly interior wind, which threatened to carry him far from the reality of things.

"That's not all, that's not all. It's worse. It's the end. It's the whole country that can't make it, that can't make it against these knots. They've always pompously covered themselves with cloaks and sashes! With vestments, fringes, fabrics, pendants, banners, pennants, steps, arches, colonnades, ugly colonnades," and he rocked back and forth to the rhythm of his words, augmenting the beat as if he had to make a jump. "Covered faces, shirts, handkerchiefs, cords, ceremonial towels! To tie everything up, everything that doesn't fall into line, that slips out tied up this way, senseless, crammed, slung, shod, belted, big sack, indeed huge sack…."

She was afraid that he would fall, and in order to re-establish some kind of contact she suggested that he drink another glass. Subissoni took this invitation the wrong way: he stopped short and began sulking, making a dull sound suggesting his lament and his reproach. He opened his maneuverable eye widely to demonstrate his amazement and his resentment too, with an infantile exaggeration that by itself could have made him lose control.

"Calm down," his wife advised him, "calm down. Be patient and wait. You're right, but your reasoning is so vast that it's valid always and for everything in democracies like this one… for all history. How many times have we said it? Now consider these bombs. Their motive is as simple as their mechanism; everything is so clear that even the police and the government won't be able to make a mistake. I'm sure that they'll find the terrorists quickly and that they came from the right. If they don't find anything it will mean that the government itself set the bombs and that it will continue doing the same until it can pretend to be forced to set up a new authoritarian regime. Gaspar, it's so simple."

"The dead ones," he – who had been only half listening, pretending to be absorbed in his glass – tried to go on. "The dead... more cadavers on the Italian boot, to... to restore it, to replenish it, to fertilize it, if only anything was still cultivated on it. Ah! the boot," and he made the gesture of biting it, "it's stuffing itself with more dead people."

"The dead," she sided up to him, "are dead. The dead are equal to all those others that we have always seen; our comrades who fell and also our enemies who fell and also the bombarded civilians. They are the same: dead, that is, they are equal and have always died for the same purpose, for hundreds of years."

"And we have to always stand by and look at these dead people?" he grumbled.

"And we then, why haven't we died?" she said, this time with severity.

"We've died a thousand times," Subissoni showed his self-pity by touching himself and by opening his coat.

"No. And we'll live to see the end of this too. Calm down. You'll see that at eleven o'clock the TV will already say something about the terrorists."

"Terrorists. Terrorists. Not terrorists. They're not 'ists,' they're 'ors'... doctors, professors, praetors, curators, protesters, laborers, director; 'ors-ers,' all guilty, graduated, respected, illustrious who trade money, whores, bombs. Government indeed. The government preaches, embraces, inaugurates, cuts... it cuts centers, scholarships, pies, prosciuttos, protocols, capocollos, intestines, salamis! Salamis! us, us," ran on the professor, while starting to sway again, "so we'll really keep quiet. In silence before this little theater," pointing to the spectacled tripod "that does everything by itself, it invents and comments and frightens." He stopped there pleased with the near rime. Vivés understood and gave him a smile.

"It may be," she said then with a conviction that she affirmed word by word, "the end of fascism. The terrifying end. If the workers stay calm. It would be a big step forward, bigger than another electoral gain. Either the government is guilty or, otherwise, it cannot but side with the workers." She followed this thought closely and went on confirming it to herself, examining it from within and without, as if she had to block out another hypothesis, of which she did not have a clear idea, but of which she must have sensed the distressing negative aspects.

Once again she stuck her lips inside her mouth and put her left hand on the knot of her hair. She stayed like that a moment and smiled with great indulgence at Subissoni who was watching her with trepidation.

The wineshop was beginning to get full; everyone was talking partly with everyone else and partly with themselves, as if to share and to conceal the harshness of the facts and to contain the painful flux that was erupting from within each one's conscience, so that it would not become a collective uncontrollable and ferocious tidal wave. Individuals and also groups prepared to wait, to evaluate and to decide. Nobody, noted Vivés with relief, took it out on the leftists, on the contrary the few rudimentary arguments that went beyond the repeated reconstruction of the facts, tended toward the fascist right, toward its plan to throw the unionist and political struggles into disorder.

Then Vivés proposed to her man that they go out, for a walk and then to supper too, and that they wait for the late television news.

Some people acknowledged Subissoni with deference, moving out of the way to make it easier for him. He breathed a sigh slapping his hands on his sides and went out onto Corso Garibaldi. He looked and turned all the way around so as to be better able to see, with his only eye, the entire view from one side to the other and to savor it as though he were in front of something new; the tiny boulevard was deserted, while under the loggia, two groups of students were rehashing the same things and raising their voices.

"It's the end of everything," repeated Subissoni taking the hand that his wife was holding on the nape of her neck. "Maybe everything has been over for some time. We knew that Russia, the USSR!! would begin to conduct its international policy as a world power. Here in Urbino it would be possible to resist if it weren't for this University!" and he nodded toward the students.

Vivés kept quiet and went on squeezing her mouth and her eyes. She breathed deeply twice and then stopped and told her companion that she would prefer sitting down. Subissoni looked around disoriented, as if he wanted to find a chair right there. He saw that Vivés was distressed, he stamped his feet, stood a bit aside and discovered with impetus the Hotel Italia, where it had always been. He turned toward his woman and put his arm around her to hold her up and to lead her. In the doorway he called out loudly and as soon as he was inside he began to do things with the authority of an occupant. He became aware of this as soon as the woman was seated in an arm chair inside the entrance and he got so red that even his blind eye was glowing.

He would have remained there on his feet in the doorway of the hotel, for shyness, but he couldn't leave Vivés alone, seated among those arm chairs, abandoned to the precarious order of that long and narrow room in front of the wooden reception desk, like a lost wayfarer, like a sick person taken in by pity. He turned to approach her and bumped into a tall wrought iron and ceramic ashtray in front of the closest arm chair. "Even this is a tripod... everything in the form of a pulpit, balcony, platform, gallows,... everything from on high, among inspiration and condemnation, holy spirit, warning, arrow or cigarette." He was confused, but by his luck he was able to gather the two unbroken pieces and reassemble the apparatus. Vivés smiled but didn't succeed in raising her lips, that drooped bitterly to the sides. Subissoni noticed it; "Don't let it get you too much; do some cursing and get it out of your system. Don't swallow this other rubbish. What can I give you?"

"I must have caught cold at the office and when I came out too. Maybe I didn't digest the tuna fish today. Winter has started so suddenly...."

"Always tuna fish, always tuna fish. You open up those cans because they're Spanish. Eat some prosciutto or some canned meat too sometime! And afterward take a minute to go out for coffee."

"Maybe you're right. But I always drink a cup of hot tea."

"Hot broth, that's what you could use. Let's go to the restaurant here, without going outside, and you drink a nice consommé. We can spend some money for once, if it's a question of health."

His awkwardness moved Vivés to give him a caress, raising her left hand that was tingling; "Sweetheart, so many times we could spend a little more."

Subissoni was amazed: "And the house? and your publication? and your trips to Barcelona, to London, to Moscow? Just for the house we still owe two million lire. And will I always be able to do four theses a year? I know that at the University, puh, puh," he spat more ruthlessly than ever, "they're starting to have doubts about the history theses. And they even say that the theses always have old themes, positivistic; next time I'll do one on a tripod, a trestle, without themes and with a coin on top, with no backing, nor causes nor effects, on a tripod. But now let's go get some broth: a bowl for each of us."

"No," replied the woman, "I couldn't eat and not even drink. Sometimes an Alka-Seltzer has helped me. I'd be very grateful to you if you could get a couple of tablets for me."

Subissoni was directed by the doorman to the pharmacist on call, the one in Piazza delle Erbe. He got ready by shaking himself and waving his arms, listening to and repeating his mission and the order and after stamping his feet in the doorway and rolling his good eye around, he departed for the corner. He knew it wouldn't be simple, that he would have to ring the bell of the private residence of the pharmacist and that the latter could refuse to recognize any emergency and the need, therefore, to come down and wait on him, especially since he didn't even have a prescription. He prepared himself to do battle, and the two or three groups that were stirring about in the piazza mumbling and cursing gave him courage; they could intervene if it was true that the pain and indignation for what had happened was holding them and keeping them heated up in the middle of that snowy piazza. The pharmacist was in the doorway of the house, with a red flashlight in his hand, waiting on a customer.

"Just Alka-Seltzer, two or three packets," said Subissoni, "just Alka-Seltzer, but it's necessary... please."

"Yes," said the pharmacist, and a moment later when he reappeared in the hallway with the package in his hand, he said, "Did you see what these delinquents have done? The death penalty, the death penalty...."

After taking the package and paying, Subissoni asked, "Who are the delinquents supposed to be? Who are the delinquents supposed to be?"

"You mean you haven't heard? Don't you know what happened? Where do you live anyway? Where do you live?" meanwhile the pharmacist turned off the flashlight and got ready to double-lock the door by pulling the iron bar down from the wall.

Subissoni took off in a hurry, careful not to slip on the slightly downhill area in front of the church of San Francesco, where the snow was hard and perhaps very icy. He cursed while imagining that people would go to church stupidly in flocks, disregarding everything, without looking... and on Friday, market day, when there are the most intense transactions, orations, novenas, oaths, vigils, frenzies, sermons, the dragging of feet and of devotions.

In the middle of the piazza he replied, "I know everything, and I try to understand something before talking senselessly or like a parrot. I live as I can, where I want, as I want, with whom I want. I live as I like, with whom I like. But I live... and I cogitate too."

He handed the package to Vivés while still concentrating on the derivatives and combinations of "as," "where," "with." He was glad to find his woman standing up and smiled at the doorman to thank him; he was surprised to see that the latter had gotten a glass of water ready for the medicine and that he was quietly handing it to her.

Vivés took the glass, decided that there was too much water and went to pour out a little on a plant at the foot of the stairs.

The plant was green and robust and Subissoni, strengthened by the persistency of those little branches, put that whole rigmarole that was still expanding along with his worries in hiding between its leaves.

4

Giocondo Giocondini was introduced into the library in the presence of Count Oddino while the television was broadcasting a program called *Italian Chronicle,* one of the favorites of the young gentleman and of his aunts who had redescended from their own rooms so as not to miss it.

Giocondini, broad and swarthy, ceremonious and slick, knew that he must pay his respects without disturbing them and wait quietly behind the three lined-up armchairs. The newscast coming up soon would be the appropriate moment to talk and to get some indication regarding the trip that certainly would be taken the following day. And so he waited, in his place with the devoted indifference of a dog, ready to go according to the movements of his master, even though he had already heard something about the bombs in Milan.

When the program was finished, Countess Marzia turned on another light, but a dim one, just right for getting a look at people's faces without interfering with the contrast on the television. Giocondini stepped forward and extended his greetings, with great respect and with the cheerfulness appropriate to his name and his work and also to his goal. Oddino said, "Taranto and the swing bridge," and Giocondini assented heartily, exalting the beauty of the place and the intelligence in choosing such an interesting destination and mechanism. He said, however, that it would be a long trip and that they would have to leave very early if they wanted to go and return in one day, but there would be wonderful sights and very beautiful countryside to see during the trip, from the windows on both sides, especially yellow tufa churches without doors.

At that moment the newscast began. It was the mournful tone, in a way sort of homespun, that caught the attention of the three, causing them to turn their backs to Giocondini.

They listened in silence. Oddino even got back in his armchair, something that almost never happened with a newscast. During the broadcast of the news he usually finished his supper, half of which he consumed during *To Know* or during *The Spiritual Hour* or during the union and business reports; at the end of the meal, having satisfied every appetite, he got ready for *Carousel*.

The news of the bombings surprised the Oddis and offended the two sisters, who immediately got angry at the television that exposed them to those events and that confusion, dragging them into a drama that had nothing to do with them. The television made them think about the facts, but they did everything they could to push them away and not be contaminated by them. Furthermore those announcements and those sights inspired more horror than pity. The official pity of the newscaster and of the commentary obscured and deformed the very images, helping the two sisters to deny reality and to shield themselves with concocted indignation.

Together they heaved a sigh and said, "Milan, Milan! Everything in Milan, oh what a city!" shaking their heads in disapproval, "Twelve dead… and you'll see that the dead ones aren't even Milanese! Oh! Milan, Milan! What do they want in Milan?"

"And always in the banks!" intervened Giocondini. "No one can live anymore with all these banks. Everybody's going crazy over money. Everybody in the bank; off to the bank, even for a thousand lire; even people dressed in rags…."

"The masses have gotten spoiled. Here's the result," said the sisters to each other.

"They don't work anymore," said Giocondini. "Nobody works anymore. Just strikes, strikes and more strikes. Right here too," he asked, "is there anyone that works anymore? Me, a small businessman, self-employed, I manage to work for twenty hours a day. People who are thinking about bombs don't think about working. People who think about working don't think about bombs. They all ought to be forced to work."

"Ah! Milan, Milan, what a scandal! Right in front of everybody... for everybody... with everybody...," the ladies defended themselves. "But why do these things happen? What is the government doing? Isn't there any police? There aren't many, and always fewer priests. And the Pope – who comes right from Milan – who knows how he is suffering, poor man! It's a direct insult to him."

These congressmen and senators that only talk, why don't we see them now?" asked the inconsolable and wheedling Giocondo Giocondini. "You're right," he went on, "there's no government, and no state. A fine republic! There's the republic."

"There is television," said Oddino gravely. The others stopped talking and looked at the set, without understanding what the young count meant with that tone and that very severe affirmation – which by itself confirmed a great truth – however, at least those three didn't understand the significance or the connection.

"You mean that television teaches rebellion and violence with so many of its shows?" asked Countess Clelia.

"Perhaps that's true too. Too much idle chatter only gets people confused," concluded her sister.

"That's for sure," said Giocondini, "Television has taught people not to work. It shouldn't be on all the time and lots of programs should be cut out. People have only learned how to have fun and when they don't have any more money for that they rob a bank. The banks too are there to be robbed. Too many tellers! Too many open doors for everybody... too many drafts!" He said the last three words smiling, so as not to be completely negative and risk discouraging the others from taking their trip.

The television changed pictures and the indignant comments of the political groups started rolling in – all of them, and almost all of them using the same litany – and then the announcement of the detailed investigations by the police, of their commitment, of the multiplicity of their plans, but also of their disorientation. The TV reviewed a sequence of terrorist acts. The April twenty-fifth bombing at the Industrial Fair and at the Milan train station and the series of train explosions on the days of August eighth and ninth.

Clelia cried out, "My God! Anarchists! The anarchists are back!" She who in '36 had had a fleeting crush on the nobleman Subissoni, who soon thereafter got tied up in anarchism, sold everything and took off.

"Maybe," said Giocondini, "that could really be. Some hot-head taking advantage of the confusion." Since they weren't talking about the trip any more he was trying to sum up the various suppositions and change the subject with a joke that would liven up the group. "One anarchist only, or two. Two underground types, with nothing to lose. The television should be more careful... to not spread panic. Just think how it looks abroad. The same old Italians...."

"You mean they are Italian in Milan? I'm beginning to wonder," said Marzia. "Really all Italians in Milan? In Turin and in Palermo and Naples too? It appears to me that the only Italy left is between Florence and Rome. Did you see a few days ago? In Redipuglia there was no one to pray for those poor heroes."

"Italy is only nice to look at," said Clelia. "Nobody worries about her. This Pope also is too sad... and he's always complaining."

"One hundred injured, an entire hospital." "Who knows how many of them will die?" "Some Milanese people too," they said in turn, partly because they were waiting for Oddino to say something.

But Oddino was silent, concentrating on the television as if he expected the living screen to be able to vary, with other announcements and other sights, those events, or to emit a conclusion that would result in the exclusion of everyone's resentment, even his and that of his aunts. The television was still on and therefore it should indeed say something else: it certainly wasn't dead, blown up with those bombs and with that news!

"Wait," he said, and it seemed very reasonable for everybody to stay there waiting for something momentous that surely would be revealed by that Cyclops's mind-eye looking out at time and life. Giocondini too accepted that reasonableness, in which he felt the weight of established authority, and he understood that it was precisely Oddino who would know how to shift gears and get the engine running again.

"You are really a count," he said. "You don't feel small like me, in front of these horrible events. I'm even afraid of television.... Maybe because I watch it so little! I don't even know how to turn it on. At my house, my wife put it in a place where it gets reflected everywhere, because of her mania for continually washing the floor, the doors, the windows... it seems to me like it's always outside, the TV, on the window panes, in the sky...."

Oddino was not distracted and stayed attentive to the screen, which was vibrating. He moved his head closer to that already-finished drama, which by then was fleeing with the ball of the globe, rotating ever smaller behind the scenes, above the desks, beyond the wastepaper baskets and the doors, in the wave of fading music that swallowed it completely.

Oddino raised his hand and pointed with relief to the empty, though still vibrating, screen, which had turned benign, like the drowsy eye of a nice uncle, whose large, myopic lens had just fallen into the grayness of the wool of his vest, but was ready to light up again with pleasantries and favors. Giocondini was reassured, even though he was a little worried about the arrival of some funereal "political tribunal."

The two sisters went on looking at each other and were about to interrogate each other with their eyes and with the pursing of their lips about the substance of that fact that had disturbed them and about how it was possible for it to come back now, at just the moment when it was being closed up, like a pie in the oven or like linen cloth being sewn together. Between their hands there remained the fastidious cushion of that event, wet and heavy, which they could hand back and forth or hold on to together.

They got more comfortable, while continuing to look at each other and to make the same gestures. "Twelve dead, one hundred injured," they were saying softly, "a series of attacks... but against whom? Whom, if there's no one in command anymore? There's no sovereign anymore."

At that point they really looked at the TV, the whole set, the big shining head and the dials underneath, its striated limbs resting on the table with the arrogance of a regal rear end on its throne, the mysterious wires and connections that nourished and bound together the kingdom. Then a big wave of affection turned them toward their nephew, the last of the Oddis, the family's hope and their hope for continuation, the living sign of their every action and of their whole world, he who would survive them and who would seal and, in fact, even arrange their death. A sovereign like Oddino would always be far away from bombings, since his legitimacy was noble and true, closed among those walls and protected by the whole city of Urbino, by every brick as by the love of each inhabitant.

They turned toward the window, looking over the portico beyond the courtyard. The faithful night closed in under their eyes, as always, and enumerated the stairs of the first ramp, there where it turned to leave them, to commit them to their sleep, with only a few thoughts about the next day.

"What do you say about these dead people, Oddino?" asked Clelia who, still holding that wet cushion between her hands, was unable to reconcile herself and wanted to calm herself under the new sovereignty.

"I'm not saying anything. I can say that they are dead... perhaps in vain.... Why? Because they were supposed to die. The bombs exploded... and they were intended to kill. It may have been communists who set them, who knows from where – international communists – but they may also have been young people... Americans, American types. But just wait... the television will tell all.... In three or four days it will tell all… it will even be able to say that other bombs have exploded. It will say everything… perhaps even too much… even with TV 7. It won't leave us alone…."

The television had started another program, and the volume of both the words and music was louder. Oddino went to check the controls, but the dials were all in their preestablished order. Then he turned on the central light and took a look at the doors and even the walls, to see if there could have been some seepage there. Reassured, he turned off the set, with a gesture of punishment, and he turned toward his aunts, certain that the punishment had satisfied them too.

He covered his supper tray: the gesture meant that he did not intend to go on with that meal, that too much time had passed from the moment in which he had started it and, what's more, time had changed.

Seldom in the last ten years had that library room been illuminated with all the lights: the book shelves, the red ciphers of the figures and of the words, the inlaid work on the backs and legs of the chairs reemerged… even the little door on the side of the hallway, completely forgotten as though it had been walled up by the dust and darkness in that empty space.

Giocondo Giocondini was framed against that little door by the stares of the three Oddis, with the uncertainty of a messenger who has not yet set forth his news. The two sisters were awaiting his words; and the anxiety made their hands quicken on their cushion. They smiled to encourage and guide that man toward giving a pleasant and reassuring message. But Giocondini didn't know what to say, that is he didn't know which words that trio would welcome with pleasure, nor did he know how to reconcile the trepidation of the aunts with the confidence of the nephew. He needed to cough but tried to control himself, even though if he coughed he could avoid having to speak, because he didn't want anyone to think he might be coming down with a cold, especially since he really did feel one coming on after that impetuous snowfall.

Oddino hit him with, "Can you make it all the way to Taranto?" and Giocondini was for the second time that evening convinced of the natural authority and ability of that gentleman.

"Yes," he said, "certainly, all the way to Taranto... and back. A very beautiful trip. I'm convinced that right after Fossombrone there's no more snow and that after Ancona there'll be nice weather."

"Good," said Oddo, "at what time will we have to leave?"

"At six o'clock... if it's not too much trouble. But if we want to see the bridge in the middle of the day...."

"Alright, at six o'clock."

The sisters extended their hand toward each other on that shared cushion, and they felt, while smiling sadly, how it had become lighter and drier: their discomfort now was due to the observation that it was so light and to the question of how it could have gotten dry, almost changing material. They stood up awkwardly and sideways because they didn't want to leave the cushion or damage it and also because they didn't want to see the television set naked that way under the overly-bright lights.

"Six o'clock will be alright," said Clelia, "But then we need to go to bed right away."

"Should we get anything special ready for you?" Marzia asked her nephew.

"No. The traveling bag, the two thermos bottles, the bottle of cologne, and the usual change of underwear."

Oddo was calm and this greatly reassured his aunts who had to assume responsibility for getting everything ready, and had to find the spirit to encourage and to challenge each other to perfection in those tasks.

"Let's hope we don't run into those ruffians who planted the bombs... who may be escaping toward the south," complained Clelia, to make her last adjustment of the cushion before freeing herself of it.

"If only...," said her nephew. "If only they were on their motorcycles, and we could recognize them and arrest them. Why don't we bring a weapon? Perhaps the revolver that you keep would be enough. You, Giocondo, do you have some other weapon?"

He was getting excited and the gilt of his bronze-like eyes highlighted their pearl trim.

"No, little bird, it's not necessary to act imprudently. If we run into them we'll notify the carabinieri and the police."

"And if there are no police there?" argued little bird, with every dimple vibrating and with his down shining in glory.

"Then we can follow them. Follow them at a distance," said Marzia, "to see where they go and notify the police."

"That sounds just right to me. We would be doing our duty completely and in the most secure way," proclaimed Giocondini with a lofty tone, so that no one could top him with another clever line. "I'll bring my binoculars and some rope, in fact chains, just in case. But now I'd better go to get the car ready with everything in place. I also want to put up the silk curtains on the rear windows again."

The sisters approved, and Giocondini began to withdraw. Clelia was taken by a thought: she turned completely toward that man and started looking at him intensely, as though she were judging him for the first time; her gaze fled toward the little, rediscovered door and she murmured, "Mind that you do...."

Not even to her sister would she confide – neither while together they were dismissing Giocondini, nor afterward while they were going upstairs with Little Bird, who was amusing himself by jumping the stairs three at a time – the recollection that had bounced in front of her, in the middle of that too-brightly-lit library, in which things that had been abandoned for years had retaken their places and provoked fear, if only because of the suddenness of their reappearance with all that they represented: a recollection that before her eyes had enlarged the luminous corners of the room and shook the curtains and the floors almost with the sound of weapons. As a little girl they had told her a story about great-grandfather Oddo Oddi-Semproni, privy chamberlain of the pope. In the spring of 1851 while he was traveling toward

Rome on the Via Flaminia, in a stretch between Sigillo and Nocera Umbra, at a fountain, he had impetuously recognized and detained two criminals, two well-known outlaws from the Pontifical State. But when these two rebelled, the three servants of the count took off running and he was stabbed with a dagger through the throat that left him dying. When the servants came back to remove him from the road, he couldn't even scold them, and they brought him to die in a nearby sanctuary.

The sisters accompanied Oddino all the way into his room, the nicest and the biggest, which looked out on the courtyard, and they entrusted him to the sadness of the Christ figure in Barocci's *Noli me Tangere* and even more to Bartolomeo Schedoni's thoughtful *Madonnina*. With her last glance Clelia unfortunately noticed how naked, tender, and long the throat of the Christ figure was, as well as that of the Madonna, who seemed to be bowing toward the two little clinging children just to offer those two elongated and stretched arteries in the Schedonian style. She trembled and prayed silently with a fervor that she hadn't experienced for years – since the last time when toward the end of '45 she had prayed to Saint Anthony – the one in her room painted by Guercino – that upon exiting from the desert and from his contemplation, he would undertake to make Count Chikiewicz, a Polish major and guest of the Oddis from the moment in which he had personally liberated Urbino, decide to ask for her hand in marriage.

For her own good, Countess Clelia did not wish to recall the result of that last fervor, so desperate that it resulted in her being the one to discover the dashing Major Chikiewicz, a little high, in addition to nude, and with his partly-white chest hair curled up, in bed with a young trollop from Urbino, a certain Mandarina, little more than twenty, when he by then was hitting fifty – in a bed in the Oddi household, albeit on the first floor. The major, with complete military tact, in order to excuse himself, had jumped to his feet, standing at attention totally naked and ruffled in front of her terrified at the door. And what's more, he went on bowing, with his palms extended along his thighs, until his first head, the bigger one, almost touched the other one, smaller, but still red and shining, not yet cooled down from the heat of Mandarina.

Clelia never forgave herself for her carelessness, to which she attributed the miserable fate of the Polish count caught in the act. In the Cathedral, a few days later – in order to worthily amend matters – he married Mandarina, covered with veils, at least as many – it was said in Urbino – as the men who first had also, although in a different way, covered her. And after marrying her he carried her off, as an emigrant, to Argentina, perhaps because he didn't have the courage to return to kiss the sacred and holy soil of Poland with that shameless thing who, favored by her new position as commandress of the detachment, continued to prefer the lower ranks of the army of Anders.

At the time Clelia had that room repainted; she herself moved the bed from its position facing the door and put it out of sight against a side wall.

Clelia, twenty-four years later, took care not to ask anything of that Saint Anthony by the painter of Cento, partly because by then she had entrusted herself directly to Jesus – and what's more painted by a trustworthy Urbinoite, who was even a friend of the family and had made a portrait, among lace and pearls, of a Clelia like her; all happy and about to become the wife of an Albani from Pesaro.

But that evening, having avoided encountering the ecstatic stare of Saint Anthony or his very realistic hands, a little sweaty – so much so that in the summer it appeared to her that she could smell the odor of that fervent sweat – she had really turned to the pistol in her most secret drawer, a big pistol with a six-chamber magazine, in silver and engraved with symbols of the Leone di Giuda, a souvenir of the African adventure of her brother Oddo. She wrapped the pistol in one of the most intimate linens of her trousseau, not without perturbation, and placed the parcel in a fur muff that she had added to the change of underwear. It would be as easy as could be, in an unfortunate circumstance, to insert her hand in that nice fur and find... the solid grip....

With a shiver Clelia quickly got undressed and sheltered herself in her spinster's bed, crowded through the years with ever more pillows, rosaries, lace, ornaments, jars of valerian, cordials, eyewash and various perfumes, besides cookie crumbs and tiny tin-foil balls from chocolate candies.

5

At 6:10 AM on the thirteenth of December, the Mercedes-for-Hire of chauffeur Giocondo Giocondini pulled solemnly away from the front door of the Oddi-Sempronis, covered the last stretch of Via Ca' Fanti, still in first gear, and then entered cautiously but easily, with blinding headlights, the descent of the Pincio. There each of the passengers looked up through the still black branches of the chestnut trees, to see what the weather was going to be like. The sky was not visible, but the field between the Vigne and the fortress, wide open and raised just like Subissoni's civic chalkboard, was turning white in front of them and then on the left-hand side. The snow on top was intact, although not everywhere. It looked like a shawl, pierced and frayed where the fabric, especially around the edges, did not succeed in covering some of the mounds and shrubs.

"We can tell better at Fossombrone what weather we'll get," said Giocondini. "Now you can get a little more sleep if you want. Everything is in good shape. Last night my wife was up till midnight cleaning the inside, the carpets and the seats with Esso spray. It needed it. Do you know who I ran into last night, right here where we are now, while I was coming down the hill from your house? Subissoni and his companion... speaking of anarchists. They were in real bad shape. He was so worked up that to stop me he practically ran in front of the car. She was completely pale – more than ever – still acting like she didn't notice anybody. They wanted a ride to their house, and I gave them one because the owner of the hotel was there. Subissoni was out of his mind and kept telling me "easy easy" at every bump, and there are plenty on the way to Via dello Spineto; and it was scary how the woman let herself go on the back seat. For a moment she twisted her mouth and held up her hand like she was going to throw up. "Hey no," I said to him, "you and the lady are going to have to get out. This is costing me more than I make. I'm doing you a favor and you shouldn't take advantage by getting everything dirty for me." But all he did was look at the woman, who fortunately got control of herself. She paid – because he doesn't know how to do anything, he can't even manage a lira – she even opened the door to their house, and he wanted to go in first to help her but was stumbling all over, and it looked like he intended to bump his head on every part of the door way. Speaking of anarchists!… But we have everything, even chains!"

By then the Mercedes was beyond the foundry down along the national road. When Giocondini stopped talking a few drops started falling. The driver got into a more comfortable position in his seat and in his leather jacket, wiped the windshield in front of him with his hand and turned on the windshield wipers. These reassuring gestures, plus the subdued conversation of the two wiper blades and the torpor of the heater, a little afterward convinced the three travelers to sleep. The rain increased gradually and was coming down hard at the first bridge on the Metauro. There was no more snow around and a dark green color made the fields, the trees and the first slopes of the hills all look the same. At Fossombrone the rain got even stronger and kept up the same pounding rhythm until Fano. After turning onto the Adriatic road and after checking to see if everyone was sleeping, Giocondini lit his second cigarette; he feared for a moment that the noise of the motor reverberating between the houses might waken his load and he slowed down. The rain continued, but it was lighter against the sea and also against the tamarisk bushes.

At Falconara it wasn't raining anymore and the sea was as white as the snow in Urbino. The traffic had started with a few carts and people on bicycles around the station. During the climb up the Pinocchio above Ancona, a sudden gust of wind hit the car and carried off all the noise. This emptiness woke the passengers, all three. They were amazed to be at that point and happily began planning where they would stop for coffee and then where, about an hour later, around nine, where they would eat a brioche or a sandwich or a slice of pizza, or who knows what fresh local specialty. They agreed that it was fortunate to be traveling on Saturday, a day favorable for everything, including the baking of brioches, and even favorable for the freshness of food in general.

"We're already out of the duchy and in a couple of hours we'll be out of the country," said Giocondini. "You're right, Countess Marzia, Italy is short."

"Yes, but on this side along the Adriatic it isn't as bad, not as lazy as on the other side toward Naples and Sicily; although it's not really Italy on this side either. It's sad, low-lying, dyed. You can't tell where anything is, where the mountains are that you can see far off, rose-colored, here and there. If I remember correctly. The earth is brown like chocolate, full of rocks like hazelnuts; the cities are cookies, cupcakes, colored like the sugared almonds our farmers use."

"Don't get us hungry before it's time, Aunt Marzia," said Oddino. "Where are we going to eat?"

"I'd say in Bari," proposed Giocondini. "First let's do a good stretch and get within ninety kilometers of our goal: after dinner we can do the rest in a hurry. Everything considered, around four in the afternoon we can turn around at Taranto and start back."

"And how long before we get to Bari?" asked Clelia.

"Just over four hundred kilometers. We can get there around one-thirty if we avoid long stops before then."

"Good," said Oddino. "Right now it's five to eight. We'll stop in an hour and a half to eat something, and then we'll go straight through to Bari."

"Bravissimo," said all the others.

"He leads with confidence," added the aunts.

"In Pescara then! Breakfast in Pescara," said Giocondini.

At that point of the descent toward Loreto, the Mercedes was passed by a big-cylindered motorcycle driven by a man dressed all in black leather, with a black helmet too and a red neckerchief; his gloves and some other straps were also red. The motorcycle was red and black too. All together they noticed that on the back seat he had a black brief case, of solid leather.

"There's the guy with the bombs whose running away," discovered Oddino, "look how he's fleeing! Get his license plate. His license is BO for Bologna; he may be a communist. Or maybe it's BO for bombs."

Everybody laughed, but with trepidation, and Giocondini increased his velocity so as not to lose the motorcyclist. Oddino asked for a pencil to write down the number of the license plate and his aunts leaned forward to help him. They had retained the usual traveling formation: Oddino in front, to learn and to act as guide; Clelia, attentive, directly behind him, ready to give him a handkerchief, a candy, or some perfume; Marzia behind Giocondini, with the bag full of provisions and bottles at her feet; on the seat, between the two sisters, the straw basket filled with changes of underwear.

"It's him, it's really the bomber who's running off now to confess in Loreto... or even further on down, to Padre Pio," said Giocondini.

They laughed, fully absorbed by the chase, especially since as far as Pescara they knew the road and the scenery well since they had traveled several times to those parts and most recently to Atri, to see the facade of the cathedral, whose picture had appeared around the middle of November in a television spot that had the obsessive cadence of a strumming harp.

They lost the black and red motorcyclist just as they were entering Grottamare, but in a frenzy they found him again just beyond San Benedetto del Tronto. They stayed close behind him making all kinds of speculations on that solid brief case tied to the rear seat with perfect leather straps. A couple of times the motorcyclist turned around to look at them with that Martian face – especially that red crossways sneer – that gave a bit of a scare to the Oddi sisters.

But at Porto Ascoli the BO motorcyclist without slowing down turned right onto the road to Ascoli Piceno.

"Farewell bomber," shouted Oddino. "You're cutting out because you know we recognized you. He's pretending to go to Ascoli Piceno," he went on with disappointment.

"Fascist places," Giocondini let slip out. But no one reacted to that assessment.

"Here ends the state," said Marzia, "and these are already places that you can't recognize any more. All those little red villas with a small tower that are on the hills and these other green ones with terraces that are on the sea-coast: presumptuous the first ones, even with fences, and the others so badly made that they're peeling and have broken steps on the sand."

"They're fascist houses," concluded Oddi, surprising everybody with his tone of certainty and disdain.

There was a pause and then they started to recognize, while going through Roseto, the street where they, rather disappointed by the facade of the cathedral at Atri, turned the last time to go and eat. That dinner was also not among those worth rememberéing, the antipasto of sausage and the liver sausage barely good and just slightly better the walnut flavored after-dinner drink from Tocco Casauria. With these flavors in their hungry mouths they arrived in Pescara at 9:20 and stopped for breakfast. The café, which was at the beginning of a boulevard that still had some flowers and that led to the station, was nice. Inside there was a relaxing warmth that even gave off a cordial sense of community, perhaps because of the presence of three or four uniformed bus drivers who were joking with the waiters, with the cashier and with three other run-down customers, who could have been porters or unemployed men waiting for some small job to do around the buses.

It was one of them who suggested the *parrozzo* instead of the brioches. Our foursome was already happy just for that welcome and kindness, but even more so for taking that suggestion about the pastry specialty of Pescara. They ate with gusto and drank their hot cappuccinos smiling the whole time at the porters and waiters, but were unable to enter the general conversation – those others were speaking in a dialect so sharp that it did not permit our party any way to penetrate it. They listened to it with great curiosity, becoming horrified among themselves. They bought two packages of *parrozzo* and then Giocondini allowed himself a closing grappa. Finally, first the ladies, and afterward, but one after the other, Oddino and Giocondini, made use of the rest rooms.

In the meantime, without looking at anybody, three long-haired young men came in, shivering more from the cold than seemed appropriate for the outside temperature. They grunted at the cash register, and they all threw themselves against the hot espresso machine. The porters from the other end of the room looked at them disapprovingly but with tolerance, and while pointing them out to the bus drivers. One of them livened things up with a joke saying, "Da bombs! Assault upon the State," in stronger Italian, making it understood that he was repeating a slogan that he had heard or read that very morning. "Assault upon the State," repeated two or three of the porters and drivers playing with the force of those words that they were using for the first time, and which had no form or authority and were not very believable, especially because of the way they were exaggerated.

The three longhairs didn't react. Once they understood they made a few awkward grimaces with those green mouths of theirs, that immediately devalued them, unable to even give a good comeback to the quip. "Assault upon the State!" they too repeated, snickering.

Our foursome said good-bye to everyone, particularly to the porters, and went back to the Mercedes. The car was shining proudly under the light blue sky of Pescara, ready to welcome them within the profound quiet of its blue-tinted windows.

They took off in a hurry and began looking at the pine woods on the one side and the olive groves on the other until they saw the sea that was flowing slowly by under a sunny break in the sky.

"The South!" said Clelia. "Even the idea is different. It looks like it's on a trip toward other shores. It's not stationary and intact, like in our parts, between Rimini and Marotta. Here I'd never go bathing."

Oddino spotted a violet-colored town high up above the olive groves and asked what it was called.

"Ostina," answered Giocondini who already knew he had to answer those questions, even if he had to make up the answer. If they already started in the central part of the trip they could go on for at least an hour, referring to any old thing: a railroad crossing, a plant, a gas station, an abandoned bicycle on the side of the road, a little stream, a church, even a man.

"Who's that?" Oddino might ask and Giocondini would answer, "The road keeper" or "the baker" or "the plumber" or even "the doctor" "the pharmacist" "a bricklayer" "a farmer."

Usually Oddino liked the answers better with the definite article, that didn't leave him, in the uncertainty of a possible series, hidden, spread out in the vicinity, invisible behind hedges and inside houses.

A little before San Severo he started the questions with a church.

"San Marcello," answered Giocondini hurriedly.

Then a river. "Tramenta," fired back Giocondini.

Even a street sign: "The Monte Rotondo fork." Then someone on a bicycle: "The mailman... off service," because he wasn't wearing a particular kind of hat. "Nobody works on Saturday any more, not even down here."

Right after that a woman: "The laundress," made up Giocondini.

"From where?" asked Oddino suspiciously.

"From here. There's a nearby village here called Lindoni, which means that they all do washing."

"And that mountain up there?"

"That is, for sure, the Crociferato, near Basilicata."

"And this other one near us? This one that's all bright?"

"Ah! that must be San Giovanni Rotondo, Padre Pio's place."

"Have you come lots of times to Padre Pio's?"

"Not many, four or five."

"How come, with all those people that used to come down here from Urbino on pilgrimage?" asked Countess Marzia seriously.

Usually the aunts did not interfere in the question and answer game and when, occasionally in the past, driven by real concern over those automatic and inconclusive answers, they had done so, they had always been severely rejected, sometimes even getting into a quarrel that had compromised and even interrupted the trip.

"They used to come down here in groups, in buses more than as individuals. Only a few came down alone: those who didn't want to be seen or who had some specific questions to ask."

"Which ones?" Marzia continued asking.

"For example, if they should pick one wife or another; if they should buy farms or a pharmacy, if they should get an operation...."

"And what did Padre Pio answer?"

"He didn't even want to see them. And if he knew that it was for business purposes, he would chase them away with harsh words. He had a loud voice that could scare you."

"And what did the ones that were chased away say?"

"They got all worked up and poured it out on the whole trip home. They would say he was a witch doctor, a quack and not a saint."

"Did you see any miracles when you went there?"

"I saw lots of people crying seriously and other happy ones, as cheerful as sparrows at threshing time."

"Did you ever smell Padre Pio's perfume?" It was still Marzia who was interrogating, with Clelia getting a little dismayed and frightened that her sister could fall into irreverence.

"No, although... one time I did smell something.... I happened to be in back of a group that was going crazy...

all of them sniffing here and there while imploring and crying, and I even seemed to smell... a rose."

"A rose? Only one?"

"That's right! One rose. Really only one. So much so that I turned around two or three times looking for it, to see who had it... because it really seemed to me – it's clearer to me now as I remember – that it was a beautiful yellow rose and that it was in someone's hand, a man's."

"There are so many roses, everywhere...," said Marzia.

"But what time of year was it?" asked Clelia, who was lighting up with hope and with satisfaction at showing off her astuteness with that question.

"Oh, I couldn't say," Giocondini disengaged himself, "perhaps," and before responding he looked hard for a pronouncement that would not be banal either in a miraculous sense, putting that rose in the winter, or in the opposite sense, setting it among so many others in the sunny season, "perhaps in the fall... early fall."

"There are always roses," said Oddino, "and perfume can be spread around any way you want."

"No, Little Bird, don't say that," pleaded Clelia turning with disappointment toward her sister. "Some people smelled that perfume hundreds, thousands of kilometers away, and months and months after their visit."

"We're right in San Severo," said Giocondini, "and we're still in time to turn off to go and see and smell, if you want to."

"No, no," said the sisters together. "It wouldn't be proper; when the Church has made it's decision...."

"On to Bari," said Oddino, "to Bari. However I suggest," he added as though he had one of his plans, "that you don't use any more perfume. What kind of perfume do you have?"

Clelia and Marzia interrogated each other: they had the usual Jean-Marie Farina cologne, for their collective use, lavender in their lingerie, and personally, the first had her essence of lavender and the second had her Mytsouko, a gift – carefully held onto for sixteen years – from that very fascinating French antique dealer, who stayed on in Urbino for almost a week continuing to cover her with kindness even after he had bought that nude Venus spied upon through some branches by a big reddish colored satyr, which, who knows why, happened to be in the Oddi-Semproni's house.

It should be said that the Venus had been painted by Nicolas Poussin toward the end of 1626, in Rome, just after moving into the house on Via Paolina. Now if we want to go back to its entrance into the Oddi-Semproni's house, we can tell how it had been acquired from the Barberini family in 1782 by the grandfather, Count Oddo, during his last trip to Rome – some say because he was in love with that naked woman… and by then really only in shape for looking, others say because he was concerned about the upbringing of his thirteen-year-old grandson Oddino, without his father Sempronio, who was run through in a duel, not on the road but still outdoors, in the park of the Imperial Villa of Pesaro, by a certain officer Valganazzi whom he himself had challenged because he could not put up with his mocking interpellation, among the refreshments in that villa of Count Tizio, Caio, Sempronio Semproni. What is certain is that that naked Venus was spied upon for generations not only by the satyr among the branches, but by all the young males of the family, who would imagine with her all the moves that then they would put into practice with the servant girls. Our Oddino was not in time to see it before his aunts removed it, perhaps compelled by a subconscious need to adjust his desires, when he was not yet five years old. At that time he could only wonder why a little girl from Ca' Fante, who was fed to him by his aunts with her pig tails ready to be pulled, had to, in those moments of greatest clamor and desperation, because of the rudeness of his attacks and lapidations, squat down to piss on herself, something that for him worked so well standing on his feet, with his knees slightly apart.

In Bari, during dinner, Countess Marzia went twice to the restroom, but could not decide to throw away the flask of Mytsouko that reminded her of the one kind gesture that she had received in the course of her past life. The antique dealer had furtively invited her a good three times to his Hotel Italia and finally, the day before his leave taking, he had embraced her and kissed her on the stairs for so long and also so furiously that perhaps Clelia herself had noticed, as she sat waiting in the second parlor near the dining room, but with both doors open toward the stairway. Because of the embarrassment that followed, M. Maurice Lingelbach must have forgotten his promise to write to her and even to leave her his personal address in Paris.

Countess Marzia limited herself to better tightening the top of her flask and to wrapping it tightly in two well-folded sheets of regulation toilet paper.

The dinner in Bari was good, but, in part, ruined by Giocondini's wandering around the back alleys of the old quarter where he got lost looking for a short cut to get onto the road for Taranto.

Between Bari and Taranto it was raining in clear lines that made everything more rose and more brown-colored: to our party it seemed like a spring rain. This was part of the reason why Oddino could not forget about the rose. Instead for Clelia and Marzia it was a reason for dozing off during the whole stretch between Sammichele and Massafra.

With Taranto in sight the rain slackened off a bit: it was invisible up high against the sky full of luminous clouds, while it was acting furiously down below among the smoke that was rising from the ground.

Taranto appeared larger than our travelers had imagined, with an immense periphery laid out in blocks, crossed by streets that were still not all paved.

"Who knows what dust, if it wasn't raining," said Countess Clelia, and she added that those new houses seemed nice looking, but, who knows why, not very appropriate for southerners. More suitable according to her would be higher, more crowded and more somber neighborhoods, and not those little houses full of windows, bright and shiny with their fixtures and frames that gave the impression of being open so that you could see everything inside. The sky was reflected in all the sparkles aroused by the rain and went inside to invade the still-deserted habitations.

"When they're finished up with a few trees around they'll look better," said Marzia, "because at least all those slabs of yellow dirt will disappear and there will be a sidewalk, hopefully a dark one."

Going along toward the center, the older houses appeared, covered over with awnings as though a strong summer sun had been alive until an hour before.

The feeling that something celestial, fateful, had disappeared a short time ago and that everything had just been taken by surprise by an inexplicable yet total emptiness, was noticed by our travelers. The two sisters were about to get discouraged, until all at once they saw the sign for the swing bridge. At that point the city also rose up, with the dignity of some almond-colored buildings and a bone-colored church, as shiny as it was porous.

"What else is there to see among this minutiae?" asked Oddino.

The others didn't know what to say but were already looking haphazardly among the streets of the center for a café, a building, a portico worthy of note, which could serve as a reference point – that wave of comfort that an important and recognizable place, even if never seen before, emits toward the traveler.

But it was not possible to stop in front of the nicest and busiest café, which looked so warm and sparkling through its windows and plants. None of them would have left the car, which made the same sounds that it made in Urbino and kept intact its precious extraterritoriality, which was especially important in the middle of that bustling and cunning street.

"On to the bridge, to the bridge," said Oddino, "afterward we'll see if there's something else."

They drove around a circle thick with palm trees and turned into a very wide boulevard, with white buildings on the left, and on the right a row of big palm trees and a perforated balustrade. At the end, above the buildings, there rose a fortress of tufa and bricks; its unforeseen profile, a little on the dark side, was softened by the clouds. It seemed to Oddo as if they had to go up again in order to go down to the sea. There was the bridge in front of them, closed, slung out toward the other shore. Oddo didn't recognize it and was upset. He ordered Giocondini not to stop, to go as far as the open area, down there where there were some closed kiosks. He wasn't able to see the point from which the television pictures had been taken. Giocondini understood that he couldn't get his bearings, but did not suggest going over to the other side for fear of getting trapped there: he too knew very little about the functioning and the schedule of that bridge, which seemed completely useless to him, indeed as stupid as a war documentary.

"It's a rather colonial thing," he said to comfort Oddino.

"I really expected more," said Marzia. "Who knows when it opens and closes?"

"Well we're looking at it from so far away that we can't even see the water below. My goodness, why don't we go closer?" But Clelia, at the end of this intervention, was herself bored with that thing that she was unable to see. For a moment the evening before she had imagined seeing a glassy bridge, at least two kilometers long, going back and forth continuously to accommodate on top carriages, bicycles, herds of animals, people in a hurry, especially women with big earrings and baskets of fruit and fish; and underneath, ships of every type and color, warships and passenger ships, the first ones crowded with sailors, lined up and saluting, through lacerating whistle blasts, and the second ones also filled, but with Chinese men in pigtails. The Chinese were laughing. And there was also a trapeze artist who was performing between one side and the other of the moving bridge and also a little boy and a little girl, in bare feet, curly-haired, who were in danger of falling and being crushed by the two parts of the bridge that were reclosing: but in the end, among

the screams of a horrified crowd, they were able to save themselves by grabbing on to a wire: an iron wire put up there
fortunately by the Red Cross nurses of 1935.

"It looks like a public piss pot!" burst out Oddino, "a
rusted one!" The association, other than by that painted
mass of iron in the modern style, had been suggested to
him by the odor that was rising up from the wall and also by
that stretch of beaten earth that ran alongside the bushes, a
favorite place for military patrols, in which he had irritatedly
commanded Giocondini to park. His aunt's Chinese men
would also have come to those strong-smelling winding paths
once they had gotten out of their junks, with the congested
smile of urethral urgency. Giocondini too, driven by the same
power of suggestion that vividly captured the truth of his
corporal condition and relative position on the seat, betray-
ing the greatest degree of his incontinence, noted with relief those shrubs and directed himself toward them, while
saying that he would see what views might open up beyond
there or find someone whom he might ask. He came back
smiling and everyone understood what it was that he had
found and how he had rapidly made arrangements inasmuch
as he was bouncing along and rubbing the tips of the three
fingers that are generally most used, and also most displayed
and also imposed in benedictions and indeed in aspersions.

"Nothing," he said, "really nothing. There's the tower.
Maybe we should go up there, but I don't know how. There's
nobody there. Should we go and ask or should I just run
over there on foot?"

"You go," said Oddino.

"Ask when they're going to open it and if you can go over
it and if from the other side you can see better. We'll wait
here," said Marzia, who went on with a thought of hers
while opening the window on her side that faced the sea.
"It's humid, but the air is good. We're really at the bottom
of Italy. Just smell this air!"

Clelia considered that gesture rather daring, or at least
too confident; she withdrew into her corner and said nothing. Oddino was watching the clouds pass over the walled

fortress, noting the difference in color between the lower ones, which he saw through his aunt Marzia's open window, and the ones that were crossing above him, on the windshield, within the bluish area. He thought that maybe the high wall too could see them in two colors, above and below, and that in the alternating of the combination it received the same impression that he did of movement and travel. In order to pursue this impression he started whistling and found among his external noises a hissing suitable for his fortress friend, for that companion of his who was strong and had a powerful and round forehead like his own.

Giocondini came back saying that you could go over the bridge, that on the other side there was a nicer view of the city, and you could find fresh mussels to eat there. To see the bridge open and a ship go through they would have to wait until sunset, or even later, without even having the certainty of being able to watch the operations. They looked at him in amazement, standing on that ground, having returned after being away for almost half an hour, in part, because of information that he had gathered, but also with concern – as though he had risked getting separated from them and from the car, getting lost or getting absorbed or contaminated somehow by that strange atmosphere of the extreme point of the heel of the boot.

They agreed to cross the bridge and take a look around there. Giocondini got in and started up the car. Marzia had the courage to leave her window open. The Mercedes crossed slowly, in line, with its Urbinoite ticking-sound, which on that construction sometimes increased as though reacting to real emotions. Oddo was looking at the rounded sea on his side, while observing every detail of the bridge. The people and the houses constituted only a testimony: the thing to see was bigger or smaller, but in any case it was he who fixed its limits and who animated or blocked the scenes. Marzia was worn out by her struggle with the window, and by that strong air that could have dragged her away; Clelia sat tensely between her window and the basket from home.

"Whoops," said Giocondini at the slight bounce of the car as it came off the bridge. "Now where should I go to park?"

Oddo indicated on one side the last strip of that sea he was dominating. Giocondini stopped before that, on the edge of the open space near the mussel vendors.

"Ladies and gentleman," he said to Oddo, "don't you want to try some? May I get out?"

He obtained permission to go and taste the mussels, but none of the others moved. Marzia was tired out by the joy that was about to bring her a sea of regrets. Oddo had in front of him his companion, who would remain there for him, with seriousness, indifferent to the highness or lowness of that bridge which was a kind of railroad crossing. He was able to determine that the fortress looked out toward the sea, toward the infinite, among the clouds, a bit obliquely, just not to be distracted by the variableness of the bridge. Clelia was taken up by the boring thought that the bridge resembled other monuments also far away from Urbino, such as the Mole in Turin; the central train station, inside, where the trains leave from, in Milan; and even, a little, the Galleria, also inside, in Milan; and that block of Via Nazionale in Rome that consists of the National Gallery of Modern Art, the tiled tunnel and the pinnacled top in the background, that you may or may not see, but which are, in any case, the ideal enclosure of that stage set and of so many other unitarian stage sets throughout Italy, of the Altar of the Fatherland.

Other clouds arrived, and the sea started getting high, at least for a long stretch out toward the Ionian, and these signs made Oddo understand that he could not hold up his companion any longer, that he probably wanted to leave, with an even more tender brow and the yellow color that was running off preceding him on the backs of the most luminous clouds.

6

"There's nothing I can tell you except to talk about it... a lot, all the time, everything; the fact itself, its separate parts, how it was done, how it's reported, interpreted. If this explosion remains integral and isolated, commemorated only in the speeches of men in power, it will become consecrated for all time like an altarpiece: it will go on exploding forever, intimidating us forever. We will follow all the news about it and we will discuss it thoroughly."

These were the words of Vivés, the morning of the thirteenth, addressed to the three porters of the Autonomous Communal Consumers Organization who had been waiting anxiously to hear her opinion about the bombs in Milan. And while they were leaving the tiny office to go to the warehouses, she added: "Do you feel some guilt? Do you feel like you made a mistake recently with your strike?"

"No," they answered from the door. "But what if they were comrades?"

"Even so you shouldn't feel guilty. There are impatient people everywhere. But I don't think the bombs are red. If they were red there would have been thousands blowing up, in lots of different places. Either they are the government's and then there will be others that they'll make go off a few at a time until they justify a state of emergency, or they're fascist provocateurs'. If we don't talk about it, the injustice will remain hidden, even inside us, until it finds its place, even inside us."

Vivés didn't eat at noon. She looked with a wrinkle of a smile at the Spanish sardine on the little can – Hah! Hah! Dolores the fisherwoman! – among her little yellow waves, more like the tails of a comet than sea swells. "The sea at Gerona, that doesn't have a sea," she thought. "The sea of land between Gerona and Mauresa." She got a taste in her mouth and chewed to get control of the recollection. She too had made bombs... and yet she had had a little girl's dress embroidered and frilled like those waves of the sardine! She had traveled by train with eleven kilograms of explosives from Gerona all the way to Malaga; down there she had put together the bombs, prepared her wicker basket, and had gone down to the docks at the right time to throw them at the ships just arrived from Morocco.

She had come away from the docks without difficulty behind some real cigar and fruit vendors, perhaps because the bombings of her two other companions had happened an instant after hers and had been more intense. Together with those women she heard the chain explosion of the bombs in military barracks and quarters; they sent a smell of dung through the whole city and it seemed like the cavalry, which had come galloping crazily out through the streets, was chasing after this smell. She stayed in Malaga for three days, always out on the streets with the problem of rejecting the passes that soldiers would make. She had gone back to Gerona on the train passing through Madrid and at every station she had gathered different news about the Republic and about sedition: the train kept going while passengers with opposing opinions argued openly. Spain was no longer divided in two, but in two thousand pieces. Vivés was making that trip like a big inspection; she was directed with her whole heart toward her little part, where she felt she had to begin. In Madrid she waited calmly for the second train, while she heard that the government was in permanent session and that the people – many were arriving at the station and shouting and threatening the trains, the locomotives, as though they were organs of the ministries capable of making decisions – were asking for arms. She got on the train and waited half a day for it to leave, without even getting off to look for something to eat.

She put down the little can with the sardine and then with much seriousness cleared off the green felt area of her little desk. She chose a sheet of checkered paper and pointed her pen over it, but after thinking for a moment she took out a notebook and started writing, in Italian: "On December 12, '69, at 4:47 PM the bombs (one bomb?) were (was?)

exploded in Milan in the Branch Office of the National Agriculture Bank in Piazza Fontana (N?) causing 12 deaths (13?) and 97 (96?) injuries.

"The public is horrified and alarmed but appears to be controlling its fear, in part because of the indifference diffused (on purpose) by this democracy deprived of any qualities, with no means of direction or control. There is no common line, other than some groupings among the opposition; but even here without any principles or obligations.

"This bomb, which has injured us (by chance?), can constitute our hope for a mass discussion of our principles and of our institutions, in addition to government policy.

"By today's press, the *Corriere della Sera* (middle class) and *l'Unità* (communist) I am informed of these data...."

Vivés stopped. The deep pain that she felt made it difficult for her to do the news-study that she had proposed for herself; instead it pushed her toward writing a diary, and with the urgency of remembering and with the intimate doubt, new for her, whether the throwing of bombs could be justified. The generic quality of this doubt was new for her, because in the past she had felt that it depended only on the specific conditions of the conflict, and she had always overcome it with the conclusions that she had been able to reach.

The diary would be a useless indulgence. How many of them had her Gaspare begun! And how irrelevant they had appeared to her, outside of any time or philosophical reference!

Instead everything should start again from the beginning, returning to the moment of the proclamation of the Spanish Republic of 1931.

A game had been started there that was still being played. Gaspare had withdrawn a long time ago, he had put himself above it, beside it, across it and was spinning his cocoon of anger and sweetness. "But me?" wrote Vivés to herself on the sheet of paper that she had chosen shortly before.

She left the office at that unusual hour and went home in a hurry to find her man as though she had to make up for the insults, which she had cast at him with her thoughts and judgments, by seeing him again and by her unexpected presence and by some affectionate gestures.

Subissoni wasn't home, but she knew she could find him under the trees of the Mill having a discussion with the mechanics and the bricklayers, filled with fervor now that they were better able to listen to him during their work break.

Subissoni was deeply moved upon seeing Vivés and went toward her swaying back and forth and rubbing his hands together: "What's new? What's happened?"

"Nothing," the woman reassured him. "Nothing. I only wanted to see you and take a little rest together with you. We slept so little last night."

They went into the house and sat down. Subissoni had not eaten but did not want to admit it to his companion in order not to show his real state of agitation.

"Let's have some coffee," he proposed. "And for resting, do you want to really go to bed in your room?"

"No, I'll just stretch out right here," and she indicated the couch in the living room-kitchen. That was the spot, next to the door of the tiny room where their inexpensive stove and sink were, where she would feel the warmest.

"This story about the bomb must be followed with great attention because it marks the beginning of the last act. We have to follow it together and discuss it a lot, every piece of it. What is the Bank of Agriculture? Who goes there? What are its rooms like? Exactly where did the bomb explode?"

She was talking as though she would make a long speech and when she stopped it surprised Subissoni who was getting ready to follow her. He looked at her and Vivés turned her smile into a communicative twist to express their mutual intention: meanwhile she raised her left arm behind the nape of her neck. "The coffee, the coffee, how about making this coffee." She said the words one after the other, but raising and lowering her voice, with her breath regulated by the autonomous impetus of her chest and she repeated the word "coffee" three times to completely free herself from that swelling.

She turned her face toward the wall, but then turned around again and right afterward took up a sitting position: "I'd love to have an omelet like they make in Mauresa, even more flavorful than the ones in Gerona," she said seriously, staring enchantedly at the door.

The revelation had it's effect on Subissoni too, who realized that something was wrong with Vivés. Meanwhile she was saying, "I'm reacting to this thing like a conventional person. Where's it going to end?"

She was still looking at the door. She lowered her eyes to her lap and then started considering the sweater that she was wearing.

Subissoni was frightened; he got up so as not to show it too much and started dealing with the espresso maker; he unscrewed it and noticed that it was already prepared, at least its filter was filled with coffee; he shook it to hear if there was water in the bottom and let it slip out of his hand; the coffee fell on his shoes, the water that filled the bottom part to the proper level splashed on his shirt sleeves and his pants.

"Look what I've become," he muttered, "I'm pissing on myself and my shoes. Last act indeed; for me it's been all over for some time, since even before I left. Ugh! this pompous and loathsome country. They'll end up arresting us again. Another prison camp, another jail, other prison guards. Bring them on, we've got to get to know them, listen to them, taste their hypocrisy and now their ferocity."

He tried to gather up the coffee piled on his shoes, but in his anger ended up spreading it all over, puffing and shaking like a fan.

"We need to get to know them, that's true. For too long we've only been reading," said Vivés, "and we've been deceiving ourselves inside this house. We even bought it, and what's more we have calculated our interest. We know nothing about who's in charge. We know nothing about industry. We know nothing about Milan. We know nothing about unions. We know nothing about workers. We know nothing about collectives. We know nothing about local government.

To us everything seems to consist of words and of that ugly milk from the television. It's like the Republic of 1931: the same constitution, the same middle-class face."

"How come you're saying these things to me? We have lived. You've been able to write and even work without serving anybody. Many people consider you their teacher," said Subissoni provoked to the point of becoming immobile. "Many people," he repeated. "And if it's because of the house that you have to suffer, we can sell it," he started trembling again with his eye still staring up in the air.

Vivés tried to calm down by getting herself more comfortable on the couch. She turned toward the window and stared at the curtain. The play of the light on its embroidery could even be a city on the edge of a white desert – a low-lying, neat, quiet city, inhabited by reserved and hard-working people – the city knew that soon it would be overcome by a terrible calamity: by a disease that was swift and unstoppable like an eclipse.

The image had been Durruti's, who spoke to the crowd at Sallent while the CNT – an autonomous organization fighting alongside the Republican Government forces in the Spanish Civil War – was raising the red flag on the town hall to proclaim the independence of that community. At that time Vivés was watching from a wide-opened window and throwing flowers on the people.

Then she had seen the civil guards reenter, but from the street where she had fought alongside of the anarchists. In the end she was worn out, convinced that she had made a big contribution, but the guards ignored her when they made their arrests. They took the men around her who were smiling, as though they were getting ready, as a matter of course, to undertake another job. Vivés had been disappointed and stayed stretched out on a wall looking at the valley of Llobregat until night, until the white light of the moon unveiled the fields.

Now another disappointment was again casting a spell over her, but her fixation was with doubt and with a fear for which she did not know the cause; it was not a fixation with the endeavors of her youth. She concentrated on the curtain with an infantile grimace across her whole face, which, however, did not succeed in canceling from her eyes the staring that was making them dilate. With an unemphatic voice, as though she was reading the end of one of the cooperative's inventories, she said, "These bombs have measured my life! This much is certain."

Subissoni was upset, he looked around the house to see where the blame might fall. His good eye hit upon the walls, the fireplace, the door toward the stairs and the upstairs, which with their material innocence made him even more emotional. "What is this fear?" he said, partly to himself. He took two steps forward and put the unscrewed espresso maker on the table. Then he saw the woman who had been since '39, for so many years, his sustenance and also the object of all his energy – the little space between her lips, the part that he felt most in that moment. That space suggested an unfulfillable void, equal to the one between the two chairs that stood on this side and that side of the table.

"Order...," he said, emphasizing the syllables to express his own feeling of impotence, which was itself suggesting many more problems and themes, "life... the part of it that remains unknown, life with purpose, the democratic republics, the history of constitutions, the loss of civil relationships... even the bombs, so many of them! So many memories! The orders, the institutional confusions, the marmalades of the masses; where should we put ourselves? Wasn't it into studying?" he mumbled. "This house we can sell, if it bothers you to own it. In fact, donate it to the orphanage, if they just let us live here till we die...."

This word stopped him and gave reality to the space between him and Vivés, as though he had fallen into it. Then he became overwhelmed with emotion, ·

"...la vida sigue,
los muertos mueren y las sombras pasan;
lleva quien deja, y vive il que ha vivido,
Yunques, sonad,"

at this point he spoke in an undertone. "Wasn't it you who

taught me this poem? How was I feeling when you recited it to me the first time? If my eye had been infected?"

Vivés looked at him and was not able to give him a smile: once again, and like always by chance, Gaspare, putting forth so many words and gestures, succeeded in unveiling for her the reason for the pain that she was feeling and in putting her in a position to be able to act accordingly. Those verses, which she had always kept as a source of courage, were telling her now that she had abandoned her life and that she had not prepared the conclusion and that, in the meantime, the end had drawn closer.... It was in front of that window and it was sending her a ray of light that brought a pain to her chest and her whole side on which it was shining.

Subissoni understood that Vivés was by then seized by the brightness from the window that was falling in front of her in a puddle, splashing her feet.

"All you need are a couple of lines tied together to enchant a Spaniard," he mumbled, then rejected: "especially if he's in jail," he added to empty out his bitterness.

His eye was tearing and so the need to go and check it allowed him to get out of that situation of feeling excluded. He withdrew to his room and approached the mirror on his chest of drawers; but before looking at himself he looked at those things that he loved, to the point of becoming emotional. The house was justified, it wasn't property, it was a refuge; and the pieces of furniture were useful and silent companions, without ambition and yet well prepared in history, and even in sociology, as required nowadays. They knew how to stay in their place and do their job. In the first drawer of that chest were his three shirts, his eleven handkerchiefs, his two pairs of cotton underwear, his four pairs of socks lined up for the summer; in the second, his sweaters, his vests, his woolen underwear and socks, respectively in the quantities of three, two, three and five; in the third drawer were scarves, gloves, partly unmatched, bandages and, inside a package, a basin for ocular bathing, a rubber container, and a pair of glasses with an opaque left lens.

In his wardrobe were hanging three suits, of various weights, two pairs of pants, a raincoat; and on the two doors, on one side, four silk ties and, on the other, his Garibaldino neckerchief and beret; in the space at the bottom were arranged his shoes; two pairs for the winter, a third more suitable for the summer season. His bed was made of iron with a yellow bedspread of cotton, whose coolness Subissoni appreciated on his neck and on his hands even in the winter. Nearby stood his night table, with his books and recent letters on top; in the drawer some pens and pencils, a loaded revolver but with the safety on, some little packets of mints, aspirin, bicarbonate of soda, the syringe for his injections and, below, in the main section intended as the austere seat of that deposed nocturnal sovereign that was the chamberpot, his manuscripts in progress, his savings account book and a bayonet, standing on its handle.

There were other things around too, but they were less important, right then, than his watering eye. Subissoni had not looked at his eye right away because he knew well that it was only filled with tears; as usual, once or twice a year since '39, these tears would almost all go gushing straight into his blinded eye, in whose space they would stay shining like an oyster in an open shell: only if his tears, as had happened not more that three times in those thirty years, had flown abundantly, would they have flooded his eye lid and then flowed, not drop by drop perhaps quickly following one another, but like little streams down along the whole side of his cheek.

Subissoni concentrated on the house, partly because with regard to it he felt free of any guilt. He had chosen it, but Vivés herself had bought it, caught up in some momentary book-keeping professionalism. He had limited himself to expressing his very pure happiness. "In jail yes," he had always added to his motto during those last years in Urbino, "but to the Capuchins – a communal home for poor and lonely old people – into the hands of the nuns, never." And he himself said that his sarcasm had the sad brilliance of a bayonet – an Italian bayonet, from imperial Italy, one, Savoyard and Mussolinian, had stuck him in the left eye during the encounter between the Garibaldi battalion, in which he fought, and Roatta's black arrows along the road to Briluega, during the first action of the so-called battle of Guadalajara.

Subissoni was attacking a villa called Palazzo Ibarra when he was wounded: he went on fighting in the second line until toward the end of the night between the twelfth and the thirteenth of March '37 when his companions took this Palazzo Ibarra by storm. The exaltation of the victory over fascist Italians kept him at the front until the morning of March 18, when in his bandages he heard the entire republican army move out toward the offensive on the Guadalajara front. Vivés was there with the anarchists of Cipriano Mera,... but only at the end, in prison, would he meet her.

Subissoni, tortured by pain, could not fight for the whole rest of the war, while Vivés would go on fighting to the end always with Cipriano Mera; but when she saw him turn against Madrid, to liberate Casado barricaded into the southeastern section by Barcelo's communists, without saying anything she laid down her arms and took off through the fields. She too had stopped on a March 12, that of '39, as they were able to determine together six months later in the prison camp.

Now the bombs marked another twelfth as the date of the day.

And hadn't he left Paris for Madrid the evening of September 12, 1936?

What day was it when he had taken the qualifying exam in Rome for teaching Italian and history in high school? He couldn't remember, in front of that mirror, overcome with amazement – even after so much time had passed – at the events that had befallen him during and after that fateful exam.

"So you come from Urbino," the president of the committee had noted. "Urbino. Pesaro-Urbino. Then you should be able to tell me with precision about il Duce's speech in

Pesaro six years ago: his brilliant speech about the defense of the lira... tell me about it with even the detail of a reporter..." – and upon his hesitation – "...But surely you were present, in that piazza, on such an important occasion! And in your own province...."

"Yes, Pesaro is the province," he had mumbled. "Urbino, you know, is far away... almost forty kilometers; and it is only nominally a provincial capital... and as a second name...," he tried to smile.

But that fascist president would not listen to reason.

"What," he got up in arms, "you did not go to Pesaro to hear that speech of such importance? Then you are a monument of indifference... and even worse... and so impeded as to not be able to go less that forty kilometers to hear il Duce? And you would like to go and teach in the schools of our Italian youth? And what would you like to teach... effeminatism or democratic legitimacy... decadent poetry...?"

"Well, look, D'Annunzio...," Subissoni tried to object.

"D'Annunzio? D'Annunzio is a hero. He flew over Vienna, he conquered Fiume, he was in the war, he lost an eye against the enemy." (Ugh! Ugh! the evil eye...! Subissoni caressed his bereft cheek.) Then he had smiled while suggesting: "But didn't he also write some poetry...?"

"That's it," shouted that president, "out with your membership card; tell me if you are a fascist, if you love Italy, if you believe in il Duce, if...."

Subissoni got up and said with livid firmness, "I love poetry, I am a Leopardian, I love Cattaneo and Pisacane... and also the *spigolatrice* – the poor peasant women who gathers up the remains after the grain harvest – I believe that Italy still needs to be created...." In conclusion the president had called the guards on duty and had had him arrested. He stayed in Regina Coeli Prison for sixteen days and then was sent back to Urbino, without a word.

In front of the train station outside Urbino three fascist squad members were waiting for him and, while he was starting toward the city bus with the other passengers, they attacked him and beat him till he bled, while calling him "the Leopardian *spigolatrice*." Luckily since they had to ridicule him that way, it limited their beating just enough so as not to be fatal. After three hours Subissoni was able to stand up and undertake the bitter uphill walk to Urbino. The whole night long, step by step, he went up toward the city, every so often throwing himself down on the grass on the side of the road and looking at the moon with the words of Leopardi: "What are you doing there, moon in the sky? Tell me what." Two months later his mother died of heartbreak, without having completely forgiven him for that scandal.

A little after that, when school had started, he noticed that he had not been assigned to any of the high schools in the province and "not even in the kingdom, and not even on the islands of the kingdom" in the words of the supervisor's office in Pesaro. So then he applied to the Free University of Urbino, the heritage of local civilization, the pearl of independence and of autonomy, for any kind of a job, even as an assistant librarian, but he was rejected, and with much hypocrisy, even too much, which affected him more than the beatings.

After a few months he sold his house and one night he left Urbino. After ten days, having undertaken a long, but well-prepared journey, he landed at Marseilles and from there proceeded toward Paris.

He settled into a small hotel called Jeanne d'Arc no less, near the Porta d'Italia. It still had a sign on the door to advertise that inside, even in the rooms, was the prodigious presence of electric lights. The hotel was full of Algerians and some whores that even the Algerians disdained. One of the whores attended to him on the night that he had a delirious fever, wetting his forehead and his lips while relieving him of almost half of his pecuniary assets. So then he took a job with an art merchant, which consisted of reading to him the writing in Italian on the borders or on the backs of paintings, or of prints or catalogues. With this work he paid for his two scant meals a day, washed down with two Alsatian beers. But he soon quit in order not to run the risk, which he felt was very serious due to his status as an indigent exile, of falling in love with the young daughter of the antique dealer. To elude the pursuit of this very gentlehearted girl he also left the Hotel Jeanne d'Arc and got a job for the summer as second watchman at an aristocratic villa in the suburb of Merly. In the café of Merly he learned how to get into contact with exiled Italians and to enroll with them in the international brigades.

He presented himself swaying back and forth like a bell, almost deaf from his own excitement. He proudly gave his personal information while expressing his contempt for Urbino, its not-very-free university, the local fascist headquarters, the organization itself, the founding duce and that horrible backdrop that was Savoyardically unified Italy: Gaspare Crescenzio Aldobrando Subissoni, born in Urbino on June 2, 1901, at 4:00 AM, with a degree in fine arts from the University of Rome; he failed to say that he had studied there while living in the Nazarene College, him, a free thinker!

"Code name?" This request surprised him and shook him with such pride that it uncovered his cranium.

"*Spigolatrice*," he answered, even successfully holding back his emotions.

"*Spigolatore* – the masculine form – might be better, comrade," the enlistment commissar tapped him on the arm.

And as a *spigolatore*, he thought, he couldn't help getting an eye injury.

"But I found," he said to himself in the mirror, "the nicest ear of corn in all of Spain." The impetus of Vivés brought him back to the conversation of a while ago and completely restored his distress. He forced himself to understand what could be grieving his companion so much; what, after years in which they had discussed and understood everything, from Stalin to Kruschev, from the Uomo Qualunque – the political party in immediate post-war Italy that appealed to former fascists and other extreme right-wing elements – to the MSI – the neofascist political party – from the Garibaldi front to Pacciardi, from the blacks to the French Maytime of the year before, could have disturbed Vivés so profoundly. He had never seen her cheeks depressed like that, that look in her eyes with no love, fury or pity; her eyes drawn inside like two watch lights. So he took it out on the government, on the Christian Democrats, the Socialist Party, the Republican Party, the Social Democrats, the unified people, the schismatics, the communists and the trade-unionists, the priests and the bosses, Italy, lower Italy, upper Italy, the Pope, oh the Pope!, yes, the universities, the ministries – and here he laughed like a crazy man – the ministers, the assistant ministers, the ex-ministers, etc., etc. with furious ramblings, grimaces, menaces – and he also added the police, the border patrol, the carabinieri, the phony regions, and also the new universities in Abruzzi, Apulia, Campania, Basilicata and Calabria and the one in Trent and the one of the Sacred Heart, and finally the one in Urbino too, yes the superb, free and binate, because of the one in Ancona, the Tambronian... once in Urbino in '46 when it was still a matter of prestige to get him up on a speaker's platform, all nice and squint-eyed with his beret and neckerchief, someone had introduced him to Tambroni... out came some profanities that could cloud up the mirror and rattle the packages in the drawer of his night table.... It had been Vivés herself who had told him to not let himself get taken in by those phony antifascists, not to get up on those platforms, where with regularity he would stumble around and risk knocking down flags, banners, posters and microphones with his swaying back and forth, "...too bad I didn't knock down the scenery of this farce, too bad I didn't destroy this miserable little theater of very bad actors...." The actors recalled him to his senses; he was able to calm down in a moment thinking about the actors he had always loved. In Paris whenever he could he went to the "Comédie" and even tried to enroll in a course on acting. "Why?" they had asked him; "actors die of heart attacks," as they watched him clutch his heart in confusion to ease the pain. He looked at himself in the mirror; he carefully felt his chest and checked the rate of his pulse, he breathed deeply and went into the bathroom to freshen his temples and his wrists.

He decided that he should get a clear explanation from Vivés: that she should say what was bothering her, what she felt like doing or not doing, and together after a thorough discussion they would decide what was best.

"Fortunately and to our credit too and also because we have had lots of practice," he said with ceremonial formality, satisfied with the decision he had made, "we know how to choose. We know how to evaluate and to choose. We're not a couple of novices! We have not been deformed by fascism, we're not like these Italian politicians.... So now we are able to discuss and to choose."

Vivés smiled when she heard him talking that way, like the rector of a seminary, and she really got a kick out of it. She made a gesture for him to come closer and then she gave him a caress and not just with her left hand, which she felt a need to exercise along with her whole arm, but also with her right hand so as to cover any appearance of egoism in her gesture.

"Sweetheart," she said to him, "I'm going to get very much involved in this matter of the bombs. I want to study it, to examine every aspect of it. Spain can serve as an example, its history between '30 and '39. I'm familiar with it and I have to make my experiences available to our most trustworthy comrades. I'm going to organize a study group with some of these people. We'll take note of everything and we'll discuss everything. Unfortunately we won't always have reliable sources; it would be necessary to go to the scene and to talk with so many people: we know well how the newspapers exaggerate and invent things. It may be that I will have to go to Milan. You won't mind too much, will you? You know that we have to pay attention to every detail available, evaluate everything without getting led astray.

The light from the window had retreated and in the shadows Vivés appeared recomposed and calm. Subissoni looked at her and the scholarly pose slipped off of his face. His companion was rigid, distinct from everything else in the room, the ear of corn erect and not cut, not picked and not knocked down by the wind of his emotions and his proposals. Vivés was performing and her eyes, only slightly aroused as they looked in his, were declaring that she knew how to perform. Subissoni began swaying back and forth as though he had been hit by a flying object: only a few moments later from within him came an impulse that made his hands tremble.

7

A few minutes after 5:00 on the afternoon of Sunday December 14, Giocondini's Mercedes was making the climb up the Pincio. Oddino was looking at the field of the Vigne. It was shining white in the fading light of the sunset; it was still snow-covered although by then the shawl had become very soiled and lacerated. Somebody must have gone out there and walked around for quite awhile and stamped down the snow to make a sign, indeed to write some letters: some A's and some S's were recognizable in this order: AS S (barely legible) A (barely legible) S; but then the writing became unclear on the line below, in the middle of the field, in a very confused stamping, as though the writer had fallen down several times and had forgotten the final part of the message.

Oddino yawned and looked at his aunts who hadn't spoken since dinner at the Passetto restaurant in Ancona.

The journey had gone on for another twenty-four hours after reaching the goal of the swing bridge because a pandering advertisement had attracted the young count toward a visit to Alberobello, the famous city of the trulli.

"Trulli or twirls?" Oddino had said upon seeing the curious white habitations, and his aunts had enjoyed the comparison: those houses really looked like a collection of overturned toy tops that children twirl. The visit had been brief; a quick little tour of the trulli section with a few comments about the cleanliness of the streets and of the roofs, about the white color of the limestone and about the small scale of the houses.

Supper was consumed in Barletta, and a certain distrust circulated among them regarding the roast lamb – precisely whether or not it tasted of game, whether or not it was from the mountains, Apulian or from elsewhere: Greek or Yugoslavian or even Albanian. The meal, as always, had been a complete one, from antipasto to dessert, to fruit, to coffee, to the after-dinner drink. Afterward followed the rest room operations, which were prolonged in view of the lengthy sitting until Urbino.

But when the headlights illuminated the signs for San Giovanni Rotondo, Oddino ordered the second deviation.

"Let's go to the convent of Padre Pio. Let's see if by chance we can smell some perfume."

"Right now, in the middle of the night? We won't find a place to sleep! And then who knows what kind of beds for pilgrims and what latrines!" said Clelia, counting on the horror that Oddo felt for unclean toilets or the evidence of, or even the warmth of, a previous user.

"We'll sleep in the car; and our other needs we can take care of outside. There's no snow down here."

Giocondini, who was very content with this additional deviation, with the lengthening of the trip and corresponding bill, solved the problem by saying that he knew of a small hotel where they would find everything comfortable and to their liking.

The women gave in, partly because of the idea that within one hour, and not five or six, they would have a warm and sufficiently long bed.

"Tomorrow morning we'll go to the first Mass and then we'll go straight home. It's Sunday, tomorrow."

Giocondini agreed enthusiastically, so much so that he went as far as promising that the next morning he would take communion; that he felt a real need to do it outside Urbino, with a different confessor, and in a climate of general sanctity. He also prepared himself for the possibility of getting a dose of perfume.

The sisters found the idea of communion a good one, but the one about perfume hazardous, especially since at that time Padre Pio had already been buried for quite a while. At that point, however, they understood why Oddino had prohibited the use of all perfumes since the morning. They looked at each other and with a squeeze of the hand they communicated their respective emotions.

A little later Oddo opened the window on his side: a gust of cool, in fact cold, wind, entered, which also instantly revealed itself to be humid and, in that first stretch, to be completely without any aroma. But nobody said anything, limiting themselves to covering their necks.

They arrived in the town, and it started pouring rain. It was just past midnight and there was no one on the streets. Giocondini couldn't find the little hotel that he had promised. There were no signs lit and in the glare of the headlights, dilated by the rain, it was not even clear how that city was formed. Small white houses alternated with immense empty spaces, as though suddenly an abyss opened up; and then some little trees arrived, bent by the wind, sparkling under the headlights and, afterward, white or red loggias that were oblong, enormous, empty like skeletons and, afterward, very tall and compact buildings. Our travelers were prisoners of the Mercedes, which was puffing unhappily, partly because of the strain of the low gears into which it was being forced by Giocondini who had finally run out of luck. With terror in his eyes and with his rounded nostrils fully dilated, partly to express sympathy and to sustain those souls, he went so far as to invoke the help of Padre Pio, to guide them and to welcome them. He was rewarded with the worst, because the downpour increased to a velocity greater than the velocity of the windshield wipers; what's more Giocondini noticed that the wheels were skidding on the muddy surface of that sort of piazza in that disaster area in which he had gotten himself lost. He put the car in reverse gear while mumbling something about not remembering exactly the way to the little hotel and while trying to bring himself alongside the houses that he had last seen. At least there the car would be a little protected and would not be blown away.

"And we didn't even want to ask Padre Pio whether we should sell our farms or repair the villa of the Chiú," said Clelia. Giocondini jumped at the name of the villa that for years had been at the top of his desires, the goal of his plans and of his servitude. But by then he was alongside the houses and had to maneuver to reverse his direction. Oddino remained impassive at his side and was looking straight ahead with the concentration of a cockswain who knows that he is near the place where he has to change direction. Marzia was troubled by the rain and by the disorientation, but seemed to be tasting them with a wrinkle in her nose stimulated by the feeling of a premonition. Other dark buildings appeared and then a loggia at the side marked by a reddish light on the inside edge of its pavement. Giocondini faced it and filled it with light by bringing the hood of the car right under the last arch. There was no one there and the vaults, crudely lit by the headlights, appeared like the parts of a poorly anchored balloon.

Oddino got out and with a couple of steps positioned himself in the middle of the loggia. His pose was regal and his figure cast a tall shadow across the entire space between the arches up to the ceiling. He raised his head and made a sign with his hand that intimidated the three inside the car, and also aroused their expectation of who knows what revelation. Another figure came out from the shadows and placed itself in front of Oddino. The three shuddered but they were soon able to see that it was a woman, a tall gypsy woman all wrapped up in a mantle. As she turned toward the car, the coral jewelry, which was shining in her hair, and also her teeth emitted rays of light.

Oddino turned around too and with a peremptory gesture summoned Giocondini. The latter moved his big buttocks, which showed clearly below his jacket, which had been pressed against his back during the whole trip. He moved his buttocks with a hesitation that emphasized the wrinkles in his pants and seemed to express all his caution and calculations in spite of his attempts to hide them. Finally he went up to Oddino, bowed, rolled his eyes, and went back to the car to get the basket of food, which represented the precious reserves of Urbinoite energy and virtue. These were the regular supplies that the Oddi's took on all their trips: in a nice tall basket, equipped with special compartments for a thermos, a flask, a bottle, silverware and napkins, and with a cover held tightly by leather straps and brass buckles. Oddino took the basket and offered it to the woman just as it was. The latter threw herself on the ground to open it and immediately sank her teeth into the chicken that had been placed on top in the form of a dome, so that its fragrance would not be suppressed or contaminated. After shattering the chicken, she got busy on the loaf of bread, sitting up a little more comfortably on the pavement at the feet of her benefactor. Giocondini went back to reassure the aunts, but Marzia wanted to get out and join her nephew. Every so often Oddino looked at the woman's hair and then looked around as though he was searching for a connection between those tufts of hair shining with dirt, but also with a gentle moisture, and the color of the city and of the night just outside that loggia. When his aunt arrived, the gypsy stopped eating, tucked the food basket against her chest with both arms and turned her gaze to the gentleman who was standing over her.

Oddino smiled and likewise the gypsy; Marzia's smile was different. Giocondini smiled too as he tried to figure out where they were, where there could be a hotel, a convent, a hospital. Without answering the woman got up and placed herself at Oddino's side: they had the same prodigious stature and the same carriage; the down on the young man's chin shined in such a way as to raise some questions among those who were watching, the same questions that were raised by the wrinkles around the ears of that queen of the road. Marzia couldn't identify any particular one, but her heartbeat suggested that the encounter seemed like a scene from D'Annunzio: in '42 in Rome with her brother she had seen two of this poet's dramas, and with her spirit rather shaken by the city, which she was seeing for the first time, but also by its heartless youth, and by the theater itself, by the excitement and the suffering of her brother who in that theater was expecting to meet the woman for whose hand he had asked more than a month before. The whole affair was hopeless; blown up with misunderstandings, formalities, delays, glasses of anisette. In the end the future mother of Oddino appeared with a pallor that Marzia never forgot, partly because she often rediscovered it, for the most disparate reasons, on the face and also on other parts of the body of her nephew.

The vagabond offered one of her shawls to Marzia, and Oddino, with the same sapient appearance, bade his aunt to accept. The rain had diminished a little and the wind that preceded the dawn of the new day was stirring it up and whipping it into currents, leaving some places untouched. Oddino asked for the umbrella and then left the loggia. The gypsy ran toward the corner from which she had come, grabbed a waterproof canvas and followed him.

Marzia and Giocondini went back to the Mercedes. The car started up behind the two of them who were walking side by side, although six feet apart, without speaking to each other. It was not clear which of the two of them was choosing the direction; they were going here and there by chance but always in perfect synchrony, even when they would stop. The three others were hoping that the gypsy would tell Oddino where to find the hotel or the church and that they would get there soon because the cold and the humidity inside the car, which was going with all the windows open, were unbearable.

At a certain point Clelia got the feeling that she had been caressed on her left cheek by a warm hand that smelled intensely of violets. She said nothing, abandoned with her eyes the two figures who were proceeding at the edge of the darkness and stared at the violet light of the dashboard: she was seeing it for the first time because until then it had been blocked out by the presence of her nephew. Now that presence seemed lost – and irretrievable – to her. Then she became frightened and started to cry. Meanwhile the two giants were in front of the door of the church.

Oddino signaled to his companion to stop and went on alone until he touched the wood of the door. God had always been for him a preceptor who had unduly abandoned his house. He was waiting for him somewhat suspiciously,

ready to forgive him and even to be generous. He was looking at that door to see what it had that was different from
those at his house, in order to find there a sign that could
explain why the divine presence preferred it.

He also went to look at the smaller side door and walked
around the outside of the church. In the back near the sac-
risty there was a big open door from which were coming
some voices; it was a group of the faithful who were waiting
to confess in the place where for years the great friar had
heard confessions. There were a dozen of them, men and
women languishing from sleeplessness and lagging faith,
squeezed together in animal-like promiscuity. They looked
at the newcomer with suspicion and started squeezing even
more closely together toward the inner door as they rancor-
ously waited for it to open, so that many of them, especially
the females, indecently showed their weighty and discon-
solate rear ends, horrendously real, as though nude and with
their organs distinguished one by one by their animal like
movements and also by the short accents of the word that
each one had emitted.

Oddino went back to the gypsy who had remained in her
place; he was encouraged by a look at her austere figure
well-composed in her garments and started off again. They
walked to the end of the city where the country began; they
looked several times toward the sky and also, bending half-
way over, toward the ground. They never spoke to each
other. They went back to the church and walked around the
convent. They arrived at the hospital and from there back
again to the loggia where they had met.

Several times Giocondini had gotten out to plead with
him to get back in the car, to relieve his aunts of their grief,
to leave that witch who was only waiting for the chance to
rob him of everything and to damn him with who knows
what witchcraft. The first two times he had answered that
he wanted to look for and see and ascertain if you could
really smell perfume. The third time he ordered Giocondini
to give ten thousand lire to the gypsy. Consequently
Giocondini was not so eager to approach him again, at least

not as much as the aunts wanted him to be. At dawn Giocondini shouted that they were about to run out of gas, but Oddino was already coming toward the car, with the gypsy at his side.

They stopped and looked at each other with joy and with an understanding of each other that shocked the spectators, even though the evidence of a leave-taking reassured them. As a gift Oddino gave to the woman his umbrella and part of their spare clothing.

"You are the lord of Italy," said that nocturnal queen to him with a broken accent that affirmed the truth.

Oddo took up his position with his usual pose, and he was not at all excited, as though he had conducted the most natural of experiments. Giocondini floored the gas pedal in order to get away as fast as possible from that place of exaltation, in compliance with what had been decided by the aunts.

At daybreak they returned to the national Adriatic road, wide open for long stretches through the plain. A blue-white sparkle made it stand out among the fields, which were still dark or covered by the black foliage of the olive groves. The speedy Mercedes with its high beams emerged from the night and signaled the beginning of the day; from behind its blue tinted windows the travelers saw flocks of birds headed inland and a little later isolated sea gulls that were trying out the wind. The sisters were still struggling against the strangeness and the fatigue of the night and against the impression of having lost something else beside the basket of supplies and the umbrella – just as happens after being frightened. But they avoided searching for what they could have lost in order not to see themselves once again in that blinding downpour, lost among the insensible buildings and arches, and above all in order not to once again have in front of or behind them the image of the witch and also that of Oddino bewitched by her company. The sea gulls that were disbanding in the wind kept them in their anxious state. Oddino, on the other hand, was carried away by a new sensation: someone else, not of his own household, had followed him and obeyed him. The church of the holy friar had not had any effect on him, and he had maintained his freedom before all those whom he had encountered, and he had dominated every event.

The first sunlight appeared suddenly revealing an open plain that followed the route, with only very gentle ups and downs every so often. Under the influence of these undulations the three travelers fell asleep. They woke up an hour later when the Mercedes stopped at a service station. They didn't fail to get their cappuccino, nor to accompany it with some almond pastries. The bright daylight encouraged the sisters and the speed that was chewing up the distance kept them closed within the familiar and reassuring car.

Oddino was looking at the coast and at the signs; at some of which he turned all the way around to continue watching. He touched his forehead with his fingers, which he then moved to his lips to make a calculation. When he had apparently figured it out, he slapped his hands and placed them at rest on his knees, like a ruler.

In Ancona they ate avidly a six course sea-food dinner and then a sour cherry ice cream, another lemon ice cream drowned in vodka, coffee and finally the sacrosanct after-dinner drink of herbs. When it came time to pay Giocondini, as always, functioned as minister: he advanced the money and marked it down in his account book.

They got back on the road and at Senigallia, already in the environs of Urbino, the sisters fell asleep again. Oddo did not sleep and went on enumerating, arranging and checking – even with a bit of cruelty in addition to staidness – those exploits of his that all concluded with regal satisfaction and then severity. Giocondini looked at him twice, with a maliciousness betrayed by his big and shifty eyes. However, this malice was abated by the admiration that he breathed in little by little through his nostrils, for Oddo's composure, for the solemn appearance of his big round head, and the healthy look of his skin. The third time he pointed out to him the walls and the castle of Fossombrone, the seat of the countship of the Oddis, of his sovereignty.

Oddo, as always, measured the bridge across the Metauro, which was on his family's coat of arms, very high, all brick, with the perfectly rounded arch of Roman origin, but with the roadway and the walls in ascent toward the middle where they were joined, according to a seventeenth-century restoration, in an acute angle. Many people had thrown themselves from that bridge: even a woman from their household. These suicides or accidents had always invigorated the fortunes of the Oddi-Sempronis, often in litigation with the bishops of Fossombrone to impede them, in their desire to break that chain of incidents, by erecting a protective chapel at the entrance to the bridge. On the other side of the bridge, toward Sant'Ippolito and Fratterosa, there remained for our Oddo only five farms of the thirty-two that in 1781 had been counted on a family map. But Giocondini was not aiming at those – far away and abandoned to the reds – he was maintaining and continuously developing his plan to unthread from that map – already frayed and full of holes – the villa of the Chiú, not too far from Urbino, on the road to the Foglia, in a nice panoramic position, surrounded by oak trees, and nearby, just a little downhill, two farm houses and a hundred acres on a gentle slope. The villa had been abandoned for a hundred years, and the farmers had fortunately all gotten jobs with the university or the city. The entire property could be sold for at least two hundred million lire to the university, which was looking for a location for the newly instituted departments of agriculture and geology. Giocondini knew that for the Oddi sisters that part of their property represented above all a weighty sense of guilt, because of the decay of the villa, and the disaster that one hundred years ago had befallen the sixty-year-old countess discovered in a pool of blood from a hemorrhage of obscure origin from an unmentionable body orifice.

At the top of the Pincio, while it was slowing down to turn into Ca'Fante, the Mercedes once again passed Subissoni and his companion who were going to watch the afternoon television news. Subissoni recognized the Oddis and nodded his head in a deferential but rather vague greeting that could also have been mistaken for a casual gesture – for example, his trying to keep his balance on that slippery street. In Urbino the cold had preserved the snow with a doleful mood, which our travelers tried immediately to repel, in part with the joy of being home. Giocondini tried to wind things up with a reference to the discredit and stupidity of those two. "If every anarchist was like them! The bombs would blow up in their hands, or even before, in their faces."

"Is it true that Subissoni was blinded by a nun that he was raping? The nun pulled out a big needle from her headband and stuck it in his eye," said Oddo.

"Oh! It certainly could be true. I think that's the most that someone like him is capable of," laughed Giocondini.

The sisters had opened the door and were getting ready to unload the car. All at once Marzia rediscovered the vacuum left by the basket and – with an even more embarrassing surprise – the gift of the gypsy's shawl under the seat. She couldn't resist picking it up and unfolding it, It was really beautiful, full of soft colors like a peacock's tail, and in good condition too.

"It's beautiful," Clelia told her, "and it makes you look younger; it gives color to your face."

A strong emotion took hold of the sisters who hurriedly dismissed Giocondini, without listening to him about the plans for Christmas, which was coming soon, or about the annual closing of their accounts. They shut the door, each of them anxious to be alone. Marzia undertook the task of putting away their things in the wardrobe upstairs and Clelia of preparing hot tea for everyone.

Oddo, instead of going to the library and turning on the television, went directly to the science laboratory to sit in front of the globe.

Clelia in front of the buffet in the little room was struck by an effluvium of violet that made her dizzy.

8

Vivés had not missed a single newscast, always in the same chair in the corner against the wall of the Paci wineshop. In the same spirit she had bought all the Milanese daily newspapers each day, both Sunday and Monday. She had pursued everything with her notebook in hand, in order to write down any new element and every statement that she considered important. Subissoni had always stayed a step behind so as not to distract her. Sometimes he underlined with derision or with anger the salient passages, so as to warn her, in addition to declaring himself present and indignant to the point of being nauseated.

"The last drop... the bitterest...," and he even smacked his lips to suggest the aberrant refinement of the new potion. Thus he ended up being considered half-drunk by many people.

Vivés was going ahead on her own. Subissoni considered this detachment as the most serious nefariousness produced by the bombs and by that monstrous head that had made them explode. Toward that head whose presence he considered obvious and certain, he was directing threatening gestures and terrible grimaces.

After the evening news of Monday, December 15, Vivés left the wineshop and withdrew to her office at the Cooperative Store as though she wanted to meditate on her papers while waiting for the late news. Subissoni ordered a bottle of wine to legitimize his staying there. He went on suffering and inveighing for what had happened and taking it out on that head that he knew well but did not reveal, not even to those to whom he offered something to drink, and while shaking back and forth he got closer to recognizing every mole and hidden intention.

Vivés was going ahead on her own and didn't wait for any of the porters and clerks, with whom she had established a study group, to join her.

Little by little as the TV and the newspapers pounded out the news, the latter were detaching themselves from any supplemental research out of fear and also out of knowledge of its futility. The feeling of disdain and disapproval was shared by all, and no other bombs had exploded within the last two days. The Milan attack remained a provocation, not the beginning of a plan of attack against democracy. So said *l'Unità* and *l'Avanti!* and even the TV and the middle-class newspapers. The provocateurs were surely fascists or working for the fascists.

Vivés was going ahead on her own: in her tiny office she continued pouring over the newspapers, often going back to *La Stampa* where it was written: "...extremism, but extremism of the left,... they are dissidents of the left: anarchists, pro-China types, labor groups...." Her mouth and even her hands were strained with apprehension, but in her eyes a look of patience was developing that still succeeded in putting order into every gesture.

"Is a trap being prepared?" she wrote in her notebook. "Is it still possible that the anarchists will be accused, after all that has happened? Death has been taken away from fate and organized by governments into production and consumption for all these thirty years. Anarchists have never made use of death or of its collectivization: they have confronted a different kind of death."

Her train of thought was interrupted by a sudden shot of pain that she was unable to control. She put down her pen and supported herself on the chair. After a moment she got up with her hands trembling and joined Subissoni in the wineshop.

The professor was lecturing: "The cities of Italy, differing as they do in character and tradition, and in the ways they are oppressed, cannot be forced into one single organization, nor be under the control of only one center...." He interrupted himself and grumbled to himself, "...but only receive help from it." This last phrase had always seemed rather contradictory to him and dangerous with that "but" that implicitly admitted the usefulness, even if occasional, of a center, regardless of its type. But with enthusiasm he started up again: "The common people who in various forms see gallows rising up," he declared with his lucid eye that was about to overflow, "and victims falling... and bombs exploding, and what's more... hear them, smell them, count the mangled limbs," he pointed to the TV, "...the people are the only judge of how citizens have to get along with each other...."

He saw Vivés and suspended his speech. With his hands still in the air he went to point again at the TV. Free from his companion's gaze he continued on his own with pride: "The citizens have their unity there. It's a unity of songs and of bombs; of useless speeches and of millions of ugly faces."

He was searching within his self-pity for other expressions, but Vivés held him back by his arm and asked him to take her home.

From the Pincio Subissoni looked in the direction of the Vigne, but the impenetrable night did not permit him to see another of his declarations, it too unfinished, lost in his anger, in his precocious realization of the absolute stupidity of those who were supposed to receive it.

"I make it so unpleasant for you," he wobbled, "that you actually have to run away? You were interested in staying to hear the late news!"

"No," answered Vivés, "it's not because of you. I'm the one that wants to go home because I don't feel well. I'm getting worn out by this hill. The television won't say anything at this hour, the revelation will be made during prime time, before *Carosello*, carefully orchestrated, tomorrow or the day after."

"Or perhaps we won't be told anything tomorrow or the day after. It's all covered up, everything," said Subissoni, already set to revive his proclamation on the general confusion and the inevitable dissolution of the country.

"Exactly, because it's all covered up, that is to say all organized, the TV will be forced to give some sort of explanation." Vivés stopped him almost harshly. This rebuke hurt him so much that he almost fell down.

"I know, I know," he said, "I'm a deplorable muddle-head, out-dated and out of touch with society. And also out of touch with truth, freedom, and the dishonesty to be satisfied...."

Vivés stopped and leaned against a tree. She was bent forward and breathing with her mouth wide open. Her eyes were covered with an earthy shadow that made the rest of her face look dirty too.

In spite of the fact that he was all wound up with his own rhetoric, Subissoni noticed. He staggered, he started grumbling louder and louder as if to let himself fall into self-commiseration, but he had to confront that symptom that was making Vivés's face look dirty. He got close to his woman, held her up, wiped her face as though it were really muddied. He didn't know what else to do. So he asked her how else he could help her. Vivés smiled at him. Getting back some light in her eyes, she entrusted her left arm to him so that he could hold it up, but without exaggerating, and slowly along the tree trunk bent down to sit on the edge of the street. Subissoni preceded her on that strip of cement and in that way took her on his knees.

"Just for a moment," said Vivés, "until the pain goes away."

Subissoni was trembling without understanding anything, drawn-up in his effort to hold her arm up high. Quickly he looked around everywhere to see what might be of help to them: the lamp post, the enameled plate over the light bulb, the windows, the balconies of the Ducal Palace, the clean snow in the trees, the door of the garage for buses.

He didn't find anything and didn't hear anyone go by, nevertheless he entrusted himself to everything, to the asphalt that appeared in dark blotches, to the nearby branches, to the illuminated walls... to his shoes, especially the right one, in the hope that they would last and would continue maintaining the life of that moment and of that scene.

Vivés coughed and told him that she could get up again. When they were on their feet, Subissoni was grateful to everything and full of energy. He took off his overcoat and threw it down on the spot where he had been sitting and asked his companion to sit down there and to wait, as he would be right back to get her with a taxi, with some kind of car. He almost fell down ten times while he was running toward the wineshop. He did not find any public cars, but a young man agreed to take him in his own car. Subissoni also got three cups of espresso and poured them into a bottle. A minute later he was back with Vivés, gave her the hot coffee, which he had brought her, and got her into the shelter of the car.

"It was this cold weather," she said, "I caught a cold in the last few days."

When they got home, Subissoni helped her up the stairs into her room and into bed. He went back down and thanked the young man with tears in his eyes: "Tell me who you are; leave your name with me, so I can recompense you in some way. You have been an angel, an angel." He noted down his Urbinoite name and said good-bye to him.

He went back to Vivés and sat down at the foot of the bed. Vivés smiled at him and threw him a kiss, and so as not to scare him altogether made a gesture toward the bottle, as if to thank him for the coffee. To that practical solicitude of his, he added others, taking care to cover her with an additional blanket, to bring the electric heater from the living room into her room, to put on her night table, beside the coffee, a bottle of water. At every gesture, Vivés's face turned toward him dragging along with it that same shadow.

"The doctor," Subissoni finally exploded, "we'll call a doctor."

Vivés raised an arm toward him. "No," she said. "Please, no doctor. Give me a week. Just a week. If I'm still not well, you can call him."

Gaspare understood the determination of his companion and stopped. He also tried to understand the reason. Her seriousness was apparent to him, but that was precisely what frightened him and then caused his distraction.

In fact, without saying anything, he started undressing Vivés so that she could get under the covers. It started raining and the sound of the rain accompanied him in that operation convincing him that it was correct and appropriate. The naturalness of that sound diminished his apprehension so much that when he uncovered his woman's breast he smiled with a touch of mischievousness, and he caressed it and kissed it.

Vivés took his head and wouldn't let him go. "You innocent thing," she said. "You're the most innocent man on earth. They'll get an innocent one like you."

Subissoni leaned against that breast without understanding everything, content that at last Vivés was saying something and was talking about him with love.

"And you who wanted to go to Milan," he said, "up there they would get you, you know, they'd arrest you again. They remember that you used to lead the nationalists out of Barcelona, along the coast, where the anarchists would shoot them. Watch out! You're not very innocent. You even talked badly about this house," he closed with self-satisfaction and turned toward the sound of the rain. "We'll have nice weather within a couple of days. It's raining and getting it out of its system. For Christmas we'll have sunshine."

"When my week is over," said Vivés without letting him go, "I'm really going to go to Milan for a few days, and alone. You understand, don't you, that I need to know more?"

"We'll see," said Subissoni, "in a week. If there really will be sunshine, and if you can get a seat on the train at Christmas time."

Vivés moved her man's head and finished undressing by herself until she was naked. Then she got up from the bed to go and get a night gown. Subissoni drew back aroused, ready to turn around, but he understood right away that that body was protected by its impassive naturalness suggested by the balance of its proportions and by the dark color of its flesh. He couldn't even get pleasure from some memory of a shared intimacy. Vivés stayed sitting on the bed for a moment. Finally she drank the coffee and asked Subissoni to put her notebook on her night table.

Gaspare turned toward the window; he scrutinized the night while he was closing the shutters, with an eye on the little trees below, they too closed in darkness. Completely invigorated he went to get the notebook, placed it on the night table, turned out the overhead light, turned on the little one by the bed and went to sit in his place at the other end of the room. A few minutes later he was sleeping with his head on his chest.

Leaning on her left side Vivés was looking at the wall moving her eyes slowly along to the window frame. Here the shadow of a cliff over the sea appeared, like the one at Stiges on the Mediterranean. Several times she had waited there until daybreak over the water with groups of prisoners condemned to death. At daybreak her companions would make the condemned men walk up to the highest point, show them the beauty of the hour and the natural beauty of the place, lecture them about not knowing how to appreciate them during their lifetime as egotists and profiteers, and then shoot them. The prisoners' deaths upset her every time. Even after a year of combat. It was a different kind of death, perhaps because they didn't understand. They would look at the early light on the sea, the very deep and distant bay without understanding, and so too at the nearby trees with their eyes opened wide with terror. Then, in order to try to understand, they would look at the guards, and even at the ones that were already raising their rifles to kill them. They all died with a painful grimace of surprise.

Vivés went on for at least two hours staring at the line from which the wall descended toward the window and there chose a point that seemed to her the clearest. Afterward she got up and turned on the big light. She went to the wardrobe and opened it to look at herself in the inside mirror.

She took a long look at her eyes and at her whole face and undid her hair and divided it on her two shoulders.

In the middle of the night Subissoni woke up, found that his woman was sleeping normally and left her room, which was too warm by then. He stayed in the kitchen, stretched out on the couch, with the window shutters still open so that the first light would wake him up, since he had planned to have all the morning papers ready for Vivés when she woke up.

He was awoken by the cold when no rays had yet reached the window. He put his feet on the ground and had trouble getting up. He found his overcoat on the chair where he had left it after taking it from Vivés's shoulders the night before. It was still wet, but he put it on anyway. He turned on the stove and tried to dry it off a little with the heat from one of the burners, stretching out the material in his hand. Outside the cold struck him in his blind eye stirring up a flash of pain from his eyeball to the vertex of his cranium to the opposite temple. This too gave him a feeling of pride as he proceeded, finding once again the pleasure of a real and concrete mission and the excitement of the clandestine aspect of the hour. He even walked in front of the University, stamping his shoes on the step that he hadn't seen for twenty-one years. In '48 he had tried again to ask for a job, but once again got only excuses and the impression, while jumping over that same last step, that someone behind him, now protected by protocol, frosted windows, and waiting rooms, was making fun of him without restraint.

He crossed the entire Giocapallone without running into anybody and even in Piazza della Repubblica everything was still deserted and closed: the public clock showed that it was five o'clock. He got under the shelter of the short loggia of the collegial palace, and there he marched back and forth until at five-thirty he heard another step approaching. As though a signal had sounded, within a few moments half a dozen people approached the piazza coming from various directions. A bar opened and a yellow light animated a corridor. Subissoni went along the corridor and entered the bar. There the first discussions got started – on the weather and people's illnesses – while waiting for the espresso machine to build up pressure. The professor, greeted to his surprise as such, ordered a grappa since he had to wait for the first newspaper stand to open up, around a quarter after six. The grappa blinded him and made him sneeze; the coffee, which was passed to him as soon as it was ready and with a little anisette already added to it, confused him even more. But his glory was re-enforced by it, even among the other customers just like him, more or less discredited yet unique, each with his own distinct trait known to the entire city. The company was exciting him, until finally the conversation got around to the bombs. Someone said that based on certain statements made by the investigating authorities one could imagine that the investigation was turning toward some anarchist groups. Subissoni trembled under the blow and twisted his mouth and was about to go on the offensive against that atrocious lie, but as he turned around he noticed that everybody was agreeing and that many were intervening to confirm that rumor. That tribunal was unquestionable, and the authority, mixed with impudence, that emanated from it intimidated him. How could he have stood up to those irregulars who had no qualifications and represented no institution? So he groaned. "Easy, for goodness sake, take it easy. Let's wait for the investigations. Why the anarchists? Why not the fascists? Why not the property owners, or the government itself?"

"We also said the fascists right away, but it looks like there is some proof."

"But really the anarchists? Do you know that it's an old trick to take it out on them?... Whenever they want.... I know all about it... in Spain...."

"Yes, of course, Professor. But the proof? And also the anarchists may have changed. They are no longer the ones with neckerchiefs and newspapers. It seems... that now there are some rich ones. Very rich anarchists. But it's right, Professor, to wait for proof."

Subissoni left the café right after that to free himself from his fright, because the newspaper man could not have opened his little shop yet. He continued strolling under the small loggia and saw the city coming to life: the milkmen, the bakers, the push carts toward Piazza delle Erbe; on the other side, the public taxis were lining up. He saw the newspaper woman arrive, he helped her raise the metal shutter and drag inside and open the rolled-up newspapers that had arrived in that moment. He bought five dailies and got disoriented among the large headlines. He also got confused because in his hesitation he had blocked up the entire shop. He stood aside and talked about the proof that he was waiting for while also looking at other people's papers, but nobody answered him. Everyone went off in a hurry, with the impenetrable faces of people going to a ceremony. Subissoni broke away, he addressed himself to the arches at both ends of the loggia, he cursed the rain that was starting up again and he threw himself back inside another café. But he didn't have the strength to open his newspapers: the first one, within which he had folded the others, was *l'Unità*. Without unfolding it he could read the headline; "FROM THE PROFOUND SUFFERING OF MILAN A WARNING AND A COMMITMENT TO DEMOCRACY." He started fuming over the words "warning" and "commitment" and went on repeating them to himself to empty them out little by little and hear them slowly acquire the most worn-out meaning – Mazzinian, risorgimental, like a Masonic, Carduccian, high-schoolish proclamation. He got as far as the University, the Urbino one, at the high point of his argument; even the thick ink smudgings of the letters confirmed his interpretation with a note of mourning that dirtied his fingers. He was mumbling to himself with no need for other people. Only after another outburst was he able to look around, at the warned and the committed people. They were sucking their cappuccinos and sneezing over their shots of grappa. Some were positioned in front of the pastries and every so often a hand would reach out quickly, but would often end up being retracted, altering its direction, and circling around before coming to rest. Few were talking among themselves, perhaps because by then the hour did not leave much room for delay.

Subissoni did everything like the others: he drank a cappuccino, selected a pastry, gulped down a grappa, but no one said anything to him. He went outside and under that loggia he felt lost, while the rain was coming down so hard that it kept everybody under the arches or inside the shops. He, however, entrusted himself to the rain and with a decisive step entered the street. The water welcomed him and he alone, courageously, went up towards the Ducal Palace, before the appalled stares of everybody. He felt himself worthy of that admiration and tried only to protect his newspapers under his coat flaps. He passed someone who was running and someone with an umbrella and they all watched him advance tall and resplendent. In the food shops the people got close to the windows to watch him go by. Subissoni was getting warmer all the time. The city, in the light of the new day, but with its street lights still on, was shining in the rain like a precious picture frame. And within this frame were the people who were looking at him.

The clock on the Cathedral accompanied him for a while, ringing half past eight. When he entered the clearing in front of the Cathedral, the rain squeezed itself enough to form a few rare snow flakes: that gave him a boost because it diminished the dripping from his hair and ears into his collar. He still went ahead solemnly, becoming emotional in front of the side-wing of the Ducal Palace. The doors were getting close to him, reflecting themselves in the puddles. The railings on the steps of San Domenico under that whipping rain were playing a children's song like the one played by the iron fence around the Subissoni's vegetable garden at Sant'Andrea, in the old house that he had sold in order to be free.

The love that he felt completely blinded him, causing even his good eye to drip with tears: his love for Urbino, for that almost sleet-like rain that happened only in Urbino, for that light that was shining around him like his joy. He ran into a group of students who came running up from San Polo: little ones and slightly bigger ones, all bundled up, with their designing boards sticking out as though they were armed. He recognized the orphans and stopped to watch them hurry away. He passed in front of the University and bowed to the Bonaventura Palace. He went close to the door and said at the height of his exaltation and love: "Perhaps I really wasn't qualified. And any way they even refused Leopardi a teaching assignment here."

With that idea he justified himself for all time and did not fear running into some professor or assistant – better still the rector himself with that balanced walk of his like a long sack of watermelons and gourds badly stuffed together, with the last pumpkin of his head bent forward on top. He would have greeted him with respect, bowing and offering him, without malice, some expression of good wishes in Spanish. While actually bowing he felt the water go halfway down his back and he took it as a beneficial test. A torrent of water was streaming down the San Polo hill and he did not try to avoid it. Three quarters of the way down he went into the bakery to let himself be seen and to buy brioches and fresh bread for Vivés. The exclamations from the help were the finest compliments he had ever received. He refused an umbrella or to have someone accompany him; further on he greeted the vegetable gardens of the Spineto – he as innocent as they under the rain – and finally arrived at his house. Vivés too had to see him in that state of happiness and strength and he went straight upstairs to her room without taking off his coat.

Subissoni threw open the door and stopped on the threshold to look and to let himself be looked at. Vivés, as he had hoped with all his heart, was awake and sitting up on the bed a little, but enough to see him right in front of her. He saw her stretch open her eyes and cover her mouth with one hand, making the appropriate ritual gestures of surprise and admiration, then frown and scold him without very well hiding in her words a touch of pride for that act of bravado.

Finally Vivés smiled with the indulgence that he wanted.

"I brought you the newspapers," said Gaspare, "just arrived. I ran back without even looking at them. Urbino is calm. There's nobody in the streets, but there is nothing to fear." He stepped forward to offer her the papers and noticed that he was dripping a trail of water behind him: the water had invaded the landing and was flowing down the stairs.

"Hey," he said, "if I had fallen down on San Polo I would have ended up like Bonconte!" and in his enthusiasm he recited from the *Purgatorio*:

rain fell, and then the gullies had to carry
whatever water earth could not receive
...It rolled me on the banks and river bed,
then covered, girded me with its debris.

He took off his coat and hung it on the staircase banister. He found the package of sweets and went to place it on the night table. Vivés already had the newspapers on her knees, but she still turned to him to ask him to get undressed, to take a hot bath and perhaps to go to bed.

"I feel good," he said, "I'm happy. In Urbino they've understood who I am. Maybe I'm harmless, but I'll never be their victim. And Urbino counts; it counts for itself. Even *l'Unità* says Milan, that is, it distinguishes, separates. It doesn't say Italy. Now I'm going to make a hot cup of coffee for you and I'll make one for me too."

He went back downstairs, took off his shoes and his jacket, dried off his head and started making the coffee. Meanwhile he swallowed two gulps of the anisette that he kept beside the jar with the ground coffee.

Vivés hesitated a little before looking at the papers. Then, little by little she let her eyes see the headlines: her desire was struggling against her fear. As soon as she had woken up, right away she found the clearest spot along the line of the wall over the window. She had remembered it as she was waking up. In fact, she had woken up as though that brightest little halo had penetrated and broken the darkness of her sleep. Her memories were confused and dampened by the humidity – rather far from the truth that interested her, which instead lifted itself up from the print, circled around to confuse her eyes, and then went back to settle on that spot in the bay of Stiges. The newspapers were screaming in the same way. They had the same surprise of so many little circles stretched open; they abandoned their limbs in the same way as those clean-cut gentlemen that she had shot. She recalled how the flies were already there, on the blood, almost together with the bullets, on their wide open eyes and on their mouths, and the irascible flights they made to get there: as her fear made to that spot on the wall. She went back to the newspapers and started understanding. She got into an almost sitting position: she glanced at the pages one after the other, she found on all of them the news that had upset her and that was suffocating her while she failed to find even a hint of anything that could diminish the truth. She chose *l'Unità* and read the lead article on the front page, breathing at every point, swallowing to confirm it to herself. "Mysterious suicide of a suspect at police headquarters. Giuseppe Pinelli, railway worker, forty-years-old. The police identify him as an individualist anarchist. The police chief's version: he was 'strongly suspected!!' There has been no report of the interrogations." Vivés was able to read the whole article, which was continued on the second page. The anarchist had been held for more than three days because his alibi did not hold up and around midnight he had thrown himself from a window on the fifth floor. The police chief had stated that since the suspect no longer had any defense he had collapsed psychologically, and his gesture could well be considered a self-accusation.

Vivés noted that that comrade already had been arrested on Friday and, therefore, as soon as the bombs had exploded the police had started hunting for anarchists with a deliberate plan. She noted furthermore that the police chief was the same one who, according to *l'Unità,* had rejected the theory that an inspector had already expressed on the evening of the twelfth to *La Stampa,* according to which the search should be conducted on the left, and even beyond, among the anarchists and the Maoists.

Vivés found confirmation in her own fear. She let the newspapers go and stared at the drops of water left by Subissoni. Even if she had wanted to, it would have been difficult because of the pain that was splitting her hip, to turn to the left, toward the window and toward the spot in her life that was coming back. She could smell the odors of the pine woods, which got stronger after the cadavers had been lying in the sun for a few hours. Even the smell of maturing grapes in the vineyards further down reached her. Some of the grass had the smell of mint, but even more sharp, since it drove away the flies. She sat among those leaves and could breath more freely. The recollection helped her. She stretched out in a natural position and concentrated on her breathing.

Subissoni came in with the coffee, still happy, still with water spots along his back and legs, which he protected and tried hard to show off as though they were the inextinguishable proof of his bravery. His hair was messed up and his face was twisted by the cold and by his exhilaration, with his neck and his forearms sticking out from his ugly worn-out and unbuttoned collar and rolled up sleeves; and what's more he was chuckling as he shuffled along in his slippers. Vivés was struck by how old he was and felt disgusted. It was one more proof of how life had betrayed her – and had betrayed everything. She slowly pulled one leg out of the bed and looked at it. She did not feel similarly disgusted and quickly forgot the reason why she had taken it out. She touched her thigh, which was still covered.

"They're accusing the anarchists," she said.

"I know," answered Subissoni. "But they're vague arguments."

"Not really. In Milan they forced one to kill himself."

Subissoni stopped in his tracks, with the coffee that was trembling in his hands.

"How?" he asked.

"He threw himself out a window of the police station."

"They were accusing him?"

"Yes."

"Did they have proof?"

"Nothing apparent. The proof is that he was an anarchist."

"What do the newspapers say?"

"That. Some of them are already rejoicing."

"And the left?"

"Which left?"

"L'Unità," for example.

"It doesn't comment. It points out some contradictions. Deep down it would not displease them either if it was the extraparliamentarians."

"No. Don't say that. The truth is what it is."

"And what would that be?"

"If it was an anarchist, it was an anarchist. And that's that," said Subissoni finding new strength and stepping forward toward the night table. "It can't be the fault of all anarchists or of anarchism either. They say that there are even rich anarchists, nowadays. Everything is so confused!"

"They're not anarchists. It was not an anarchist, much less a group of anarchists. An anarchist would have fired at the Prime Minister, the Pope, the President. How everything has happened for nothing! The Spanish War, the World War, the atomic bomb, Stalin.... Everything has to start all over again." She remembered her leg and looked at it for a moment. "Who knows if I'll be able to start up again. One thing is for sure. Everything is as it was in '36. 'History is flat,' Argote used to say when he gave us our rifles. The Marxists are wrong to glorify history; they lose themselves in it. History is flat, at least since a hundred years after the death of Christ. Nothing changes. Only a few holes have been made here and there. There is no history; everything is the same in their devotion. There is he who commands and he who dies. Neither will you make history, not even with these rifles; at the most you'll make a hole in the curtain. There is no history yet: there are governments, assassinations, disasters, but not history. There is no God and history is like a shawl thrown over a wooden cross. There will be history afterwards, if we succeed in making a hole through which we will all pass; on the other side, beyond the curtain. History will be the history that we will be able to make, in anarchy, on the other side."

Vivés looked at her leg again and at the even more deteriorated spectacle of that old man who was trembling.

"Who is going to be able to make that hole? It would have been better to have died the day I left Cipriano Mera."

Subissoni was rocking back and forth, he impetuously gathered up all the newspapers and went to throw them down the stairs, where it was wet.

"We," he shouted. "I. I'll make that hole. Don't worry! We're in Urbino. History doesn't touch us. Not even Italy's. This is the curtain that suffocates everything, at least here around us. Rest assured, I'll make a plan for where to make that hole. Don't get upset over that anarchist. Perhaps he wasn't really an anarchist; perhaps he was just pretending. How old was he? To be an anarchist he had to be at least sixty years old. If not he was a movie anarchist. He did kill himself, however. Did he have any accomplices?"

"They're not saying anything. They talk about anarchist circles. We'll see in the next few days or even this evening on TV."

"No, you're not going to see anything. You're going to stay home for a few days, until this storm has passed. Do you want to end up like last night again? You need to stay in bed. I'll bring you the news and the newspapers, and I'll notify your office. You're pale and you're worrying yourself too much about these bombs, anarchists or not. It happened in Milan. Have you ever seen Milan?"

Vivés tolerated these comments with the same forced self-control that she used for so many other arguments: "Why then did you come to Spain? Because you were looking for a place to lose your eye? Milan or not, it happened here, to us. But you – do you understand it? It's the last time it's going to happen to us. Should we do something or pretend that it hasn't happened? You know – right? – that we're going to die soon? What purpose did our lives serve, our battle?

We have to take the final step. What did you say to those who wanted to take you away from the front? What did you say? I feel like I'm starting up again or starting anew, and don't you do a Feliciano de Silva to me, my fine knight. This evening you will escort me to the television, and I will be good and stay in bed until then. But now take a bath and take an aspirin and comb those… locks."

Subissoni didn't know whether to be insulted or proud of himself. He swung back and forth and looked out the window to follow the tenderness of his mood. He managed to see the tips of the trees below.

"That's right," he said, "I was just looking for a place to get my eye torn out. And I was successful and found it. I remember only that there was a garden, that he screwed me by jumping out from behind a tree. But I found you; I saw Africa, Provence. And I can tell you that I have never stopped fighting. Many times," he said while looking at Vivés and drawing close to her bosom, "it was my happiness that enabled me to go on fighting." He did not feel the warmth of her bosom because by then his hands had gotten numb. "At the proper moment I too will know how to throw myself out the window."

She hugged him and pulled him toward her. "I know my love, I know. We have lived until now just for this; and we have always known it. But who would have said that they would be waiting for us on December 12, '69? You know that they have waited for us and that we have been ready for some time. Come on, jump in my bed, embrace me."

Gaspare got in and hugged with all his might the beautiful prisoner of Burgoz, who had been the first to talk to him and had said to him in Italian, "where are you going, you fugitive Ghibilline?" Then she had taken off her beret near the water of the fountain and had let her hair fall down to her waist.

9

A broken eaves was spurting water on the large vase in the courtyard, some inside some outside, with an alternating sound, modulated in such a way as to seem like an admonition. Its rhythmic noise awoke both of the Oddi sisters who were sleeping in the two rooms immediately above. On December 16, according to tradition, the preparations for the Christmas celebrations began, accounts were settled with the occupants of their rural properties, taxes were paid, as well as the occasional household servants, and the capons and turkeys that would be served at the five big festive dinners were closed in their cages, while the eels that were to be roasted alive on Christmas Eve – and also on the evening of the second day of the new year, according to a particularity of the family – were placed in the appropriate tub. Of all of these only a few now remained to be done, even though this time were added those necessary for the celebration of a very important event that was coming soon – the coming of age of Oddino, which would happen on January 8, 1970.

Plans had to be made very secretly. Arrangements had to be made for everything: the part-time help had to be hired, the invitation list drawn up, the invitations prepared and sent out at least by the twentieth – written by hand on little cards with the family coat of arms.

The previous evening the two sisters had already exchanged concerns about money: they needed to settle accounts with Giocondini, as well as with the butcher and the other suppliers; pay the city taxes, the national ones; prepare for the holidays, for the birthday celebration; and also arrange a gift for Oddino. For that celebration the sisters would have to have at least two new dresses each, one for the afternoon and one for the evening, and an overcoat too for the solemn Mass in the Cathedral, at the Oddi-Semproni's altar, in the left nave, at whose base was placed the family tombstone, by then reduced to the state of a relic since the tomb had been closed along with all the others during the restoration of the Cathedral.

Marzia and Clelia were in the kitchen where they had gone to prepare their coffee and milk. For five years they had not had a full-time maid, and by sharing the chores evenly they managed everything. They called someone in every so often to clean out the cellar, to beat the larger rugs and to pile up the firewood and coal. Cleaning the highest vaults of the ceilings was the specialty and joy of Oddino who had invented a system of tying poles and brushes together, which was perhaps complicated but certainly efficient, at least for his entertainment.

The sisters consumed their breakfast of coffee, milk and Lazzaroni cookies looking at each other with an occasional smile – shivering from the cold – and yet prolonging every gesture in order to put off as long as possible the moment in which they would have to begin talking about money. Oddino's birthday was worrying them too. It had already been a couple of days since Clelia had hinted at a certain fear, rather vague, as though this date was not coming at the right time, as though there had been an error or, worse, as though other serious, as much as confusing, errors might follow it. In short, it didn't seem possible to her that Oddino had arrived at his twenty-first birthday.

Marzia understood the twist but had not explained it, except a little to herself and barely clearing up the most uncertain extremes of her worrying, which was perhaps a result of her affection – of her wish to postpone an event that could distance her nephew from them – and not necessarily because of any doubt – that is, that Oddino might not be ready for that date and for all that it implied. Oddino did not seem like – and this could even be one of his virtues – a young man of twenty-one years. It was said that at twenty-one some already had earned a degree, some were already on their own in Bologna or Rome, some already had fiancees and presumably others on the wrong track even had mistresses, some were already driving automobiles, some were traveling the world on their own. For several years the aunts had been brooding over these affectionate doubts about their nephew, but they did not know how to resolve them, because of, among other things, their embarrassment about confirming them by even enunciating them to each other. At confession they revealed very little, and for some time now they had stopped going and instead had taken up the habit of providing for themselves some penance and a few rounds of supplemental rosary. They had spoken about their nephew with one of the priests at the Cathedral, who had hastened to respond with a maxim in Latin according to which Oddo would not be late, as a fine offshoot, in expressing all the strength of the paternal oak tree. Lay doctors have the vice of looking for money and of shaking their heads with irony and even with the contempt of freemasons. Women doctors had little more to offer than they did and once they were alone in the library or the science room with that overgrown and naive boy, behind the curtains, with their legs under those tables where it would be possible to hide the encampment of Asdrubale on the Metauro, who knows what they might have gotten into and what subject they would have brought up....

Marzia and Clelia had also taken up reading a few years before, experiencing some ugly encounters and undergoing serious insults on so many pages. But in the end they had found what they liked. The first, in Italo Calvino, in his noble characters who were more or less integral, but always correct and genteel, worthy of their family and of the old virtues – all described so well, with a dry and subtle pen, which followed its accurate and attentive reader... like the sound of humming... every second, in bed, while she was getting up, in front of the door, on the stairs; even at the table, with those lace-like plots... with those words that knew how to knock and let themselves in. The second one, in the domestic virtues of Natalia Ginzburg, where the family was well organized, each of the members with his own qualities, even with his tics or whims... but always very aware of the importance of proper authority, of common sense, and of contributing to the strength of the family: each protected in that way by the good words and by the bad words too, by the rules and manners that might be a little odd but always of the family; far from the wickedness of this world, which seldom appeared, and then always beneath, and not worthy of the family nor even of that pen;... or if at all, it might be looked over, judged, and admonished.

So for the last few years Oddino had been secretly nourished by common sense, but also by some courageous, not well-defined, but certainly not senseless, hope. If Oddino had ever given any sign of abandoning the rules of good common sense – or even wished or just thought about it – his aunts were confident that the fine, clean-cut world of their readings would show the way to handle the problem and keep it under control. Hope, hope as intention; I'll go further up; I'll take a nice cold bath; I'll encounter a vassal and together they'll take us... we'll all go to the mountains with Gino... etc. etc....

But fortunately for him Oddino had some irreproachable qualities and being superior to them, was unaffected by all that Savoyard cajoling. However on his own he had read *Don Quixote,* and he loved that cavalier so much that he cried every time he suffered a mishap or misfortune and was saddened for several days when he saw him come back to his home town and meet the hare that was fleeing from the pursuing dogs and when the women put him to bed. For many more days of sadness he awaited the strength to read the last chapter, not only for the grief that he already felt in learning of the death of the cavalier – and that would be magnified by reading the actual words of the recounting of that irreparable event – but also for the annoyance and also for the envy and for the remorse and for the pain and for the unbearable delusion that he would feel upon reading that he was not cited in his will.

It is still not known whether Oddino read that seventy-fourth chapter. Once during a trip to Lourdes, in 1967, with his aunts and Giocondini, he let it be understood that he was actually afraid that in that final chapter someone might have made a joke out of his cavalier, and he turned threateningly toward Spain. Oddino had the impression that this book could have been written better, even if it was already marvelous: that is, that Don Quixote actually deserved more than Cervantes. And it is known that aristocrats are there to be portrayed and served and that their virtues are always superior to how they are expressed, narrated, interpreted, portrayed – "corporate images" by their subordinates, lackeys, reporters, informants, ushers, secretaries, boatmen-coachmen, toilet-flushers, auditors, speakers, ministers, directors, seminarists…. Try to ask any sovereign, president, managing director, section chief, high commissioner, general manager, secretary general, general! Ask how he feels served and respected and ennobled, even the head doorman of the ministry for bureaucratic reform or the head janitor of the institute for the preservation of artistic treasures!

The only sovereign worthy of his scepter and who does not complain about his subjects and who has a clear relationship with the latter who spend their lives watching him while he spends his working for them, in addition to watching them, allowing himself once in a while to look beyond, toward heaven, beyond the tents and poles… is the cleaning man – with his ragged jacket that is nevertheless red and appropriately decorated, at least on one side – of the two smelly animal cages of the smallest circus in the world, with dark blue writing on a crapped-up table of a cart drawn by a clairvoyant mule, by a talking donkey and by a drum-playing horse: the Universal Circus.

Just that morning of December 16, at dawn, when the rounded mouth of the large vase had not yet made enough noise to awaken the Oddi-Semproni sisters, all the members of the circus troupe – men: 1, women: 1, dwarves: 1, children: 1, and animals: 6 – had died of hunger and cold during a snowstorm up along the curves of a steep and secondary road in the Pyrenees.

Once the anxious mood of worry that accompanied their reawakening passed, the Oddi sisters – unaware of the trained fox of the celestial Universal Circus, who was dying as he chewed on snow, the last of the group, closed in his tiny cage near the hen who had already been dead for a few hours, companions for years in the same number and of thousands of crappings on those innocent bars – addressed each other. In their words they found other worries.

"What should we do?"

"We'll sell something."

"What would it be wise to sell?"

"All we have is land, or the villa."

"I don't think it's wise to sell the villa. Money is always losing it's value."

"We always need more of it."

"Today we could ask the advice of our cousin from Pesaro. He has to come to arrange the celebration and to introduce his daughter."

"We could get Giocondini to make us a loan'"

"We already have too many debts with him. I don't trust him very much. He's good, but too eager for money."

"A loan from the bank."

"Perhaps, a mortgage. But will they give us a mortgage just when Oddino is about to reach his majority?"

"Sell gold, some necklaces, furniture, books?"

"Perhaps we'll do that. Let's wait for Ganganelli."

"We have to pay for Oddino's celebration and pay off our debts with Giocondini and our dresses, which will arrive from Turin tomorrow or the day after."

"Do you have any idea what the bill will be?"

"No. But it shouldn't be any higher than last year's. Only one dress is silk. And the overcoat is one of those ready-made ones."

In short, the sisters were rather uncertain, obliged by who-knows-what astral current to suffer a part of the pain that the end of the Universal Circus had scattered to the wind.

Oddino came down in his bathrobe and put an end to those discussions. He sat at the head of the table and waited for his bowl of barley to be followed by his cup of hot choco-late. Seeing him clench the spoon in his fist with the fingers of his other hand grasping the silver napkin holder with such authority, Marzia remembered that at his majority her nephew would automatically come into possession of the cash amount of ten million lire. This could solve all their problems and permit the celebration of his birthday. For the moment they could make another debt with Giocondini.

The latter arrived overflowing with compliments for Countess Marzia. Wasn't it she who had immediately understood that the bombs had been set by the anarchists? No, it had been Clelia. Anyway, fortunately they were about to catch them, and so the public well-being would soon be reestablished and refortified.

The countesses called Giocondini to the back of the dining wing and even invited him to sit down.

"We need two million by tomorrow. Soon we will pay our bills, and we will give back this sum too, by January 15 of next year."

"Very well," said Giocondini. "I am at your service, as always. And it's not necessary to worry about deadlines. You already owe me two million and six hundred and fifteen thousand lire for the trips and the advances of the last eight months; with the two million that I'll give you we're beginning to build up an interesting little sum of money. Why don't we use it as a partial payment toward the villa? It's better for everybody. You have valued the villa with its land at twenty million: on January 15 it will be me that gives you more money for a total of ten million. Three more I'll give you within the year; three, more or less, you'll spend with me on trips for '70; at the beginning of '71 I would have a debt of four million. I'll pay you two by March and the other two we'll use up with trips in '71. Naturally I won't count the minor expenses for short trips, from here to the piazza and from the piazza to here, errands, mail, prescriptions, etc., etc. With modesty and with the pleasure of serving a family such as yours...." Giocondini would have gone on, but Countess Clelia stopped him: "No, we don't want to make any sale agreements. We couldn't do that when the heir is just reaching his majority. We can sign a note to you and pay some interest."

"Why can't we prepare a bill of sale for the villa, for what's left of it, that interests me only because I still love the countryside and would like to go back to it? We could predate it, for last year, or even earlier. You'll free yourself from a burden and get a good price for it, in addition to my services and my gratitude. Don't you understand the times? And what if they were to expropriate uninhabited houses? There are lots of farmers and southerners that are demanding just that."

"No. The villa is the Oddi's. As for expropriation, it wouldn't be the first time that our family would be robbed and that Monarchies and Republics would remedy their own guilt and misery by using our virtues and our wealth. Stop thinking about the villa and tell us whether you can give us what we have asked for."

Giocondini was about to rebel, seeing his dream go to pieces, but before he could find the words and the insolence, the countess went on: "There's another favor we have to ask you, and it will show you how much confidence and trust we have in you. Oddino is a man now and we are thinking about his future. But there is something that we can't do for him. Already just bringing up this matter shows you that we consider you a faithful...," but Marzia couldn't think of a substantive.

Giocondini was glowing with new hope exactly because of those hints and those hesitations... like a chain at the bottom of a well that has hooked onto something big!

The countess got it all out in one breath: "You would have to escort him to some girl in Pesaro or Rimini that will entertain him... teach him to dance, give him instructions. Since he left high school he hasn't met any girls, except with us, and he has never wanted to go out on his own."

Giocondini was melting from happiness and really began sweating from all the well-stored-up lard in every part of his body. He coughed tactfully, several times, as one who has understood as much as necessary and who knows how the words of the message must not be spoken in their entirety or by themselves, but only ambiguously, so that they won't have actually ever existed and can therefore disappear quickly and easily. Meanwhile he was consenting with his eyes lowered so as not to show the lightning of his eyes that was burning holes through his eyelids to his shoes. He knew that it was with a stroke of luck that he had caught his prey by the throat, and he didn't want his prey to notice that it was in that position and attempt to free itself with its last burst of strength. Taking his time, without losing even one drop of blood or one gasp, he would devour it giving the maximum time to his own pleasure.

Clelia closed her eyes as though she really didn't want to see the dragon's mouth. Her sister's speech had confused her, even though she understood its significance. Even Marzia, who had expressed it with complete awareness, saw it growing before her and getting heavier and crowding them so much that she began to fear for the orderliness of the house.

"When you have time and want to, of course," she said, but by then she had given in to the inevitability of the event.

In fact, Giocondini was able to overcome, with no problem, that attempt at postponement. "Tomorrow, right away. Now, before the holidays. It's the best time. People are more in the mood for a good time. And even proper girls... with school on vacation... shopping to do...."

He noticed that he was terrorizing the sisters.

"Yes, tomorrow," he confirmed. "I'll come to get the Count around three. I'll be like a big brother to him; permit me to say so. And tomorrow I'll also bring you the two million."

While he was going out he went on paying compliments to the two sisters, wandering from one thing to another, as though in his amazement he went on talking to himself, but finally he said, "And what if, on his own, Count Oddo had fallen into the hands of a woman like the one at San Giovanni Rotondo?"

The sisters withdrew to their rooms waving to each other at the top of the stairs with their eyes swollen. They cried for two hours without stopping. Clelia sunken into her pillow and every so often turning to look out the window at the clouds that from her window seemed to have greater speed than when seen from any other place. Whenever she had opened the window the clouds had immediately slowed down. Marzia, standing in front of her mirror, every so often lifting the edge of her skirt like the curtain of a tiny theater. They were crying because Oddino had to become a man. They were crying about time; and every little medicine bottle, light, book, frame, stool, or drawer of the room supplied an ever-renewing and varying reason.

Looking at those things all together very often they became bewildered, irritated at first, to have been distracted from the liberation of their crying and then by another pain that came over them – for which they didn't know any more whether they should cry – because time had passed and too quickly or because it had never passed for those objects. Every so often in recent years, in this confusion, both of the sisters had put their hands on these same objects twisting them and breaking them. Marzia, from her little theater around her legs, moved that morning in front of the door of her closed room and threatened it with clenched fists, but she didn't dare to touch it. The walnut door, in eighteenth-century style, with its internal framing in the form of wings, emitted rays from the star-shaped trimming around the key hole, and from the key itself, a bronzed light as straight as a sword. Closer up, the door laughed nastily, withdrawing itself space-wise through its woodworm holes. Every other detail of the doorway and of the whole room – the window, the bed, the slippers, the light switches – was aware of being part of an inviolable space.

Clelia's window was flying faster and higher than usual when Oddino knocked on the door for his dinner. Clelia got up from bed and reassured him.

Marzia went back to the mirror while Oddino was knocking. She looked herself over, especially her face, and said that she could not come down, that they should excuse her, that Clelia could prepare the meal by herself, that they would see each other after their afternoon rest.

Oddino withdrew without questioning her. Marzia stood there in front of the mirror and from her own gigantic eye went on to consider the objects that she found reflected nearby, for the first time independently from her, autonomously placed and arranged in another system. But after a while she noticed that she herself could compose or alter this distinct system, by moving her head slightly.

She didn't go downstairs until five o'clock when her sister informed her of the arrival of their Pesarese cousin, Count Terenzio Ganganelli, accompanied by his daughter.

10

The uproar over some arrests made in Milan even reached the interior of Subissoni's house. People coming home even an hour after dark were talking loudly and what's more each one seemed convinced of the rationale of the motives and, above all, of the extravagance of the arrested characters, already identified by the police as common delinquents, among whom stood out a male nightclub dancer, imagine! Practically an old man already and a complete failure – it had been some time since TV had dumped him.

Subissoni went to the window to seek confirmation of the news and he got it, feeling it enter within him with the reality of that hour, of the few enveloped lights, with those even more convincing human halos of theirs. The image of the ruined dancer, talentless and jobless, actually infuriated him, so much so that a hot rancor covered and squeezed everything inside his head and inside his stomach. "Ah! Ah!," he was forced to bellow with his mouth wide open. "Aaaah!" and he pounded his chest repeatedly to help expel the heat of that rancor. He rejoined Vivés to address her directly with that outcry that expressed both his disgust and his satisfaction about having been right better than any other argument or demonstration.

"Aaaaohoh," he went on ever more raucously and even threateningly as if saying "I told you so" to his woman. "Ahahahah," scratching himself more and more, emptying himself out until he gasped. Out of breath, "A dancer," he said, "a show-hall dancer. Here's the guilty one! Here are today's anarchists. What do you say now? What kind of exploits are these? What kind of men? What do you want to start over."

Vivés, to free herself from the pain of the news and from the equally strong pain thrust upon her by Subissoni's enormous injustice – in which she was unable to distinguish the portion that he himself was suffering from the portion he, on his own, was committing – got up, went to the window, went around the room looking for something that might help her to begin. She was still groping around overcome with pain and then she headed toward the bathroom. She pushed aside Gaspare with a force that was not hers. He wobbled and had to support himself against the bed in order not to fall. Vivés slammed the bathroom door, maneuvered the faucets and began filling the bathtub. That strength did not come from her will nor from her body since she was unable to control it comfortably or even to keep it from turning against her. Vivés stared at herself in the mirror, and her stare became intense because she didn't know where to direct it or what to look for. She got into the tub and tried to concentrate on her own body.

Subissoni came to the door and said, continuing in his rancorous litany, "Yes, get yourself ready. Let's go watch TV... Let's go watch the dancing!"

Vivés was lying in the tub, she was sweating but couldn't get warm. In her throat she felt a membrane that interrupted the flux in all her limbs. It was an effort to control her own mind and to feel as hers the shield of her forehead and the sweat that was dripping from it. Her attention was fragmented and every so often she grasped a detail.

Subissoni insisted and this time his voice made her feel a clemency that invaded her entirely. But such clemency did not take long to transform itself into very deep pain, both inside and outside, with such dullness that it completely subdued her, but also with sharp pangs that exploded in particular parts of her body. She dried off as best she could, with an alarmed eye to the mirror. She took a long time to dry her feet and then she went slowly up her shins to her knees, in a scrupulous journey, full of curiosity and of discoveries that were supposed to hide her nostalgia. But finally she moved her lips to form the last two words of a song that had already started in her memory. In the room she found Subissoni who was waiting for her with a cup of coffee. She threw her towel on the bed and stood naked before her man, while taking the little cup and starting to drink. At the halfway point she raised her head and looked at her Gaspare who was trembling. "You harmless thing," she said. "You are harmless and the world is full of harmless people like you. Now go out because I have to get dressed."

Subissoni waited for her downstairs, fully dressed, armed with two umbrellas and also with a walking stick, which he had pulled out of who knows where. Before going out he warned her that no matter what, she should stay calm in front of the TV – anarchists or no anarchists; to wait, but not to withdraw from the evidence. "If it's true that he's a dancer," he concluded, "a good-for-nothing, an incapable crook, arrested at his first attempt…. He's not an anarchist, anarchists are something else," he added to affirm his own defense and that of his woman.

Vivés smiled at him and leaned on his arm. They arrived in the piazza around eight and they stopped under the clock as though they had met there that evening just like on so many others. The piazza was black, sunken, and a bitter wind was passing high above the buildings. It's roar could be heard even higher than the Fortress. One of the workers from the Cooperative came up to Vivés: "How are you? I'm pleased to see you. An ugly story what's happening; that is, ugly people. People like that aren't any good to anybody," and off he went. Subissoni didn't say anything but he tried to make up for that encounter, which seemed to him an attack against Vivés's ideas, by proposing that they go and get something to drink before the newscast, perhaps at the closest café, which was the nicest.

The café lady greeted her too, showing her concern about Vivés's health and recommending that she take good care of herself. Subissoni felt as if everyone was looking at him, felt exposed to ridicule partly by the fact that he was holding in his hand two umbrellas and a walking stick. But at that hour people didn't linger much. Vivés slowly drank a rhubarb liqueur and asked for a pastry too. Subissoni realized that he was hungry and said that they would have supper afterward.

They crossed the piazza again and Vivés was walking with the attention and air of a convalescent: she was breathing with her mouth half open and the fresh air broke the membrane in her throat.

The wineshop was crowded and the two of them stayed in back, next to the door, partly because Vivés understood that Gaspare would not have had the courage to break through that throng in order to go and claim his usual place. The far-away screen appeared sharper and more cruel, and from behind that crowd it gave the impression of spying through a hole directly into the reality of an event. Everything was confirmed by the murmuring of the people and by some shouted accusations: the arrest of Pietro Valpreda– thirty-six years old, individualist anarchist, ex-dancer, already known to the police – and the detention of eight other persons. People were wavering back and forth and every so often our two made contact with the talking window. There even was an interview with the police chief of Milan. By then the voices of the people there drowned out those on the TV, and at a certain point someone suggested turning it off. They all found themselves satisfied with each other, exhausted as though they had undertaken an enormous burden. Many of them went out in the open, to look up in the air, relieved. The consorts Subissoni went out too; he behind with his wings spread, with an umbrella in each hand and, in addition, clenched in his right hand, his walking stick.

Vivés wasn't saying anything and Subissoni joined her to look her in the eyes and to listen, in case she might whisper something.

They entered the Hotel Italia and this time they went into the dining room. They sat down at a table without even taking off their coats – Subissoni still with the umbrellas and his walking stick. They were asked to sit, given the time, at an easier-to-serve table, and to put their overcoats on a nearby chair. But they were not at all willing to be hurried. Vivés's hair still fell undone to her shoulders and she realized it, with a smile, when she spread her arms on the table: that nice white linen table cloth inspired her to confidentiality. Then she became lost in her thoughts.

Subissoni interrupted her, "... a dancer," he said and took a breath to straighten and twist so as if to not see anything, "a dancer...."

"I was also thinking the same thing," said Vivés. "There was a dancer among the anarchists that I joined in Madrid after the first year of fighting... small and courageous, with lots of lipstick and eye make-up because he was also a homosexual."

"Was he a gypsy?" scrutinized Subissoni.

"No, no, a dancer, from Madrid, courageous and small and all made-up, even in combat. He never had time to do everything because he also cooked for lots of people."

"But not a Wanda Osiris dancer!"

"Who knows?" said Vivés. "And who knows if it was him."

"But if the taxi driver recognized him. Why get a headache trying to recall the past? A shitty dancer, Italian, in night clubs, on TV, planted those bombs! An idea? Not one! Italian confusion, the bordello, the operetta, the puppet-show, bombs here and bombs there, with no discipline, no science, no doctrine, no history, no virtue: a colossal three-colored bordello. There is no Italy! Italy died at Teano. Only Duke Valentino could think about doing it and after him the only great unitarian hero was appropriately another Valentino, Rudolph, the king of Brilliantine. And therefore it was right that a dancer...."

"He really was a dancer. He used to come to me to get injections," continued Vivés. "Always injections, he was crazy about injections...."

"Like all whores," said Subissoni. "In the bordellos from nine to ten in the morning, always injections. And this Rumor, with his cute little mouth, doesn't he look like he gives himself a restorative prick every morning? Farewell Italy, she's all there outside the boot offering her big buns for an injection, so many buns, red, green and turquoise, white and yellow, white and yellow!... On each of them Franceschetto

119

Cibo is chewing. Nice name, eh! A son of Pope Innocent VIII and he married a daughter of Lorenzo de' Medici. The father pope was mostly concerned about having a good time after having made and lost only one war. When he died he was succeeded by Roderigo Borgia, a Valencian native and an arrogant type like all you Spaniards. He had more children than fingers – and well brought up judging by what they managed to do. They even got the idea of unifying Italy, which until that moment had been doing so well and had been so wise, it had actually constituted a confederation. Can you imagine? A peaceful confederation, the Italic League of 1455, including the Duchy of Milan, without bombs or ballerinas, the Republic of Florence, the Papal State, the Kingdom of Naples and the Venetian Republic. They reconstituted it in '80, but Venice no longer adhered. And then Franceschetto Cibo arrived and then all the other sons of priests, male dancing sons of ballerinas." Subissoni tasted the wine.

"The dancer, yes," said Vivés, "but what did the TV say about the railroad worker? It doesn't seem to me that they said anything about the railroad worker who threw himself out the window."

"He threw himself out when he saw that they had found them out."

"But did they know each other? Did they work together?"

"They belonged to the same group. They knew each other. They did the job together. But you're worrying too much. Are you by any chance on their side? It's probably better that they found them out! What kind of a revolution are they making by killing at random? Why are you defending them? Who did you used to shoot at?"

"Does it seem to you that this middle-class republic," Vivés looked at him, "is not capable of lying? Does it seem to you that this clerical republic is not capable of making accusations at random, to conduct an inquisition, to suffocate? Doesn't it seem to you that it has found a way, the most convenient? I'm only trying to understand; because, I repeat, that in any case, even if it was them, it seems right to me to start up again. We cannot stay out of it if these facts are redoing the pieces and scenes from '36 – the same ones that I saw break up and fall! How can we stay out if it is now the beginning of the end? And there's something else that I want you to know because it grieves me very much: that once again, and with so much anger, the anarchists are being aimed at."

Subissoni listened, placed his glass on the table and his shining eye that betrayed his bitterness proclaimed: "You're even sorry not to be with them."

"Yes," answered Vivés, "you're right. But I am with them, as are you too! I mean that these bombs have put us back on patrol. The patrol had gotten lost, it was walking some place else and now we have found it again in the open. But I'm not sorry, as you want to think, not to be with them in preference to you. We two are together, even if I go to Milan, for a week or two."

Vivés was breathing better and that big clean and white hall gave her a comfortable sense of space.

"There are two points to clear up," she went on, once again placing her hands symmetrically on the table. "You who are always quoting, do you remember Ivan Karamazov? With what disdain he distanced from himself his step-brother Smerdjakov, not considering him worthy of being his disciple? We too have been proud. Distant with pride and almost with scorn from politics and action; isolation as though anointed with superiority, as though around us were only the deformed creatures of those whom we once raised. We have kept many truths to ourselves, satisfied with our experiences and with our superior capabilities, and we have been offended by the arrival of others, by different routes and means, at our conclusions. We have barricaded ourselves in our pride. The second point is fear. You have to know that I fear that this pride has forever distanced me from life, from the possibility of getting back into it. And fear takes still another step – and it gets bigger – that there is no more life left for us."

She stopped talking and started looking at her hands and then went on, just so that affirmation would not take up all the room inside and in front of her: "As you see I'm talking about both of us." But this unity – that she constructed materially by squeezing his hand in hers – suggested another concept to her: that their two hands together no longer were touching the rest. But she didn't say so. She replaced her hands on the table cloth as if to entrust to this gesture her intention to reenter the world.

Subissoni did not say anything, being content with that squeeze: behind the timidness and the mildness of the aristocrat who for generations had been stripped of every taste and prerogative for power, he could hide incumbent and royal obligations. This game, into which so much disillusionment and solitude had forced him, had ended up by giving him a certain duplicity of spirit: here he could withdraw to play with his own pusillanimity, or else charge himself up to explode through his various complicated exercises in verbal aggressiveness.

Vivés on the other hand could not hold herself back, with her eyes on the straight line of the table: "By now the game is almost over."

They ate without talking, concentrating on the food, preparing each mouthful meticulously, chewing slowly, lengthening the pauses between mouthfuls. They were hungry too, because it was the first complete meal that they had eaten in three days.

They were hurried by the waiter who wanted to finish up. They excused themselves but went on with the same rhythm until they were finished, and after that they ordered a grappa. In the kitchen the irritated waiter commented: "The condemned man's last meal."

The two of them put their coats back on in front of each other, both attentive to each other's gestures. They stared in each other's eyes, but with nothing to communicate. Subissoni sighed as he took up his walking stick. They went outside separately – Gaspare with his umbrellas as wings. But the wind had come closer and the first gusts were blowing through the loggias. In front of the theater it was sweeping the street with whistles that ended up in the barrel vaults of the Mercatale. Gaspare caught a blast, and for a moment was poised like a poorly made eagle. Vivés went tranquilly ahead, still content to walk with a nimble step, such as she hadn't had for years. Subissoni passed her, all squeezed together with his umbrellas under his arms, then he stopped to get a better grip on his walking stick. After that he positioned himself behind her.

When they got to the cobblestones of Via dello Spineto, Vivés felt her ankles get slower as though they had become untied and then they started to hurt. This pain aroused the one in her chest and her arm, which, however, after a few moments, was so light as to make her think that it had reappeared just to show its lightness and its rheumatic muscular nature.

Subissoni entered, as always, before her, after having promptly opened the door with a precision in every gesture that made him proud every time. That evening too he emitted the usual ah! of satisfaction. He turned on the lights and went down the two steps to the left toward the kitchen-living room. There he started to untwist himself from the umbrellas. Seeing him ruffled up that way, inside that small low room where the black toothpick of his figure assumed an improbable and unhappy proportion, Vivés felt a pang in her heart. The whole house, the stairs that she was going up, the two windows in front of her, the door against which she was leaning and the sequence of the rooms that she didn't see but that fell before her like a picture, thrust upon her a wave of sadness that forced her to sit down on the first steps. That dismal and well-ordered place did not belong to her: she tried to recognize it, to judge it and, after a moment, the possibility arose before her, although very remotely, to free herself from it by jumping like a horse through those two windows. They probably weren't anchored too firmly in the wall of turquoise mortar. It was she who had recalled the Universal Circus that morning, while looking in the mirror at the light blue and completely unfamiliar nightgown on her shoulders and the turquoise cracks in the frame of the mirror at the same height.

She let herself go on the steps and felt like her chest was detaching itself from her, as though it was entering alive in the reflection of a mirror that someone had inserted in the collar of her overcoat.

Subissoni came running while hurling aside his umbrellas. Vivés lifted her head and looked at him to stop him, so as not to have him on top of her.

"You're always like this in the evening," he said. "This time I'm calling the doctor."

"Don't you see that it's the cold? Just like yesterday. Leave me be! I still have five days before the doctor. You promised," and she held her left arm, which felt heavy, out toward him; then she closed her eyes to make the door and the room disappear.

In the middle of the room, a discouraged Subissoni went to sit between the table and the stove. He was so tired that he spread out with his head and arms on the table. He just had to wait a few minutes and then help Vivés to get in bed.

The smells of the table, on which his forehead was resting, began to interest him and gradually established a profundity that aroused him. He recognized the odors and scents one by one, each in order in its different place. He looked at the slit in the middle of the table: not more than a millimeter, but open, alive toward the bottom of the drawers. He continued on with his eye as far as the stove and then in a circle he went and stopped at every part of the furnishings or of the walls that were at that height. He found that he was certainly able to help Vivés. He felt the solid strength of his own feet that gave him the proof and a signal. He got up and everything followed him rearranging a new order of relationships, still at his command. Subissoni whistled like an obeyed animal tamer – not a song, but just two or three unarticulated verses, some longer some shorter, but on key. He had found in the back of the pantry a jar of chamomile and after placing it on the table went to get, with another whistle, a pot, a cup and saucer, a teaspoon, a napkin, the sugar bowl and the medicine.

When everything was ready he emitted with a whistle two more affirmations and then he took off his coat. He went back to the stove and began the operation.

Vivés opened her eyes in that moment and saw her companion bending over the stove while with his other hand behind his back he was keeping time and leading his men.

She understood instantly – as though looking through a suddenly torn curtain – that that man and those gestures belonged to a rhythm different from hers, with which she could no longer keep pace; that the whole scene, the actor, his movements and his instruments would outlive her.

She continued looking with that awareness until the end, until Subissoni – although trembling – poured the chamomile from above into the cup, put down the small pot, took the cup in both hands, and turned toward her. She also saw his amazement increase and cover his whole face when he realized that she was awake and waiting for him. The fragrance of the chamomile was so strong and so self-contained that it convinced and helped Vivés. She drank it and got up by herself, while Subissoni stood below, three steps down. Vivés undressed and put on her light blue nightgown with affection.

Subissoni stayed downstairs a little longer to lock the door and take leave, with his eye, of each object, helped by a big shot of anisette. Ah! Ah! he sighed and planted the empty glass in the middle of the table.

He went into his woman's room and took up his place at the end of the bed. He limited himself to smiling at her, with the gestures of a soldier who was getting ready for guard duty. Vivés did not have time to begin a thought before he already was sleeping sideways in the small easy chair with one arm hanging over. This detached arm stayed alive, even more so, as though it was his insignia.

Vivés went on looking at him until she cried: that awkward body, old by then but never matured, of fine stature, but always squeezed together, tightened up as to be un-manageable, always with something swollen, always in some different place – a shoulder, a curve, a flank, an elbow, a knee – in some positions it made him seem like he was made entirely of legs and sticks, in others his back made him look like one long sack. The arm that was hanging out was very beautiful, the hand that came from it was stupendous and alive, with naive trust in every finger and wrinkle that made a strong claim on time, days and happiness.

Vivés went on crying softly and that arm was giving her a thousand memories and reasons for crying or for consoling herself. It could be a shadow of Gerona, a farmer who greeted her at sundown, her Orfeo love, Orfeo's boat that betrayed her, her rifle, her battalion, Cipriano Mera's legs, the line of the first rifle unit, the entire revolutionary army deployed around Madrid. Every part of those formations was made of the same stuff, had lived and rested in that way, had dis-appeared. That hand corresponded to a million faces that she had seen and that she recognized one by one. And she had not known how to love them all and to die with them.

Subissoni was sleeping crossways on the other side and his sleep was going up and down his body like a puppet theater, but a lot of times it thickened and got stuck, as though it couldn't find the stage or script. His face had a knowing and ironic grin, but his shoulder – stretched out in a full arch, barely touched by his collar – cursed the useless-ness of life.

Vivés got up then and directed herself slowly toward the wardrobe in the back of which she kept the box with her documents and her studies. She put the manuscript that she considered most important in order and placed the whole thing on the left side; then the letters that she had saved and the ones received in the last few years about her translations and about the plans for a work that she agreed to with the Federation of Frankfurt; and finally her completed transla-tions, which were lacking only an introductory essay.

She took a white sheet of paper and with the pen that she kept in the box wrote: "Dear Gaspare, my love, you already know everything and will not be surprised if you look inside yourself. Take care of yourself and of these things that I entrust to you so that they can fulfill the intention that initiated them. I love you and I am grateful to you for everything: for so many years you have been my country, as well as my lover. You must go on, and now I touch your shoulder. The unification of any country under any external authoritarian or unreachable power – as in the democracies with a central parliament – is always an obstacle to the freedom of common people. Don't take it out only on Italian unification, but fight on so that the possibility to make decisions and, therefore, everything else of value doesn't get accumulated far from the head and hands of each man. Keep on loving me and keep on doing for me the things you know how to do.... The end is easy, even too easy, it approaches you as though you had already seen it lots of times; and you even recognize it, and you even regret not having given in to it before. It's happening to me this way too, although I didn't do anything. Don't start waiting for yours, but when it does arrive embrace it as though it was me and as I embrace you now. Your Vivés."

She wrote on the box in a kneeling position, shielded by one of the wardrobe doors, which she moved twice, accidentally banging it against Subissoni's foot.

She didn't put away the letter or the box. She waited quite a while in that position, but Gaspare did not wake up. She left the folded sheet of paper on top of the others and, before closing the box, she took some of the notes for the essay that she was writing. She went back to bed and held them in front of her. After a moment she gathered them and arranged them on the night table. She looked at the spot on the blue wall like the bay of Sitges. The wind was whistling far from the window and only once in a while did it suddenly get closer and make a horrendous rip in the big canvas of the night. But Gaspare's abandoned arm was stronger: it reached the center of the earth and, protected by it, Vivés fell asleep.

When the ripping of the wind repeated itself, Subissoni woke up under the impression that he had the cup of chamomile in his hand. As he sat up he saw that Vivés was sleeping and then was encouraged, content to have performed well his duty with that liquid. However his body was aching all over and he had trouble getting up. He went up to his room to go to bed, but while taking off his wristwatch he saw that it was past seven o'clock. He couldn't miss the glory of the day before and almost falling down the stairs he went down to get himself ready to go out. The glass in the middle of the table was asking to be contented and the shivering Gaspare grasped it, filled it with anisette and made communion with it.

He was able to go on challenging the biting wind for the entire stretch of the street between the houses, then he let the wind at his back push him all the way from the Pincio to the piazza. He stopped in the wineshop to say hello and to drink his first coffee. The rough but trusty hands of the porters and drivers who greeted him encouraged Subissoni and sent him excitedly into the activity of the city.

In the piazza he was greeted by others. Even the newspaper man recognized him and greeted him with an understanding nod. Everything was working like the day before and the latest news was making the rounds without affecting him. The newspaper headlines confirmed what the TV had said the previous evening. But Subissoni was primarily interested in that beehive that was getting back in action. The satisfied and cruel comments were increasing its strength and varying its form. Everywhere there were more people than the day before. In the large café the waiter clinked his glass for good luck before offering it to him. Subissoni greeted him and thanked him – trying to participate in all that happiness and to be with them. Milan and her massacre were far away and also condemned: above all the futility of the spectacle and of those ballerinas. He moved closer to the bar and the people and after mumbling something about the contradiction between history and TV, he went back toward the middle of the room to sway back and forth and enjoy the pleasant atmosphere of solidarity. His only regret was that Vivés was not there to partake in that happiness.

He stayed so long that when he went outside he saw the school children who were crowding around in front of the entrance to the school, his school, fifty years earlier. He walked through the groups and got emotional when he saw the berets, the books, the lips not yet tightened into their faces. He stayed there until the children went in, tempted to strike up a conversation, but not finding a way to begin. On the way home he thought about the words that he could say approaching them the following day: one word. He ruffled among the topics and he didn't notice his tears provoked by the cold, unbuttoned and trembling as he was, with the roll of newspapers in the left pocket of his coat that unbalanced him like a bird with a broken wing.

He went into the house and found Vivés downstairs preparing herself another cup of chamomile.

"Vivés, Vivés," he shouted, "This time of the morning is the most beautiful in Urbino. They're starting off to work and everybody seems young. An infinity of children are going to school with a rascally look about them. Their faces are filled with rebellion and also sweetness, and also knowledge, and irony. You're right, we have to do something for them: so that they don't fall into the net."

He hugged his woman and helped her to sit down, for he would take care of everything. At the stove the newspapers were getting in his way and so he put them on the table: "There's nothing new," he said. "It's the same as yesterday. Everything's done."

Vivés got closer and started distinguishing one paper from the other; then she leafed through each one, glancing at the headlines. She did not move her eyes, held back by a suffering that was implacable. And the suffering increased and became gradually more confused as she became forced to give in to the apparent proof against the anarchist ex-male-dancer. It really could have been anarchists, among other things because the police were talking about a master plan and about correspondence between various groups. But why didn't they put the bombs in Parliament or in the barracks, in police stations or in court houses? She found the news about the suicide of the railroad worker. Two workmen confirmed his alibi and the police were softening their accusations against him. The magistrature was forced to open an investigation into his death, while the Milan police chief was swearing to journalists that it had not been the police who killed him. Vivés felt the disgust of an episode equal to millions of others, many of which she had seen close up. In fact, the face and the ceremonies of the assassins were identical.

"Punishment and injustice," she blurted out. "This is what you have to tell those children. And the injustice is not death. It's dying in the midst of lies, without ever having been able to tear off the crust of injustice from life, not even from one spot. I'm afraid of dying in this moment that really could make me die. Tomorrow I'm leaving for Milan. Help me leave."

Subissoni was frightened by Vivés's tone; he glanced at the newspapers, but he didn't understand. And yet for the first time Vivés had asked for his help: "No Milan," he said. "No Milan. What would you do in Milan? I'll help you, I'll help you, come with me tomorrow morning. We'll go in front of the school. You'll be able to talk." And filled with emotion he went on: "You, you! I know I don't know how to do anything anymore. You'll help everybody, here in Urbino, mornings and evenings. You'll talk with everybody. I'll go to Milan. I'll be the one who goes to Milan, to throw myself under a streetcar. I'll throw a bomb at the statue of the king and I'll throw myself under the streetcar. In Milan they have to know that the disaster is Italy, that they should have stayed with Cattaneo, with Maria Teresa, with Switzerland, with Cardinal Borromeo, with Don Rodrigo, with the Unnamed… but never with Italy, never…. I'll throw myself under a streetcar…."

11

Shortly after dinner Giocondini's Mercedes left the city walls and headed toward Rimini. There the appointment houses were more comfortable, and also the trip would be longer.

Starting the previous evening after their talk with Terenzio Ganganelli and with his daughter Lucrezia, the aunts had been urging their nephew to accompany Giocondini on an important errand.

Oddino was enjoying the trip, seated for the first time in back and by himself, looking at the scenery on both sides in search of patches of snow that were still left: with those triangles or stripes, piled high or sunken in, he could construct a game of signs.

Giocondini didn't waste any time bringing up the subject of women, especially since he was the only one doing the talking, asking the questions, answering, and every so often breaking out in an exclamation of admiration.

In high school Oddino had learned a few things, partly because of the presence among his classmates of the very beautiful Guicciardi girl, who had dropped out during her last trimester just like him, not because of superiority like him, but rather because of a scandal that had overwhelmed her – "dragged her down," they said in Urbino – actually with some students and professors from the University. The Guicciardi girl had been his seat partner during the first two trimesters, placed right next to him through the intervention of the principal – just so his stillness and paleness would compensate for the vivaciousness and color of the impetuous Gigliola.

That girl had done nothing but tease him, and not only with words. For whole hours she had held her hands – and not motionless – on his buttons in front, but without succeeding in exciting him; and when she had tried to invert the situation she had disgusted him enormously.

Perhaps ever since nursery school, in which he had spent no more than eight mornings of obstinate silence, Oddino had managed the maneuvering of his buttons on his own. He had an entire film-like repertoire for this purpose, of which he was the sovereign and projectionist. The omnipotent Oddino would rise up upon himself, choose his reign, the object of his love, would undo his buttons, unsheathe his scepter and crown his omnipotence by blending together, as only the chosen few can do, legend with history, fantasy with reality. He had no need of anything or anyone; his reign was so vast that so many images, situations – like very beautiful palpitating butterflies – would go and entangle themselves in the nets at his borders. He would capture them, dispose of them, store them away in a neat and perfectly organized file which it was possible for him to consult under various categories: wall, hour, sun, rain, voice, hip, lace. It could be said that any word from the best nourished dictionary could be a sure key to the entrance into this grandiose archive of video-cassettes, of odors, of flavors, of sounds that comprised his unlimited and regal possessions.

Under the reign of his omnipotence he was listening to Giocondini's scurrilous and miserable speeches. That one was all lit up, at the height of his power as super-counselor, by his desire to take advantage of this enormous opportunity to dominate the count and his patrimony: "Once I get him started, he'll be mine," he said. "It's well known that one... hair has more pull than a hundred pair of oxen!... than a hundred, a thousand of these Mercedes."

Long before arriving in Rimini Oddino understood that they were bringing him to his first confrontation outside his realm, but he did not get frightened because it would be happening in neutral territory, far from Urbino, where no one knew him; and what's more, in a clandestine place and with professional women, who – who knows why – he had always imagined perennially reclining and tired, fat and with opened legs, breathing difficultly with their whole throat, mouth and cheeks, like bellows, half-suffocated in make-up, so that they did not have the strength and not even the use of their organs for speaking. As for seeing, they weren't able to see, positioned as they were with their head thrown back, their foreheads covered with curls and their wigs pulled down in front and with a pillow positioned like a bridge under their butt. Those of that type that he had desired, and therefore met and possessed in his omnipotence, were Spanish, tall, with flowers in their mouths, large combs in their hair, big waves of hair that enveloped them. Underneath they had lots of lace and lots of things that were round, warm, sweet, so many, rotating, smiling, tiny, gentle dolls, who one by one recognized him and embraced him as sovereign, desirous of touching his scepter and of drinking from his globe – half way between an orange and a piggy-bank – in any case, swollen with liqueur and with seeds.

Nobody in Rimini would take away his scepter and his globe, symbols of his sovereignty. What's more, they would not see them. His omnipotence had always been valid in and of itself. He had devised and tested his system of taking trips in such a way as to avoid ever exposing his omnipotence to the challenge of the outside world.

In Rimini, Giocondini followed the ring-road and just before reaching the sea he turned toward the inner city, toward the third row of little hotels and pensions. In front of the newest and most impressive of these he stopped and got out, advising Oddino to wait for him, that it would be well worth the waiting. Oddino noticed that there was no one on the street, that there were still a few leaves in the trees and that even some flowers were still alive around the fences. Giocondini came back in a good mood, offering him a pastry soaked in rosolio wine, which to him seemed immediately and without any amazement, a tongue. He followed his chauffeur into the hotel and still further, to the end of a corridor where Giocondini brought him into a room, asking him once more, with lots of promises, to wait for a few more minutes.

Oddo remained standing right by the door, and right there is where he was found by the entering prostitute. She was startled by the sudden encounter and this did not displease the young man. When she got herself together she could not help admiring the beauty and stature of that overgrown boy who had frightened her and who continued to remain motionless in that position.

"What a handsome beard," she said, without daring to get near him. "What nice big hands. Who knows what lovely caresses you can give? Pardon me, Honey, but I didn't know you were here. I came in to get undressed and get in bed. You don't mind do you?"

Oddino smiled and encouraged by this she began taking off the white sweater she was wearing, meanwhile she was sighing pathetically pretending to be hot and rubbing her hands on her chest and hips. Then she took off her shirt. After more words and gestures, her brassiere; she had on a pair of underwear that covered her higher up than her belly button, perhaps to hide the scar of some operation. She never risked approaching that silent soldier with his face shining like a medallion. She turned toward the bed and lay down there and started wiggling around and calling him with increasingly lewd names. She kept up that act for about half an hour, until she got completely numb from the cold.

Oddino had hardly turned toward her, with his opaque eyes. The whore was humiliated and began coughing and moaning, no longer looking at that statue, she put on some of her clothes, gathered the rest, and left.

Five minutes later a little man entered the room with a tray of liqueurs. He placed everything on the dresser and turned around to go out. Oddino asked him to bring a Coca-Cola. The old man came back with the bottle in his hand, disappointing Oddino who wanted it ice cold. The door reopened again and this time a girl dressed in an overcoat and hat with a big handbag came in. There was something about her that pleased Oddino, who made a gesture to invite her to sit on the bed. She cautiously went and sat on the edge. Oddino went toward her and sat down beside her – he too had his overcoat still on. She put down her bag as if to start undressing but Oddino stopped her. He began putting his hands under her coat collar and touching her. Then he pushed her down on the bed and embraced her. The woman was intimidated by that big loaf and let him do what he wanted, barely separating her legs. In that tangle of clothing it was difficult to move, but she soon felt a warm bundle that was pressing against her thighs: she looked down with her eyes and with her hands she pulled back the edge of the overcoat and of the covers that must have gotten rolled together and tangled up, but to her great surprise she encountered Oddino's luminous scepter.

"Wow!" she said, and encouraged by the boy's smile, "I've never seen such a big beautiful bird."

Oddino found the expression correct and appropriate to his regal status. He got on top of the woman and even before she could receive him in the natural way he rose the steps of his throne and settled in with an impressive outpouring of coins, well pleased by his own generosity.

"Mamma mia, what have you done to me," said his lady companion. "Whose going to get rid of this soup now? You should have warned me, you lovely hunk. But what kind of a glove could I have put on you? A big sack, one of those plastic bags from the supermarket, I would have needed."

Oddino got up continuing to smile. The lady asked him to get her a towel from the bathroom.

"What did you do to me," she went on saying, "it's as if you operated on me."

She cleaned herself as well as she could, with her hat still on, but unsaddled and wounded, and with Oddino looking on contentedly.

Whores often behave like what they are and so our lady couldn't wait to get out of there and tell all the others what she had seen and what had happened. Forget about impotent whimps! Forget about gigantic big babies! She got undressed and redressed as well as possible and went to get the other three house members who didn't have the courage to go in alone because they were afraid of making the same mistake as the first one – who had come out sneezing as though she had embraced a polar bear. Giocondini was still busy in another room, trying to warm her up a bit.

The four of them came back in a group, and Oddino was not at all surprised to see the door reopen. The four of them went well together and his first lady looked even better without those waiting-room clothes. And what's more, they were in a festive mood and approached him with admiration.

They started taking off his coat and jacket and then his shoes: they settled him down on the bed and took off his pants. Oddino could see them working against the background of the ceiling, like the merry muses painted on the vaulted ceiling of the upstairs room. The women gathered around him and started looking at his face, his skin, his shiny down, at his big fleshy violet colored lower lip: they were frightened by his eyes, deep and gilded like behind the hole of a burial mask, befitting a horror or a science fiction movie.

Between his vivid cornea and his eyelids there was a black separation, flowing with a substance equal to dense liquids found in phials for injections against anemia; between his eye and its socket there were hid lovely eyelashes and a depression that looked like a shiny seashell. The ensemble shined like ivory and coral knickknacks under glass, like the tiny silver spoons kept by mothers, or by the madams of these ladies, on the dresser with the teeth marks of children who died at the age of two in an excess of convulsions. The mother held the spoon so that the child would not mutilate his tongue during those painful contractions, until the spoon in her hand became covered with saliva and the imprint of mortal pain. The psychological dowry of these whores always included such a spoon. Oddino's face, with its oval shape and fixity, belonged to the same dowry, together with the photo of the faces of cousins who had left the seminary almost at the end, overwhelmed with passion and soon after died from TB; or of sailor cousins with chin straps blown in the air with the powder magazines of vessels in various glorious places of *mare nostrum*.

Here there was a superior nobility: that glazey secretion of the skin that made you think of a museum with shadowy and feminine abundances that could pass for Leonardian ambiguities. To the whores of course. The more discerning reader could refer to the portraits of Angelo di Cosimo di Mariano, called il Bronzino, one of them done in 1532, in Pesaro, in the Villa Imperiale, for the likeness of the Duke of Urbino, Guidobaldo II della Rovere, and now exhibited in Florence in the Pitti Palace; the other, in Urbino, a few years after, for the likeness of the last of the Oddis, not yet joined together with the Sempronis, Oddo, sixteen-years-old, handsome and studious; and who three years later would be dragged and trampled by an enraged bull, apparently by design of that Semproni who had already killed his father, forced his mother to marry him, and raped and become the lover of his sister. The painting that depicted this Oddo was quickly sold by the usurper, in part not to have to see the haughty disdain of his eyes every time he went up the stairs. Still with staring and painful eyes, not at all worn out by time or by the impoverishment of the Oddi blood, as in the case of our Oddino, he is exhibited as a portrait of a young man with a book in no less than the Metropolitan Museum of New York. Whoever is able to view this picture will learn much about our Oddino, but will also have the advantage of seeing how il Bronzino must have known something about the sexual attributes of the depicted person, and what a great artist he must have been, able, like a fortune teller, to dispense and prognosticate, even for the descendants, similarities and correspondences in their virtues, even in their most secret ones, so much so as to have painted him, following an innocent scherzo of clasps and ornaments around his belt and then sliding lower down, a kind of letter H right at the lowest point of his groin, toward his left thigh, where he generally positioned and rested that head that had many lives and even more names. Il Bronzino had the qualifications and the tendency to understand such equipment so that on the one belonging to the 1535 Oddo he painted an H to perhaps indicate *Huh,* a Latin interjection expressing amazement – and it is known that at that time cultivated men and pansies still used Latin – or even to say *Homo, sic et simpliciter;* or else *Honos, Honoris,* god of honor; or else *Hinc:* from here, from this place, from now on; or else

Hinundo: swallow; or else *Historicus, Honorabilis, Hirtus,* or else *Hippomane*: fleshy excrescence; or else *Hisco,* which means to open one's mouth especially to sing the praises of kings and the feats of military heroes; *Hiulco*: to open, to split, to cleave; or even *Hilaro*: to render merry, to make happy; or else *Hio* (intransitive and transitive): to open, to open for oneself, to split, to split open for oneself, to have one's mouth wide open, to desire ardently; or else *Hercules, Herculeus;* or even *Hic, Haec, Hoc*: this (pl), this (m), this (f), this thing; or more clearly *Hasta*: staff, rod, cane; or, with hope, *Habeo;* or, with determination, *Haereo,* an intransitive of the second: remain attached, to be affixed, to adhere, to hang, to hesitate, to remain, to reside, to stay; or else even, *Horreo,* an intransitive and transitive of the second: to be erect, to spring erect; or even, *Hospes*: he who receives or is received. Or *Hymenaeos*: nuptial song, wedding.

And this was the kind of song those ladies were singing when, like the artist, having made a quick sketch of his chest and positioned his arms with his delicate fingers to the side, went directly to his *hinc* and his *hic.* They found it partially awakened, still sleepy with its hooded head resting in the usual place, already identified by il Bronzino. Still singing and expressing their joy they turned it around like a person and woke it up completely. Its arousal made them jump away because of their surprise and their fear of getting hit by that jack-in-the-box. Oddino, who was pleased and attracted, positioned himself better, stretched his legs apart and raised all his arches and the heraldic lunettes of the Oddi-Sempronis.

The four ladies stood in contemplation with their hands together and full of emotion. Considering that the gentleman was not part of their family, nor of their people or community, they were induced by their amazement at other people's magnificence and then by the miserableness of the comparison, first to cry because of their family and societal destiny, with tones that denied any hope, and finally because of their own wretched destiny, in that dark month of vendettas and fears, of government uncertainties and hysterias, of all of Italy.

They cried and sighed for quite a while, these four provincial women liberated by the bordello, until, once again, grasping from reality that awareness that pain often reinforces – especially if it has been prolonged to emphasize a fasting and to increase the joy of the first act of resumption and encounter – they threw themselves all together upon their guest fighting among themselves for that object with furious blows and with the danger that it, suddenly escaping from the embrace of the first contender, might spring back and hit the first one that was trying to get close. The not-so-young-anymore regional pugilists, friends of those likewise regional ladies, would have said, saddened by still-noisy memories in their ears, "a knockout punch." But they all managed to get their hands on it and little by little even dared some other gestures, nevertheless brief both because those who were momentarily excluded insisted and because each actress was anxious not to stay too long away from being able to admire – simply look at – that sovereign who had stopped there by chance on his way to who-knows-what crusade.

But that king nevertheless had to be served and so the provinces proceeded with the elections. Those who came out third and fourth felt cheated and were already looking for a pretext to throw everything into confusion. But with a gesture the sovereign restored everything to order.

They completely undressed Oddino and slipped him between the sheets, since those ugly covers were bothering him. The first elected got in beside him while the others formed a circle around them as is proper for those excluded from the administration in Parliament. In a matter of seconds, although tenderly and delicately, Oddino made use of her. Since he was, as we have said, by means of his own omnipotence, used to fusing together quickly, and without problems, fantasy and reality, once reality had quickly descended to his level – actually proposing itself even ahead of his fantasy – the consummation happened naturally and contemporaneously with the attainment of reality itself.

The first contented herself with having been just that and took up the position of the second in the semicircle. The second lady entered with plans for reform and equilibrium – but not even she had the time to accomplish all her projects before the sovereign had already issued another edict.

The provinces in semicircle found it appropriate to hold a consultation and to prepare a program that might give the king a chance to meditate, to raise up his head and to face the problems of the country; after which the third lady entered with the conviction of a possible democratic reform. And, in fact, because of the natural evolution of these historic events something of the kind did happen that at least had an influence on the length of the debate.

After this they were served refreshments, liqueurs and coffee by the usual little old man.

The fourth lady was getting anxious to be subjugated and united with the others. Her fate was the happiest. Oddino was beginning to get a taste for this democratic relationship, which gave to his reign a few more items for his archives, longer film clips, situations that were more narratively extended, sequences that went beyond the clack of the first take.

These pages, as the reader has probably noticed, reflect the admiration of the author for Prof. Subissoni and for his ideas and were written according to his thoughts on Italian unification, which that very afternoon the professor was entrusting to the ceiling of his room, tired as he was and poorly nourished and even a little benumbed from having tried to compensate for his improvised and scarce meal with a couple of his abundantly-sugared cups of espresso, which were even more abundantly perfected with anisette. In short, he had drunk two tea cups and not espresso cups, filled with a little coffee and lots of anisette. He was thinking precisely about that horrible nineteenth-century of Italian history, about that herd of rich kids and loafers who were the

Carbonari; about that presumptuous Mazzini who considered himself a living compendium of the virtues of Cincinnatus, Catone, Caesar, Brutus, and Caesar Augustus: the same virtues, which then were unfailingly taken up again and fixed in the fat head of il Duce, the Italic compendium and model Roman; and before that, about that Christian Democrat Gioberti, the Lamb of God, but also of any old master's stable;... and one by one about all the others... including that Victor Emmanuel II – who always appeared to him in his underwear and at the entrance to a latrine with a wooden and crapped-up (royally) hole from which Gaspare could see the departure of a long railway that enclosed all of Italy, bringing to her that small amount of regal product that had passed beyond the boards, and destroying forever and all together her coastlines, coastal towns, landscapes, beaches, piazzas, arches and columns.

What had been the mark of distinction of this Unification? The decadence of customs and a herd of little poets, cracked up literati and hemorroidal librarians, conformism and emulation.

Our provincial women would have agreed, although for customs they would be thinking about those practiced in their coastal environment. They would add disfigured coastlines and beaches to the professor's bitter reality. Even regarding their Rimini, with only one bridge, there would be some painful comparisons to one of those excrescences or neoplasms produced by the superabundance of the impure and disorderly impulses of unitarian vigor. No difference of opinion regarding those little grieving poets, professors, and academicians. Awkward but authoritarian, fearful of venereal disease but dirty and bad smelling, demanding and presumptuous and ready to blame anybody else, even a fly, a sigh or an external noise, a lipstick, a newspaper, a picture, a fold, a reflex, a bed squeaking, for their wrinkled and gray impotence – and who even wanted to maintain at the end, while putting their underwear back on without ever having taken off their shoes, that that ashy gray color of their miserable side kick, that dismal urinary tract of theirs, was a sign of distinction as well as of equilibrium and of desirable and demanding maturity.

In the meantime the women went on adoring that sovereign who was still able to hold an audience without having himself protected and masqueraded by protocol, ceremonial trappings, attendants or chamberlains. They nourished him with exquisite mouthfuls, they washed him and perfumed him, they sang for him, they confided to him many of their secrets and taught him some of their wisdom – and a few tricks too. The one who had been first to embrace him followed him into the bathroom for a statutory amendment to the preceding rather succinct declaration of unity.

All together they followed Oddino to the door and invited him, with such devotion, to come back and to protect them that it frightened and worried Giocondini, who in the meantime had caught a nasty cold. A success of that type could rob him of his prey and make it autonomous and wise: that enigmatic noodle might turn into a libertine capable of squandering his entire patrimony in bordellos.

"No more going to Rimini," he thought to himself, "next time I'll take you to some sad whore for priests and prefects, in Fano or Fossombrone: to one of those that won't lose her head, those who are used to suffering in silence and to pretending to enjoy with an even deeper silence that comes close to the symptoms of agony. That kind doesn't have dressing tables or knickknacks: they leave pills and papaverine on their night tables and those little spray pumps for their asthma.

The city of Fano has always been against the Duchy of Urbino and in more recent times always in favor of Italian unity, of the Savoyard monarchy, of the Italian Army, so much so as to have caserns – and of various specializations – sufficient for a Balkan state or for popes; devout, but without the imagination of even a sanctuary, like Saltara; theologically black, with a regional seminary; extreme in opposition to divorce and to any freedom of research, so that it has more boarding schools than regular schools, and is so miserable that every year it sets up a carnival celebration with a costume parade and with lots of throwing of chalk confetti: and then every summer it repeats the same celebration, with the same floats, with the same papier-mâché caricatures and with the same confetti.

Giocondini knew that once an unfortunate young man from the Urbino countryside along the Metauro, who had gone down to Fano on an errand and had stopped by one of the most accredited whores of the place, had felt in her bed, as he was getting ready to embrace her, some kind of hindrance around his knees which turned out to be, after an immediate and anxious examination by the young man himself, the very complicated, plush-covered and mended, hernial truss left behind by some previous patron. The young man withdrew sick to his stomach and for some months was unable to get close to any woman. His companions, in fact, had to take him to Rimini and get him sufficiently drunk before he was able to start up again.

During the drive back home Giocondini certainly did not enlarge the luminous halo of that success with compliments or any reference whatsoever. Meanwhile Oddino had rediscovered the stripes and checker board patterns of snow that here and there broke up the night that was awaiting him. Those turreted ladies or muses of the bel canto had been gracious and kind, but he preferred those of his reign, who were plentiful, silent and always lying down, and whom his omnipotence could break apart and illuminate in a minute, and it could also make all kinds of miracles spring forth from their wrappings, and all for him alone.

That is why Giocondini could have saved himself the haste with which he planned to bring him promptly to supper with his aunts: to return him quickly and close him back up in his environment, where he would have him under his control.

12

Vivés had stayed in bed the whole day putting the papers back in order that she had taken from the drawer during the night – passing them from one hand to the other, with an occasional glance at the words.

She knew that everything was going well, but that everything was mediocre and, worse still, useless. If the anarchists were the kind that left those bombs in Milan and if the world was what it seemed to her for some time now, dominated and divided by industry so as to leave no room for free communities, what difference was there anymore between Franco's Spain, which little by little was acquiring legitimacy because of its order and its progress, and Czechoslovakia, even the United States of America and the USSR?

She thought nostalgically about Africa, about the flies of Africa, so motionless that you could make a game out of them or use them as company... sort of like those words of hers on those sheets of paper. She had seen how it was even easier to die in Africa.... Someone who was dying first looked at the wound to see if it was mortal; when certain of this, he turned the other way and died; or if he was too tired he covered his eyes right away and died; or if he was afraid he stretched out his hand toward a camel... for help... the camel barely had time to take a step or raise his lip or ruminate while turning his head, that the fellow was dead... and as soon as he was dead he did not become a cadaver, but a monkey... or a little bagpipe... or an abandoned wine skin, or the trunk of a fallen palm tree or who knows what desert wreckage.

In her search for these familiar and comfortable images, bracelets or hair pins, or else the back of her childhood violin, and how she would leave it upside down preferring not to meet it face to face so as to not be interrogated by it about her love and her progress, she who would have preferred a drum, she could only run her eyes back and forth along the walls and the window of that room in which she had been living for sixteen years now.

There was no room for death in there and nothing domestic, other than her own body. She looked at it and saw with grief that it was not dry and that it was not in any way nor in any place similar to a handle, that would be easy to grasp and ready to use…. She felt like a prisoner and she filled up with hate as well as fear, the more so because her window looked out toward the mountains, toward the interior of that country that was not hers. Her fear continued to swell so much so that she was afraid she would die right then. She squeezed her papers and waited. Little by little her fear melted into pity, for herself and for her things and then into guilt for having forgotten and offended her Gaspare with that hate…. Then she called him and was happy to find the walking stick that he had left by her side just so that she could call him by banging on the floor – before, while looking for some way of knocking, she had not seen it behind her night table.

She grasped the stick and banged and immediately Gaspare arrived looking as if he had jumped out of bed to get there on time. Vivés stretched out her arms toward him and made him sit down on the bed. She got close to his chest, which in that moment was puffed up and stiffened as though it had been overdosed with starch, and kept on looking at him from below, along his jacket up to his forehead – when she arrived at his bad eye her feeling of tenderness increased.

"You're right," he said, "you're hungry. It's almost two o'clock, and I still haven't brought you anything. Maybe it would have been a good idea to order dinner at the hotel, with a nice dish of broth for you."

"That's not why I called you. I just wanted to see you. I'm not at all hungry. I just wanted to tell you that time is standing still for me in here, that I'm almost afraid to be alone, that I wouldn't even know how to take a trip by myself. I'd be afraid of becoming immobile and of getting lost. When I go to Milan I'd like you to come with me. You would help me in so many ways. Some things you've always understood better than I have. Will you come to Milan with me? We both need to get a closer look at what is happening. The students are barking! And then? The contracts need to be renewed! And then? I'm almost proud that in Spain already in '30 we knew what to do! It seems to me as if the world doesn't know what to do anymore. But we haven't forgotten it, right? Is it true that we've placed ourselves in here to wait? To wait for our next departure, right?

Subissoni didn't answer and Vivés tugged on his jacket several times. He was slow in answering because he had realized that his companion was suffering. With a smile he finally spoke: "It's all so true that there's no longer any need to wait or to go to Milan either."

He worried about having disappointed and even offended her and so he went on: "We'll even go to Milan, if you want. And to other places too. So many times I've thought about going to kill Franco or the Pope; but I've always given up the idea partly because, when I started looking at them, they already seemed dead to me. You were right in Spain when you were killing each other among yourselves, among yourselves who were thinking about the future in the same way. It's worth more to kill traitors than enemies. Sometimes the enemy is right – and then they are always on the other side and not among little people like us. You shouldn't have left Mera, and I should have stayed in Urbino and blown up the Fascist headquarters. The hell with becoming actors on the stage of history. Every man carries his own scene with him. Anyway, we'll go to Milan."

"I've read all the newspapers, "Vivés said, "and I've been thinking. You're right to say that Italy does not exist. It's not there. Even now it reacts in so many ways, by chance, and jerks around like the chopped off tail of a lizard."

"Nice," said Subissoni, "it's true. The headless snake. And so it can become a procession, with everyone under the banners, with their heads lowered – or a race, a road – but it never knows where it's going, it never raises its head, it never looks at its body. Cultural unification, and then linguistic and then so many republics: that's the way the best ones thought about it, even Manzoni and Leopardi. A united nation is always the possession of somebody. Jacobinism by always pushing further, trying to clear up everything, wanting to renew everything and raise itself as high as possible, has always ended up by creating the throne of a tyrant. Between Buonarotti and Mazzini it's been one big caricature in this country. How could those chocolate-makers from Savoy not arrive here? Think about it, on Lorenzo's seat, in the halls of the Venetian Republic. Thus everyone in Italy is an exile. Who more than Leopardi and Manzoni? We'll say this in Milan."

"Yes, but other things too. Most of all we need to look, in Milan, and listen. I know the value of what you're saying. The only Spanish unity is in the wandering of Don Quixote. But I think that today's means of production have created something else, perhaps some new provinces. All Jacobins, and then Marxists, have seen unity as the measure of social justice. We should not be content with a lesser vision – that is not as partial as it is regressive."

"Those nice, provisional, revolutionary committees," said Gaspare. "I always took off whenever I encountered them. I could always spot the rabble that would suffocate them and that would use them. And then who says that these means of production are the right ones?"

"That's what we have to go and see. We've been talking too much about countries and men, almost like Mazzinians or religious poets."

"No, no. I have in mind Cattaneo and Pisacane and if I want a poet I'll take Leopardi, and I know how to read him – and if I want a utopian I'll take Campanella and I know how to read him."

Vivés was having trouble supporting Gaspare who in his excitement let himself go against her chest. His speech was weighing on her too, reduced like the room and the surroundings that were closing in on her. She mentioned something about the false autonomy of rural societies and felt like she was saying the truth for fear of that land. The light that was coming in through the window was also material, with a border that reduced the breathable air. She asked Gaspare to open the door to the stairway for a moment and to prepare a cup of chamomile for her.

When he had left, she took the walking stick back in her hand and waved it at the window. She leaned against her pillow half-stretched out and was suddenly struck by the beating of her own heart. She felt it against her throat and in her ear – so distinct that it seemed to be coming from a different place and even from a different body. "Bird, bird," she murmured, "don't go away." But she understood that it would be unnatural for it to stay there and obey her. Her will did not reach it and this was the conscious grief that she got out of it. The heartbeats were pounding, pounding and, like all allurements, they could disappear. She was frightened again by that peasant land that must have started getting dark in front of her window. The milky way could not have risen yet and not even Roland's sandal, as she used to call a constellation that as a child she had composed in the sky above her home. She had found it again in Urbino, but fixed toward the south, while above Gerona she could see it go where it wanted: every so often the sandal changed direction: Rome, Africa, Paris, Madrid.

She moved and took the stick while thinking that Roland probably had one with which he supported himself while sinking in the ocean or with which he reached out to touch Brazil. She stuck out her left foot and looked at it for a long time, and it was still grayish and sweaty. She did not see it change – as she was expecting it to – and so to separate it a little from herself she leaned it against the stick. That way she was bent over and still having difficulty, but at least the effort kept her company.

She turned around toward the cups, which Subissoni had already deposited a few minutes ago, without her noticing, while she was finding Roland's sandal. Who was Roland? A knight, a shepherd, a navigator, a mathematician – whatever she wanted – a Greek, a Sicilian and often a Babylonian. His face never appeared and he understood numbers. Roland enumerated and counted.

Subissoni had made a mistake and instead of chamomile he had made her some tea, very dark, with the usual cookies from the Cooperative. Vivés moved the stick in front of her eyes to hide her crying. But with the help of the stick she did not show her emotion. She gulped down one cup of tea and even chewed a small cookie. She turned over again in bed with the intention of sleeping until it was time to get up and go and watch TV. She tried to let herself go in order to be able to fall asleep, but from the inertia of her thought slipped out a reprimand for her own weakness. She straightened up and started breathing deeply. Still not satisfied, she went to the window and opened it. She glanced quickly at the hills and withdrew toward the wardrobe. She opened it up again and pulled out her heavy box in the middle of the floor. On her knees she rearranged the manuscripts and the letters, several times, without ever finding the right place for the sheet of paper intended for Gaspare.

After several attempts, which were truthfully quite hasty, she took it out altogether and without rereading it she tore it up. It took a big and painful effort to get up to go and hide those tiny pieces. She couldn't find the right place until she got the idea to throw them out the window. She opened it again and the wind and the cold of the countryside were right there huddled together waiting for her. She tried to touch them just enough to scatter her papers, but they seized her, grabbing her by the hair and by her clothes with the force to drag her out the window. Vivés clutched onto the window sill to keep herself from falling out, but that way she could not close the shutters. She did not call Gaspare and kept up her resistance, with her eyes toward the sky so as not to be swallowed by the sea of hills. She spat twice in order to breath better, aware that her strength was giving out. But a change in the wind caused the door of the room, which opened onto the stairway, to close, so that the wind current on her shoulders, that was reducing the strength in her legs, diminished. She was able to press her knees against the wall and grip the shutters with her hands. She still had to struggle for quite a while to get them both shut.

She threw herself exhausted on the bed and a moment later succeeded in getting back under the covers.

The last struggle of her life had taken place like a child's dream: against the wind, against an invisible face. Now the cold was keeping her company and giving her courage. Even in her dreams the cold had always been real and helpful. Even on the battlefield the cold gave soldiers a feeling of victory. As her heart slowly got warmer it grew smaller.

Then Gaspare emerged with more little plates and cups in hand. She was breathing deeply a breath that barely reached her throat and he too, was all disheveled and pale. He turned his whole head this way and that way to see the confusion of the room. Even the cups from before had fallen and broken. He became frightened without understanding, getting even more pale in spots like a drunkard. By luck the box was closed and the papers were safely inside. Vivés was no longer pale and her cheeks were blacker than her eyes: her hair covered the whole pillow and fell halfway down the bed.

Subissoni said nothing. He moved some things that blocked his way, but without trying to put them in place. He put down the new tray and gathered the pieces of the first one. Bending over beside his companion's bed he heard nothing, and yet, already in that moment, he was surprised to have noticed something without understanding what it was. While he was straightening up he thought it might be the feeling of cold, or an odor. He went out without saying anything, closed the door, went slowly down to the bottom of the stairs, straight toward the cabinet where he hit the anisette again, and with no need of filling the coffee pot or disturbing the sugar cup. He understood that upstairs he had been afraid – afraid that Vivés had gone crazy. In Spain the insane asylums and the convents are full of women who cover the beds with their hair, dribbled from their mouths and their privates and whinnied like she-mules. He took another drink and then decided to go back up. He entered the room and found Vivés in the same position as before, but immediately noted with alarm that she had the walking stick in her hand. He stayed near the doorway and spoke up, asking where he should put that box and if he should put the room back in order. Vivés smiled, with the black of her cheeks that pitifully covered her mouth, and then said: "Leave everything as is and I'll straighten it up afterwards. Don't wear yourself out. Why don't you go out? I don't think I'm going to be able to watch TV this evening. You'll watch for me and then tell me about it. Get ready for another official ceremony and don't get upset. Eat something first and don't drink. If when you get back I've fallen asleep please don't wake me up."

After hearing her speak with such good sense, Gaspare got emotional and went toward her to embrace her and to confess in tears his shameful suspicion. Vivés saw his mouth twisting and his eye shining and intervened by saying, "I don't feel well. You can't embrace me. Put away the box and fix up the end of the mattress."

Subissoni took care of those tasks enthusiastically and then stopped stiffly three feet away from his woman. She lifted the stick and struck him lightly on his left side, which in that moment was the bulging part of his body.

"Go on. Listen carefully and stay calm when you talk. You are the best and not only in Urbino. Drink something, but not too much. Come back when you want, don't worry about me, but don't catch cold tonight."

After he was touched by that stick, like a knight, Subissoni stood up straight, with no bulging and no trembling. He blew Vivés a kiss and went out. He felt as if he was returning the favor of that investiture by closing the door more carefully than usual. With his mouth closed he tasted all the flavors of happiness and intellectual pride, walking with large strides toward the piazza.

He encountered some people who were coming back for supper in the downhill neighborhoods and he exchanged greetings with all of them. He got to the piazza a little after seven and stayed there to enjoy himself, going from one group to the other, without speaking, barely shaking his head, until supper time. He caused a stir in the restaurant where he and Vivés had been eating for several years when he went in for the first time in about a week. He gave some reassuring news about his companion's health and went into the kitchen, taking a certain liberty that he had never allowed himself before, to select his food. In addition, he ordered a bottle of Albana and offered some to his neighbors.

"What's going on professor?" the proprietress asked him. "Did you win the lottery? Or did you get a job at the University?"

"Brava," he said excitedly, "the lottery and the University! There you have the two banners, the two elements of subjection and ignorance. What kind of a republic is this that preserves the gambling of the lottery and leaves its universities in this condition?"

He waited there for the newscast, but he didn't follow it very attentively, partly because he had seconds on the Albana. Nevertheless he understood that the anarchists were to blame, those ballerina-type anarchists, so foolish and spoiled that they take a taxi to go a short distance, letting themselves be noticed, they conspire with fascists and police informers, they throw themselves out the window right away, before they are even proven guilty, thus unmasking themselves completely.

"I'm going to Milan soon," he said forcefully. "I'm going to go and make some contacts and give some history lessons. It seems to me that we all need it, including the proletarians and most of all the gentlemen anarchists,... because I'm told that nowadays they are well to do...."

At that point from the little adjacent room, the one used by non-regular customers – it too half-deserted and with only one light – the peremptory and southern voice of the two students who had been silently looking through the door was raised: "Why don't you shut up and forget it? You don't know what you're talking about and you're only saying nonsense."

Subissoni staggered and stared toward that corner that should have been empty. He saw the faces of the two with long curly hair and how they were distinctly different from the faces of the Urbinoites, how different was the very place in which they were.

"You shut up," he struck back, "you who don't speak our language. Who do not even belong to this Italy. On the contrary, you're a bureaucratically fabricated Italian. You don't know anything about federated Italy...."

One of them got up and actually threatened him. "Sit down, idiot, and drink! Drink so you can warm up the membranes on top of that pole. What the hell do you know about Italy.... What are you, a civil servant? Or are you a papal policeman? Like everybody in this noble city? No, we're not Italians like you. So what about it? Don't you understand that you threw those bombs? You threw them, so don't worry about federated Italy and the lottery...."

Subissoni was unable to respond. He sat down trembling, not knowing what to do. He looked around, but no one was helping him, not even the host – not even those who had been drinking his wine.

"Me..." he said, "me...me...." His disappointment and his shame were worse than his fear, and so he tried to run outside bumping into everything. He started up the hill so as not to show himself right away in the piazza under the blows of that attack and of that defeat. In front of the Cathedral his anger took over again and he threatened the stone statues and the door of the City Hall. He even considered going to the police and so he turned around and headed for the police station, but when he saw that he was really going in that direction he stopped and got mad at himself.

He turned around and went back the same way and when he was back in front of the Cathedral he continued on to the Ducal Palace. The pitch black darkness blocked out the internal spaces of the facade and therein, right against the main door, poor Subissoni went to console himself and to cry. A motive for getting hold of himself could have been the recollection of those two faces: besides being young and dark they were rather handsome and also serene. The crusty tone of the one who had gotten up to speak the second time was not offensive but almost inspired, like a teacher's, and even his words, at least some, were not banal insults. He had also admitted that he didn't give a damn about Italy, much less about being Italian, and even less about the middle classes and the powerful. He had expressed – even if in an impulsive way – Vivés's idea that the bombs had been placed by well-to-do hands, by time-honored arms, and that perhaps someone else more stupid had exploded them.

Subissoni raced home hoping to find Vivés awake and to be able to tell her about that encounter. On the way he prepared himself to omit the first part and to sweeten the tone of the lines, as though it had all taken place during a discussion. But he found Vivés's door closed. He stood still and listened, but didn't hear any signs of Vivés being awake. He tiptoed back down to the living room. He once again went to work on the anisette bottle and from a discrete dose of the stuff an unexpected wave of self-approval reassured him. He threw the anisette down puffing and clicking his tongue. His head was still crowded and so was his stomach, and to reestablish the entire circulation of his own blood he prepared himself a boiling foot bath.

A little later, while he was waiting to fall asleep, the recollection of what had happened was coloring itself with glory, and the image of those two young men – especially the one who had gotten up to speak – was becoming increasingly pleasant. He fell asleep with the hope of seeing them again.

He was awakened by the banging of Vivés's stick and he ran to see her right away. His woman had gathered her hair together, and also the bed, on which she was sitting – a little raised up against the headboard – was tidied up. Even the room was picked up, with everything in its place, sustained by the strong morning light.

"I was late," Subissoni said. "But I slept in good company."

Vivés smiled, but it also might have been the light or a small movement of her body, that altered the creases of her lips. For years even Gaspare wasn't able to tell for sure whether Vivés was smiling deliberately or if the smile was only by chance formed on her mouth – often half-open – by a word she pronounced or by the bubble of a thought.

"It went well last night. Nothing new. The guilty are guilty, proven by an infinity of other evidence. They found explosives in their homes, maps indicating the location of their attacks, and other stuff. It's a little history of these times, out of proportion but not big. Unfortunately, the number of deaths has increased. How are you doing? Two days until the doctor. But you do look better to me this morning. You've fixed yourself up. Everything here looks nicer. It's even a beautiful day. Unfortunately I missed the time for the school kids,... maybe I'll wait for them when they get out. Do you need anything?"

Vivés gestured a "yes." "A newspaper," she said an instant later, "just one – *l'Unità*."

"Okay. I'll go right away. But in the meantime don't you want some coffee, tea, chamomile?" And since she was saying "no" with her head, he went on joking: "Some anisette, some rum, a nice glass of port?"

Vivés raised her stick to threaten him and Gaspare fled.

He went off full of courageous ideas, only slightly insecure for fear of meeting those two immediately and not being ready yet to question them and to undertake a discussion. He noticed the sun as he was losing it by going under the loggia. He turned to see it, but by then it was blocked out by the theater. In front of the hotel he thought about Vivés. He consoled himself with the fact that she was feeling better, but then he started wondering about the way she had looked at him. He wasn't even sure that he had seen her eyes. He went into the wineshop and greeted everybody, but he realized that he had been risky because they weren't the same people who were there at dawn. He ate his breakfast in a hurry, covering his mouth with his hands while eating the pastries, and he left with just a nod for the waiter.

He bought *l'Unità* and folded it in his pocket. In the meantime, next door they were opening the communal clubroom and already professionals, proprietors, and employees were standing around waiting. The city was not as spirited as it had been at dawn on the preceding days and, what's more, the sun had a diluting effect. Subissoni gathered himself between his shoulders and went straight across that wingless stage. He retraced his steps directly to his home, stiffly grasping the newspaper in his pocket.

His hooked figure cut a straight line up the street, but it leaned to one side as though it was trying to escape the force of that journey. On top his head was rolling around furiously. Thirty yards from home he cursed, raising his free arm like a whip. He opened the door and the sun in the living room repelled him as though he had the wrong house. That sun put everything in disorder with an equalizing light on the cups, on the dishes in the sink and on the small glasses that ended up all placed on the left side of the table, toward the stairway, hurriedly, and not well-placed in the center, which he – defenseless and also humiliated by the crude transparency – considered doing each time. He stood still there for a moment and then closed the door.

The light of the stairway was cooler, and without moving he turned in that direction. The stairs made his head spin, and he had to support himself and then go up two stairs so as not to have the whole thing ahead of him. The stairway step by step – each one with its bricks laid on end, enumerated in that invented position; each brick cut to order with an earthy dusting, but quickly tricked into serving a common cause, slightly less important – impressed him and moved him.

At the top of the stairs, on the landing there was the turquoise curtain with one side opening to the hallway and the other to the continuing ramp of the stairway – useless but always there just like in Spain. Subissoni understood that everything depended on the outcome of Vivés's illness. Once before he had fled from a house with those indications, and after so many years he ended up in another, just like the first.

He went back downstairs and rearranged the glasses. He put away two without washing them. He left the third right in the middle of the table and used the fourth for anisette, twice. He noticed that the bottle was almost empty. He measured the dosage that was left and felt that it was appropriate. He went up to Vivés and found the door open. The room was tidied up and looked like it usually did. Then he got stirred up and began wavering back and forth. "Nothing, nothing," he said. "No news, and Urbino is as you know it. I had created some false illusions yesterday and the day before. Anyway, who opened your door? Who's been going in and out? Who's been coming to see you?"

Impressed by the reality of that other presence, he stopped. "Here's the newspaper. Your *Unità* ah hah! You, who were supposed to convert all the communists! They're all marching so beautifully... toward the conciliatory republic. This is what's new about Italian unification – the new formula. The cardinal legate is going to come back and tell us who can play the violin and who cannot. And when the most stupid person plays, the happy people will applaud. You think I'm kidding? Do you know that with an edict the cardinal legate prohibited the Jews from playing the violin? Do you know why? Because the violin is a heavenly instrument, or celestial. Here's your violin. I haven't even turned a page. There's little to read, judging by what I got from the front page. The republic has swallowed it. True or not. But I'm not paying attention to you, I'm just saying it to say it. To say that this republic would swallow everything. And I don't care if by this I'm conceding that you were right. You know I've always admitted when you're right. I'm only sorry that I brought you here! But where could I bring you? There's Franco in Spain, yes or no? And the pope in Rome. Isn't he always flipping his skirts around with his hands inside and out? And in Milan aren't they charging three thousand lire a meal? And Paris? Maybe the Marseilles is still running Paris?"

He wiggled and tried somehow to interrupt the orderliness of that room. The light dimmed a little, with a little jump that gave him a bit of hope. I'm going to break another pact. Tonight I'm going to call the doctor for you. He'll tell us when we can leave for Milan – if you can. No, no, it's not that I want to go alone. And now I'm bringing you some coffee."

He moved something else and then went down to make coffee. On every step he bumped against the wall and almost tore down the curtains. Downstairs he started singing and then he remembered the anisette bottle. He took it out, shook it to check the level and held it ready.

Having poured the coffee in the three little cups according to the measurement of the espresso maker, he poured anisette into two of these and barely half a tiny spoonful into the third. While he was conducting these operations he spilled a little liquor, with curiosity he watched it expand on the table to see what final form it would take. He couldn't make out anything in particular and so he said, "A territory, a duchy, the duchy. If we don't do something here fast the only thing left will be the laundry-day duchy... bleaching itself increasingly whiter." He gulped down one of his two small cups and with the other two he headed back up the stairs. Vivés was reading the newspaper.

"THE SENTENCE AGAINST VAJONT HAS NOT DONE JUSTICE," declared Gaspare reading a headline. "Oh wow, what expectations! They're expecting nothing less that justice! If they knew about just one of the trumpets of our prison camps!... How it sounded in the evening... it made the night larger than any I have ever imagined. They came down like pigeons, by the millions. They went up like fish with their mouths wide open from the biggest pond in the universe. What an accent those trumpets... to say that justice has died forever, that they shouldn't try to dress her up and to bundle her up, and drag her up, all broken up as she was. Ta-ta-ta-ra-ra-ta-ra-ta," he made a trumpet with his nose and drank his second espresso. "Ah I'll read some more: HIGHLIGHTS AT THE QUIRINALE OF THE.... Highlights? What highlights? Ornaments? Cornices? A sash of blue silk highlighting the forehead of the republic? HIGHLIGHTS AT THE QUIRINALE.... Highlighting the Quirinale. That's the problem. To highlight or not to highlight? Quirinal or Viminal? Or Lictorial?"

Vivés put down the newspaper and looked at him smiling sincerely with a look of pain that seemed an excessive reprimand to Gaspare for those jokes. The woman's forehead was more pale and relaxed, even though crossed by a ripple of sweat. Gaspare was forced to think that her whole face, even the part that he couldn't see, was acquiring a flavor. He kept looking, and Vivés smiled again, with less pain.

"Let me read," she said, "it's not true that there's nothing new."

"Drink your coffee," said Gaspare still attracted by the honey of her face. He noted that it went well with the trumpet and with the pond and that her hair was detached on her temples like the wings of those pigeons that had passed through his mind. Still hanging on to those images he spoke, "When you get better I know what we're going to do. Once and for all. We're going to go and throw a couple of bombs in Spain, in Franco's bed. Then finally they'll shoot us and in the evening we'll first hear the trumpet again and then everything will close up and a nice shroud will come down."

"They'll have us garroted," said Vivés.

"Fine, better yet! As long as they play the trumpet the night before. This much someone condemned to death can ask. And I like the garrote. It's more cruel, it's more noble, it's more monstrous, you feel it more... and meanwhile the trumpet...."

"That's enough," said Vivés.

He got up and took the cups. His woman's face was a little twisted to the left – just like when he had met her – thin, with her cheek bones out over her thin and protruding chin. The upper part was all eyes – very black, coming at you from every part, making it difficult to comprehend them. When they stood still in the back of their disproportionate spaces they quivered as they looked out like two turtle-doves on the same branch. Now her left temple seemed twisted too; but it too was always involved in the machinations of those real and false smiles. Now the black of those huge eyes was less shiny but made them seem closer to him.

He moved away and turned toward the light of the window. In that moment the midday bells started ringing.

"Do you want to eat?" he asked. "Do you want your box? Do you want me to help you go downstairs? Aren't you getting tired? Who knows what new ideas you've gotten! You have always read differently than I have. I'm going to buy something to eat, near here. Isn't there anything you need? Toothpaste, soap…?"

Vivés looked at that poorly executed caricature of Don Quixote with a feeling of love and of pain that moved her in her bed. She pulled herself up so she could see him off better and gestured toward her stick, as if to tell him that it would keep her company. She did not try to speak because she was not sure that she wouldn't cry. And then she waited for him to go out so that she could dedicate herself better to her reading, entering completely into that concoction of ferociousness, of lies and of naiveté that was expanding… toward something very noble and grandiose, however, that could be read between the lines and would soon appear.

The paper itself of the newspaper was already a part of that advent. She read line by line the first and second page and several times, with increasing hope, the news about a letter from intellectuals and students that asked for the truth about the death of Giuseppe Pinelli. She slowed down to read the names of those that had signed it: those real names, lined up, in a group, alive, who had been able to think and decide, and who would not give up. The lists of comrades entrusted to her had always given her strength and she had always taken care of them as though they were innumerable and invincible. The effort to read those names made her tired. She did not want to sleep and, even if it was difficult, she kept her eyes open to prevent the darkness of her eyelids from animating apparitions and recollections. One can hope to reach a line of unknown and living comrades. She let her eyes fall upon the various things in the room, but she could not concentrate on any one thing before it would quickly sink into the deep silence that was also submerging her bed. From the window a very distant sky could be seen, which didn't even seem to be part of Urbino. It was blue and flat like a wall and with no roof above it.

Vivés was so worn out that she had to close her eyes and was forced to see the fox of the Universal Circus, clearly, with the blue boards behind him. She was forced to shut them even tighter and see the two horses mounted by soldiers – she had always been afraid of these encounters because she didn't know how to distinguish between the uniforms.

She was able to reopen her eyes at the feeling of remorse for having ripped up her letter for Gaspare. Just in that moment she heard him coming up the stairs making some inarticulate whistling sounds – a usual sign, as much of impatience as of satisfaction.

Subissoni had put a new bottle of anisette in the cupboard and had thought it proper to bring along the old one to pay honor to its end. He got on the bed and looked at the ceiling on which might fall the blows of Vivés's stick. He pulled up two covers and a pillow on his stomach and then, protected in this way, he turned toward the bottle. The little bit that was left would not bother his stomach protected by that tightly-held pillow. But here he interrogated himself. "How long has it been since I started drinking? Have I really started drinking? But if for years I never drank more that a glass of wine a week?" He became ashamed of thinking about himself and went upstairs to Vivés. In that moment she had her eyes closed. He stared at her and noticed that her face was swollen in some places.

He went back down to think about his own room. He couldn't even stand the pillow anymore for the anguish that gripped him. He got up again and opened up a couple of drawers but soon sat back down discomforted. Then he went down to get the alarm clock and decided that at four o'clock he would call the doctor. But he couldn't stand the wait and he went back up to his companion. He found her looking toward the window, with one hand on the newspaper. He couldn't figure out where she had her other arm. He didn't know what to say both because of his grief and because if he had spoken he would not have been able to keep quiet about going to call the doctor in a little while. He heard the rustling of the newspaper and saw that his companion had started reading again.

Vivés was no longer able to look far away, as though that would require a longer breath. She wanted to say something to Gaspare, but his composure on the chair impeded her, so she took up her newspaper again and started the cultural page. She read the whole thing, concentrating on the report of the committee for the defense and struggle against repression. She was happy that such a committee existed – even though it was made up mostly of lawyers. She was even happier to read that some international anarchists were going to look into Pinelli's death. She turned toward Gaspare and with a gesture indicated the page. He approached and took the newspaper. Vivés had both hands lying on top of the covers now. Gaspare realized that she was frightened by the way he had taken the newspaper from her and started looking at her. Then, as if to justify his bending so far over, he picked up the stick and handed it to her. He went back to his stool at the other end and showed his obedience by starting to read. He looked at the newspaper with rancor, just waiting for a convincing opportunity for leaving it. He held the whole thing in front of himself so that it would be out of focus to his only eye. He closed his eye and leaned his head back behind the sheet of paper in order to follow the woman's breathing, which had been a little noisier than usual, as though she was about to fall asleep.

Concentrating in that way he heard the stick hit the floor. He got up and saw that Vivés had turned her face on the pillow with her eyes closed and that her mouth was shaking from repeated sobs. He ran to her and called her. He waited an immense moment for her to answer or to make a gesture different from the one that was twisting her mouth. He called her again and got close to her face, taking it in his hands. All he saw was one eye open slightly with a long shiny streak. He waited for it to open completely and to recognize him. Meanwhile he was calling more quietly, while softening his grip. Her face fell backward with a decisive gesture of abandonment. Subissoni had a tiny sharp sensation of fear, in the middle of his head. Only a moment later he breathed and understood that Vivés had entered into her agony.

13

Giocondo Giocondini – he too, perhaps of noble origin, inasmuch as his family had come from the outskirts of Arezzo in the retinue of an excise officer in charge of conducting investigations in the Urbino legation – like all servants and adulators, could not bare that his master – the jerk entrusted to him by chance, for the satisfaction of all his needs, and also to test his will and capacity to completely reverse their respective destinies – might be in some way superior to him.

Giocondini was driving himself crazy with the fear that Oddino might be sufficiently equipped and capable of succeeding in becoming independent some day and, in any case even now, to be stronger and more admired than he and especially regarding those delicate subjects for which so many women-travelers and others, had always recognized him as unbeatable. That's what he had the Mercedes for! Not just to make a more comfortable ride for the relatives of sick and dead people, court witnesses, university assistants... nor only for the noble Oddi Trinity – to which the very trademark of the great German industry referred, with its three points shining brightly on the radiator... like the peepsight of a machine gun and of power!

Giocondini acted like nothing had happened the day before and adroitly rolled his eyes between the discouraged aunts on the one side and the desirous Oddino on the other, for the purpose of proposing another try. In this way he succeeded in embarking the count and taking off toward Fano.

"It must be done again," he was already saying near Fossombrone, "eh, eh, learning everything all at once would be too easy! Repetition for maturing, strengthening and giving proof of real virtues... all the more so for a nobleman with a family like yours, which must not be extinguished. One strike is not enough... eh, no! How many strikes did your ancestors probably make in order to occupy this whole valley? This is yours and you have to be worthy of it. You have to cover it all and then you have to prove it and re-prove it and keep in form."

Oddino was pleased with the beautiful day. He saw lots of people on bicycles, lots with carts, lots of old-fashioned cars, so much so that seldom in the past had any trip given him such a strong sense of freedom. Freedom to stand over his little theater, always like the omnipotent one that pulls the strings and moves each scene and actor. The things he saw by chance gave him material, but to become real they had to enter his theater: that bus, for example, or those road workers, or that road sign. He was secure and felt no fear, not even of Giocondini's fastidious scholastic speeches, since his theater also had a curtain that he could use to close off and suffocate any show that he didn't like.

Giocondini looked at him furtively, confused, if not intimidated, by that monument of Olympic serenity. He was asking fewer questions than usual, and less inappropriate ones, and even the sun seemed to have come out just to make him happy – as happy as an unleashed dog running along the banks of the river and the road.

But Fano was as sad as ever, just as Giocondini had expected. And he went looking through the back alleys with their rubble and rubbish and abandoned military barracks in order to get to the oldest and worst part of the city.

At the end of a street, in front of a rubbish garden, was the small rose-colored house of one of the city's most worn-out prostitutes. The woman was always in the window, three feet from the street, right by the door; busy preparing food or sewing, partially hidden by a curtain. If she wasn't at the window she was upstairs in the bedroom, at work.

Giocondini went and parked the Mercedes, half on the garden, and told Oddino to wait for him. He wanted to make things clear to the whore – that she subjugate and intimidate the young man and that she then tell him everything about how he acted and especially about that particular subject. The woman was not at the window, but the door was ajar. As soon as Giocondini pushed it, an enormous spring operated bell over the door rang out like a parrot.

"Who is it?" asked the voice of the woman from the top of the stairs. "What do you want? I'm sick."

Giocondini went upstairs and found her in bed: "I can't," she said, "My sciatic nerve is killing me, I'm burning with fever. And I'm anemic. I can't do anything."

The room was swollen with balsamic medicinal smells, but also with her breath, so that it prevented one from sticking one's head inside. Giocondini immediately grasped that scene of horrors and decided to convince the woman at all cost to work something up for his purposes. But this gentlewoman, honest and charitable, beat him to it by saying; "If you need some service I have a maid here that helps me and who might be willing to accommodate you. She's kind of small, but she's very young and you might say that she hasn't even started yet. For sure, she has no experience. And I haven't been able to help her, immobilized as I am. Any way it's up to the customer. If he's looking for refinements, he won't find them here. Dirce," she called, "Dirce."

Giocondini turned around and saw a girl and Oddino appearing together. Their eyes were different but they were both staring with the same look of amazement. Since they both stared in the same way they both got the same shadow in the middle of their forehead and the same light at the base of their nose. Standing together like that on the landing they had the painful appearance of two outdated comedy actors. Everything in that little house was in proportion to the girl, from the stairway landing to the doors, to the narrow window over the door; while in that tiny space, he, big and solemn, seemed stuffed inside a box.

It all seemed propitious to Giocondini, who hastened to reassure the woman of their acceptance of the service and to indicate to Oddino the lady assigned to him.

"The count...," he addressed him that way to frighten her even more, although she already appeared to be the most timid and most unprepared prostitute ever, "...will bite an unripe plum; but this is the way for him to sharpen his teeth."

The two of them were pushed into a tiny room across the hall furnished with a bed, which almost took up the whole room, a chair and a portable bidet with the appropriate water pitcher.

"It happened by chance," the old prostitute was saying. "I really got her as a maid. I certainly wouldn't bring a professional into my house to take away all my customers. Has the young man come to lose his virginity? Do such innocent types still exist in the countryside?"

"Uhm!" said Giocondini, "we'll see," and he went downstairs.

Shut up in the little room Dirce and Oddino looked at each other in the light from another tiny window almost blocked out by his shoulders. The girl had curly blond hair, cut short to her very pronounced neck muscles; she was looking crossways at that young man, partly to be able to see his face outside of the confusion of light from the window that caused different hews to affect the clear flesh of his shoulders and his hips. She tried to smile and from her drawn mouth several pale dimples formed and went forth like so many circles of sweetness. She even smelled of sugar.

Oddino bent over and kissed her. Taken by surprise she giggled and reacted awkwardly. They both had to wipe the saliva off their mouths. Oddino sat down so he could move more comfortably and so that more light could come in. She understood and turned on the nightlight by the bed. They smiled together and took a better look into each other's eyes. He made her come closer so he could start kissing her again; she was standing up and he was sitting down, but with the back of the chair in front, between them. Dirce grabbed hold of her dress, and he realized that it was not so much to take it off as it was to protect it from the rough corners of the chair. He laughed out loud, stood up and started kissing her again. They squeezed each other with an affection that both were feeling for the first time and which they still thought was hidden by flavors, by material, by odors, perhaps by kindness. Oddino was not embarrassed to take out his scepter and to offer it to her. She took it in her hand and caressed it. Afterward, when she wanted to remedy the situation, she apologized while undressing in an instant. Oddino was profoundly touched by that gesture of stripping herself without being in bed, standing up in the back of the room. There were cold spots visible on her white body, especially on those neck muscles, which went down her whole body, gradually softening, but still pronounced halfway down her buttocks. Oddino like a real count covered her with his own coat and then he too got completely undressed. When he stood up his body cast a pearly light inside the whole room. They embraced and got into bed.

It was Giocondini after quite a while who knocked on the door. He had stayed there eavesdropping for a long time and after he heard them often talking he had hope that things hadn't gone all that well; apparently there had been no repetition of that exaggerated admiration of those dirty Romagnole whores, always ready for a spectacle.

Dirce got dressed first, but Oddino indicated that she should wait. It was he who presented himself, with her behind, led by the hand.

"My dear lady," said the young count addressing the half-dead madam in her bed," I want to ask you for the redemption of this girl Dirce. That is to say that you should not assign her to anyone. For a few days Dirce can still take care of you, but in the meanwhile you should see about finding a replacement. On Christmas Eve around noon I will come and get her."

That big old whore, who in Fano liked to be called the Leopard, was cut through to the most painful part of her sciatic nerve by that surprise. And the only thing she could do was to turn toward the Madonna. Giocondini – who had stood beside the door to let in that big puppet, who was looking kind of surly and in the mood to spout off a question or an enumeration, by chance, of the architectural history of the church of San Rocco or of the dotal property of

Vittoria della Rovere or of all the times he had eaten smoked prosciutto – staggered down the stairs and felt his giant camera-like eyes squirting out of his head. Redemption? Christmas Eve? And his tone! Then he went back up the same stairs partly driven by that speech, but not all the way up, owing to innate prudence. "But really," he said, "I don't understand. Perhaps something did not go well, and so the count wants to try again. Certainly he will find the girl again. She will still be here I imagine. And in a few days the rested count can have her again all for himself."

"No, no, my dear Giocondini," said Oddino. "Dirce must no longer go with anyone. The time necessary for the lady to get better, six days, and then she'll come away with me...."

"Away where?" asked the other one with eyes that were getting bigger and bigger.

"To Urbino, home, with me."

"Home... but... but your aunts.... I couldn't, I mean, I couldn't conceal... I wouldn't want to be responsible...."

"Come on. Don't act like an old parish priest," said Oddo perhaps a bit too hastily.

"A... what? who? a pa... pr...."

"A parish priest. A curate. You look like, and now you're even acting like, a priest – the kind who doesn't know how to say Mass and who is always blowing his nose and always rubbing his hands. Dirce is mine. In a few days, on Christmas Eve, she will enter my house. My house, which is a palace."

"But the girl...," the other one tried to object.

Dirce looked toward the madam, sharply, squinting her eyes and her lips so as not to lose anything and – as though convinced by the spectacle of that broken down bed and of those double chins that did not quite reach that point of her enormous sciatic buttocks that would have enabled her to move – said, "Yes, I'm going with this gentleman. I'll wait until Christmas Eve."

Madame Leopard crumbled even lower down on her back and there touched the ultimate position of happiness and purity; from all the flab of her neck she offered praise for that miracle of love to the Madonna, who justified with that sign her entire life of prostitution – even though often at the service of the father rectors of the regional seminary.

Giocondini, on the other hand, lost control of his eyes – that is, those two movie cameras inside the big box that was his head and which he usually used to review films that were pleasant for others and even more so for himself. And once again, working on the same principle, during the trip home he designed another plan, the application of which we will see point by point further ahead.

The separation between Oddino and Dirce took place with a kiss, almost hastily: as though both wanted to get it over with quickly so that they could better await their next encounter. But the eyes of both went on supporting each other in their certainty and afterward they conserved the wonderful image of the other in the vagueness in which they had become enchanted of each other.

Only after Fossombrone did Oddo rub his. Then he emptied himself into sweet sleep.

Giocondini did nothing but repeat to himself, while working on his plan, that that ox had fallen in love. He had planted his kisser against that straw doll and who knows what it would take now to put an end to that – a cart full of railroad tools.

Oddino woke up in front of his house and right away rediscovered around his neck the embrace of Dirce's loving sweater and between his mouth and nose her sugary smell. He threw open the doors with a heart as big as his palace and announced to his aunts even before seeing them – while they were coming down the stairs – that soon he would be married and that before that they would have the pleasure of the company of their new niece.

"Ask Giocondini," he said and went and closed himself in his room.

Giocondini narrated, giving more importance to some things and leaving others less clear – both because he didn't want the aunts' surprise transmuted into anger to be dumped all upon him and because he was still not sure of all the elements of his plan and above all the part that that straw doll queen would have in it. He confirmed the news to the aunts but left them unclear as to the circumstances; and about the girl he said only, beside her name, that she was tiny and graceful, that she seemed like a country orphan, and that she couldn't be more than eighteen years old.

With that detail Giocondini stopped himself. The two women looked at the ground and then the courtyard and the stairs as though they were looking for a real trace of the passing of those eighteen years. They found nothing except the idea to lock the door even tighter behind Giocondini.

"Dirce," said Marzia entering the kitchen to make herself coffee – and the name sounded like the tiny espresso spoon she was using.

"A country orphan, from who knows what countryside?" said Clelia and her glance fell upon the first lemon plants between the courtyard and the garden. She consoled herself by looking at the earth that the rain of the previous days had splattered from the vases onto the surrounding columns. Afterward, when they looked at each other alone, each one understood the feeling of hope that was growing in the heart of the other.

Giocondini on the other hand was heading home like crazy down through the streets of Lavagine. First point: go back to Fano and collect from the Leopard and elsewhere as much information as possible on that Dirce. Second point: with this information, for sure negative, and with the aggravating circumstance of her minority, blackmail both the straw doll and the old whore into disappearing. So that, third point: that ox will find the manger of Bethlehem closed on Christmas Eve. Fourth point: take that Trinity on another trip, as soon as possible – and toward some sanctuary – or else frighten them with a trip to Milan amidst the bombs or to Rome amidst the bombs and all the trumpets and papal robes and stairways on their knees and a visit to the Pantheon, to Raphael's tomb, with a rekindling of the usual noble disdain of the family at the sight, right there, of the tomb of the Savoyard kings, who were presumptuous in addition to being usurpers. A visit to Florence, to the Pitti packed with stuff from the Oddi family, and then pay their respects to the nobleman Giulione Battiferri, chased out of Urbino by the fascists and reduced to poverty personally by King Victor Emmanuel III and to the point of having to work as assistant doorman, because of his stuttering, which got worse when he had to loosen up his tongue to speak French in one of the hotels along the Arno, a little out of the way.

The idea is, concluded Giocondini, to confuse them with politics, get them all worked up, drown them in their fear of debts and of expenses… and, in the meantime, get them to spend recklessly without letting them notice it….

The following day in Fano, Giocondini found the Leopard – who looked like a miracle had befallen her – seated on the bed leafing through *Novella 2000* and so many other nice magazines to see whether any other story was as beautiful as the one that had happened to her and also to select Dirce's bridal gown. And it was just here that she wanted to ask Giocondini about a bridal gown – from so many years ago, from the time of her youth and of the liberation – that a certain Mandarina or Canarina had worn in the Urbino Cathedral while marrying a Polish prince before a chorus of two thousand soldiers: a gown and an event in which were represented and liberated all the whores of the Marche region, and even beyond – as far as San Benedetto del Tronto, and northward, as far as Imola and Ravenna.

Dirce wasn't there.

The Leopard was unshakable in her dream and with the proof in front of her. She was the one who was asking the questions to find out whether the young Oddo, besides being a count, was anything else, and how many rooms he had in his palace – perhaps with the idea of a possible stay in one of those so-called guest rooms.

Dirce's last name was Badalocchi and also Toccaceli, and she came from a town on the Metauro near Fossombrone, from Fratterosa or Sorbolongo; that is, from the countryside between the two. Criminal record, debts, abortions: nothing. Diseases? None. Poverty, just poverty. Sweet, mellow. Virgin, or not virgin, it wasn't clear even when she first came there and not even she knew. She had never been one and she had never lost it. Very capable of working. Two pale little hands capable of lifting two hundred pounds. Having seen a nurse only one time the first day she had learned how to give an injection very well.

What could Giocondini do after all that news? Driving back toward Urbino he had to invent another plan: corrupt that Dirce and make her serve his purposes; or else get her infected right away by some good-looking bum.

14

Gaspare fell to the side of the bed, holding on to Vivés's hands. He was thinking that he should get up and go call for help, but every instant might be the one in which Vivés would expire. He was straining to listen for her death rattle and to look at the black and white line of her eyes turned toward the window. He was still waiting to be looked at and, at the same time, hoping that perhaps she kept her eyes that way just to see him with the last laborious gesture left in the corner of a pupil.

Vivés withdrew one hand, the right one, opened her mouth wide, so that even her head bent downward, and ceased breathing.

Gaspare observed those gestures with the calm that precedes the storm, until death locked them in place. Then he got up on his feet and went to the end of the bed, he raised both arms up to the ceiling and began emitting a sound that gradually became a howl, until he fell down exhausted. Only his eye remained fixed on Vivés's forehead. And it was his eye that prompted him in all his subsequent actions: going to his companion's side and adjusting her better on the bed, wiping her mouth with his hands, positioning her arms along her body, arranging her hair behind her head leaving a little on the sides, closing her eyes better. He also closed her mouth, while he kissed her and spoke to her. His eye took care of everything as it imitated what it had seen done in analogous cases, without understanding what the voice was saying. He shifted the scene outside the room down the stairs up to the door. At 4:30 PM Subissoni announced from the doorway of the house to everybody and to nobody that Vivés Guardajal had died.

Three physical education students, who were out running, found him there where he had fallen down. His body had kept the door from closing, and the wind had gotten into the house and went on banging things all around. In order to close the doors the youngest of those students went in and so found the woman stretched out on the disarranged bed, with her light blue nightgown turned up to her chest. All three of them covered her back up, they picked up the things that had fallen down and broken and then went back to get Subissoni revived. One of the three went to tell the hospital.

The first to arrive was a municipal policeman, then a young doctor, then a porter who worked with Vivés, then a sales person and two other porters.

Subissoni had to answer a lot of questions and did very well, supporting himself on the youngest of the three students.

Someone asked if he needed candles or women to watch over the deceased or a priest. Subissoni shouted angrily and guffawed waving his arms threateningly. Other formalities were expedited and after approximately one more hour the three students asked if they could go while promising to come back. Subissoni bent over the table and cried until ten o'clock. Only the two porters had stayed, one with him and the other upstairs. A little after ten the one upstairs had to go. The other one stayed until eleven, then he got up and left after pointing to a dinner of soup and wine that they had ordered from the restaurant.

At eleven o'clock Gaspare was alone, behind the closed door of his house. This time his actions were prompted by his entire head. He got up and filled the espresso-maker, looking toward the stairs. He mumbled and turned on the burner. After watching the gas flame, he turned around to look at the living room and went and rearranged the chairs. When he heard the coffee boil, he went and got the bottle of anisette. Next to the new and unopened one he found the old one that still had a small amount at the bottom. In his effusion he took it out and embraced it as he began again to cry.

The whistling of the coffee snapped him out of it. He prepared two cups and once again taken by emotion he washed his face under the faucet of the sink. Then he turned toward the stairs. He had to confront them, as if he had to open the window and fly away in the night, which was compact, difficult to break through, tightened around that death. But Gaspare went up the stairs one by one, with his nose and eyes dripping continuously on both flights of stairs, and when he was at the top he pulled up his head and presented himself.

Vivés was submerged in the black of her hair because when they had arranged her they had taken away her pillow. He didn't like that and decided to remedy the situation, but when he came closer and bent over her he saw her so serene in that position, so secure, that he was subjugated by it. Death had not overlooked any details of her figure and had sealed everything in perfection. He noticed the width of her forehead – even more subtle than usual – the extended space between her eyes, her upper lip slightly raised by one of her two middle incisors. This stiffness emphasized the forceful look on her face. Gaspare noticed it for the first time, and even her ears and neck appeared in a form that he had never been able to see.

Her hands, however, were easily recognizable, and had the delicateness that they always had. Death had not taken or added anything. He was afraid to touch them, while before he had gone and touched her forehead naturally. He noticed that her hands had been placed in the position of a cross, according to ritual, and so he took them one at a time and stretched her arms along her body. The new position was a better measure of the femininity of Vivés's body. Gaspare remembered how proud she had been of her own Catalan beauty, like a guitar. Then he started crying again and talking to her.

He sat down next to her with the window in front of him. The night was crossing over without stars and without storms, calmed by Vivés's serenity.

Every so often Gaspare moaned, as every so often a vague light shined in the sky. A little before dawn he rested his head on Vivés's hand, pushing as though to enter, and a clement sleep opened the door for him. At dawn the wind picked up again and woke him up. The light was already high in the room. Gaspare looked at Vivés and, disappointed that she had not been affected by those events, shook his head and said, "How proud you are," and then he mumbled several other affectionate reprimands at her. With the increased light he saw that Vivés had some black spots on her neck and he once again felt desperate. They knocked several times on the door and he went and opened it. It was the doctor from the night before accompanied by a city health worker. After a moment the doctor asked him where his room was. The two of them took hold of him and brought him to bed and there they gave him an injection.

Gaspare woke up at five o'clock in the evening. On the stairs and down below there were people from the Cooperative, together with other unknown people. In his amazement he climbed up to the top of the stairs and in the doorway of Vivés's room he found a bunch of red carnations and some young people standing there. He had to go by them to see Vivés. She was still there, immobile and recognizable. Her color had changed and her features had softened slightly, but the weight of a big distance was already pressing down over her whole body. Gaspare tried to measure it with years and with sufferings, but he got only a partial result, partly because he sensed in his mouth the chemical of the injection that was still restraining him.

He turned toward those young people and recognized among them the one he had had the discussion with in the restaurant; "There," he said raising an arm toward that death bed, "the war is over. You'll have to find your own now."

He sat down and realized that he had finally said something right, that even Vivés would have approved. He got right back up and went and got out her box, stirred by a sudden command. He opened it and took out the manuscripts and the letters. He called the student and said to him, "Here, here are some studies and important depositions. They are Vivés's. They need a good philosophy student to get them in order and to bring them out."

"A group," said the student.

Subissoni looked at him with appreciation. "There you are, a group," he said, "that's right."

"Could you lead this group?" asked the student.

"Me?" said Subissoni. "Me? I would only cause confusion. And besides I have another project. Can I give it all to you?"

"Yes," he answered, "we'll look at the material and we'll discuss it in the collective. Then we'll let you know."

"Do you know who she was?"

"Not well. We learned something today. That's why it would be useful to meet again with you."

"She was the best. She started when she was fifteen years old...in '26, and she stopped yesterday...in combat. She fought till the end. How many things she could have done...in a different place...and I hid her here, in this house...."

He cried and went back to his room. At that time official delegations of the city and of the left-wing parties and many more young people started arriving. The mayor went to shake hands with Subissoni, who said, "I know you are good and I too can say it. But you are forced to serve Rome more that Urbino. And Rome is strangling you...."

Toward night, among the students, arrived a female Greek student in exile who quietly sang a song.

Subissoni went back upstairs and asked everyone what they would like to have from that heroine; books, clothes...that it all should do battle again.

The students and the others looked at each other in a moment of disorientation, but then they understood and some actually took some things. Subissoni opened the wardrobe and took out her overcoat which he gave to the young Greek woman.

A little later a policeman told him that the funeral would be the following morning at eleven o'clock, at the expense of the city administration. In the evening the doctor came by and gave him another injection.

In the morning the same doctor woke him up and administered more injections and pills and also advised him to eat something. They called him only at the moment when Vivés had to be placed in the casket. He discovered that upstairs there was a group of young people, who were helping the pall bearers, making that operation less painful. Subissoni stopped to look at that body in the coffin on the floor and again felt like he was kept at a distance: even her hands had gotten smaller and were hidden beneath her clothes. His love for Vivés was moving him in a different way: closer, still banging around and within him without finding a place, a handle. His student arrived and led him back to his room. A little later the coffin was lowered to the ground floor and he heard it, bumping lightly against the wall, as well as the unreal words of those who were giving instructions for the operation. The nearness of the student sharpened the sensation of the emptiness of his grief, which was welling up with a thousand reasons and which he was unable to control.

"What's your name," he asked.

"Nicola."

"A southerner?"

"Yes. Pugliese."

"Why did you come to Urbino?"

"Because this is supposed to be a Marxist university."

"Is it really?"

"No. But it's okay. It has a Marxist dimension."

"That is?"

"It's workable."

The funeral was ready. Subissoni put on his beret and his militant neckerchief and presented himself. The small procession walked down through some tiny streets to Porta Nuova. Students and porters from the Cooperative carried the coffin on their shoulders.

At Porta Nuova the coffin was loaded into the hearse, which left while the little group was saluting with closed fists. Subissoni got into a car to go to the cemetery beside the city official who was in charge. When he saw the hearse being driven toward the entrance gate for the burial ground he said, "No, stop it. Not there. Go to the crematorium."

The city official was dismayed, "Where? But there is no crematorium. The burial is planned in a tomb...."

"No, no. Vivés must be cremated. That's her wish, and mine too. There's a written deposition for this purpose, just to avoid problems like this. So let's go to the crematorium."

"But there is none. Not in Urbino."

"Then it must be built. A pyre must be prepared."

"A pyre? But what are you saying...."

"A pyre. Yes, a pyre. Are you afraid? You know very well."

"But it's not possible. The law...."

"There," shouted Subissoni, "there, right to the end... and even beyond."

"Italian law...," the other one went on.

Subissoni swelled up with rage, "That's enough," he shouted even more loudly, "there is no law! Me, I've been outside the law for many years. Vivés too, she...," and he pointed to the hearse, "and she's not even Italian. And I never wanted her to become one.... I'll take care of it myself. Call some students. Together we'll make a suitable pyre, we learned how from Homer. And you can watch, if you want... because you haven't learned anything."

"But Professor, that's impossible. You can go to Pesaro. There should be one in Pesaro. Wait, let me do something." He got out and went to telephone City Hall and got approval to ask Pesaro. He called Pesaro and was informed that there too it would be impossible. Maybe in Bologna. Another telephone call to City Hall, while the hearse stood still three steps from the gate. Then a telephone call to Bologna, with a long wait, and then another... until it was finally learned that there they could do it, but only the following afternoon. The hearse could proceed to its destined place. The coffin was sealed in the presence of Subissoni, who was leaning against the wall under the weight of that other injustice. He wasn't watching. Every so often he turned his eye, when the noise got louder and when the blue flame seemed to expand. He was gripped by the feeling of disgust that cemeteries had always given him and he went out. The city official told him that the coffin would stay in there until the departure for Bologna.

"And me?" he asked, "I can't wait in here."

"You can go home."

"Home? And leave her in here. Give her back to me. Give her back to me immediately so I can keep her here outside with me."

The head of the monks who took care of the cemetery intervened. He was a bright young man who proposed placing the coffin in the church of San Bernardino.

"No! Here outside!" retorted Subissoni. "No churches. You're a sly one. But not in church." The monk smiled and the sweet honesty of his eyes surprised the old man: "Why are you afraid of that roof? God won't ask anything from you for this hospitality."

"Fine," said Subissoni. "Neither am I asking for anything. Let me stay out here with my woman. It won't be the first night that we've spent in the open."

"Why are you so hard on yourself? If you don't want anything from God, can you take something from me? If the city official agrees we can place the corpse in the courtyard of the convent. It's in the open and outside the cloister."

Subissoni went to see the courtyard, a square one, completely of bricks, even the columns and the pavement and even the well in the middle, with clumps of weeds and moss on the north side. He said "yes" and bowed to the young monk, who opened his arms with such a burst of joy that it confused Subissoni. The coffin was transported on a kind of wheelbarrow pushed by the porter. Subissoni put his hand on the edge. The monk opened the gate and waited for the old man to indicate the place. The city official and the pall bearer withdrew and Subissoni remained seated at the edge of the courtyard to look at the coffin on the pavement of the corridor immediately to the left of the door. The monk asked him if he could bring some pots with greenery that they kept in the garden and he accepted. The monk had the young and enormous hands of a farmer. He was arranging the earth of the pots and the leaves of the plants with such natural ability that it touched his heart. Since his time in France he hadn't seen anyone working.

As soon as he had finished, the monk started respectfully withdrawing, so Subissoni stopped him with a gesture: "Pride can be a big sin," he said, "but without pride one is lost forever."

The monk smiled once again and said, "I cannot judge, before you who considers himself as powerful as God. I can, however, tell you, since you look upon me as a brother, that your words are mistaken and your sentiments are confused. Pride is a sin and it loses everywhere. What has saved you and this woman is not pride, but love."

The monk withdrew and Subissoni got closer to the coffin. It was peaceful in there and he felt Vivés's company united with time, which was flowing limpidly over every brick. At noon the monk returned to invite him to eat, but he refused. A little later he saw the monk leave on his bicycle. Then Nicola arrived with two companions to invite him to go back home.

"Tonight," he said, "but not home."

That evening Nicola came back and accompanied him to Urbino where he let him choose between the hotel and his and his companions' hospitality. Subissoni accepted the latter and found a bed in the students' room. He ate the things that they offered him and also swallowed the medicine that Nicola recommended. He slept the whole night, and in the morning those young comrades had a bath ready for him and helped him shave and get dressed. Nicola even lent him a clean shirt. Then they accompanied him to San Bernardino and left him in front of the coffin. "I have found some comrades," he said, "now that I'm at the end. It's thanks to you, who always kept on teaching. Now they know what they have to do."

The monk reappeared from the other end of the courtyard, toward the cloister gate; he smiled and raised his hands so as to point out the first blue sky in more than two weeks and the sparrows that were celebrating it on the roof tops.

Two hands like his in wrought iron closed the arch of the pulley over the well.

A little later the hearse arrived and Subissoni endured all the operations of the new transport and of the embarkation with a tranquil conscience. He noted, with relief, that the hearse was more modest than the one from the day before and instead, with displeasure, that the monk remained at a distance out of discretion. He turned to salute him waving both hands, like him, in the form of an embrace and took his place beside the driver who had already started the car.

15

During that period Oddino went out twice all by himself to stroll around Urbino and let himself be seen, but also to orient himself regarding two acquisitions that he had in mind to make – a ring for Dirce, cleaner than the ones that his aunts would have pulled out, and a five-shot automatic rifle for himself.

He went into several stores and was welcomed everywhere with deference. Even those who saw him pass by pointed him out, with curiosity, but most of all with congeniality. The events of his last two trips, to Rimini and Fano, had somehow leaked out, and the citizenry had taken notice of it with pride, considering him like a new communal endowment, in which everyone could share even if indirectly, for example, with a sense of trust that generated tranquillity. In short, Oddino was looked upon as another battle tower and he rightly deserved the title of count and lord.

While parking in the piazza Giocondini noticed this new behavior and a few expressions bounced around him and led him to twist his lips. Who had talked? He wasn't forgetting that he, himself, had blown off steam the first night in the wineshop and many of the managers and waiters of the hotels along the coast, especially those on the back streets, are Urbinoites from the countryside who have gone down there to try their luck but always with the idea – and as soon as they had even half-a-day to actually do it – to go back to Urbino, or Cavallino, or Montefabbri, or Schieti. He, himself, had brought dozens of them back and forth at the beginning of and during the season.

And now he was forced to see that big salami walk through the piazza with the austere serenity of a powerful and beloved lord.

What's more, everything was going well for Oddino. He traded an old vegetable garden beneath the walls for a diamond, and two old arm chairs from the science room for a Browning automatic with an embellished grip and butt.

Like all omnipotent beings our very young lord had with things, and also with human beings, a rapport that was not saddened by the weight of contingencies, by differences or even by the rational calculations associated with life insurance policies; in short, by the burden of history, or if you wish, by any connection with time, space, society – as in a series of sequences in a movie. Instead he had a very simple and handy collective rapport, consistently his, and dominated by him alone, as though – thinking again about a movie that replays continuously without possible variation – he could pull the photographs out of a box one by one, not according to any order that might make sense within his box-like kingdom, but just put together generically and by chance. And the photo that came out did well every time. It was just the one he wanted, that deserved to be enlarged, lengthened in its perspective, animated, colored and turned into a talkie.

The only principle of omnipotence is, in fact, casualness. And for the rule of transitivity, he who succeeds in organizing his casualness becomes omnipotent.

Poor Giocondini went on biting his fingernails bloody turning here and there with his big cinematographic eyes that were full of so many links, which increased his anxiety and his spitefulness. He saw and heard the following scene, for example: Oddino exiting haughtily from the loggia of the school; and the arches, which, until then, were empty, filling up with people, who came in order to see him exit and traverse – but who were visibly upset by their doubt regarding the direction of his traversal and the reasons for it – and who were illuminated and rendered happy by their admiration for his walk or for his stature and for his manner of holding his head high without revealing the point to which he was directing himself. Many of those people subsequently left to follow Oddino at a respectful distance while speaking in a raised voice to make themselves heard by him, and then they even had the courage to start hurrying in order to touch his halo of air and then to get ahead of him so that he might see them.

Oddino would stop in the middle of the piazza and all the groups of stationary people immediately would get bigger and even become lively with the excitement of his nearness. Standing in the yellow-marked zone for taxis, Giocondini heard people coming from the long loggia murmuring about that apparition, hoping that this enormous, living and protective statue might turn toward them so that they could express openly their devotion: the count, a lord, what a lord, the lord, Oddo Oddi-Semproni, the greatest of the lords of Urbino, a lord... oh! the lord!

In the end that was just the way it seemed to sound to the distended and reddened ears of Giocondini, who was perhaps envious because he had come – and not so long ago – from outside Urbino,... and maybe he could even be excluded from the completely Urbinoite enjoyment of their lord – aside from the fact that all those concerti were spoiling his cantata per flauto solo, which he had been sucking and whistling for years as the exclusive soloist and interpreter, with the goal of enchanting that same water snake and his two aunts... they two of the aquatic kind.

And what then if, close to defeat and desperation, he had taken the initiative of that turn of events to lead it, with a couple of slight turns of the steering wheel, toward just the result that he had anticipated; or, in any case to influence things so that he would be present at the moment and at the place of the coronation... and not too far from the crowned one?

So he paid his respects to Oddino several times from a distance and decided to put into effect his very new plan. He chose the most discredited groups of those present in the piazza – who were also the noisiest ones – and he approached them, circling around like a falcon who gets increasingly daring as he decreases the diameter. He started with the most discredited and lively and gullible – full of explosions and hand-waving for anything at all – and also the group with the biggest number of pauses and of brief migrations toward the bars down below; that is, with the group that stations itself by the iron railing on the edge of the piazza toward Valbona, also very close to the biggest, if not the only, public pissoir in the city. This group is composed of loafers, but from old Urbinoite families – common people or minor artisans or small merchants or unemployed husbands of employed wives. It is not a very politicized group, but it is optimistic and inflammable – it gets emotional for every civic ceremony and most of all for those of the culinary, lyric, meteorological, and heraldic type.

Giocondini got closer and, while taking a cigarette out of its pack, he waited for a pause in order to express his agreement too, nod his head and change the subject, as though it would be impossible to say anything more or better on that subject than what had just then been affirmed by the last orator. "However...," while looking impersonally toward the middle of the piazza and toward that halo that was moving behind that holy man. "Man, what a lord that Oddi-Semproni is. What a fine young man, what glory for Urbino, what nobility. Someone like him should be in command.... Urbino would regain her splendor... with a lord like him.... Pesaro would go back under.... Forlani would come up here to kiss his hands... and to ask his advice.... A lord."

Right in the midst of its confusion the group found conviction, and it got inflamed... and just because the matter was not very clear, it had to get inflamed in order to better illuminate it.... With the light concentrated in the middle, it was easy for Giocondini to withdraw little by little and disappear from the edge of the backs into the shadows. He put out his cigarette butt in the middle of the piazza and advanced toward the second group: this one also on an iron railing, and this one also without much standing in society. It was constituted of lower-middle-class Urbinoites with partly rural ties and also of people who had migrated from the rest of the province, united under the banner of employment and of calculations about ways of retiring, of redeeming years, of obtaining benefits, of prolonging vacations, and also under the banner of gambling, of style, of comparisons between Rimini and Riccione, Inter and Juventus, American movies and Italian movies, Romagnola female students and the ones from Abruzzi, Signora X's butt and Signora Y's glance, Rumor or De Martino, Mancini or Fanfani, Alfa Romeo or BMW, the Rector or Montanelli, *Oggi* or *Gente,* and so on. They leaned against their iron railing, which bordered the part of the piazza that extends toward the Cathedral, between the street that goes uphill and the level part of the last two arches of the small loggia.

These people, who had always thought of Oddino as somewhere between mentally ill and half-witted, were now admiring his cock – the astonishment of the news was too recent to be already contaminated by envy – which had aroused amazement in every luxury hotel of the Adriatic Riviera, and, therefore, his nobility, which probably had who-knows-what domains – even hidden – who-knows-what underground petrified golden forests, who-knows-what treasures piled up in a tunnel dug beneath the Oddi's garden and extending beneath the Cesana until it comes out above Fossombrone. That kind of a cock – excuse my saying – had to necessarily sink its roots among the coffers of historic treasures, urns, arms, phials and filters.

Giocondini went closer and said, "I was there."

He had to tell everything, several times, to satisfy their most detailed questions. He made up two other luxury hotels and said "yes" that among the women there were some Germans, who were the most admiring and the most content, and a Florentine noblewoman in tears, on the upper floors, to see how that discovery of hers was contested and how her hopes of keeping him all for herself and making him lord of who-knows-what territories between Siena and the Maremma were dissipated. "What do you mean lord? – Lord! Lord, boss, governor!"

Everybody agreed that he could be a lord and – so they would not reflect too much on the significance of that affirmation – Giocondini immediately invented a series of amorous sequences in the rooms and on the stairways of the

hotel, which often lengthened the field, beyond the un-
bridled lust of the lady whores and non-whores, because all
the other female guests, in addition to the Germans, also
came running, because everybody was curious to know who
was the bearer of that natural wonder, of that full-rigged
ship or young eagle, or jet or locomotive, of that bridge cast
to the other side of any bank, Bosphorus or Dardanelles;
who was that Atlas, from what prodigious family and nobility and, above all, where was he from.

Giocondini grinned as he recalled, still emotionally, how
the name of Urbino resounded, how all the women were
reveling in the taste of saying "Urbino": "Urbino, Urbino...
yes from Urbino like Raphael," and how they were all exalting the beauty of the city, not only the ancient one but the
living one, and how they considered it the most abundant
and fortunate. And to close on a note directed toward the
characteristics of that group he affirmed that that evening –
in just one evening, if he had wanted to – Count Oddi could
have earned more than five million, just for letting it be
seen and perhaps lending it to one of the richest ones. Meanwhile there was the risk that in Rimini they would want to
take him away; that is, to appropriate him for themselves
like a big tourist attraction. In short, a weight like Oddino's
fertile cornucopia would be a pretty nice income for any
balance sheet, even for the Italian balance of payments. "Just
like always," they all said.

Meanwhile the unwitting producer of wealth was still
walking around the piazza enjoying his maturity – that new
and splendid one assured him by Dirce – with the modesty
and the precision of sewing a button on the front of his
coat.

Oddino was walking around well-protected and covered,
looking around without the need of finding anything. At
the opportune moment he would pull out his usual perfect
photograph to put in that little apparatus, which, when he
was a child, his aunts would give him in the dreariest moments of winter Sundays to see enlargements of the stations,
the fountains and the colonnades of the cities. What was

that apparatus called? Count Oddino was wondering but was saved from asking whomever he might happen to encounter among the men or the groups in the piazza by the sound of Giocondini. Once he had left the second group – all excited with their calculations – to its iron railing, he appeared in the most luminous part of the piazza while bowing toward Oddino to proclaim to him his deference.

"Lord," they kept saying all around from the first to the second group, "lord" to the amazement of those few isolated people crossing the piazza as though it were a thoroughfare and not recognizing it – at least not in that moment – as the center of a new historic development.

Oddino without having found the word he was looking for was even more haughty, with an air of slight irritation, in which his subordinates hastened to recognize the supreme preoccupation of their lord. Giocondini could already see him cloaked and enthroned, with himself by his side to accept taxes and tributes and to administer justice, the treasury and even the regulatory plan.

Oddino was making his last rounds, aware by now of the general deference, of the bows and of the greetings to the "count" and to the "lord." Then he stopped and raised his head entrusting it to the nocturnal gusts; when he drew it back he leaned with clemency toward the groups and ceremoniously gestured his farewell, even using his hands, aware of and grateful for their sentiments, but also for their distance and for the inevitable fact that many of those subjects he would never see again.

He put aside his sense of royalty and, after one more go around, he inserted into his apparatus the white and yellow photo of Dirce, who was very gracefully raising her arms. Her doll-like substance was shining brightly in every fiber, even in the most hidden ones, and grew larger to the point that Oddino was able to pet it with his hands on the border of his own overcoat and then on the linen velvet of his easy chair in the library, where he had arrived just in time to catch the national news on TV.

In the meantime Giocondini hurried to the appropriate place to prudently request his membership card in the Christian Democratic Party.

16

Subissoni had calmed down. He got a good feeling from the fact that he was taking Vivés away with him. The man who was driving was young and gray and was doing everything with naturalness, but he was going so fast that before the fork in the road he had already passed the students who were going back to town.

During the entire trip Subissoni sat in that hearse as though it were his own entire world, the only part left and worth saving: not just Vivés's coffin, but also the two seats in front. He was also possessed by the completely mad hope that he could go on traveling forever in that hearse. Headed anywhere, to the Finnish lakes or to the Pyrenees.

Up ahead he found the three quills of the mountain of San Marino and he noted that they were out of proportion: a crest, a geological curiosity, fastidiously in competition with Urbino... and, what's more, completely false, like a trick water pitcher.

He became enthusiastic about the trip and felt some anxiety as he got on the super highway for the first time. It was a very cleanly manufactured product, worthy of a modern hospital. The flow of vehicles was burning, like certain television episodes. Subissoni felt like he was being introduced into another world and starting out with a certain satisfaction. It would have been easy to continue on to Hamburg and then descend by sea to Gibraltar and then enter Africa and arrive in the middle of the Sahara. From there proceed to the Middle East and then to the Urals, greet the comrades in Moscow and then go spontaneously to Siberia, he and Vivés, or else take a Swedish boat and arrive at Hamlet's castle, and then London, greet other comrades, count those who are living and drink with them, and then from London by ship toward Labrador. The countryside too – that now, on both sides of the road, was intact, well-ordered in rows – invited him to work out those itineraries. Continuing his journey he would have died at the bottom of the globe, in Tierra del Fuego. It wasn't for nothing that as a boy he had given away all the rest of his stamp collection for three from Tierra del Fuego. Vivés, by now with that rigid look in her coffin, was ready for sure.

He invented other trips until when the car reached the exit for Bologna and entered the streets of the periphery. The city was as it was supposed to be. Subissoni felt a slight tug at his heart caused by the idea of arriving immediately at the crematorium where the operation would be performed right away with that air of efficiency that he saw in everything around him, which was held together and, in fact, made cold by a compact, although not brutal, indifference.

But nobody in those streets knew where the cemetery equipped with a crematorium was. It must have been an old one, maybe behind the funicular for San Luca. As the car got closer to the center of the city Subissoni's suffering started up again and increased. It occurred to him that the cemetery would probably be horrible, all in rusty iron, and inadequate for the operation that it was supposed to perform. They traveled painfully from one end of the city to the other for about half-an-hour and the old man was becoming furious, no longer even consoled by the confidence of the driver, who had shown some signs of disorientation.

"Italy…," said Subissoni. "You have to come to Bologna in order to honor a deceased person. The country of Lucretius and Pliny, the land of Horace and of Ovid. Near here the Duke of Urbino with his own hand stabbed the Pope's cardinal legate with a dagger as he was fleeing from the French and the rebellious Bolognese, in 1511, on May twenty-fourth… mute… like the army that was passing by. The Pope defended his throne, but it was a piece, just a piece of Italy, and he was allied with the Venetians who had a long tradition of autonomy and of republic. How many should get knifed today? We should clear the place out with our swords…."

Subissoni tried to go on ranting because he had seen a gate that could have been for the cemetery. Extending from the gate there was a little brick church, with the rose window almost attached to the roof. The gentleness of that architecture placated him and renewed his disposition toward pain. The hearse approached the gate and Subissoni got out to ask. That was the place, but it was closed and it would not reopen until four o'clock.

Subissoni was happy that there was that kind of a modest and beautiful facade, completely befitting Vivés. That was her last appointment. There were other times when they had to wait – each time she had taken his hand and calmed him, with a slight movement of her lips, in the language of the swallows. This one could be a church for swallows. He had the feeling that Vivés had walked her whole life directly toward that church. He had waited there for her without knowing her. She had arrived in that box and he was curious about seeing her. He started crying and his eye immediately overflowed.

"What should we do Professor? It'll be more than an hour," the driver asked. He lifted his hand and rested it on the hearse to get to know that woman that he had waited for his whole life. The church was open like the mouth of a mother who calls from a distance, but the child doesn't hear, since he already knows what she is saying. The surrounding space, leveled out by that one feeling, which diminished even the awareness of itself, was like a notebook, with a short obligatory reading. As always Vivés understands. He'll understand too. First he'll give a few kicks here and there and then he'll understand, and he'll follow Vivés as always.

He went to touch the walls of the church, to lean his head against it. The driver joined him and questioned him: "But you're not religious. You're an atheist, right?" The old man turned his head all the way around so he could see him, because the driver had approached him from the side of his blind eye, and said "yes," partly to join in the discussion between the facade and Vivés.

The driver had been frightened by the first eye full of liquid, which was listing like a jar in the current, and he would have liked to withdraw his question.

As he leaned against that wall the old man thought about dying. Where would he have found a haven like that one? It could even serve as a ladder, as a table, as a boat, as well as a book. On the other hand, the gate on the side was ugly, just an ugly unhinged gate. With its black paint it gave the impression that you would get your hands stained if you touched it. The path beyond it was better, with more earth than gravel, but it turned quickly behind the church toward an unknown clearing. The church was probably beautiful in back too.

At four o'clock the custodian arrived and when he saw the hearse he asked what they wanted. The driver showed him the papers and Subissoni listened to make sure it would be handled properly.

"Today?" said the custodian. "Today? But that's impossible, nobody told me anything. We don't have any ovens ready. For sure not today."

"So when?" asked the driver.

"Not tomorrow either. Maybe the day after, the day before Christmas Eve."

Before answering the driver had to go and hold up Subissoni and once again was frightened by that eye that was throwing out water. Subissoni embraced him.

"But I have to leave," said the driver.

"Yes you," responded the custodian, "you can go. Leave us the coffin and the spouse. And I'll have to consult with the authorities in order to proceed in this way."

An assistant to the custodian arrived and stood next to Subissoni. In the meantime the hearse drove in and went behind the church. The coffin was once again placed on the ground at the moment when Gaspare arrived.

The driver explained everything to the custodian, urging him to have as much pity as possible for that old man who for sure would die soon from all that was happening to him.

"He'll stay here with us. In this nice yard, in front of the ovens," the custodian said to Subissoni. "He'll stay here, and there's nobody else. Anyway let's register now in case someone else should come. There are people who have waited for weeks. You'll have to stay in Bologna because you need to be present when we open the coffin and move her toward the fire. It's required. We have to know who is being burned. During these two days if you would like to come and watch over her, come whenever you want, when it's open. Otherwise be here on Wednesday morning, the twenty-third, at nine o'clock and in a few hours we'll take care of everything. What sign should I make? A cross?" but in the meantime he had already made it.

Subissoni reacted furiously and went and erased the sign; he took the chalk out of the amazed custodian's hand and on the coffin wrote the two initials of Vivés's first and last name. That gesture saved him from falling into desperation.

He asked if the church was open and if there would be any objection to his being in there even at night, even if they knew that he was an atheist. He was told that the church had been closed since 1939. The coincidence touched his emotions but also stirred him up. "It wasn't destroyed," he said, "it was closed. Its facade remains pretty as a picture, and clean."

The Urbinoite driver announced to him that he had to get home and that he would, therefore, be leaving right away. The custodians saw to some of their chores until around six o'clock and then they went off toward the gate and alerted the professor. Subissoni stayed in front of the church for several more hours, in part because beyond the gate there was an area that curved in toward the church and was closed off by a wall only in the beginning – a little further on the wall ended and a wire fence began, which must have been as old as the closing of the church. Along the fence there were some climbing weeds still growing vigorously. From there Gaspare could see – while he was holding his hands on the wire mesh of the fence in the midst of those weeds – the oven building where Vivés was sheltered: the door, the grating, the upper edge of the facade.

After a few hours of night he went looking for a hotel and set off in the opposite direction from the church. He found lodging only in the center of town, at a price that made him shiver. However, in the room he was surprised to find a very nice bathroom in addition to a bed and some very comfortable furniture. He undressed and took great care of each article of clothing – cleaning and recleaning them with all the convenience that that room permitted. He figured out a way to use everything profitably in that cleaning process. Then he took a bath with equal meticulousness, he dried himself and laid out the towels in such a way as to get to the bed without ever letting his feet touch the floor. He fell right to sleep and stayed asleep until morning, when he got ready to go back to Vivés. He wasn't sure that he could find his way, so he decided to take a taxi.

The cemetery was open and he went and took his place in front of his companion. The coffin was on a kind of mobile catafalque that could be raised to the level of the mouth of the two upper ovens. For the whole day until closing time he went for a walk every so often around the church, conversing with the facade. Whenever they encountered him, the two men from the crematorium reassured him, but he avoided paying attention to their work. After closing he stayed on in the open space in front of the church, and when he couldn't stand any more he sat down and leaned against the fence and the weeds.

In the hotel he repeated, even more scrupulously, the procedures of the previous night – only his bath wasn't as long because he interrupted it to go and ask to be awakened at six o'clock. He had already paid his bill before, when he came in.

On December 23 at seven o'clock, an hour before the crematorium opened, Subissoni was in front of the gate, facing the church; a moment later he moved toward the fence. At eight o'clock he went in with the custodians. They opened the door of the building where the ovens were and Gaspare saw his companion again. No other coffins had arrived and, according to the custodians, everything would take place in the simplest way possible. They would get the oven up to its maximum efficiency, the first on top to the left, in line with Subissoni's blind eye. Then he moved two steps. At the same time the custodians started some procedures, among them the lighting of the oven. They put on gloves and masks advising the professor to do the same. Gaspare refused – the calm that, since the moment of his discovery of the church's facade, was protecting him, prevented him from yielding and even from becoming indignant. The custodians started unsoldering the coffin. This procedure was necessary and was carried out rapidly. Gaspare caught a glimpse of Vivés's shirt and resisted. Meanwhile the custodians were gesturing that he should go outside. He withdrew and waited while trying to find the weeds that had kept him company. A few minutes later one of the custodians came out to tell him that he should go back in because he had to look at a certificate and sign it.

Some other people had also arrived, two or three, and he had to consult with one of these. The crematorium appeared larger, and its structure went in joint perspective with others toward the interior of the cemetery.

Subissoni was led to the proper place. After every stop – accompanied and interrupted by the noise of the fire-irons – he had to go down a hallway. There he found the man in street clothes from before who gave him a paper. He even lost sight of the custodians and found himself on a different road, with neither church nor fence. The door that he had come out of was almost invisible in the wall. He moved to the other sidewalk and waited. When he was tired he sat on the ground.

That's the way the second custodian found him toward evening. He pulled him up and brought him to the first-aid office at the central station. He already knew a lot about that man and suggested to the doctors that they get him in shape for his trip home.

Subissoni spoke up and said, "Send me to a concentration camp. I'm a prisoner of war."

They gave him some injections and stuffed him with pills so that by midnight he was able to take the train for Pesaro. The next train, scheduled for around one o'clock, was more than two hours late. He endured each of those minutes, one by one, walking back and forth on the platform, in the open and with that cold air, scaring the other passengers. Trains were arriving from every direction, overflowing with gloomy people; others were leaving with screeching noises. The sound of iron beating on iron was everywhere: doors, tow-cars, switches. Subissoni didn't know what to do with his hands. He was chemically saturated with that stuff that they had stuck under his tongue and in his veins, but he felt like he was missing something. The trains got more and more crowded. The banging iron sounds were multiplying and drowning out the shouts and the train whistles. Subissoni started fantasizing: war, the new war, communications, the front. This was the station for the front. With these images in his head he suddenly found himself beside the train for Pesaro, which was being assaulted by columns of refugees and deserters. Of all the trains that had passed through, it had the most mild and most stupid face. He recognized it; he saw it materially ready, shining and panting, and in that same instant he realized how much he missed Vivés, especially her calm voice, in all that confusion. He got on, desperately trying to enter with the crowd, but barely managed to get a place standing near the door. The train left and he saw the city of Bologna pull away – with its buildings and trestles getting lower and lower – but before those blocks that could hold back his desperation disappeared completely, the train stopped at a switch. He became hopeful that it was being called back expressly for him, so that something could be handed over to him. Instead he saw the rapid and express trains, which had precedence, skewering through in both directions; as the white placards on the sides of those trains went whizzing by he read the names: Rome, Milan, Naples, Venice. Then his train woke up and took off.

"Damn them," he screamed, "who knows where they're going. The railroad, the ruination of every town in Italy, up and down whistling and taking on loads: the great unification. From Italy they've taken only the advantages, in fact its skin: because there's nothing else left anymore. Yes, the Apennines. And its skin will last as long as ours lasts. I'm alone and won't last long." He noticed that everybody was looking at him in amazement and then his energy was kindled by that attention: "None of us will last very long and, therefore, how will the great unification hold itself together? If it has skinned and boned the South in a hundred years of slave raiding worse than what the Saracens had done in a thousand years? If it has devoured all the customs duties, excise taxes, salt taxes, and tobacco taxes, and has castrated itself with its self-sufficiency? What will Italy do if it doesn't have the good fortune of a war pretty soon in which it can sell itself to somebody or other? It won't be long before we'll be talking about progress while chewing on misery. Every postal officer, every magistrate will come into court pale with the taste of having tortured his district in the name of unity and misery. And that paleness will be fused into the new Roman teston, the colossus that will go and sit down in the middle of the station, there, where the trains come in. That's the one that will sell more slaves and knock down more walls in our cities.... We should set up barricades with our suitcases. Empty your suitcases, open them up and scatter the contents. What is this republic other than the cardboard box left behind by the king? And furthermore, even his box was already an old one. They were all elated by the idea of getting to Rome. Oh! oh! Mazzini marched on Rome too and that's why he didn't understand anything about Italy. He even said that only in Rome could the absolute destruction of the old unity begin! The old unity!... The one that consisted of nobility and culture! And why not look negatively on someone who talks like that and raves on about a fatherland as if about some mystical body detached from whatever verity? At the price of ending up in the hands of Cavour. And that other character knew whom he had to serve and what was meant by industrial exploitation! Ih! Ih! Ih! From fathers like these how could Mussolini not be born? And Gioberti was left there waiting. Who is Rumor if not the same face charged with new slogans?"

The people – all crowded in the hallway and by now established in and resigned to their individual places, even though in some cases it was a very precarious one – were looking at him and getting increasingly interested in what he was saying. On both sides the clear night was unraveling in the train's lights. At the end of the corridor, black and tall, that old man who was talking enclosed the scene and became identified with the power and noise of the train. The ones closest to him were also the ones most attracted by that gleaming eye and by the variously colored spots spread around his face, just like what happens to crazy people when they get all worked up. He even had a bit of white cream on his cheek under his good eye. His oratory touched the heart, partly because of his exclamations and his gestures, and he made everybody feel more secure about their own mind and their own suitcase, and more judicious about various ideas.

"Aren't all those who govern us, with an occasional serving of bombs, and with their backs turned toward history and toward us as individuals and as peoples, members of the Academy of Syllographists? This is not the century of virtue, of virtue that is preached and licked; but of truth. Just as Count Giacomo always said. He, for sure, listened to what the earth and the moon had to say and understood Theophrastus's lesson on men's perspiration and about what should be sung to fools and how toads go around with medals or crowns on their head. From there Italy's second nature should have been born – the broader and more general one! Old unity indeed! Today who, in fact, believes in this country? Only arrogance, vanity, envy, speculation and fear believe in it. When has – I'm not saying all of Italy… not even a region, or even a city or a town… but even one man, just one – ever succeeded in beating these principles that hold up the boot's underwear like a big safety-pin? Now I'm not going to tell you, here by the train toilet about these underwear and how many people have used them to clean up all kinds of filthiness and organs, including their rods. I am the only Italian who has won a battle, just one, really fought-out, routing the enemy. The only winner still alive. And do you know why I won? First, because I fought by myself, with the conscience of Brutus before and after death, and then because I was fighting Italians who were led by institutions.... Ih! Ih! Ih! Against the militia and against the army too, which were fighting for the fatherland."

Subissoni saw how the people were listening to him with a look of amazement, but how, at the same time, they were becoming enlightened, and in that light he found the glow of his own triumph.

The train stopped for the umpteenth time and in the clearness of the night the slopes of San Marino appeared.

"Look there," he said getting even more excited, "San Marino. There's a little country that everyone goes through as if it was his own; there's a country that is not being turned upside down."

The train started shaking and then took off again. "Watch out! Friends, comrades! Watch out, companions for a night and for all nights! Watch out because Italy could be turned upside down again. It's up to you to keep it in balance by recognizing and enjoying freedom. And on freedom I could make a long speech – that will be for another time! On the way back!... For now I can tell you only that freedom is a thing and that it must be used on behalf of others: by coming out of one's own self one encounters freedom, by giving oneself to others one possesses it: like me now talking to you.

"But right now – because in a little while I have to get off – I'm more anxious to tell you that if you don't pay attention to the balance of freedom for yourselves – without expecting anything from this republic – Italy is going to fall on itself, crushing us all, this time by the millions, with the extermination of entire populations. The example is in the two world wars and in all the events that accompanied them in each nation.

"The schemes of national authority, the old shackles, the more they are broken and on the point of being dissolved, the further away they get from reality and the more they bring about destruction. When authority loses authority it starts killing in order to find itself a body."

Subissoni neighed like a horse and then drank from a bottle that was brought to him.

"An incision made on this still-birthed republic. It's worse than the Spanish one in '31, worse than Weimar's. It's as if it had been made by a committee of Buonarroti, Mazzini, Gioberti, Cavour and the Prince of Canosa. And then it was brought up by the same preceptors of the royal family – the most ignorant priests and prefects. That's why you've got to get your hands on it – because it has become that empty authority that I was talking about before. How? What to do? Go on traveling, don't lose your suitcases, get water at the stops, hot coffee with anisette tomorrow morning, and meanwhile think about it. Each one of you has a head capable of putting the world in order. I can assure you of that. Think about it and then do what you think is best! Don't start right away doing what others do. On the contrary, *don't* do it."

Subissoni was sick, a captive of his own triumph, which by now was speaking for him. He drank some more from that jug and looked at the jam-packed corridor. People were even coming out of their compartments to look at him and listen to him. A white light from the sea touched his black coat-collar. His blind eye was shining in one point while the other one was going all over the place with the speed of his thoughts.

The spots on his face, though even more livid and irregular, underlined that fierceness that was dominating everybody. The train was about to arrive in Pesaro, so he stood up, even more erect, and with his full voice solemnly said, "So go ahead comrades. And remember that it's not true that the sun covered itself with rust because of Caesar's death. It didn't care at all. And it's the same for the statues that we obstinately go on considering with terror and reverence. The mountains won't tremble. And as for the scales, we have to take them and control them and then weigh whatever we want. What's true instead is that when one of us is missing, the stars and the planets fail to rise and to set."

The last sentence touched him. The train stopped. Gaspare was near the door and still he moved with such energy as though he had to break down the walls. He got so ruffled up that he had difficulty saying good-bye and hearing the people's good-byes. When he was on the platform he stiffened up as if he had come down from the moon. He turned toward the train and opened his arms.

"Your suitcase," screamed some of them who saw him alone and empty-handed, "your suitcase. Didn't you forget your suitcase?"

The train was leaving and he answered, "Nothing," and then even louder to cut through the cold and the noise of the train: "Nothing. I have nothing."

17

Since ten o'clock Oddino was ready with an imaginary photo of the happy encounter between Dirce and his aunts and was awaiting the arrival of Giocondini.

His aunts had undertaken the job of preparing the Christmas Eve dinner, according to the rules of the household: chick-pea broth, boiled codfish and then, once their religious contrition had been satisfied, the jubilation of a nice big eel, arranged almost devilishly with its tail between olives and bay leaves, and many other meatless delicacies, among which in past years were not lacking French oysters, Russian caviar, sturgeon, salmon and even frogs from the Metauro and wines from the Rhine and from Champagne. Fish had always been a clear favorite of the Oddis, and Christmas Eve dinner had always been the most important one for them. This time other than the eel the aunts would only be able to add some fried cod filets and canned salmon slices.

Giocondini finally arrived, with the excuse of an adventurous trip from Pesaro, and Oddino was able to leave, impatiently anticipating the animation of his photograph with Dirce's entrance: the exclamations, embraces, words and with him taking his place at the head of the table, where the crystal and silver and also the gilded ornaments of his armchair shined most intensely.

During the trip to Fano Giocondini was more obsequious than usual, very often calling him lord, count, lord of Fossombrone and of Urbino. But Oddino had already, on his own, thought of putting the ducal throne, which was usually turned around in empty contemplation of the globe, at the head of the table.

However Oddino was also more refined due to his lightness, having fasted that morning, and even more due to the image of Dirce, and of the solemnity of his own arrival in the little rose-colored house and then of his taking possession of that doll made of cloth and gold.

Never had the valley of the Metauro seemed so wide, with such subdued colors and gently sloping hillsides. Fano was scattered here and there facilitating his entrance, with a sky marked by a blue line, which was really the first sign of a celebration: that is, the joy of creating one.

Once again the Mercedes went all the way into the garden, and Oddo preceded Giocondini to the door of the house. Dirce was in the tiny kitchen standing next to the stairs, waiting for him, blond and curly as she was supposed to be, dressed in green and with her pale hands clenched in front of her. Oddo approached and kissed her once again with his saliva, and, after him, she laughed too. In the darkness behind them, silent, in spite of the fact that every fold of her body was shaking, was the Leopard, dressed in red and violet and held together with veils. She approached them twisting her big lips nervously. She couldn't bear the happiness and perhaps for that reason had tied herself together with those ribbons. She didn't know what to say, nor what to offer, nor when they would bring Dirce back to her, and not even what would happen to her. Oddino looked at her and said nothing. He brought Dirce out into the middle of the street as if to assure himself that she could move. He left her there to go back for a moment to say good-bye to the poor Leopard. Meanwhile Giocondini had taken possession of Dirce's luggage and had withdrawn behind the car. For years the Leopard had been terrorized by the fear of being abandoned in the middle of the street or even on the door step, and so, shocked as she was, she twice withdrew into the house.

During the first part of the trip Oddo just looked at Dirce beside him, sunken so deep into the upholstery of that big blue car that she had to hold her feet up, but with much dignity, with her eyes only slightly squinting out of fear and curiosity. Oddo's eyes were serene as, further along, he looked calmly out both sides and enjoyed what he was seeing, with no rearing or tearing. Giocondini was observing, in his rear view mirror, the reigning couple that was holding hands.

In Fossombrone Oddo showed his bridge to Dirce, who smiled without understanding. The curves were making her get pale and feel uncomfortable, with all that springiness. Oddino embraced her to hold her still. Another thing that made Dirce uncomfortable was the blue tint of the windows, especially in its various shadings. Oddo advised her to close her eyes and ordered Giocondini to stop. Then they went on but took several short breaks until they were just below Urbino and had to stop at the entrance. Giocondini went and got some coffee with Fernet in it, while Oddo kept the doors and windows open: after that Dirce only would get out in front of the house.

Dirce managed to take all the curves of the Pincio. She just had to gather her forces a moment before getting out of the car, which had already stopped. Oddino went to open the front door and waited for her on the threshold, offering her his arm. They went in, silent and solemn, even though she was trembling and forcing herself to hold her head up straight.

The hallway was wide open and illuminated. The high artificial light lit up the yellowish brown of Oddino's raw silk shirt-collar, while all the dim afternoon light, clung down below to Dirce's green color and the paleness of her neck and hands.

The aunts were waiting in the first sitting room, one beside the other on the same sofa. They had not turned on the lights there and that forgetfulness attested to their need for protection.

Oddo entered and ushered Dirce in. "Here," he said, "my dear ladies and aunts, is the guest and the bride that I promised you."

Then the aunts got up and approached the girl using all their energy in doing so. Another moment had to pass before they were able to greet her and shake hands. Once again the natural light favored Dirce, reducing her paleness and softening the contrast between her colors. Her light blue eyes – with that subdued tone that poor young people and cats have, but which can stand up to and become impenetrable by any fire and can turn back any light rays by slightly closing themselves – were wandering well above those simple gestures.

Oddino asked the three women to sit down and began looking at them and smiling, as if he had completed a set.

A hired servant brought the tea.

No one spoke as the light was fading. They remained silent as it got dark. Oddo was satisfied and the aunts had forgotten about the electric lights in the presence of that little puppet dragged out of some attic unvisited for decades. The elderly servant reappeared and surprised them all when he turned on the lights. Oddo got up and also Dirce, to whom the aunts addressed some compliments.

The preparations for the dinner had to be looked after and the guest also had to be shown to her room. Oddino went to the library and got comfortable in front of the TV. At dinner time Countess Clelia went up to get the girl who hadn't dared to move.

In the dining room all the lights were on and the four of them, still without speaking, got ready to dine. Dirce's green harmonized with the lace of the table cloth and with the form of the glasses, and her blondness stood over the rest, neatly like the chick pea broth in its cups. The conversation that each of the three women might have started got confused in that play of colors, in which each of them participated in a different spirit. It was a good sign for Clelia, sad for Marzia, who even foresaw the comparison between the white color of the fish that would be served and the arms and neck of that girl.

In that intimate paleness of hers Dirce was ill at ease and made only indispensable gestures, almost as though she were afraid that it might slip away from her. She had thought that Oddo would meet her in her room right away and since she was waiting for him she hadn't washed or powdered herself.

Oddo asked her if she knew a Christmas poem and she said "yes," right away, lying. The aunts were pleased and expressed the hope that it would be a new one for them. Dirce opened her mouth, but Oddo said that that was not the moment to recite it. The conversation started up even though Dirce answered everything with a precipitous yes or no, still frightened by the thing about the poem. In an attempt to straighten things out she told a story all in one breath about how one time along the river she had been frightened by a black snake with its head raised and two eyes filled with poison sticking out at her and she jumped and ran away, but then her uncle who wasn't with her told her that it was an eel and not a snake and that since the eel hadn't jumped back in the water but had followed a rivulet toward the gravel and grass, that she should chase it and catch it, and how she was afraid to do it and how her uncle who couldn't do it because he was lame threatened her with his stick and finally about how disgusting it was to pull it out of the mud and throw it at her uncle who almost got hit by it and so was able to capture it. Swallowing their eel became difficult for all of them. Oddo proclaimed that he would like to go some time to see that place where she found the eel and asked Dirce if she would be able to find it. "Oh! Yes, sure," she said, "it was just below our farm."

"Yours?" asked Marzia.

"Yes, ours."

"Do you still have it?"

"Oh, no, they sent us away soon after the death of my father, when I was eleven years old."

"Sent away? But then you worked there?"

"Yes, we worked there, right; and good too, because it was a nice farm with seventy-five acres and a nice house, even with electric lights, and we even raised tobacco. Then bad luck threw us out. What hopes my father had when he left the Tarugo to go down there to Fratterosa! I was little, but I remember it because he even gave me a horseback ride on his shoulders."

Oddo was getting uneasy and didn't show any curiosity for knowing how that story went on to finish. For his aunts it would have been impolite to insist.

The supper went on much longer and every so often something was said because the elderly servant mixed up the order of the courses or the wines. Marzia had to bring him in the kitchen to put things back in order and arrange for the final course. The last course was the ice cream prepared by Clelia and upon its arrival Oddo got up to open the bottle of champagne and serve it. After he sat down again he asked Dirce to recite her Christmas poem. Marzia intervened to say that those poems were supposed to be recited in the parlor and after coffee. Then all three Oddis remembered that they had not taken out the Nativity scene: all three looked at Dirce whose arrival had caused that lapse, but nobody looked like they wanted to reprimand her.

Oddo ran to get the Nativity scene, which was a little machine animated with chimes. He treated it with the excitement and the precision with which one treats the well-known mechanisms of one's personal equipment – which are, in fact, known by heart and from which one expects immediate and unfailing gratification. When the chimes stopped playing he asked Dirce again to recite her poem. Dirce frowned as if she was going to cry. She had trouble talking... and became enchanted by that Nativity scene so small and real looking that it scared her.

"This Nativity scene...," she indicated.

"Yes, it's a machine," said Marzia, "but it's holy. It's a mobile machine from the last part of the 1700s. It's made of iron and silk, but it's holy. The stable is made of china. We all discovered it as children...."

"Okay," said Oddo, "it's a Nativity scene like all the others.... Go ahead, Dirce, your poem."

In the presence of that Nativity scene, Dirce, who didn't know any Christmas poems, wasn't even able to speak. "I can't remember," she said. But Oddino went up to her and took her by the arm, firmly so that she would stand up straight in front of the Nativity scene to recite her poem. So she closed her eyes and said:

Oh baby Jesus, who has just been born,...

...who has not been clothed...

...but laid upon the straw...

...just barely dry now....

She stopped talking and closed her eyes.

"What kind of a poem is that?" broke in Oddo. "Is that a poem? It's a very stupid country poem. It's so stupid that you're ashamed to go on. There's no lullaby and no tenderness. Where's the devotion? Your right not to say it. Listen to this one," and he recited his, beating the rhythm with his foot so loudly that the chimes sounded three notes.

"Beautiful," said the aunts. "It played by itself together with Oddino. What a beautiful sign! Very beautiful."

Dirce was again looking at that little machine with terror. She was frightened by the harshness of the jerking and exaggerated movements of the body parts of those shepherds as they bowed and offered gifts. St. Joseph moved his neck to look at the crib and seemed decapitated, just as the Madonna appeared to have both her arms mutilated when she held them open.

Dirce raised her eyes toward Oddo with the hope that he would understand the monstrous deceit of that machine, but she found him irritated and at the same time excited by the two poems.

One after the other the aunts recited theirs and then Oddo a second one, as he stamped his feet even more loudly. Then all three recited one, the longest one, together. Oddo wound up the chimes and taking Dirce by the arm made her repeat, to the rhythm of the music, word for word, the first one that he had recited.

"I wanted to give you something," he said, "very beautiful, but you don't deserve it yet. We'll see if I can give it to you tomorrow."

The aunts looked at each other lowering their heads. It was already time to go to midnight Mass at the Cathedral.

In the street the three Oddis walked ahead, with Dirce a step behind. Just before entering the Cathedral some men who were standing in a circle turned toward the Oddis and greeted them with some words of devotion and repeatedly called Oddo "lord." The little group had been organized by Giocondini who had been following the scene just out of sight.

211

The Oddi-Sempronis went to take their place in the center aisle and Dirce had trouble keeping up with them in the crowd. As soon as the organ struck up the traditional pastorale, or "pastorella" as it was called in Urbino, written and put to music by an Urbinoite aristocrat, Oddo stood up and in a good, strong voice sang every word, the only one in the area to know them all, let alone sing them. That courageous and knowledgeable exhibition was followed by a rather strong whispering. In the back of the church Giocondini lost no time getting out of there so as not to hear the comments and to avoid making any himself. Dirce was surprised by that tenor voice, but her soul was already predisposed defensively and she had already proven this by cutting through the crowd behind those three and following them to their family pew. She sought refuge by looking up in the air, at the highest point of the big white dome, and then casting her glance around to all the gilded rays of the decorations on the various altars and to the luminous footwear of St. Crescentino, which girded, above the turrets and bell towers of Urbino, two rosy infantile feet, too small for an enormous saint like him dressed like a military commander. The three-quarter-profile of the face had a vaguely holy look, but Dirce couldn't help thinking – and most of all feared that everybody thought – it looked like Oddo's.

At the end of the Mass lots of people congratulated the count and his aunts and not only people from the well-to-do pews, because some young members of Catholic Action approached Oddo and had him dictate the words of the pastorale. "Only we in Italy are ashamed to pray, to pray together and to sing in church," they said, with several of them contributing parts of their statement.

The walk back home was taken slowly by our foursome, as though they wanted to be the last to leave the piazza of the Ducal Palace. Oddo took Dirce on his arm and explained to her how the heavens are arranged on the night of Christmas, how the constellations move toward Bethlehem and others try desperately to flee, and how so as not to be attracted they burn up all their brightness a few moments before midnight, then when they are burned out they fall, leaving behind those deep black streaks that can be seen at the edges, especially in the east.

The whole night, with a new nightgown on, Dirce waited awake in her bed for Oddo to show up, but that didn't happen. She fell asleep at dawn and much, much later she was awoken with an invitation to come down for breakfast. She got her second outfit out of her suitcase – a blue skirt and light blue wool sweater also selected by the Leopard in the supposed style of Grace Kelly – and she put it on and presented herself in the hallway. The others were already downstairs. Dressed like that with matching colors and complimentary materials, which was unusual for her, and going down that greenish and odorous stairway, she felt different and understood that she was walking into a trap.

The greetings were cordial and lengthy, even though there was another banquet to get through, with panettone, family sweets, candied ricotta, tea, coffee with anisette. Then the women withdrew to the kitchen to prepare the midday dinner. The aunts invited Dirce to take the cloth off the cappelletti, which had been ready since the day before, and then to separate them and to gather them up – activities which, because of their delicateness, were intended to make her get into the spirit of the family. Afterward they showed her the fireplace, the big burner where the broth was boiling in a large soup pot and they listed for her all the ingredients that went in with the boiled meat, with particular attention to those that were considered exclusively part of their family's cuisine. Then they joined Oddo in the library to watch on Eurovision the Papal Mass from Vatican City. They received the benediction contritely and on their knees, but immediately after that they started feverishly looking at the gentlemen around the Pope to see if they recognized any of them. They were uncertain about the one with the feathered headgear and sword and two others in knee-length pants. Marzia told Dirce that Oddo had the right to become a Maltese knight and even a chamberlain, a bursar, an attendant and bearer.

Oddo announced that for New Year's they would go to Assisi and that they would spend Epiphany in Rome. When he heard that Dirce had never been in the capital he specified that they would stay there for three and perhaps even four days.

Meanwhile that day went on equally divided between dinners and television sittings until the cessation of programming and the complete fulfillment of every family ceremony. For the Oddis too, the night of Christmas opens the season of Carnival, so that in the kitchen after midnight the threesome plus Dirce shared two tankards of punch, one flavored with tangerines, the other with oranges.

Dirce had remained in the background – seated on a chair in the library that had been taken from behind the TV – in a corner that no light had touched since the time of the glowing and dazzling light of the war in Africa. The healthy atmosphere of the time and the appearance of some modern object: a pack of cigarettes, a radio, a vase had opened up the hallways and the windows of the Oddi household and, in the examining light that had come in, everything seemed a little discolored and claustral compared to the little novelties, accents, commands, clicking of heels that were inevitably brought in by occasional guests. Perhaps better put, everything or something gave a sense of enclosure, if not actually a real sense of claustrophobia, to the count of that time such as to cause him to decide to embark for East Africa, whose maps in *La Domenica del Corriere* were strewn with gold, silver, platinum, tin, copper, and iron mines and very fertile cocoa, coffee, tea, and hibiscus plantations and virgin forests full of game.

The only uncertainty remained petroleum: the presence of petroleum deposits. Oil wells, in general, never seemed to have great appeal for the regime. These concerns had, however, hardly grazed the courtyard of our palace and, when the count had returned, the effects of its drafts and the fluctuations of its humidity had lost little time in consuming the straw of the Abyssinian warrior's shield, hung up somewhere, and the wood and fastenings of the spear. The scimitar ought to have still been around someplace, if Count Major Chikiewicz – who in his large Polish and warrior chest concealed some minor childhood defect – hadn't carried it off.

On that armchair Dirce dozed off a couple of times and had to endure Oddo's reprimand the time he noticed it.

In the hallway and up the stairways Dirce – with the senses of her nose and her tongue rendered more acute by sipping the two punches and with her heart sharpened by their heating effect – was able to see and even more clearly hear, like an untiring and monotonous rhythm, a slow scraping on the plaster covering the walls and her own breath taking form, and how the light was changing into a suspended and floating mass of water that, little by little, was rising and soon would reach their throats, or at least hers; and how having arrived at that point it would have gripped her and squeezed her, making her struggle in vain to get away, and to avoid being forced to suffocate. Some of Oddo's words about plans for the day after Christmas, and some of the following days too, floated on that water like little wax ducks: the same as the ones that the children of her landlord used when they would come out to the country and play in the puddles and that they would leave for her – or more precisely on the edge of the puddle – when they were broken and could barely float on their sides, if they didn't just sink altogether. Dirce, even though she knew nothing about it, heard the steps of the count leaving for Africa. In short, she understood here too, without knowing anything about it, that closed-in feeling that might have induced someone to walk toward the exit if not, in fact, to flee in a hurry.

She waited another night for Oddino, in vain. She waited until dawn, until daybreak, until finally her hope turned into fear. She got dressed, packed her suitcase and, when she thought that the others were about to wake up and begin another day, she went quietly down the stairs, through the hallway, up to the front door and was able to open it, even though her hands were trembling because of that water from the day before that was splashing down around her.

18

Subissoni on the platform let the entire train go by, so that he could see it off with affection for his own enthusiasm and be entirely convinced that it was real and that it was going. The lights of the station just ahead revealed an equally real scene. On both sides there was the cloaked night with just a tiny collar of clarity toward the seacoast. Subissoni started walking, still warmed by the puffing of the train. He caught up with a little man weighed down by numerous suitcases and two bags. He offered to help and got stuck with a very heavy suitcase. The man looked at him with two small dog-like eyes, from below, through clusters of hair and toil, and as though he wanted to excuse himself said, "There's always hope. Each time we hope. Today, too."

"Right," said Subissoni, "today, too. It's still true today. Those who don't know have hope and those who know have no hope for anything."

To emphasize the h's of the quotation he had stopped and bent his head forward as if to go through a curtain. He started moving forward again and said, "Is it difficult? Does it seem difficult to you? Those who know means the ones who know things and who are powerful and do not hope." He stopped because of the beauty and the force of that negation, which was like the archway of that interminable night: "they don't hope for anything, nothing; neither ideas nor things." He got to the deserted platform covering and sneered, "Here are the great baldaquins of the unification. I'm hoping. I'm hoping," while setting down the suitcase and raising his fists. "And I'm doing more than that. But why is it that what I quoted and repeated from the time of Filippo Ottonieri is still as true and as fresh today as it was then? Because it was the unification of the kingdom that left things the way they were, that created vain hope among the ignorant, always, and nothing to hope for among the knowledgeable, and that left them comfortable in their area of non-hope in contact only with their own power and with the illusion of their authority. In fact, the authority of the kingdom constituted itself on all the already-existing ones, consolidating itself and consolidating them in a horrendous process of symbiosis and metastasis. And so, the divisions were perpetuated and the monarchic unity didn't become – not even in form – the unification of the whole country because all its centers and branches, offices and departments, were immediately occupied by the old non-hoping bosses, especially those of the fields and the factories. And since we are in a station, in front of the waiting rooms, it is probably not improper, but gently refined, to say that it has been a unification of classes, of first class, with heating and sofas, very different than the one for second class and above all for third class, all tattered and without doors, exposed to all the winds... including the ones of hope, however."

The little man thanked him and asked him if he would watch his baggage while he carried one load at a time outside the station toward the place on the sidewalk where the bus for his town stopped.

Once alone Subissoni went and presented himself to the whitewashed windows of the first-class waiting room and was tempted to start searching among his black clothes and his forehead, his pallor, his spots and his left ear, which stood out so well, for his own personality. "Huh huh!" he said, "I suppose I have to prove that I'm not crazy? I haven't had any ideology... for some time now!... Since before Vivés was aware of it. But I do have rebellion. My personality? It can fly off like a rag torn away from me by the wind, especially here in Pesaro. Subissoni is ready to disappear!... But under his overcoat there is a critical conscience."

The waiting room for first-class was closed as was the one for second class "to prevent vagrants from sleeping there" one of the railway police told him.

Subissoni was surprised. He appealed to his rights as a citizen and formally asked that a room be opened for him.

"I am a disabled veteran," he proclaimed, "and I am one of the few that fought on the right side, and I am still prepared to fight for the same side."

After these declarations the second-class room was opened for him – and was immediately closed behind him. He noticed this and shook his head disheartedly, like a resigned prisoner with no hope of escape. He went and placed himself in the oldest armchair. A little later the station was opened up and so Subissoni was awakened. He stayed seated for about an hour longer and then he headed for the coffee shop. There were already some people there and not just people about to leave, but porters, drivers, newspaper vendors and waiters, and among them, half hidden, the policeman from before who was keeping an eye on him. Subissoni felt that it was better not to expose himself and only ordered an espresso and, shortly afterward, a cappuccino and avoided, with a smile, the provocation of the policeman who came up to him while he was getting the change from his cappuccino and said, "What war were you supposed to be in?"

He went on smiling and that's all and showed his innocence by dunking his mouth into his cappuccino. Afterward he timidly said good-bye and left the station.

He felt as if he was overflowing with the awareness that he had gotten in front of those painted windows, and also with something else that the view of little houses and gardens had suggested to him – more precisely an embellishment, an extension of the Feltrian fortress, of which a rounded side appeared in the background. He walked still further away from the station both to distance himself from the policeman and to venture into the exploration of that view and of the suggestions that it had thrown at him. He had to unwind for himself his own awareness and then he had to unwind the coil of those suggestions, which, in the meantime, had formed a consistency and order of their own until they clearly showed the end of the coil, precisely that cord of bricks that encircled the fortress.

A little further ahead he again met the little man at the head of his flock of suitcases.

"What holds together those things and his toil too? Hope: his hope of saving them and taking care of them and sharing them. We already said it! Knowledgeable people on the other hand…. Have a good trip, my friend!"

Further ahead he opened his coat to look at himself and check himself out. He walked to the central piazza with the last push of those medicines and on the stairs of an archway he sat down, leaning against a small lion of pink stone. He recognized it and kissed it. His blind eye started pouring. All the night watchmen who were heading home on their bicycles came close enough to sniff him and one of them asked if he needed help.

"No, I'm with Pisacane," he answered, "and we're about to stop at Ponza."

The first shift of workers started arriving at the Post Office, which had its main office in that building with the small lion. They too stepped around him while wrinkling their noses. One of them asked him why he didn't go sit somewhere else.

"Why is this lion here? Do you know his name? He's called 'the spigolatore.' He's stranded here, with his red sandstone – if that's what this stone is, but I don't think so. Anyway he's here and here I must stay because I am his companion."

But his tiredness was about to burn up those proud images. He couldn't feel his hands anymore and only his forehead and his lips comforted him, receiving the coolness of the stone of the little lion. "Who knows who made you," he said. "You're probably from the early years of the 1300s – a little passé for the times, like everything else here in Pesaro. These people have always lived off others and have always copied. You come from Modena, or from even further up. I'm coming from Bologna. Your stone must be Istrian. How have you been in Pesaro all these years? Not too good, not too bad, huh? Who knows how many times I've seen you before without looking at you? Who knows if Vivés ever saw you? Did you ever see that Spanish woman pass by who was always staring straight ahead as though she was leading the carriage of truth? She had two dark eyes that reached her hair... and a stiff upper lip that gave her the same stony look that you have."

He started crying and hugging the lion, with his mouth on its short mane that was twisted like Vivés's hands. There he was found by the first patrolmen of the day, and they too went and sniffed him. One of them questioned him, when there were already some people around. "Do you need something? Can we do something for you?"

Gaspare turned around without letting go of the lion. The confusion stirred his emotions so that without answering he went on crying. "Come, come," said the officer. "Where do you want to go? Is your home here? Are you sick? Can I bring you some place?"

"I would like to know," he answered sloberingly, "if Guidobaldo II, the Pesarese, is in his palace and if he could grant me an audience."

The policeman took him for a drunk and was about to lose his patience, but someone from Urbino who was passing by recognized Subissoni and explained what had happened. The Urbinoite, who was a kind little foundry worker, went to get an espresso and brought it to his fellow townsman. Gaspare drank it and thanked him. The officer and some other bystanders decided to bring him to the hospital. But there they didn't want to admit him. They gave him two more injections and supplied him with more tablets, advising him to eat something and not to drink anything alcoholic until the evening.

At eight Subissoni was again out walking around in Pesaro, with no ideas or plans, but filled with a rage that shook him more than usual – so much so that he didn't try, even for a minute, to respect the prohibition of alcoholic beverages. His pockets were full of money – partly because in Bologna the crematorium workers did not want to be paid, offering instead their work as their contribution to Urbino's public tribute. He drank two rhubarb liqueurs in one gulp and threw himself back out on the street. He arrived in the piazza in front of the Government Palace, which had been the ducal seat of the Della Rovere family in preference to the one in Urbino. He was offended by the words he read on it – Government Palace – which meant the central government in Rome, in other words the prefecture. He went on walking at a distance from its loggias thinking about what he could do in opposition to that masquerade. The hour was not well suited for a political rally – maybe more for a revolt, but not of only one man and certainly not one who was blind in one eye. Most probably... he laughed, laughed at himself... he wouldn't even have guessed the right stairway. He would probably have presented himself to some lousy rubber-stamping official, or even more likely to the door of the latrine. He turned his eyes toward the half bust of Terenzio Mamiani, patriot. The injections were stimulating him to a strange taste for irony.

"Maybe they gave them to me only to make an ass out of me, but at least I can laugh about it, illustrious Signor Terenzio. It is you instead who can no longer laugh and who contemplates from that half-bust, half-cock, the sad things that you brought about. You – the half-Giobertian, half-Cavourian, half-republican, half-priest – entirely devoted to the great fatherland. You did not understand – just like all the Marchigians along the coast – not even one of poor Giacomo's lines, whom you made completely unhappy here with your skittish little countesses. They were looking for some cock, never mind poetry! And the literary parlor they kept as a preamble to the bed; and their desire for unification was their cupidity for stuffing themselves with some big cock noble from Turin or from Palermo! And who knows what voyages attached to those wings. What a cuckold, Signor Terenzio! Don't you hear the trains from here that go up and down ruining Italy? They transport heads, arms and cocks and bring back prison mates, disabled and enfeebled people. You stay here, dear count, and behold the palace of the government that you generated."

221

Subissoni walked around the fountain and wet his forehead, then he went to get a cappuccino with some pastries and, at the end, also drank a cognac. And hearing beside him two voices speaking with a southern accent, he turned toward the prefecture and announced that he was drinking against the central government. Fearing that he hadn't been understood he repeated his toast: "These plucked heads with Brilliantine on their necks are the real sign of Italian unification."

Outside he saw a group of children and followed them for a while. The strength that it took to behave well in front of them made him realize, little by little, what a state he was in. He understood that he was alone, wandering aimlessly because he no longer knew where to go. "Vivés, Vivés," he yelled and then said to himself "where have you gone? Where have you stopped? Where are you hiding?"

He looked at the houses of Pesaro, the facades and the doors, and while his grief was increasing those same houses and the whole city began looking like a transformed Vivés. She herself had arranged that cruel game and now she could no longer stop it or get away from it. He thought of Vivés and Lucrezia Borgia as relatives – both were Spanish and could have communicated in the name of Pesaro, which Lucrezia had chosen as the seat of her deliriums.

He became ashamed of himself to the point of commotion for having followed that perverse thought to the extreme, and in reaction he felt lots of tenderness for those houses. They were Urbinoite, of the duchy, gentle and meek, and they could be retaken and led.

He started running behind the children, but by then they were heading toward a grassy clearing in a predetermined formation and also in places that excluded him completely. He stopped and watched them go out of sight, with regret, beyond the little wall, on Vivés's side.

Along the bushes on the edge of the clearing appeared a dumpy looking woman who was wet and rumpled, with makeup smeared across the middle of her face. She took a few pointless steps, while she considered that old man with a professional air: "You don't look like a worm to me," she said. "Why don't you come with me? In the middle of that field there's a tin hut behind that tree…. And anyway at this time of day who do you think would be looking! I'd do it for you off schedule, because you look like you need to pick up your spirits. And at this time of day even you could cut it… even in your condition."

He looked at her and approached her incredulously. He kept looking at her and opened his mouth in amazement, without saying anything and without taking the final step. The woman felt insulted by that look and also by that silence: "Get out of here old man," she said to him, "get out of here! You smell like manure!"

Gaspare smiled then, but the woman, who felt even more like she was being ridiculed, went on: "Where did you escape from? From the crazy house? From jail or from a poor house? Look at this nut, on Christmas Eve!"

He went on smiling while she insulted him with increasing disgust. And to vent her anger she took a stone and threw it at him. Subissoni spoke gently to her. The woman started backing off while cursing at him sideways. He too made a move to follow her, still smiling and saying yes with his head. The woman started to get scared and began screaming. Gaspare raised his hands toward her while moving forward more decisively and with a bigger smile. The woman took off screaming, but an instant later he took off after her with the intention of reassuring her and introducing himself. The woman took off her shoes whose heels were too high for running and was quickly able to disappear around the corner of a street. From the same street emerged Giocondini's Mercedes.

"Professor, Professor Subissoni! What are you doing down here? How did you lose your way? Where are you going?"

Gaspare recognized the taxi driver from Urbino and stopped. The first time she became ill Vivés had gotten into his car. "I heard," said Giocondini. "Poor Professor, you're alone now. I have to go back to Urbino, why don't you come with me?"

223

Subissoni could not escape from this recognition and from an awareness of himself that this recognition had caused to re-emerge, and so he quiveringly got into the auto. He was trembling more than ever as he was drawn toward this new torture. He let himself go on the back seat and for a long time he didn't feel anything. Then he articulated several times the reality of being about to return to Urbino once again – this time as important as the first, when he was coming back from life, with no more youth. Urbino – so neatly put together – a scene in which he would soon fall through the cracks of the stage or where the wings would fall on top of him.

Giocondini stopped because now that the professor was awake they had to pick up their spirits by getting something to drink together. Subissoni ordered a mint drink and on the insistence of the driver he had to accompany it with a medicinal cognac. Then back in the car and this time seated in front. He paid no attention to the phony speeches of that greasy fat man but was impressed by the words "little theater" repeated several times. What did he mean by that? Giocondini gave a confused explanation of how Count Oddi seemed unreal and superior to him, for his courage, his extravagance, and the way he dominated everything.

"There's no more theater in Urbino," said Subissoni. "Somebody's needed to take charge of it. Maybe I'll get to it soon. I was just thinking about it. Ih! Ih! In part because Urbino seems like a real theater to me. Ih! Ih! Ih! That is, real like a theater." He sighed and clapped his hands: "What is more real than to exit from the ordinary and to make a different speech? Abandoned theaters are the mark of these cities; they have been emptied and knocked down by Italian unification, which even ridiculed and killed their characters, besides dispersing their audiences. Precisely they – with their empty boxes – give the most exact image of the country: every day a piece of it falls. Patapumfety! Among the ruins and the rats. And the Republic thinks it's secure in Rome, glued to the television; it thinks it's in control of everything, because it films, photographs, and analyzes everything. Tz, tz, tz, zzt," went Subissoni filming – with his hands in the form of a box – the landscape, already close to Urbino.

"Then what needs to done?" asked Giocondini.

"Theater, theater… we said it," Subissoni sang under his breath.

"Make Urbino a province; set up industries, attract money, construct buildings, don't let any more farmers in… put the strongest people in power?" This time that witch doctor had put a touch of hope in his voice. But Subissoni didn't take his interlocutor at all into consideration and emerged from his thoughts with a: "And how is San Marino?"

"Happy, clean, rich."

"Well then why don't we make Urbino like San Marino?"

"That is?"

"That is autonomous, independent, with no province, no region, no national taxes. We'll act in our own theater… perhaps directed by… young Oddi, who would at least be better than a central government – partly because in the end we could always plant a knife in his throat."

Giocondini was startled by his realization of how that nut's speeches were so close to his own schemes.

"But is it possible to think such a thing?" he risked. "You who are educated, do you consider it a possibility?"

"Certainly, with courage, with persistence. By starting to do and to want to do things for ourselves," said Subissoni, with a tone mixed between irony and disbelief.

Giocondini felt the steering wheel get lighter with that answer, and he started planning a way to put those two characters in contact, each wrapped up in his own way… and with drafts and shadows that he didn't understand but which he disdained, although with the certainty that they would enable him to extend his hands without fear of punishment and to maneuver… underneath.

"Count me in," he said. "How beautiful to have an independent Urbino again!… Naturally…," he moderated his tone and even reduced the speed of his Mercedes, "it will require good acting – knowing how to act to keep up a show like that for the whole city, its tradesmen, proprietors, the educated."

"Certainly, good acting," said Gaspare secretly looking over that very bad actor. "You will have to act well. For me it'll be different. My life is already exposed, inspired. It'll be easy to follow my lines, even for you."

"Good, good," said Giocondini, "and when would you like to meet the leading man, the one with the role of the lord?"

"Whenever. I told you I'm already ready."

"What role will you play? That of the prime minister? advisor to the duke? ambassador...?"

"For now that of the conspirator... together with you," he calculated the fear he was seminating. "Here we are conspiring against the State. There's no need for a cloak nor for a lantern. These blue windows paint the scene. Two conspirators. One old, emaciated and blind, the other one younger and rotund who sees everywhere with his eyes, who is searching...."

"Searching for what? Eh eh, in a little while, as soon as we arrive, I have to bid you farewell counselor conspirator," Giocondini skirted the subject, "because I have to bring the lord to get the leading lady; the duke to get the duchess, eh! eh! eh!... between you and me, in a bordello." He added this gossip in spurts thinking that it would attenuate the enthusiasm of that old man, who was perhaps starting out in too much of a hurry."

"Good! Never was there a place more suitable for the choosing of a lady. Provided that the lady won't want to make us pay for having taken her away from such a paradise, or even worse, won't want to organize us – like inside the bordello where the fortunate ones pass through, the wayfarers of desire, unappeased travelers... going in every direction."

"Agreed," said Giocondini reassured by the jovial tone of the other, "you'll be hearing from me. I've noticed that you go to the wineshop so I'll look for you there."

"And where can I look for you, in case I come across something urgent before you do, or even if I should decide that the time is right to take the initiative? I certainly can't go looking for you in the public area that you occupy as a driver for hire, since that would make a bad impression and discredit both of us, since no actual trip would come of it. It would look like you are too expensive and I am someone who wants to take long trips without having the necessary means."

"The wineshop for me, too," admitted Giocondini who was often there, too.

"Or else, as I'm going through the piazza by your car I'll act like I'm blowing my nose if I have something to communicate to you and then you'll follow me into the blessed wineshop or else just under the loggia, a little beyond the first arches...."

They were just below the walls of Urbino and Subissoni asked to be let out at Porta Nuova. They said good-bye and Gaspare got out still exaggerating his tone and gestures: "Ih! Ih! Ih!" he clapped his hands in front of his face and emitted one of his soundless whistles. The wind was whirring around there too. With his legs spread, planted firmly but swaying, with his eye acting like a windmill, he realized he was entering the city in the exact place from which Vivés had left it. He took a few circular steps to overcome his emotion and then set off for home. He stomped his feet and bent his knees to comfort himself, still with a theatrical air. How else could he have walked up there? He stopped and cursed that driver and his high velocity automobile, too.

On December 24, 1969, in Urbino, behind the mill of Porta Nuova, every color was disassociated in the damp air from its own material: so it seemed to his eye. A pile of leaves was heaped up against the first wall of Via dello Spineto, and this already startled him. He was forced to look higher up, beyond the bare branches of the lime trees – a miserable landscape, which got wrinkled in the insinuations of the fog. But everything turned toward him and recognized him.

Vivés's skirt invaded the countryside, just below, at the level of his hands; he pushed them as far ahead as he could, even bending forward, in his longing for that protective cloak, now lost. It was large and poorly made, but enclosed therein was the synthesis of everything, even of his mind. And still he struggled against showing his desperation to everything, against starting to ask a lime tree or any one of the bricks in the wall to give him back his Vivés. A little white snail, the kind that the fog brings out, expressed in the sharpest way possible how much he missed her. The entire Apennine arch could fit into the emptiness between his stomach and his heart with just one color, similar to certain expressions in Vivés's face.

"Snow," he affirmed, convinced by the image and the possibility of shelter from it, "a big snowfall everywhere, silent and strong…," but as the image grew it revealed itself to him and startled him, "like Vivés," he screamed in his throat, "like Vivés, quiet and strong.…"

He hurried bandy-leggedly toward home and, when he was on the brick pavement of the street, "Guess," he said to himself.

A theater person stomps his feet and can have another head that watches over him: he is divided between actor and character. Such was Gaspare as he arrived at his house. But the door, when it was in front of him with its peeling wood – its knots and the marks left by hands, like a word or a step or a certain hour of a certain year of Vivés's life, Vivés with a notebook – almost knocked him to the ground. He looked at how the walls and the corners were made. He went on looking at them and then murmured, "Where are the real ones?" and again, "Where are the real ones that you never see? Where are the ones that stand with those two or three capable of saving the world and that never meet? Or that no longer meet?"

Gaspare went in and threw himself on the nearest chair. The house still showed signs of the passage of Vivés's coffin. He let a good deal of time go by, then he retraced his steps still not touching anything: the living room table turned a little to the right, the curtain on the stairway landing raised over the curtain rod, the cloths from the floor that had been placed over the edges of the coffin as it made the turn on the stairway. Everywhere there was a white light, that, as though it was surprised, withdrew as Gaspare approached and became increasingly concentrated as it went up, until it was all in front of the mirror in Vivés's wardrobe. He smiled. A moment later he ran back down, he crossed his own room, jumped several stairs bracing himself against the wall with both hands, opened and shut the lower window, and ran the water in the kitchen.

He couldn't resist and went back upstairs and when he was on the point of sinking into that emptiness that every detail and every odor was placing before him, he opened the windows and leaned out still trying to smile ironically toward the scene, toward the fate that was filling it quietly with light. Like a tragic hero he prepared himself with that irony to fulfill his destiny: behind him the things in the room accompanied him by playing in the wind.

19

Oddino also ran to the window when he found Dirce's room empty. He was happy to find it closed. He patted the curtains and readjusted them. He too was impressed by the density of the light, which descended in blocks leaving some empty spaces – one bigger in comparison with his aching stomach. He went to look at all the windows on that floor and then the ones on the courtyard, but he found no cracks or holes. His aunts were returning from an exploration of the small toilet at the end of the left wing of the hallway, that, too, with no results.

Oddino, insulted, was on the point of bawling and gloomily directed his rancor toward that mechanized Nativity scene, as well as toward his aunts. But he was consoled by the thought that Dirce might simply have gone out to buy something… perhaps a gift for him or even for his aunts. He waited until eleven o'clock and at that time he went and checked the front door. A few minutes later he opened it, stepped onto the threshold and after a slight hesitation advanced along Ca' Fante as far as the curve of the Pincio. He did not see Dirce and started to chew the fog and to follow it beyond the Cathedral leaving his aunts in a state of agitation. The certainty of inflicting this punishment gave him courage and brought him as far as the piazza and to Giocondini, with whom he could initiate an automobile search in every street and in all the places around Urbino.

Giocondini obeyed, taking care not to show what he thought about that escape or kidnapping, but instead setting out with maximum zeal to remedy the problem. He suggested starting in the cafés and continuing in the nearby churches.

Those first investigations produced no results, and the following ones extended toward the hotels, restaurants – even though still closed – and the public baths. Right after that to the bus station, where perhaps it would have been better to look first if Oddo hadn't insisted on the fact that Dirce might have gone out to buy something. Between seven and eleven that morning only two buses had left – one for Pesaro and the other for Urbania – and the porters felt able to exclude a blond and green girl, with a cream-color bag, from among the passengers. Also, all the more distant churches gave negative results, and the same for the two open pharmacies. Then Giocondini, on orders from Oddo, turned his car toward Fano, first taking care to make a detailed tour of the inner and outer circles of the city.

They did not find Dirce and continued on toward Fano with ideas about a charitable motorist who might have happened by. During the trip Oddo never ceased looking under every tree and behind every bush or house and even further away, into the fields. Often he raised his eyes to the hills and even further up to a point that a little girl like that – without so much as the weight of a Christmas poem – would be capable of flying to.

"Here," said Giocondini upon entering Fano. He got out and headed toward a truck drivers' hangout but found very little among the chairs there, other than the certain absence of any green clothing. The Leopard had picked that very civil and very timid color from her repertoire so that it would disappear at… the first sign of trouble! For what reason? Giocondini asked something but didn't get any answer.

"Do you want me to go alone to the pink house?"

"Why there?" answered Oddo.

"Maybe she went back to get something she had forgotten."

But Dirce was not at the little house either. The stupefied Leopard was there, slowed down more than ever by the miracles of the last few days, by a malicious return of her sciatica and by the spiritual beating that she was taking from her first touch of envy. When she understood what had happened, which was very little, but also very clear and all negative, she aroused herself just enough to emit a sigh of pleasure.

But in the meantime Oddo and his driver had gotten back in the car. The Leopard lingered in the middle of the street a moment longer than usual and for the first time in a long while sniffed the air and found it not unpleasant.

The Mercedes drove slowly through all the main streets and arrived at the railroad station. Only Giocondini got out, and he came back shaking his head. Other visits were made to the principal cafés, to the front of the military barracks and to the bus station. "There was a little blond here...," indicated Giocondini, but Oddo's look eliminated any idea of proposing a substitute. The Mercedes left Fano and took the Adriatic road toward Pesaro. The first stop was the bus station and then, systematically, every street corner, piazza, café, and restaurant. Oddo, who hadn't eaten since the previous evening, was implacable. Giocondini was helping himself along with an occasional pastry or sandwich, which he stuffed down while making his inquiries.

They went back to Fano and parked for a good half-hour in front of the little pink house and also in front of the regional seminary – still with no results. They listened to the most senseless opinions and chased off after anything green that appeared on the horizon or near them: even a shopping bag or a bicycle.

At the hour of the Ave Maria the Mercedes was entering Fratterosa taking all its inhabitants between the church and the wineshop by surprise. No one knew anything about that Dirce, nor had any girls from other towns appeared there since the beginning of the Christmas season.

"In Fossombrone," said Giocondini hitting himself on the forehead. They scrupulously went through every street, and this time added the hospital and the carabinieri barracks, too.

At the exit near Urbino, Oddo remembered his bridge and brightened up while stopping Giocondini, who put on the breaks apprehensively. Oddo was convinced that Dirce, feeling that she had lost him and remembering his bridge, had gone to hide there and find him underneath it. Oddo, himself, climbed down that ugly embankment through the bushes and garbage. He risked falling and rolling into the river, but when he got to the edge he found no one. There were green reeds and the smell of shit so human and recent that it pierced your heart. Why couldn't Dirce be up above or on the other side? He went back up and crossed the entire bridge and then forced Giocondini to maneuver his Mercedes to the edge of the bridgehead to shine his headlights on both banks of the river and on the tiny road, which went gracefully off among the vegetation on the other side.

They took off again inside a completely green night that wrapped around Oddo's heart. He grasped it with both hands like a votive offering, without knowing to whom and where to bring it. "These blue windows should be removed," he said, and Giocondini assented. They stopped below Urbino in a wineshop and Oddo, pale as his votive offering, drank a little wine mixed with soda. In Urbino, the Mercedes stopped on top of the Pincio and only Giocondini got out to ask the aunts for news.

He came back once more without any news and then, following a pre-established plan, the two of them went and made another tour of all the cafés and, this time, the hospital and carabinieri barracks, too.

Oddo got home just before midnight, haggard and hushed. To console him Giocondini said, "It's easy for a whore to hide – any old doorway or gutter will do."

Oddo turned on him indignantly: "You, Giocondini, are a vulgar and stupid man. You don't understand that Dirce has been kidnapped or that she ran away because someone frightened her, which is the same thing. You too are to blame. And you too will have to pay." He closed the front door in his face and turned to his aunts. "You are the ones that had her kidnapped, out of envy. For sure it is you who frightened her with your Nativity scene and your meanness. You never said a word to her. You offered her neither a gift, nor a hug. Consider yourselves my prisoners and go stay in the closet until Dirce's return."

He was so grief-stricken and furious that his aunts obeyed him and really got in the closet. Oddino turned the key and imprisoned them. He went to the library and sat in his place with no particular picture in his head.

At two o'clock he was aroused by a flock of marine thrushes that landed in the courtyard and were fluttering from one laurel tree to the other. He noticed that it was snowing and then the thought of Dirce placated him as though it was she who was sending him those snowflakes. He had always read the kindest messages in the snow. He went to liberate his aunts and went upstairs with them.

The same snow, with slightly faster-falling flakes, because they were higher up in the wind currents, was watched by Dirce, who was unable to fall asleep in that strange little house in which she had ended up. She had kept the window blinds open so as to have the company of the night and during the first few hours she had been able to identify two very high stars, which formed a very tiny pin. Then she had lost them… but when she started to get afraid the snow had arrived. First, she had heard that old man downstairs coughing and moaning, but hadn't had the courage to go and ask him if he needed something. He had been so kind that she naturally had accepted his hospitality. Fleeing from the palace she had taken the streets going downhill, convinced that they would be easier. Instead they had proven to be terrible both because they were steep and because the brick pavement was irregular, and, what's more, she was not very accustomed to high heels. She had fallen forward without letting go of her suitcase, which had to be protected, and she had bruised both of her knees – sixty feet from the door of that man who had appeared immediately. He had helped her get up and ascertained that she would not be able to go on, with her knees bruised and surely about to swell up. He had taken the suitcase from her hand and had helped her reach the door. She had refused to go to the hospital or to a doctor and so he had offered her hospitality, had taken off her stockings and had given her some medicine. Her wounds were deep and both knees hurt even inside. The old man had started making coffee. Without having said much to each other noontime came, and he offered her something to eat. Then, since she was hurting even more, he had gone to the pharmacy to get her some more appropriate medicine. For the rest of the day he stayed near her, asking questions every now and then about life in the country. She had confessed that she was running away and this had been sufficient for him. In fact, at that point he had offered to hide her there and had indicated the room. It had been painful and difficult going up the stairs, but he had helped her. She was so alone and unhappy after having left that prison, and he had a face that she seemed to recognize.

The snow consoled her and intimidated her, deep in that bed where she had found shelter. She felt her wounds and hoped to get from them some indication of what she should do. She fell asleep in the security of her own body and of the comfortable shelter in which she found herself. She woke up with the first light of dawn and found everything as she had left it: the same intensity of pain, the same just-right weight of the covers. It was still snowing and there was already frost on the window panes. At first it gave her a slight feeling of happiness; but soon the thickness of that frost and, even more so, the reflection that connected it to the one on the bottle of water on the night table, discouraged her. She hoped that daylight would come soon and that that old man would come and tell her what she should do.

The day entered the Oddi's with the flight of the marine thrushes that had found the lemon trees. In the dark they had flocked together high up in the laurel trees, attracted by the southern wind currents. Now, with the light of day, they could spread out on violent short-range hunting missions.

Oddino gave another immediate demonstration of his authority by asking only for coffee and refusing the milk.

He proclaimed his solitude, and he even exhibited it to himself, agitating himself from one room to the other, consulting the noblest of his books and furnishings with half-developed ideas. He had been called to battle and left alone;

but he who had abandoned him didn't know what weapons he had beneath his cloak. He opened the glass doors and went out to take in the lemon trees. He stretched toward the sky to check the hour. He had two or three photos in his visual apparatus that, for the first time, were related to each other, even if only by perspective mass – buildings, doors, loggias – and by the presence of himself. This was incumbent and canceled out many perspectives and even the ultimate meaning of the representation; but, in the meantime, it encouraged his sense of security. Thus he was able to greet his aunts with the news that he was leaving. He was going to get Giocondini to start searching again and he wasn't able to say how long it would take.

In the piazza he couldn't find the driver, who was busy with some other service. He considered this absence another obstacle in his battle and, therefore, altered his plan with a different undertaking. "The nuns!" They had not looked in the nuns' convents. He was happy to have thought about this, even though an oversight of this kind demonstrated his driver's enormous ignorance, at least of literary tradition. He went and knocked at the convents of Santa Chiara and Santa Caterina and, without saying that he was Count Oddi-Semproni, he asked very indirectly about the possible admission or recovery the day before of a frightened girl under the influence of some promise or threat. He found himself back in the street having difficulty deciphering the similarity of the answers and evaluating the weight he should give to the common obstinence of their denials. Hide out on the roof of the courtyard? Enter disguised as a confessor, as an archbishop, as a police officer? He saw the blue Mercedes appear, coming through the snow directly toward him.

"Nothing," Giocondini said right off. "Nobody knows anything. She didn't sleep in any hotel in Urbino or in the province, because I asked at the police station, where I have some friends. I don't know if she might have gotten as far as Cattolica or Senigallia, outside the province. You would need a higher-up authority. But are you still looking for her? For pride if for nothing else, right? You want to find her so that then you can throw her out, right? Like she would deserve...."

"You're being vulgar again. Dirce deserves all the things that you'll never have, whatever honor and decorum. I don't even think her last name was real. Why did she end up as that woman's servant? Does this seem possible to you nowadays when there are no servants for even the Oddis? The search must be extended as far as Rome, Florence. We must be prepared for whatever comes, even for fighting, even for stealing. Introduce me to your policemen friends, if they intend to put themselves under my command. Dirce is somewhere waiting for me, and she knows that soon we must celebrate our matrimony. Dirce is crying and thinking about me." And Oddo stopped talking in order to concentrate on the photo that he had before him.

Giocondini left the Mercedes running, parked under the obelisk of San Domenico. "Introduce you to the policemen?" he said, "Okay. Someone will put himself at your service. And then what else can I do? Go and look in Rome and Florence: where, at what addresses?"

Oddo turned around satisfied. "Yes, this evening you'll introduce me to the policemen. Tomorrow, if nothing has happened, we'll leave for Florence and for Rome. We'll leave to the police the mission of covering this province, even the convents."

"This evening where?" asked Giocondini breathlessly.

"At my house, after *Carosello*." Oddo sensed his hesitation and sighed, but without showing any lack of trust: "Ah, if I could issue a proclamation, an appeal to the people...."

"An edict?" It seemed to Giocondini that he was leading the events – with that word whose meaning he did not entirely understand – to the crucial point of the discussions held and the projects made with Subissoni.

"An edict, yes," answered Oddo. "And in such an edict I would express not only the will to liberate Dirce, but other ideas as well...."

"About governing the city?" Giocondini anticipated. "You could be the lord of Urbino, by now everyone is saying so."

"Not so fast," said Oddo. "You're always impatient to rush everything. Is it perhaps your eagerness to perform several services at once? I must, first of all, govern myself, and for this I need Dirce. I shall search for Dirce. If others with other goals wish to join me they must in every case give first priority to my goal, and they must obey me. This I could say in the edict."

Giocondini said that it was all true and that the admiration that he felt for the count, together with his concern for his grief regarding the girl, caused him to anticipate and even to confuse his hopes and his duties.

"Shall we go," he said, "shall we go to Pesaro? I know of a street corner between two or three cafés where about this time are gathered a lot of... a lot of young ladies whom it might be useful to question.... Since that young and lovely girl was in the service of an old whore like the Leopard?"

Oddo turned down the trip to Pesaro and asked Giocondini to let him out in the piazza and to show up at the established time with the policemen. In the piazza Oddo waited for Giocondini to open the door for him and then got out ceremoniously. He proceeded slowly to the middle, facing the small loggia to show everyone, in lieu of an edict, the calmness of his face. It had stopped snowing a moment before and the sky had pulled back just above the roofs of the piazza like a big role of dark velvet.

Oddo turned toward each corner and street with measured timing. Thence he directed himself toward the long loggia to belie the expectations of the majority, which was moving instead toward the short loggia – more lively and filled with people who were naturally and socially more in conformity with that difficult young gentleman. He had grown too much, for sure. He even had some signs of a tired complexion; sometimes his lip was swollen by ancient rancor and his large topaz-like eye was turbid, but he was certainly handsome. In fact, his body was well-proportioned and agile but seemed as if it always needed to take one more step – incapable of stopping and being content in one place. Was he intelligent or half-witted? Too clever or naive? Sometimes with just a glance he had judged and silenced the Sunday discussion of an entire group, right there under the short loggia. In certain moments, by the way he looked down from above at his own feet, very erectly, he could even be compared to the magnificent rector. Apart from the difference in age, the same sadness, the same vagueness – confirmed by the same obstinate silence – had been captured in his eyes, especially when both walked the length of the entire loggia, by eyes and curtains, plants and lively tables, without looking at anyone.

Oddo remained in the piazza until two o'clock on that half-workday, moving finally toward the confluence of the Monte, of Lavagine and Valbona to see the arrival of undulating squadrons of country people and the very hurried faces of the more restless townspeople, who had already consumed a meal with their families and who – after bidding them good-bye with a grunt, were heading with their maximum sporting zeal toward the rummy and poker tables of the welcoming and charitable civic clubroom.

He went to the club's bar to restore himself and was welcomed and greeted with deference. At three, when everybody had already taken his habitual place in the club itself, in the cafés, in the cinemas and in the wine-shops, and only a few, and really less-important, people would go on strolling through the loggias, Oddo started out toward home with that extra step of his that created so many questions for the community. In that moment, the roll of dark velvet descended from above the roofs halfway down the facades around the piazza.

20

The malaise that spreads out at that time of day along the loggias or in front of the public buildings comes, not so much from individual bad conscience or tiredness or delusion, as from the increasing political tediousness through which worn-out and stagnant middle-class freedom is transformed, right in your mouth, into subjugation, greed and compromise. The thought process, once the source and safeguard of that freedom, is getting complacent and goes around, when it comes out and shows off, praising itself and listing its accomplishments, in its enormous pride at being exactly the same as everyone else's in Urbino, in Pesaro, in Rome... in Milan... in London, in Paris, in Berlin – instead of roaring with expressions of autonomous research.

Subissoni had gotten to the piazza at that moment and was pondering these ideas to himself while looking at that curtain lowered half-way. It did not deserve that he should begin acting. He had gone out only to show that girl that he had things to take care of and friends to meet. He couldn't let her see that he felt lost – just as he couldn't hang around her the whole time. Often you put a toy away just for the pleasure of finding it again. Gaspare was zigzagging in and out of the piazza, approaching the cafés, but without ever getting to the point of ordering anything. If he got too absorbed or lonely, Vivés's absence quickly overtook him and all around him were spread out her steps and the pleats of her last skirt. If he hung around people, it could happen that they would start asking questions and he would have to talk and maybe unintentionally confess the secret of that girl who had come to him by chance – or those wise guys might be able to figure it out from something, even the smallest thing. Nevertheless, he went to get a cup of tea at the bus station, confronting the difficult descent of Valbona, secretly hoping that someone in the bar or the waiting rooms might be looking for or talking about that girl. For the moment Gaspare knew only that she was from the country, at least originally, and that she was twenty-three years old, even though she looked less than twenty. He also knew her name and that, besides being physically hurt and headed who-knows-where before she got hurt, she was also driven by loneliness and fear. She was staying there, aside from being forced to by her wounds, also of her own free will. And anyway, he could keep her there without much inconvenience, and secretly, as he had understood that he must... in part so that he would not be alone in that house – as he was on Christmas Day and the day before when several times he had been on the verge of joining Vivés.

But what could that bayonet do other than make him feel even more hopeless every time he went to get it? And who would have taken him to Bologna again? And why not first say where the blame lies for so much unhappiness and, above all, for the historical, economic and cultural waste into which this poor country has been thrown upside-down? And then, wasn't there the theater? Hadn't that Dirce arrived at a certain time of the morning like in a contrived theatrical encounter? Wasn't there some fun to be had in writing another thesis, this time an active one, for that Oddo, who could really and legitimately reclaim the lordship of Urbino? Wasn't the unitarian state already, from the very moment in which it was born, expressing almost only – and above all its own – historical negation? It was right to start attacking it any way possible, even by trying to reconstitute the lordships of the first Italian league.

Warmed up by the arguments of that long descent, he was pleased with himself and his courage. He admired his own strength with the same complacency of an actor who calculates and listens to a display of his own skill.

He asked for a confirmation of that condition from the walls and objects, whose murmuring he could hear. He was trying to understand what they were saying, to establish communication with them – meanwhile, he enveloped them with his ideas. With this emotion he pushed open the door of the bar. He found himself in a long L-shaped room with a rather low, although vaulted, ceiling: it must have been the wing of a ducal stable.

It was full of people, at the bar and at the tables, standing and seated. Those near the bar were talking about the death of four serpents, which was caused during the night by the fumes of a heating stove improperly operated by a circus worker.

The circus had stopped in the town of Trasanni, blocked by the snow while it was climbing toward Urbino. The caged serpents were absolutely dependent on heat, more so than the monkeys or lions. They were four long and very valuable serpents: two were trained. A while before the owner had looked in there for someone who might know how to preserve their skins. He was desperate; if he could at least save their skins and recuperate a little bit of what they were worth. The people were united by this hope, with their glasses in hand.

Subissoni entered the crowd with a calculated step, tottering, but with an open mind. He too was grieved by the misfortune of that circus. The Urbinoites were talking about the serpents, with increasing pity. "And to think," said one, "that if some certain serpents were to die we could all save ourselves. And there'd be no need to preserve *their* skins.... Those four snakes in the government.... They're not even trained, and all they know is how to frighten and disgust us." A chorus of agreement was heard and more arguments against the government were expressed in even harsher tones.

Subissoni was hearing that revolt for the first time. He was impressed by the density and wealth of emotions and images. Many were talking furiously and simultaneously. Gaspare was waiting to intervene – he was preparing himself and wanted a slightly quieter moment, which might permit his assault to make room and be directed at everybody. He would begin by blaming every evil – every evil that the people there were enumerating and chewing on – on the unification made with the kingdom of Italy. But the arguments around him were not diminishing and continued exploding beyond their words. Subissoni interrupted his plan and positioned himself better for listening. He noticed after a while that he did not understand half of the arguments. He didn't understand many words or the use that was made of others. He couldn't follow the allusions, while entire phrases regarding labor and parties were new to him; he was unable to see their targets. He got closer to some but saw in their faces a violence that repelled him. He was disheartened by the fact that they talked so much and threw themselves into it without knowing anything, stuck at the level of their ignorance and physically pulling everything down to that level.

"Serpents for serpents," he found the indignation to say, "don't you understand that the problem is the cage?" He went on awkwardly while some of them glanced at him: "The problem is the unitarian confusion... because of which the serpents are no longer serpents... who live happily on their beaches and in their caves but become travelers and are sent through the snow." Some of them started laughing. "It makes you laugh, but this is the problem, the real problem of confusion. What's our situation? Where is Rome with its ministries? And where is Milan with its industries? And where are we? Who takes the measurements and plans the trips? What revolution will you ever be able to have as long as tropical snakes go on traveling through the snow?" There were bursts of laughter and jeers of varying intensity. "Who," Subissoni went on, "will determine when the revolution will have arrived at the proper point? The liberation of whom? Of each of us? Wealth placed within reach of each of us, everywhere, every place in Italy, in every season and according to our desires? Who will control the meals in the zoological gardens of Palermo and Milan? I mean the portions, the schedules, and even the number of square yards of each cage? Will the dispositions come from Rome? And who will sit in Rome? Caligula's horse or Kafka's talking ape? If it's true, as it is true, that today snakes sit there." The laughter decreased.

"Comrades, the politicians are not stupid and are perhaps not the worst of us. The government is stupid, and even more stupid is the republic that is the daughter of the monarchy. It's an absolute and blind force that sends serpents through the snow or bombs into the banks or factories onto the streets of its cities or laws between the feet of its people or progress to the top of Mount Nerone like an ugly Carduccian poem.

"The words and their targets must be rediscovered. The first word is unification. What does it mean other than poison, misery, plundering, war, ignorance, barracks, prison, cage, death... even of poor serpents? Unification as constriction, chains and forced travel, or obligatory transfer... not as the free union of peoples and cities."

"And so?" some of them screamed at him.

"So," Gaspare said, "the target is unification. This unification whose reason for being and whose mechanisms are anti-liberal and, therefore, whose programs and goals – however started and achieved – produce servitude. This unification must be broken and the pieces that fall from it must be looked at...."

"Too far backward," was screamed clearly at him. "It's enough to change the government. A government of the people."

"Which people and which government?" said Gaspare. "Would it have been enough last night to change the custodian so that those poor serpents wouldn't have died? Even the most loving of custodians would have had the same results if the heater was broken and the cages were where they should not have been according to the laws of nature."

"Too far backward, too far away. It's a useless go-around."

"No," shouted Gaspare, "you are making useless speeches. If the circus was at Trasanni last night at one o'clock, and if we had wanted to save the serpents, we should have gone to Trasanni and *before* one o'clock. Here and now, in fact, all we can do is try to preserve their skins. It's exactly what happens to us – everybody just tries to tan our hides and fix a price for them and save on the tannin and then decide whether to make from them belts, whips, lampshades, jackets, handbags, briefcases, shields, badges, gloves, magistrate's capes or office chairs in Rome or in Milan. Office chairs in Rome and in Milan, in every office, court of law, study, consultation room, registrar's, police station, party... with our hides...." Many of them had turned their backs to him and so Gaspare added; "mine at least." He was terrified by a piercing thought about Vivés.

"That's enough," said some others, "don't listen to him. He's an old middle-class anarchist, an individualistic anarchist.... All they do is spread problems around... they're dying out...."

Subissoni tried to throw himself against the ones who had spoken so coldly but was held back. "That's enough, professor," they turned and said to him. "There's a difference between yesterday and today, and there's another difference between a worker and a serpent... maybe you don't understand them... or you've forgotten them. Calm down and think about it. Meanwhile we'll make it clear to the government and to the middle class with facts...."

Under the pressure of that indulgence Subissoni moved gropingly toward the bar. "It's time to find a history...," he mumbled, "one single history; while evidently there are many double consciences going around.... I believe that serpents don't have double consciences... and that they deserve their place in history.... Or are there some trained serpents with a double conscience?"

But nobody was listening to him anymore. He closed his good eye and tried to withdraw sadly inside himself. Yet from this operation he got a measure of himself that reacted autonomously: "For whom do you take me? Shall we try to measure our consciences? And our days too and also what each of us has done for the freedom and well-being of the workers, as you say?"

One of them turned around with his mouth half-open and, after overcoming a certain indecision, said, "You are good, we know that. Certainly better than us. And what does that count for? Why should we turn backwards? Everything is clear now. All it takes is moving forward. Thanks also to you, because you are one of those who have made things clear. If you want to come with us, you have to keep quiet and march: we're marching against the government. This awareness is already revolution. If you don't want to come with us, stay behind and suffer and write books about your suffering, like all privileged people. More books that will kill time and will help the middle class, which always wants to be mixed up in suffering and in complaining. We've had enough. We know where to go."

"What is your connection with history?" objected Subissoni, with reticence and also with fear for having used those words.

"I already said it," answered the young man, "None! None now, because now we have already taken off. Where have you arrived? Well, we want to go beyond that or in any case to reach a different place."

"You'll end up the same way as the serpents if you don't change the cages and the whole circus. And in order to get in there and blow them away it is exactly history that you need."

"No, professor. No. History, as you talk about it, stands on an altar. It becomes an untouchable truism, a divinity, in fact... and it begins to dictate.... Do you know what it is in the end? This society! Just as it is, full of so many unquestionable truths, upheld even by science... this cage, to use your word. Knock everything over and come with us if you want to get out of the cage. Have courage, bandage up your eye and come with us. We have learned that we have to use our ideas to run over history if we don't want to get ourselves screwed – and run with our legs too, and often off the road, because even the road is a truism of this society, not ours, of our travels and commerce...."

"Do you see that you're agreeing with me," said Subissoni. "You don't want the structures of unification... but it's not enough to just get out in order to be free – not even to start running away from the roads.... History – not the one of power, but the one that stands in opposition, in negation; the one of the defeated, of Cattaneo, of Pisacane – teaches us how to flee and where to hide ourselves and what to prepare.... Or do you want to run forever? Or is it enough for you to run... what are you... ponies?"

The young man said yes, while laughing; "We can be everything, even ponies.... That might even be nice. But don't you see where I am? How would you define this place? Is it a study center or a history classroom? I reject the thought-system of the school, and I'm searching for one in here... that will be valid for everyone in here – to liberate all of us and give us the real tools that we need for the struggle against the government.... The government is there, and we won't get lost because we will always turn toward its face and toward its movements... and we will always speak out against its arguments with words that differ from its words."

"It's not the government... it's the unification of Italy," Subissoni tried again.

The young man shook his head: "Italy? And who's talking about Italy! What is it that bothers you? Its postage stamps, its coins? What is it? Another topic of capitalistic rationalization?" And he waved good-bye while rejoining the group, which was getting increasingly worked-up as it listened unwillingly to that discussion.

"Professor," a familiar voice rose from the area near the doorway. "Professor. It's good that I found you. Come with me so I can tell you something." Fatter and smiling more than usual Giocondini elbowed his way through the crowd and shook himself off in front of Subissoni like a dog coming out of the water. "What luck... finding you here. I was outside there, and I heard that you were speaking.... Don't bother with these people.... he's a crazy student. He's always in here... just think: he didn't even go home for Christmas. You've really chosen the worst place to come for discussing politics... you, with your talent. Not even the ones from the Communist Party come here... it's a hell hole, this place!"

Subissoni was looking at that whispering courier with a bit of gratitude, partly because with his bulk he blocked from his sight and hearing that frenzied dough into which he had stuck his head... all the more because he was getting too embarrassed to look at that young pony... who, in reality, was invisible by then, mixed in with the other shoulders and the obstinance of the long hair on those heads. Giocondini was talking and laughing benevolently, protecting him with the saliva that he melted into his words and with a solemn maneuver of his eyebrows.

Subissoni felt himself being pushed toward reaching that pony, but he also felt like he was sliding into the protection of that witch doctor. The latter placed a special glass of wine in his hand, a Portuguese one in fact, "to really leave Italy in a serious way," he said, "not just with words... and also to see it better, more clearly through this... Mateus." He accented the "m" exaggerating the pleasure of sipping and opening his head to a sudden idea, a bizarre idea that might be refreshing even though it came from the depths of his Brilliantine.

Subissoni was able to reassume a more detached pose and begin considering his situation outside of that scene – and with that marvelous double-energy characteristic of actors, who are there, who get all worked up, but who also know that soon, somewhere else, just beyond there, they'll have another secure opportunity.

"I need you," said Giocondini. "Some things are happening... that directly affect our project. Come on outside. We can talk better in the car. Don't you have to go somewhere?"

As soon as they were in the car Giocondini told his story: "Our lord is upset and humiliated too. His lady has run away from him, like the real whore that she was. We've looked all over for her but haven't been able to find her anywhere in the province. The count is wavering here and there in darkness and might even abandon the idea of governing.... But, at other times, he regrets not being a real lord just so he could conduct a search for his consort with edicts and proclamations and threaten revenge against some neighboring state that may have kidnapped her and may be hiding her. He wants his straw doll back!... What can we do to give her back to him? Could a manifesto be made up, or at least written? And what if he gets discouraged and forgets about everything? He's capable of closing himself up and not taking any more trips."

Subissoni was getting to the truth, but he didn't want to interrupt that middle-man. Giocondini felt that he was being listened to and went on: "I don't know if he can support the idea of an independent state. Maybe it would only be a joke. On the other hand, with your help we could get Oddino in with the Christian Democrats... and get him started in his career... and get him elected mayor. With an advisor like you he could do it. I'll find someone else, some authority from the Cathedral or the University. But in the meantime he wants his doll. Why don't you write the edict? At least it will serve to console him and demonstrate to him that somebody takes him seriously and is helping him."

"Alright," said Subissoni. "What is this run-away girl like? And why did she run away?"

"She's small, blond, all curls, she comes from Fano. She's called Dirce Badalocchi, but she has another last name too... she has a sad air about her, she doesn't breath open-mouthed; She has a dull face, but her legs, especially from behind...."

"That's enough," said Subissoni. "I think you've described her with more enthusiasm than necessary.... But where am I supposed to find her? If you weren't able to find her, with this big car.... Youth can hide itself, especially if it's sad, even under a leaf; and then, if it doesn't even breath,... what can we do?" he started humming, stirred by the great discovery that he had made. "But why did she run away?"

"That's what I'd like to know," retorted Giocondini. "Why? She's crazy? She's a whore? She was afraid? She was mistreated? That enchanted ox didn't suit her anymore? She didn't like the soup, the bed, the scenery? She came from a whore house and could hardly stand up and that guy had already declared that he would marry her.... Just think, a countess! From a whore house!"

"Perhaps she's a whore, but not a greedy one," proposed Subissoni, partly to hide his own emotions. "Or else she realized that she didn't love her fiancé. Or else she loves someone else whom she wasn't able to forget, or else the whore house is buying her back; or else she didn't like the aristocracy; or else she didn't feel worthy of that whole palace; or else she's afraid; something must have frightened her. However real whores don't get easily frightened, and then, before getting frightened, they try, in any case, to get something out of it. Did she steal anything? Did anything disappear with her?"

Giocondini was following him restlessly – with his motor still off – and negated everything with his head.

"Or else," went on Subissoni, increasingly content with his discovery – partly because through this game he had understood the reasons why Dirce might have run away. "Or else…" pressing Giocondini even more, "someone kidnapped her. If not some neighboring state, at least not for the moment… some relative interested in Oddo's patrimony and therefore in Oddino's celibacy… or else in giving his own choice of wife to Oddino…. And his aunts? Couldn't it have been them – jealous and offended in their nobility and purity by the entrance of a whore – who made her disappear? They could have corrupted her, filled her up with jewels,… or with some toiletry junk that can be very attractive to a whore; or they might have threatened her and forced her to run away… or else, my dear conspirator friend,… and that would be a real problem, especially for her,… they might even have killed her, slaughtered her in her bed and then dragged her into the kitchens and into the laboratories… they have them in the Oddo house, right?… and there dismembered and burned, or else sacrificed…. Ah! what things two virgin and jealous aunts are capable of doing! Have you ever read *Arsenic and Old Lace*? Was there anything boiling this morning at the Oddi's? Was there, by any chance, a lot of laundry? Or else they might have buried her in the garden, in a half-hour's time, before dawn, with their ability for gardening that is a certain heritage of our agrarian nobility…. Wasn't there some displaced grass, especially under the trees, perhaps the finest tree, the most beautiful… upturned earth around it with the excuse of fertilizing it?… Or else they walled her up in the library behind the Doré *Divine Comedy*. Is there an oven there?…"

Giocondini was hesitating, and it was just his luck that Subissoni threw the villa into the discussion. "Don't the Oddis have a villa somewhere around Urbino? It seems to me they do. So it's very likely that the aunts, for some reason, or the nephew himself, for an opposing reason, needing, at least for the moment, to cause the disappearance of the… fiancée, might have been able to shelter her and hide her… or sequester her, imprison her perhaps, in the cellars of that old building… and leave poor Dirce there in chains to die of privation…. After all this, what kind of edict can be issued? Is it wise to attract the attention of the police? In any case, it would be better to first invest Oddo, immediately… and then proceed according to what happens… if Dirce never does get out, the lord, as such, would have a much more ample selection for replacing her… perhaps acquiring some advantageous alliance in the process… if not exactly with other states, with some bank… with some land holdings… real estate… or fund or stipend… or perhaps with grammar, if not actually with pedagogy, by means of some school teacher enrolled in the noble institute of education…; if Dirce were to come back he would have a way of re-enforcing his authority by punishing her or pardoning her; or better to edit the epilogue and the epithalamium, to reconsider her… if Dirce were to reappear as a cadaver, then his royalty could help his position… indeed granting him impunity…. In that case most probably someone else would be incriminated in his place… someone close to him, a squire, a… coxswain, to use a more up-to-date term. That's the way history is," he said, out of breath.

And he repeated, "That's the way history is," just to show that that raging pony from before was right. He said it benevolently and with the desire to see him again to explain to him that what he meant for history was revolt, or, at least, the revolt of certain ideas and projects running breathlessly alongside history, shouting and teaching, often ending up in a noose or at the stake. The monk too had told him that what he called pride would be more correctly called love. Now how would that pony, who wouldn't even take part in the Christmas holidays, have altered for him the meaning of history or of planning or of revolution? New men and new times were on the move and new names too that made him shiver inside his cassock. He clapped his hands with satisfaction.

"In any case," he said to Giocondini, "if it's to do an edict or a proclamation or for whatever advice, I am always ready to present myself, with your guidance and recommendation, to Lord Oddi-Semproni. Advice for climbing the ladder to power as well as on the way to find Dirce... or even for putting oneself at the mercy of the very nicely democratic will of the Christian Democrats.

"You frightened me with that girl... and for the rest of it you seem really smart... maybe getting in with the Christian Democrats now...."

"Don't rush into it. Stop and think that in that way you lose your historic plan, my dear fellow. What would happen to the lordship of the Oddis and the independence of Urbino?"

Giocondini answered with a snort and took off very rapidly bouncing the professor around in those super-soft seats just so that he would not be able to go on talking. At the Mill the Mercedes stopped and Subissoni got out again with his mind on the result and the effect of Urbino's independence. "That Oddo is certainly no Valentino...." On the other hand he thought with affection about the pony. He had already broken up the unification of Italy and there were many more like him... including that Nicola, for example. Although this Apulian Stalinist Nikita – Gaspare smiled, – had admitted that yes, it was necessary to break it up; break it up, yes... but to remake it better, on the principle that popular unity is an efficient tool precisely because of its unitarianism and populism, for renewal, progress... elevation... even elevation? Yes or no? And who does the elevating? Who moves the lever of the elevator and who is on the plate of those being elevated, or better in the masses to be elevated?"

Subissoni couldn't wait to get back to Dirce, who had painfully bumped against his door, fleeing, however, from power and from the all-powerful, with an angst *"ab omni materia separata,"* away from the spatial and ideal city, down the stairs, outside of humanity and also outside of the theater and outside of history. He grumbled, waiting for the chance to clear things up with the pony... the jousting pony. Dirce! Who had come down the hill to him with bruised knees and poetic rhymes.

What was she, if she wasn't an apparition?

He hurried home squeezing Vivés with infinite love for the discovery that he was going to make.

21

Dirce was in the living-room cleaning. She was brushing off the stove burners with great care, perhaps caught up there with the thought that it was about the time something should be boiling in a pot or frying in a pan. Even Gaspare understood: "Oh!" he said, "I had so much to do that I forgot to buy anything. What are we going to do? Because I can't even bring you to a restaurant. All the stores are closed and there's nothing here. Do you see how busy, and even distracted, I am? Is there a can of something? Or an egg or some cheese at least for you? For me a nice espresso with lots of sugar and a bit of anisette will do. Or if not, I could run down to the mill bar and see what they have. So young as you are, you can't go without eating."

"I can go three days," said Dirce.

"How come? Did you eat so much yesterday?"

"No. I've gone without eating other times."

"For a diet, for a sickness?"

"No, because there was nothing at home. Nothing, an empty cupboard, the last slice of bread gone. No more bread soup, no more walnuts, no more lard or crab apples. Nothing."

"Did it happen often to you?"

"Yes, lots of times. More often when I was between ten and twelve-years-old. It started shortly after my father's death."

"What did you do at those times?"

"Nothing. We waited."

"Who were you waiting for?"

"Nobody. We were waiting for something to eat."

"And did it arrive?"

"Yes?"

"How?"

"In the end my uncle or my mother would get up and go to the neighbors or in town. Or else they would go together to sell or to trade something."

"What?"

"The plough, the mattocks... even the sheets."

"And then did you eat?"

"Of course, we ate. As soon as the food got there, and the next time too, each of us went to eat alone... outside, even if it was raining, under the eaves, against a tree, each of us alone... but my uncle would go to the back of the kitchen, where it was the darkest."

Subissoni was so moved that he even felt hunger himself. He made a gesture and Dirce felt herself commanded to look inside the cupboard. She moved things around with care on top and underneath and found an opened one-pound package of spaghetti and two cans of tuna. She showed all this with a smile and said that she could make a good pasta dish with it. She didn't find anything else; only the anisette bottle and one more package of coffee; even the sugar was gone. Subissoni accepted Dirce's revelations as proof of her dignity; and he could also make them known to Nicola and to the pony too. He even got the rather rhetorical idea of opening the cans with his bayonet. In any case, he went and got his weapon, even though Dirce had found the regular can-opener.

Dirce was not shocked and did not attach any glory to that bayonet that Subissoni went on showing her, gripping it in his fist, as he went around the table. He couldn't keep quiet: "Do you know what this is?"

"A dagger."

"Almost. It's a bayonet, different from a dagger because it's longer and heavier and because it gets attached to a rifle. It's a military weapon, for war; while a dagger can be used by any bully. I made this madame's acquaintance in the war... it is she who kissed me on the eye, and she was an Italian lady... because I was on the other side, against the Italians....

I was with the Reds in Spain, with the people, with the International...."

Dirce smiled, showing clearly, by her attraction to those words and to their tone, that she knew nothing about those events. Subissoni was standing there waiting, but she was unable to say anything other than to politely ask him if there was any possibility of finding a little salt.

Gaspare was fixed with this enormous idea – which he was unable to put into action – but then it seemed as if he had fought for that salt, and it appeared right too that he should still find it. He even imagined Vivés who was telling him so. He shouldn't look for it in the house, and in the neighborhood there were no stores open at that hour, only the mill bar. He said yes and went out. At the bar before asking for the salt he bought three cans of beer, three packages of cookies and three chocolate bars. The kind barkeeper, along with the salt rolled up in paper, suggested some crackers that would go well with a meal. He took three of those packages too and with all that stuff in front of him he didn't know where to put the miraculous salt. He thought about tying it around his neck, but then he found his jacket pocket. He went back accompanied by a comforting tremor... of which he also heard the distant noise that was rumbling on the other side of the valley, in the fog. The same kind of noise precedes the trains in deep gullies, like there were in Spain....

Gaspare felt at peace with the world and placed Urbino at the center of his own earthly history, which was still open and had good roads. Also the smell of that meal, almost ready in his house, was opening up those roads.

He found things with a more quiet and confident appearance. Even his observation of himself was less impossible – he had often tortured his life by observing himself uselessly. And in this way he had offended Vivés's presence. He could ask her forgiveness through that girl, by sitting down at the same table.

They ate in silence, with Dirce watching for Subissoni's occasional reactions. After the tuna they didn't know what to eat of those things that were bought at the bar. Subissoni piled them in front of Dirce and got up. He made the coffee and while he was pouring it he said one thing after another but with kindness: "What do you want to do? Until when can you stay? How do you feel? Where do you want to go… and how will you get there? Do you really want to go away and hide? Is it just for a while, to then go back to Count Oddi? Or do you want to run away for always? How will you be able to do it?"

Dirce heard those questions all at the same time, painfully. Even though the tone was kind, their reality was mean. The pain increased because she didn't know how to answer. She dropped the chocolate she had taken and put it back with the others.

"No, no," said Gaspare, "you can do as you wish. I will only try to help you. You can stay here until you have decided. In the meantime, it's you who is helping me. It seemed right to talk to you about this, also because I have to tell you that they have done a lot of searching for you, everywhere, and they will go on doing so. They even asked me if I would write a kind of edict. But you can stay here for as long as you want, even after you get better, because I'm not going to say anything to anybody.… If then you want to go back, I can always accompany you… and the same if you want to run away.…"

"No, I don't want to go back," said Dirce.

"Okay. Anyway you have time to think about it. You can't go any place with those knees."

Dirce was discouraged, weighed down by a pain that was stretching her eyes against her forehead. She was so frightened that she could have lost control and given up just so as not to have to resist that arrogant power, not even in her thoughts. She was already leaning exhaustedly on the table, as though by then it was blocking every escape route. Gaspare was sorry for having asked those questions too soon, driven by his desire to appropriate that talking and living thing. He had wound her too tightly and now there was the danger of breaking the spring and destroying her forever.

"Don't be worried," he said, "don't worry. You've got lots of time.… We'll help each other, for as long as you like staying here. I'm not demanding; I'm more lonely than you are… and I have always fought against arrogance."

Dirce got up and felt calmed down as her forehead relaxed in the light coming through the window.

"…And the secret for fighting is to talk," went on Gaspare. "That is, to look at things beyond oneself; to talk… even without telling a story." And he was talking in order to get back his hope of having found a *res nullius,* a tiny floating island in the river, after the flood, that had come and gotten stuck on his shore.

Dirce didn't say anything, but with two movements of her mouth as dignified as they were awkward she showed that she was grateful and even admired that eloquence that regarded her – even if she didn't understand it all and heard it as if it was flying over the head of her problem. The problem was still hers and, as always, she would have to decide for herself… even though everybody had always done everything for her, bringing her here and there, commanding her or abandoning her.

Problems and pain had always been the same substance. She had nothing to say, she could only do and meanwhile trust in the protection of that house, in the fact that it was there. With that man she would behave according to the demands of the moment, but without even imagining the possibility of opposing him. He was kind and gentle, like a kind doctor. You could even see it in his hands… and just like a doctor he had his words, instructions that spilled out of his head falling like a current… into which she would not be able to enter. To make up for that she thought about something else. She had found it on the top shelf of the cupboard while the man was out: the metal flask, which barely stuck out of her fist; the screw top was so well made that it gave her a sense of satisfaction; the tiny space inside was lined with glass, a kind of shiny phial with a white rubber stopper. It contained nothing and had no smell. Strong and handy as it was, it could hold and protect the most precious things with absolute security. It did not cloud up with her breath as though it were silver. She had immediately desired it, and she had appropriated it by hiding it in the belt of her skirt. Now she had a desire to look at it again and hold it in her hand. Almost immediately Subissoni left; and she could take out that treasure again, try the top again, the rubber, the glass with her finger... and then blow inside it, listen to the sound, blow again, put the stopper right back in, screw it closed again, hold it in her fist, rub it on her forehead, lick it. She was happy about that possession and the whole house, including that man who was whistling upstairs, was becoming magically warm and full of life as she wanted it to be.

Subissoni was upstairs looking through Vivés's clothes and personal things for something that the girl might be able to use. At a certain point he threw himself on Vivés's bed, he too gripped in some kind of magic, that was nothing other than his consuming faith in his own ideas.

Dirce had calmed down and was already beginning to enjoy, as she took care of some chores, her loyalty to that new roof and to all that it covered and that could be seen from its windows. The man upstairs had quietly acquired the authority to decide her fate, and he would certainly not betray her by turning her over to that crazy trio who lived in the ghost palace. She felt a slight touch of nostalgia for the giant full of saliva that introduced her to his aunts as soon as she arrived, when she still hadn't seen anything of the palace; and a touch of nostalgia above all for the sound of his words, which dominated the vastness of the rooms, in which she had immediately begun suffering. But afterward even the sound of that voice had become frightening, always accompanied by the whole palace that played on all its glass and space.

One is afraid of every musical instrument if one has shared Dirce's situation; music itself is the voice of death. A violin, a piano, an organ and even a guitar are mysterious images of death. One must sing so as not to hear the music. Some sudden sound of iron, a slammed window, a noise resonating through the forest are instantaneous alarms. One can only bare a small orchestra that would arrive all at the same time, sustaining itself as a group and exalting itself... and if it arrives from a familiar place. Girls give it away immediately, out of terror, before a bagpipe or a saxophone; with less desperation before a drum. They run away for sure or go crazy in front of a violin – girls like Dirce. Later on, after 1960, the music on the radio and in the dance halls stuns them and then deforms them like a disease.

Dirce was confident that this man, who must have gone to bed, would not turn her over to the musical trio, partly because there was some advantage to him in keeping her with him, advantages that her mind, liberated from fear, was starting to suggest to her, with a touch of maliciousness.

Upstairs Subissoni was analyzing the cruelty that some new ideas and hopes had poured over him. Maybe it would be right to turn that girl over to the count... perhaps in exchange for an ideological commitment and... in the context of an assured political solidarity! However, he would first need to know the intentions of that girl and also get to know the young Oddi-Semproni. Therefore, he would have to go downstairs to see Dirce again.

He found her looking out the window, keeping herself behind a curtain. He was much encouraged by that cautiousness but nevertheless waited before speaking. He went back to making more coffee and when it boiled up he started throwing out some words about Urbino. He took a long pause after the coffee and then asked the girl if she liked Urbino. She answered by saying she didn't know the city. "True," said Subissoni, "and you won't be able to go out to see it now. Right?" She agreed.

"Fine, how is Fano then?"

In her response Dirce expressed no judgment, no evaluation. The same for Fossombrone. They were all places on the earth, real ones; places for people; and of these places there was one for her; one assigned to her.

"And Italy?" asked Subissoni, anxiously this time. An undefined movement of the mouth was her answer; even though quickly reabsorbed, in its place remained an air of guilt mixed with curiosity.

"That's okay," Subissoni reassured her, "it's not important. Italy as it is isn't worth much more than that. On the contrary...," and then, in a reignited tone: "Do you know who is to blame for the hunger that you have suffered? For all the days that you went without eating?"

Dirce wanted to answer – partly because it seemed to her that in the words of one of the musical aunts there was a touch of reprimand toward her father and her family when she was asking her about the farm – thinking that she was proving that she had learned something in that world of... educated people: "My... par... ents?" she syllabified the question, to distribute the blame.

"No, no, please," exclaimed Subissoni. "It's Italy! Italy is to blame. It exists, affirmed in its unification, it insists... and lasts... but it's not there. It's not there when you need it... because it can't walk, nailed as it is by stations of every kind, by railroad crossings, by districts, on the cross of unification. Has it ever come to your table? Has it ever done anything for you other than to number you in order to forget you immediately afterward? Other than insult you? Other than to provide a bare table and a soup bowl and... walls, walls badly whitewashed for unhappiness and death?"

He stopped, in order to search for other more concrete reasons. He got hung up between tables and train tracks and there appeared before him a railing, which extended into the sparkle of an ambiguous glaze and then went off toward the latrine of Victor Emmanuel II. He raised his eyes fearful that the girl might have the same vision. Dirce's face was a surprise because the brightness of her features gave her an appearance of lively attention as he looked at her. Vivés's face was always as solid as a coin – even in his memory she sprang forward with a look so serious that it caused him immediate pain.

He felt himself being judged and turned to the window and then to the espresso maker. He measured the little table and the tiny step by the window sill.

261

"Unfortunately," he said, "I am very small and my idea is small like me. You don't even have to think about it. I only wanted to tell you about it."

He turned back toward the girl and with an air of excusing himself added; "...but it is the truth," and he stayed by her side.

Dirce's slightly moved white eyebrows indicated such profundity that Subissoni felt himself returned to his own proportions, with his idea that covered him completely, as wide as the new overcoat of an adolescent. Vivés had always kept a dose of fear close by for him... and in the presence of that invisible half-filled glass he had often gotten confused; and what's more he would be intimidated by one of his companion's eyes, or by a wrinkle, or her index finger, even though he was filled then, as now, with an infinite devotion to her. Perhaps Vivés, with the authority of certain of her conclusions, or just by lowering her shaded forehead toward him, had diminished many of his arguments, and many of his accomplishments too.

He went back to the espresso maker and worked with it for a few minutes.

He went up the stairs stumbling several times; the last times on purpose. The walls reminded him – with their spaces and measurements – of Vivés and her death; they also helped him to bear it physically... just as they supported the presence of Dirce.

22

On the morning of December 29, around 10 AM, accompanied by Giocondo Giocondini, Gaspare Subissoni was entering the presence of the young Oddi-Semproni.

He had to struggle against the cold inside those rooms just as he had had to do earlier on his way there. In fact, the cold inside there was worse than outside, stiffened as it was by ancient odors and filtered through timeless dust.

Subissoni was made even more vulnerable by his emotion and by the fact that that night he had slept very little, just a couple of hours before midnight.

He had dreamt about Vivés who was scolding him, at times with a smile and at times by showing him an immense mouth that was dilating to give emphasis – with its rapidity and with the monstrousness of its measurements – to the rancor of the accusation. From that mouth, which changed with increasing rapidity into so many images and that, in the end, was an opening in the curtain across the heavens, he had come out, falling head first onto the green fields of his infancy. But there he was already an adult, with his books and with his nose broken by the brass knuckles of the fascist squads – the brass knuckles, while he was looking at his own nose in pieces and bleeding, were flying and playing music in the air, transforming themselves into stringed instruments. A man arrived and stared at him: as shiny as the underside of fly paper was his look, which was already affecting him, although the man turned the nape of his neck to him. While he was trying to recognize him, he started to talk and said; "Everything that it has given us, life takes away from us entirely and all at once."

He was surprised by the banality of the dictation, on which, however, he was slowly attracted to concentrate, partly because the unknown man went on repeating it. When he convinced himself that the phrase was beautiful, he had to suffer simultaneously because he had recognized the voice, but he was unable to attribute it to anyone.

He stayed there wandering around the fields, which were getting wet, conscious of the conquest of the principle of that phrase, but shaken by his fear of attributing the voice, whose sound continued even though the man had disappeared. Until in front of an unforeseen branch – on which the voice had come to rest – he was awoken by the surprise of recognizing that it was his own voice.

He woke up as he was pronouncing the last word. Following that, he associated the branch that had touched him with Vivés, but as his consciousness got clearer he was able to add that it must have been his mother.

For the rest of the night he was unable to fall back to sleep. He was afraid of forgetting the phrase and he repeated it to himself in those moments when he was most tired. At a certain point he decided to wake up the girl to tell her so as to save it forever – "it or her?" he questioned in his torpor. He didn't get up, held there by his effort to remember if the phrase was constructed from two verses of a Latin poet translated in high school: Martial? Catullus?

"By sleeping," he told himself, "I sink ever deeper into my own depositories." The indulgence of this confession and the vision of those soft depositories that the pillow gave him brought him to a blank moment of his own youth when he was deciding to leave Urbino. He felt like it was his fear of Vivés that was lifting him up, even though he also felt grateful to her. Staying with his mother would have been easier, and there would have been no need to try to immerse himself in sleep: his mother was old, having passed away more than thirty years ago, dying as she had lived, with a gesture of disappointment. Not even the black silk bonnet that they had arranged around her head and face and not even the weight of death after more than a day and a night had succeeded in relaxing that petulant grimace. But she died in such a way that she almost broke apart in the hands of those who that morning moved her from the bed to her coffin.

At six o'clock Gaspare, calm and with much determination, had gotten up. He had gotten dressed and gone right away to buy the newspapers. (The male dancer was guilty, no longer with any shadow of a doubt!) And this had made him calmer and even more anxious for action. In the café there were just the right people who had looked at him with smiles.

Now the sidereal dust of the Oddi house was turning him cold and giving him another image, deep in his own bones, of the depositories of his life.

When Subissoni came in the young Oddo was already in the library, standing next to the TV, with his right hand opened toward the apparatus as if to point it out or hold it up. He was dressed in a dark suit from a few years ago, which made him even more imposing by leaving his wrists uncovered, as well as his ankles up to his shins. It also gave him an impatient air, which contrasted with his face dulled by a yellowish swelling.

He greeted the professor talking in spurts in a loud though nasal voice. "Did you prepare the edict?" he asked. "Do you want to let me read it? My fiancée must be found before those who kidnapped her can do her any harm. They are aiming at my family, at me… partly to take away from us the support of the people and then to steal our name and our goods. Have you prepared the edict?"

"Not yet," answered Subissoni. "I thought it might be worthwhile to talk with you first to get to know your problem and your intentions better. To whom do you want to address the edict and with what principle objective?"

"Oh great!" said Oddino, "the edict goes on the walls and the object is for me to find Dirce."

"That's all?" asked Subissoni. "Why then are you talking about the support of the people and your name and your family? I seemed to understand from what Giocondini, here present, passed on to me that your intentions were more extensive than sticking up an edict and finding a girl. For example, now when you talk about those who are aiming at your family, do you mean to refer to some group that wants to steal something from you and from the Oddis... to some unidentified person, or some unknown individuals, to some abstract forces... to some organisms that could be defined as political, in short to some institutions, the same ones that have confused and upset the appearance of the country, and therefore also the position of your family?"

Oddo became perplexed but drew his eyes out of his pallor. Giocondini had stopped wagging his tail and spraying good feelings from his big eyes, and from his collar too, having become suspicious of that reference to a thief... identified or identifiable. He stepped forward and cleared his throat and shook his big shiny head negatively behind the professor's back. Subissoni saw him reflected in the television and was intimidated by his vulgarity. "Isn't it that you want," he added hastily, "with the edict, to open up a political problem... to deny the legitimacy of the unification of the Country, that is, of the mortification of its real right to be free in the differences between its states, each governed by its own voice, drawn tightly around... around...." He got confused and stared at Oddo, whose eyes slowly moved, truly like those of a sovereign who was coming back to life after centuries of distance and fixity. But Oddino did not speak; and finally he turned his gaze toward the television.

"If you don't want to talk to me about your projects, tell me then who might be your enemies, the kidnappers of... of the girl, and to whom, in reality, you would address the edict?"

"The edict to the entire population," said Oddino, "to everyone. My enemies are the communists, the anarchists... and even the priests and also the police who pretend not to find Dirce. This is not the end of the Oddi family. The people will come to call me and to ask me what to do."

"And what will you say?" The professor's curiosity was dissipating, partly due to the annoyance that slob still standing behind his back was causing him.

"I will say what I have to say, with the help of television. Have you noticed that those television people talk better than the government ministers?"

"But will you let the people speak too?"

Oddino stopped and assumed his previous pose; a moment later his face exploded and his voice shot out from every part. "Do you want to ruin me?" he asked. "How could I speak with the entire population? How could all the people talk together? Has an entire population ever spoken? One, or two, or three, speak for it."

Subissoni was pleased with that scolding, because he was starting to become ashamed for having gotten to that point. What was developing for him was not the role of a rebel or of a political advisor, but rather that of a quack doctor. The only virtue of the overgrown child that he had before him was his insanity. Subissoni sneered at the television.

Oddino was waiting for an answer. His face was shaken even though his eyes pierced through it as through a mask. The light inside the room suddenly increased because outside it had started to snow. The three of them noticed it all at once and looked around themselves for an instant as though their positions might have changed. The brightness inflated that big room beyond its measurements, and the uncovered gestures of those three increased the theatrical character of the meeting. The television screen no longer reflected anything, suffocated as it was by the thickness of the new light.

Subissoni moved forward to take a closer look at Oddo and started playing a more worthy role: "I was expecting from you the proposals of a lord determined to reassume his command! The courage of a pretender, supported by all the reasons for the very existence of this city. Why must we renounce even the idea of being able to change our destiny, and be afraid, and abandon even within ourselves the obligation to fight for such an outcome? I was hoping that you would want to place yourself at the head of a formation sustained by this commitment. Instead you even avoid talking about it. I'm not saying today or tomorrow, but within a season something could come to maturity! It's beating even beneath this snow: inside here I hear it resonating above every vaulted room! These books are waiting for men who having read them will know how to follow through with their ideas. Isn't this the Country of the Prince? Haven't they all waited, at least those of pure heart, for Don Quixote finally to be right and to be able to encounter and defeat enemies and diseases? Did Dante really walk through hell? What did Galileo see through his pieces of glass?"

Oddino stiffened up now and in the hollow dimples on the sides of his mouth his astonishment was condensing and would soon turn to anger. Even Subissoni read his impression and changed his tone to a more didactic one: "It would have been sufficient for us to stage the first act; put it on in front of the people... and perhaps withdraw immediately afterward. Inscribe the first letter. I can tell you that only some cultural bastards used Rome as a measurement for Italy, and, what's worse, imperial Rome. This boot has been shod only by the power structure, never by a lord and his people, much less by the people alone!" He was animated by his own image. "Why can't we come together and proclaim that Urbino and her territory would be better off on their own? We would only need to break our subjection to a principle that has been imposed on us like a sacrament; to unmask the lie that sustains it. Athens, Sparta, Rome, Albalonga were free cities. Did Socrates or Aristotle ever think about the unification of nations? The proper size is the city. Against this, depicted and described by centuries of city civilizations, a small ignoramus with some French stuffing wanted a colony for his king, a colony. Urbino, Rome, Venice, Naples, Florence, colonies of Turin, or better, of the Count of Savoy. Unity of the people. Never, never. Only in armies, in penitentiaries, in the stinking hold of a ship, in courts of law. Unification of production, of commerce, of culture? Never, never. Ah! if the communists would only fight city by city! If they would drop the myth of the great production platform! If before private property they would fight directly against the sham of political unity: there, in its wrinkles is hidden the virus of monopolistic power. So much so that the country has decayed to the point where even the oppositions have been dragged down and overrun... even the center of culture; even the nature of punishment has been altered, injustice… even misery, the teacher of so much liberty. Almost everybody – but for sure the lower classes, the middle classes, the imitators of the middle classes, who are as far removed from the advantages as from the shrewdest wrong doings of the power structure – is waiting anxiously now for a signal, a star, a teacher, a head… anybody… so that it would be sufficient for someone to shout a little louder, independently or within the context of a performance, and everyone would start listening to him and following him too, if the latter would move… even if with a fake beard, or crown, or saber, or industrial scepter, wheel or wheelbarrow whatsoever…. It could even be a standard-bearer, a song, a trickster, a novel, provided that it be announced by a shouting courier, by a witch doctor or a school teacher for everybody to pay attention. From an impossible republic… for a moment… to a prince, contrary to history; and then from the prince… move indeed to a pseudo-popular dictatorship, a necessary step toward a popular democracy."

Oddino stepped back and lowered his hands. "What do you want from the communists? What do you want from me, trembling as you do, like a defrocked priest? Giocondini," he appealed, "why have you brought me this revolutionary with the excuse of the edict? I am already in command. In Urbino everyone is already devoted to me and obeys me. I am just looking for a girl dressed in green. My power is my family and if it will be possible for me I will also do something for Urbino and for…." He stopped talking as though he had been intimidated by this proposal. "Where are my aunts?" he asked himself between his big lips. "Where are they? That they shouldn't hear these discussions!" He looked at the door and the two windows up high toward the hallway. He reassured himself by considering the door of the prison that he had temporarily imposed upon the aunts and almost smiled: "I know how to keep order, I do. I don't like the carabinieri and I never see the police in the streets doing their duty; but I also don't like

269

the bomb-carrying anarchists. Are you an anarchist or a communist? What kind of edict would you have liked to prepare? To whom would you have appealed to find the kidnapped girl? What would you have promised? In what way would you have committed me? What would you have written to frighten the kidnappers?"

He became sad and lowered his head, slowly, helping himself with his hands, as though he had to move a head of stone. His lower lip hung down, damp and dejected, while his hands were joined on the first circle of his thorax, which was rounded off in three distinct sections before his belt line. "I attach no importance to Italy, nor to all her cities. I have lost lands closer to me and more mine. There is an Italy, here and there, and I travel there… and I have always come back thinking that I was better off. But now I no longer could… That girl," he said, "is very important for me and for my family. With her nearby I could begin. This palace thunders under my footsteps and in the night it trembles to the point of frightening the thrushes in the garden. I want Dirce brought back to me."

"Why?" asked Subissoni touched by that shapeless grief.

"Because she's mine, because no one must take her from me… and because she would also help me to command, if that is what she wants."

"But you, are you in love with her?" Gaspare was trembling between jealousy and pity.

Oddino lifted his head back up and opened his eyes so wide that they became round and blocked off as though they were not supposed to see or even be seen. He did not answer. An intention was moving his lips, but he was unable to open them.

"Do you love her? asked Gaspare again. "Do you care for her? Would you know how to make her happy?" After having said those words he once again was befallen by a feeling of shame.

Oddo did not increase that shame because he did not respond. Giocondini mumbled something about the duty of one who writes, to write according to the will of his patron and without too many questions. He said something about the style, but even Oddino understood, without listening to him, that he was talking about things he didn't know anything about and wouldn't even be able to tell apart. Subissoni turned toward him, challenging him with his look.

"You're not proposing a government," said Giocondini, "you're proposing a revolution! A mixture between communism and anarchy. And all this because you can't write an edit," he pronounced without the "c," "an edit so that they'll bring back the fiancée and understand that she is indispensable for our lord and for his plans for the lordship and, therefore, for the whole city. Why do you want to take advantage of the situation by bringing the communists into the picture?"

Subissoni was irritated but was able to swallow his hate for the greasy servant, all made out of half moons of fat and sweat. He heard the screeching on the distant sky of crows, chased off by the snow, who were returning from the countryside to their nests on the ancient bell towers.

That screeching and flying, way up, in an unnatural way, in the sky over Urbino, for quite a while now, he had taken as a sign of the decadence and of the Italianization of the city: stuff from Piedmont, from Basilicata.

"How right you are," said Subissoni, "You're right! It's true, I'm bringing the communists and the anarchists into the picture. How true and how prophetic you are! If at least, in fact, they were the same thing. Or, better yet, the communists should disappear. Disappear not as revolutionaries, but as unitarians, with their religion of the masses, and also of the nation, which is in principle contrary to every community. You're right, the communists must be beaten and made to understand that the idea of nation is old, the product of military and industrial power. England, Spain, France, Germany, in their turn, and now America, have always made the rest of the world pay the expenses of their unification. Italy, more stupid and inferior, dumped it on herself like a kettle of boiling water. Unification is the terrain of monopoly. Marxism did not understand this, perhaps because it is intrinsic in unification, that is in the centralized state, and in the industry that prospers arrogantly therein. What a fine trinity. These crows are proclaiming it. Can you hear? Screech screech, screech... what a fine trinity! And my purpose here was, in fact, to break it, write an edict indeed. The girl is outside the trinity; she is somewhere praying against it. I was here to find her and to entrust her to someone who could in some way, even if as a joke, fight against the trinity of power, chase away its messenger crows. Now, however, its all clear to me, because if I don't recognize power, I do recognize its servants."

Subissoni was exalted by his clever line and searched between his hands for Vivés's invisible but solid coin, for a confrontation that would encourage him even more.

Oddino said nothing and went to sit down gravely in his armchair. An enormous sigh accompanied him, as though he was conscious of subtracting himself from a reality... which, however, would return, implacable.

Giocondini tried, with one of the half moons between his head and neck – there where the Brilliantine gets mixed up with sentiment – to assume a threatening pose toward that crazy old man; and he even moved closer and with his eyes popping out of his head. He had understood the heresy from his tone, from his gestures, even though he had not understood the meaning. With rancor he extracted some words of threat and with threat some others of rancor.

Subissoni stepped back, feeling sure of himself by then. "It's the servants who work for the masters and who make them feel like masters even to themselves, even against their own nature. And the servants go on pretending that there is always a master. Look at the Christian Democrats today. What do they do other than serve, serve, serve a nonexistent master? Why do they keep this unification on its feet other than to serve it and revere it... without understanding any reason for it?" He abandoned Giocondini and went to take a look at the books.

"Even the bombs," he said – excited by the red bindings in Moroccan leather of some collections – "they're placed by servants! But is the male dancer a servant?" he asked more slowly. He looked at the television. And once more he looked for Vivés's coin.

"Please excuse me," he said after a pause, I'm very sorry. There has been a misunderstanding, and I am certainly to blame. I'm getting too old." He had turned toward Oddino. The latter in his amazement had become quiet and was looking toward the screen of the still silent apparatus.

"Have no regrets for that girl," said Subissoni forcing himself to show his good eye. "Perhaps she wasn't kidnapped; perhaps she went away on her own: she may have been afraid of your power. I can also tell you that you will soon find another, even more beautiful and noble, on your level. May I come some time," he added to render less difficult his leave-taking and also out of a fondness for that place which had illuminated him and brought him closer to his little truth, "to see this library, to examine the books that are here?"

Oddino answered yes, and assented with his head too, before entrusting himself once more to his easy chair.

The brightness of the room diminished, while the three men were no longer together. Subissoni kept toward the outside in order to reach the door, to observe Oddino to the end while avoiding Giocondini.

Oddo's face was getting darker and sinking into the shadow, which had overtaken the middle of the big room. The light that was still coming through the large high windows focused on the television screen, which reclaimed its presence – the very sound of metal, with which the door opened behind his back, seemed to Subissoni like a command from that apparatus. The hallway was empty, with its cracking plaster and swollen beams one after the other above some unreachable paneling.

Turning the corner, Subissoni found before him Giocondini who had taken the small rear door in order to come and see him out. At the street door Subissoni bowed and smiled at Giocondini's livid salutations; with an even greater sense of irony he contemplated his victory and the destiny that he had assigned to himself and that was already awaiting him.

Finding the street, the walls, the light snowfall, which was still spreading a few flakes around, was for Gaspare almost unbelievable, and it gave him a little feeling of happiness. He walked at a brisk pace, boldly, as far as the Pincio. From the broad summit of this place the city descended, subdued and tidied-up by the snow's geometry according to the sloping order of the roofs and streets. From the emptiness came a light, disheartened noise.

Gaspare turned toward the piazza of the Ducal Palace but found that empty too and almost invisible because of the fog that had come up with the first gusts from the direction of the sea.

He thought nostalgically about Dirce and squeezed once again with certainty Vivés's coin – this coin between his fingers was miraculously firm and bright across the whole piazza, beyond the fog.

Further ahead the obelisk in front of San Domenico's appeared before him with a haunted look, which expanded with the image of an ugly dream, with its stone getting slowly bigger. It was getting wider, and yet it was pointing, but it didn't have anything to do with his new plans, nor with Vivés, nor with the glory of that moment. It was an encounter and a painful recognition – the copy of an ancient Urbinoite fear. At closer look, the yellowish monolith, although of African origin, shined through the snow with the same color and the same fixity as the young Oddo. Their solemnity and their symbols remained as vague as they were hard in the framework that they imposed upon themselves.

Subissoni got up his courage and approached the monument. He placed his hand on it, trembling... but with clemency... with the clemency of a pat... on the round head of a column at the base.

Meanwhile Oddino had turned on the television and was listening to the Sunday Mass being celebrated in San Ciriaco's, the cathedral of Ancona. He had liberated his aunts, who were now kneeling at his side, still with many worries. Oddo regretted that since he had already seen that stone church on top of Ancona he did not receive any stimulation for another trip.

Giocondini was at the back of the big room with no orders or commands, but, little by little, according to the liturgy that dragged him mechanically along, he pulled up some of his half moons and began thinking about how to convince Oddino to enroll in the Christian Democratic Party. Finally, as they were all getting back up, liberating knees and sighs, he decided, in any case, to put forward the request for a membership card in the name of the young Oddi. This decision gave him a lift and relaxed all his bowels and bladder – all of which had been upset by the voices of that nasty morning – even more than the rubbing he gave himself and the belch that he succeeded in emitting with his final morsel of devotion. He felt his mind at ease, and also his stomach, which was already looking forward to Sunday dinner.

23

Subissoni arrived in Piazza della Republica while everybody was preparing to leave it, heading home for midday dinner: already the fringes of the lower-class groups were going down toward Valbona and Lavagine and even the circles under the minor loggia were thinning out. This displeased him because he would have liked to have circulated among that society and communicated in some way his own opinions and the latest revelations of that cornice of dead time, left to turn pale with its varnish... right over his head. He stood looking from above, leaning against the iron railing of the civic clubroom, and in a few minutes he saw the piazza become completely depopulated. Only a couple of professionals, perhaps with their families in the mountains, were left talking in front of the entrance to the school. Then they too disappeared behind their various words.

The empty piazza was invaded by the fog that had come up suddenly and all at once from Lavagine, as though it had had to wait quite a while for that moment. This caused a feeling of nostalgia to pervade the mind of Subissoni who left the railing to go toward the piazza with his arms outstretched, almost as though he wanted to impede that invasion and that disappearance, which he was forced to witness. He was disoriented and yet he stopped in the center of the piazza – in the center, wherever that place might be in which an external force had placed him. By breathing heavily and concentrating on every breath that he took, he was gradually able to recognize that the energy was his, accumulated by him throughout his whole life, and that now it was gushing forth to help him, to be finally used and spent.

It was right, he thought, while considering that revelation, that he was alone, that he had no dinner table, that he choose his own place, that Urbino disappeared in the fog, that Vivés was dead, that Oddo was a demented ignoramus, that Christmas was celebrated, and that the poor people had humbly –

rubbing their hands grateful for whatever heat they had –
taken routes that were different from those of the upper
classes; that that stage was not at all unified and did not
repeat the same lines every day; it was right that the fog,
which had come from who-knows-where had soaked the
scenery and the rain had torn it down. He associated the
rain with that which bathed the fields of his dream.

He raised his head for a second. Only the pigeons were
cooing on some of the cornices, but at least at that level
there were no crows screeching. He threatened the silent
crows with his fist in the air toward the bell towers where
they were nested, penetrating during each of their periods
of rest ever deeper into the walls and the garrets until they
destroyed and devoured the nesting places of the pigeons
and also of the mice. He was conscious of that fist, of the
defiance that exceeded his irony. He pronounced a few words
against the crows, grating them between his throat and his
teeth, as he thought the crows must do with the great vo-
cabulary of the crow's beak, which, as is well known and
heard, consists entirely of words that end with gry, for example liber...gry, civili...gry and all verbs that begin with gr...for
example, gr...ating, gr...easing, gr...verning, gr...gramming,
gr...abbing. He repeated these words with happy buoyancy,
conquering them in the same moment. After Giordano
Bruno or Pisacane it had always seemed base and inappropriate to him to say "revolution," as though that would be
using something that was someone else's and was strictly
connected with and linked to them. And yet he had fought
for the meaning of some dicta that, for him, were unpro-
nounceable.

In that liberating moment he assigned the blame for his
own reticence to his long, constant attention to history,
which could have consumed for him the present meaning of
those words.

Was he perhaps beginning to understand – with his blind
eye regaling the crows and with the other, the live one, fluttering toward the invisible pigeons – that he had been deprived of those words by his own social extraction, by his

whole childhood behind his mother's skirt, in a skirting game of affections, of suspicions, of pulsations, of penalizations; and then by the terrible two-part school, pupil-teacher, by his very ability in Latin; by his whole youth, by the light of opaline lamps and of curtains, made of temptations and of shams, with its interior language so private and at the same time so capable and quick in defining and burning simultaneously any external object, sentiment or view that it could be read at a glance, swallowed with just a slight taste of remorse or irony? And already with the consciousness of amassing the guilt of those tasteless meals for future judgment.

Subissoni had always been afraid of the theater, so much so that as a child when he was invited to try out for a play he was overcome at the entrance by an attack of convulsions. He had always been distrustful of novels and always hated the opera as the highest expression of national vulgarity. He had considered it – in its vulgar corruption of the purity of the music of other times – as a consumer product emblematic of the quality of national unification. In any case, even before articulating this judgment, much before, he had hated anyone who was able to sing. Especially if in a loud voice, and even more if in a group or in a choir. He had put his own bombast into his search for maximum freedom and into his own fugue.

He heard the pigeons cooing again and this time in harmony with himself. Then he thought about Dirce, who was hidden in his house and who was waiting for him and who had nothing to eat. This feeling for Dirce immediately revived for him, but with the jolt of an erroneous print: his image of Vivés, which he never let go of. However, he would have to raise it up from that implicit expanse of sublime dust, with which she had covered over all his potential. That's why he had always felt Vivés close by, like a stroke of good fortune, which was wasted on him, and with a presence that intimidated more than appeased him, because he was never able to feel as if he was on an equal level of interaction with her. And he had never understood the renunciation she endured to live with him,... as proof of her great pity, in addition to her love! He felt a bitter resentment toward Urbino, miserable as it was. What a hard imposition it must have been for her!

And that's where he had let himself get covered over with the very dust of the Oddi family. Indeed where he had nurtured his attraction to Oddo and the madness of his project.

In his fury he forgot to go and get something to eat, and he stumbled hastily off, with a few running steps, because he wanted to bring along, intact, out of the destruction of that hour, the scandalous spectacle of the consciousness that he was able to give to himself, to Vivés, to the pigeons, to Dirce. The fog bathed the waving folds of his overcoat and he tried to hold them down. Even the pavement of the loggia and then of the Pincio beat under his steps with a note of incredulity. He shivered to think that that very morning he could have considered placing himself at Oddo's service and entrusting his plan to him. He thought back to the obelisk in front of San Domenico, a monument of one faith, raised back up after more than three thousand years in the service of another!

He had to get back inside his house as quickly as possible, where he would be able to analyze, without fear of any encounters, the result of that examination, which finally he was able to give himself. He tried to distract himself while he was walking, in order to prevent himself from undoing the examination and its results with a too-hurried rational arrangement, which then would be much too vulnerable to the shots from his head at the next test, when, once more, he would be looking for perfection, entrusting himself to the game of every possible comparison, according to every rhyme or noise.

Walking, reducing the distance to the door of his house was his first conquest. He arrived full of emotion and waited a moment with the key in his hand before opening it. He took three deep breaths and then went in. He found Dirce standing in front of the sink. The girl's mouth was white now, twisted with uncertainty, and she was demoralized in

PAOLO VOLPONI

that domestic position, as though she had been looking for something to do and hadn't found anything.

Subissoni understood and overcame that uncertainty with his new strength, which now enabled him to look at things. Dirce was there, and real, even though she had her back turned to the house in a shadow of uselessness; and her presence was sufficient to establish proof of her reality.

"Don't worry about anything," he said right away, addressing her informally. "There's nothing to eat, but I'll go out in a minute to get something. I wanted to first tell you that I saw the young Oddi and you are right; he's not for you and he can't do anything for me either."

"We were wrong together," he went on while taking off his coat, "but we can make up for it, exactly because we realized it before putting ourselves in the service of their fallacy, which would have been irreparable. Like all the others that they have always committed! All irreparable, for them."

Dirce looked at him with amazement but calmly, partly because she too could make use of her own rapport with the words: she could let them go away, while her attention was entrusted to the face and to the gestures of the person who was talking, or she could become completely distracted by the sounds. In the first case, she could be moved by her attraction to or fear of the interlocutor, make a note of them and even remember some of them; but if she lost herself in the assonances, she just played around with them in her head to the point of being forced to think about her own concerns and fantasies or even to start moving in a kind of dance.

"I say 'them,'" continued Gaspare, "because Oddi is the same as so many others, similar to all those who command, and in the end he acts according to their rules."

He explained with conviction and with gentleness: "These enchanted people, if they're not truly crazy, are never alone, as it seems; they endure the silent company of crowded gesticulating people. Silent because we don't hear their messages: maybe the enchanted people hear them. In fact, they hear them for sure because they obey them." He stopped and smiled and for this reason Dirce got ready to pay attention.

"We can make things right," he started up again with a sparkle, "and do a good job of it, at least with our mistakes. Either alone or together." He suspended this last phrase with an uncomfortable feeling. "I mean that you could save yourself alone, if you want, or with me too. What is certain is that they are looking for you, dressed in green, and that if they find you they can really make your life difficult. That servant can't wait to be able to make someone else serve him. All you need to do is flee and I will be able to help you. But you must flee far away and to a place where they don't go and where they wouldn't think of looking for you – not as a housemaid, not in a convent, not with a seamstress, not on a farm,… in a factory, for example. Not Rome, but Milan."

Dirce left her place near the sink and walked around the table to the side opposite Gaspare. Against the light of the window her face was full of color and her perforated curls re-enforced Subissoni's magical talkativeness. Outside, the fog had lifted and it had started snowing again. Then Gaspare thought back a little, in his victorious head, and affirmed: "I figured out a lot of things this morning, after having seen that obelisk, and before that the dust. I considered easy," he wanted to make it simple for Dirce and also for himself, in order to establish a defense, material and real, like that window sill before the snow, "easy…," he repeated, "even useless… with a superior attitude… the simple things that people believe in – the words that still get people worked up," he said with more liveliness, "I believed that they were surpassed by my cultural superiority, by my cultured impatience, by my condescension…. I thought they were worn out… and instead they are real – they are in the actions as well as in the spirit of the people – in their hands as well as in their mouths…." He sat down all heated up, and with a gesture he invited Dirce to sit down too. Dirce obeyed, and her curls had a smell for her teacher.

Gaspare took in that smell of straw and went on: "Maybe because I was driven by impatience, because I felt that I was superior, because I knew what was the right prescription for Italy... it had already been there, beautifully written out, for so many years... if someone had only known how to read it. But nobody knows how to read anymore; nobody takes the trouble to read anymore... they prefer the gramophone or the magic lantern... and since things were going in the opposite direction, in the hands of the crack-pots, I broke off... instead of throwing myself in and taking up and defending those major truths, which really must be defended...." He got up and went to fiddle around with the espresso-maker. Dirce looked at him and understood that she shouldn't follow him. In fact, a moment later he came back and put the partially unscrewed pot on the table. He went back to get the coffee jar, opened it and dipped the spoon in.

Dirce showed her attention by saying: "There's no sugar."

"It doesn't matter," replied Gaspare. "It's not, however, that I haven't done anything...," and he looked at the stairs, toward Vivés's room, "anything at all. I fought, I let my suffering mature... if now I can say these things. I bought this house that is saving us, but I am also ready to leave it. What would I stay here alone to do? Or else should I stay here to protect you, you who would never be able to go out?"

He watched how strongly it was snowing. "I have to get going," he said with his head held high. "I have to get go-ing."

The second time was serious, with his blind eye shut as though every sign of life had left that wound. The compact light of the snow showed the lines of his face annulling every shadow: it revealed his anxiety, which accompanied the truth of his affirmation, in the brightness of his forehead, in the violet color that crept along the skin of his cheeks until it vibrated around his nose and his upper lip. The lower part of his face was, instead, dark and dry in a uniform way, drawn under his chin inside his collar.

Dirce stood up so that her savior could see her. She had no need to say anything. She had gotten up and this signified her adherence. Anyway, she added other gestures: she too paused for a moment to look at the snow; then she went and stood next to Subissoni, unscrewed the espresso-maker and handed him the part to be filled. Gaspare trembled as he put in the coffee and fled again with his eye toward the stairs. Dirce didn't understand that he was emotionally moved by what for her constituted only happiness; she feared that the trembling and detachment showed an uncertainty and so she spoke: "Okay," she said, "I'm agreed. We have to run away together, if we can't stay together here. For sure, it's better some other place, because I'll be able to go out and work."

She screwed the espresso-maker back together, arranged it on the burner and, after lighting it, turned around to smile. Subissoni stood for a few seconds near the stairway before turning to Dirce; when he did she broadened her smile.

They drank the boiling coffee seated next to each other, both of them blowing on it and every so often taking a noisy sip.

Finally Gaspare couldn't bear it any longer, he put his arm around the girl so as not to leave her in uncertainty and went to the shelter of his room. He threw himself on the bed to contain his exhaustion and his commotion. But after a lot of stressful thinking, in the midst of which was mixed his weakness and his grief, he found again the truth that he had discovered that morning and consequently how secure the decision was that derived from it. "Vivés had said it!" and with this conscious affirmation he felt himself restored at her side, as an equal. That Dirce downstairs, who was trying to make some noise to communicate her presence to him, was a creation of Vivés – alive and well as she knew people were... and with a need to defend herself, to run away from those tyrants, to find some companions and to work in peace.

Subissoni fell asleep and slept deeply for more than three hours. The cold woke him up, even though he found a blanket over him. He shivered a few times before noticing that it was already dark. He went to the window and saw that it was snowing and that the layer of snow on the vegetable garden, and even further away, still held some of the sparkle of the sunset. He walked around the room feeling numb and thoughtless. He couldn't even remember when it was that it had started snowing. The cold was painful for him and led him to consider each wall and piece of furniture in the room as though he had to check their suffering, with a bit of suspicion that they might be the cause of his.

His first internal reaction against that cold was his grief for the death of Vivés. He went to sit back down on the bed and wrapped himself in the blanket. He waited and endured stiffly, opening and closing his mouth, until that grief put order back into everything in that room and extended the windowsill to the snow. After that he started trembling, reclining his head gradually toward the memory that was overtaking him. He waited, before shaking himself off and getting himself back in motion, until he had recuperated all his blood; partly because he knew that he had before him a decisive time and a problem. What's more, he had to endure the lack of Vivés as punishment for having understood too late those fundamental truths for which she had died. He deserved to wake up and be alive only to be a witness of Vivés's truth and to serve her until the end with whatever strength he had left. He abandoned the bed and the blanket and started to go downstairs.

Dirce was waiting for him smiling at the bottom of the stairs, with a gesture of hiding something behind her back, which she quickly showed him. She had some fresh bread in one hand and in the other a can of meat. Out of kindness she did not react to the bewilderment that still was twisting Subissoni's mouth and preventing him from smiling at her playfulness and she said; "I went out while you were sleeping. I thought that with this weather there couldn't be any cars in the streets or gentlemen either. And then, I didn't wear my green dress. I put on a jacket and a hat, too, and I went alone to the closest bar. And then I'm twenty-three years old and I can do what I want and even report those who are harassing me. But rest assured that nobody saw me. I too had to do something, and it looked like you were going to be sleeping until tomorrow morning, judging from the way you were knocked out. I'm happy you woke up. I even found a couple of bouillon cubes to make some broth, because it was a bar that makes meals for the students."

The room was warm and from the window was coming that vivid brightness that snow has on holidays. A pot was boiling on the stove and the table was set for two.

Subissoni, who was slowly recovering, noted with a jolt that the table had been set like Vivés usually did it, with the two settings facing each other along the axis of the external wall, in such a way that each of them sat beside the window and could look out. He instead set the table in the other direction so as to have the stove more convenient and the door in front.

"Even when you eat you want to be moving around," Vivés would say to him, "worrying about the burners and the door, as though you were expecting someone... or as though you were afraid that they would wall it up on you."

That coincidence seemed too big to him to have been by chance – so much so as to weaken its sense of uniqueness. The suspicion was already swelling up that Dirce had done it on purpose to draw him into a trap. He wanted to walk past the girl to mess up that arrangement, and while going by her he caused her to drop the bread.

24

After the end of the Mass Oddino stayed there looking at the TV and with a gesture stopped his aunt, who dared to try to turn it off. He continued pursuing the cloth of that mind that was unfolding, just like his, without being able to compose a picture or an idea – that produced a light that burned without reaching far enough to touch anything. He got up when they called him for dinner and not even then did he turn off the set, intending to leave it in that state of impotence as punishment: in spite of knowing so much, it hadn't been able to help him against Dirce's kidnappers and not even against Subissoni. After eating he stood for a moment by the door of the library to hear it sizzling and scraping. And what's worse, during dinner he had started worrying that in his house there might be some secret doors and someone probably knew about their existence and use.

He asked his aunts not to leave the room, he reassured them and urged them to see to some tea and hot water, and then he started his rounds. The back doors were closed – and also the ones to the garden. He looked for quite a while at the trees and at the flower beds: the birds had held a banquet and left the berries and seeds of holly and laurel all over the pavement. At that hour they had flown away and only just before dusk would they be back. In the meantime, he would have to find what he was looking for. He checked the kitchen carefully, the pantry, the storage closet and the library too. Here, so as not to be distracted, he turned off the television. He continued along all sides of the downstairs hallway and then went into the science room.

This was the one place in the house, along with his aunts' rooms, where he spent the least time: he had never used instruments or tools, not even the fret saw. What's more – just like his aunts' rooms – that large room kept the presence of the family more alive from the past: the smell, the distances between one thing and another in an arrangement that was still alive and prepared for a wait that he was never able to understand and to measure. In there he was not capable of searching. He lingered a moment with his gaze on the alembics; he passed his hand over the globe and, once again, he was intimidated for reasons that were lost to him in the face of some superior obligation.

Some birds had come back to the garden. Their flights were interrupted by the snow, and one was fluttering near the windows, as though it, too, was in search of an opening. Oddo ran upstairs into the room that had been Dirce's, but nothing had been changed since he himself had locked it up. In front of the curtain of the window that was closed he cursed the mechanical Nativity scene and once again became angry at his aunts, to the point of thinking about going and imprisoning them again. At this point, however, while prolonging his anger toward other people, young Oddo began painfully to fear that the reason for Dirce's running away might lie in himself. He was unable to search for her according to her appearance, and it was much more difficult for him to search for her according to her status and her upbringing. Even that crazy old man had made it clear that it was his fault, and not because of his face or of his behavior.

He continued looking around the house with disillusionment and rancor. Perhaps the anarchist was a little right. He had not been able to understand even one bit of any of those possible reasons, and inside him there had remained a troubled confusion, within which he now could find a desire to see and to talk once more with Subissoni. He thought that he might be the only person capable of having him find Dirce or, even better, of making her come back.

In the upstairs hallway, opposite the door of that room there was the seventeenth-century portrait of a scholar – painted in a three-quarter pose, on a slightly-bigger-than-life scale – with his eyes planted directly on the painter and, therefore, on any successive interloper, with an air of challenge, reabsorbed, however, by a higher and more skeptical clairvoyance marked by the red that elongated his eyebrows toward his temples. Oddo was blocked by that look. He stood there in front of it without closing the door of the room for at least a half-hour to consider that novelty.

When his aunts, who had apprehensively listened as he made all his rounds, no longer heard his steps, they could not hold themselves back and hastened to the stairs to call him, but he did not answer. They looked in his room and in the other rooms, dragging themselves desperately and breathlessly along, and then they embraced each other so as not to fall when they saw him out of the corner of their eyes at the end of the corridor.

"Oddino, Oddino," they threw themselves at him crying and covering him with kisses, "why are you suffering so much?"

Oddino happily accepted their embrace, and the fact that he did not resist increased the passionate outburst of his aunts. "Poor little bird," they said still crying, "why are you suffering and why are you making us suffer? We'll go barefoot to look for that girl – barefoot through the snow. And afterward when you have her, you can even punish us for the fault that you have found in us. Now, little bird, try not to suffer."

"Calm down," said Oddino. "No fault and no punishment. Let's go downstairs." Arm in arm the three of them went down the stairs to sit in unity at the round coffee table on which the tea water had gotten cold.

"No suffering," said Oddino, "I'm looking for.... I would like to know more about some things: Until now I have only seen."

"That's right, that's right," said his aunts. "But you have so much time ahead of you. You're barely about to reach your majority."

He was encouraged by the discovery of the painting that depicted a certain Origine, and he was thinking about Subissoni with a bit more clarity. If he had eliminated the left eye of that portrait with an ink spot Origine and the professor would have been equal.

"Do you know," he asked, "where Professor Subissoni lives?" But his aunts, even more worried by this question, did not know what to answer.

"It doesn't matter," said Oddino, I'll find him myself." He looked outside and added: "Now it's snowing, and in a while it will be dark. Tomorrow."

Some other birds arrived in the garden, with flights so rapid and direct that they shook the snow from their chosen tree and even rattled the glass in the windows of the last sitting room.

Meanwhile a crow, who that morning had ventured further away than the others, flying against the wind on his return, was unable to reach the bell towers and the large cornices of the center, and so he went, in silence, to rest on a less-snowy part of the Oddi's roof, beside the chimney.

Dirce had set the table hoping that her protector would wake up in time for supper. She wanted to give him a nice surprise with the things to eat and she wanted to hear him talk some more. As soon as it got dark she made some noise around the stove and also up the stairs as she went to put away the clothes that she had used. A short while later she joyfully heard the professor at the bottom of the stairs. Finally she saw him looking chilly and foggy, but her joyful sense of hope was stronger than his comportment. She showed her surprise and told the whole story.

She was still excited about the story when Subissoni came awkwardly forward, almost against her, so that he made her drop the bread from her right hand. While she was bent over to pick it up, she feared that she might have mistaken everything and she stayed down there to hide her desire to cry. A hand from the man landed rather heavily on her shoulder; but it was to help her get back up. She did but with such trepidation that it shook her whole face and affected Subissoni more clearly than words. The old man staggered and abandoned all suspicion and even all the uncertainties that had followed his awakening.

He hugged Dirce and thanked her. He worried that some-one might have seen her, but right away even he agreed about their strength in addition to their right and laughed about the idea of reporting them.

"Let's report only the servant," he said, "not the obelisk. The obelisk stays there."

He let Dirce indicate where he should sit and she promptly assigned him the place near the stairs, with the window on his left and the door on his right. This, too, troubled him, but it was an opportunity to react and to understand that he must not give in to his own character; that even in that moment he could find the entanglements of his own faults, perfectionism and skepticism – the ropes to tie him up with again and suspend him forever from that ceiling, or into some bottomless pit... or pity.

So he defied the ceiling and also the wood of the door. He considered the light from the window and the gleam on the dishes, swearing to himself, grumbling in agreement with the ancient discourse of the pot. He was shaking so much that he almost pulled the table apart.

"Things...," he said, dragging his voice, "at this point! Only things now. I can't go back to frittering time away or to shedding my skin like a snake, since I wouldn't change anyway. My decision has to be made rapidly against my own self. We have to leave!... Immediately, soon, tomorrow. We have to go to Milan, to Milan... if not we'll imprison our-selves here forever, till we collapse, till we hate each other. I have had an example, a big example. Either I take a risk, and maybe die because of it, or I become a servant."

Dirce had remained standing in the position in which he had embraced her. She entrusted herself completely to the enchantment that the gestures and the sing-song of that man gave her. "To Milan...," she repeated, "...to Milan."

"Yes, to Milan. We'll work together and we'll look the reality of this world in the face, and we'll fight. You can get into a factory, me in a school or in a... newspaper, or in a union."

Dirce agreed and began getting supper ready.

They ate eagerly, passing the dishes to each other, confirming with each gesture their mutual decision and the urgent need to put it into action. When he was filled with food Subissoni calmed down and started thinking carefully. "Tomorrow is Monday, and I can withdraw the money from my account. That's all that needs to be done. Tuesday is the last day of the year and we run the risk of not finding a seat on the train. Tuesday we'll get ready and we'll close out the year in Urbino, with a bottle of champagne. Meanwhile I'll call a taxi from Pesaro, because the ones in Urbino would tell Giocondini. Maybe it's better to telephone on Wednesday morning, around eight. At nine we could leave – anyway I'll look at the train schedules for Milan."

They got to the end of supper exhausted and noticed that the water on the stove had boiled up and evaporated and that they had forgotten to put in the bouillon cube to make the broth. They laughed for a long time, holding hands under the table. Subissoni got up to take care of it and went to get the bottle of anisette. While opening the cupboard he turned his thoughts directly to Vivés, with pride and pain. He stomped his feet on the floor and looked at the window so as not to see the bottle right away. It was still snowing, thick and calm, and it seemed like the streams of snow reached the base of the lamp on the table. He filled the glasses almost to the brim and gestured a toast as he threw down almost all of his in one gulp. Dirce impulsively imitated him. Immediately after her Subissoni finished off his glass and sprayed a reddish gleam from his blind eye; "The books!" he said. "I mustn't forget some of the books. We'll have to take along a little trunk. They are my weapons," he pronounced with emphasis. "Yours are your innocence and your youth. I'm just afraid that I'll spoil your individuality!" he said a moment later while looking at the snow, "the wonderful individuality of youth."

He moved and drank some more. "The books, the books, I have to start picking out the ones to take along. The useless ones, and also the painful ones, and also the indulgent ones must be left behind. By the way, even the individuality that youth sometimes concedes is an indulgence, it's a sin that subtracts from life. Even my Leopardi committed it and was unable to live long enough to be able to mend his ways. But he, however, did write – and not for self-commiseration, but for a great banner. I'll read Leopardi to you when we're in Milan and then you'll do whatever seems right to you."

He turned and went toward the stairs with out-stretched arms, groping worse than ever on the side of his blind eye. Dirce tried to help him, but after the first set of stairs she passed out and fell inebriated at his feet. Gaspare understood what was the matter and arranged her head better on the floor. Then he went to pour himself another glass of anisette and went back to drink it beside the girl. Before finishing it he went to get a pillow and two blankets. While taking care of those operations he felt himself strong, with a desire to drink some more. He went to drink another glass, half-way. He also closed the window-shutters and turned off the lights before going upstairs. He took another look at Dirce and called her. She opened her eyes once and immediately afterward turned the other way with a grimace of disgust. Gaspare drank a sip and went to sit on his bed with the door open in order to continue looking at Dirce, wrapped up in the blanket.

Dirce woke up half-way through the night, when she heard a strong wind. Gaspare was snoring, and she got up slowly to go to bed, but then she didn't dare go into that other room, which must have been his wife's – judging by the clothes and by the way he stopped to think in front of it and by the way he paused silently inside. She laid down beside his bed, but she didn't sleep anymore for the rest of the night and not at dawn either. She squeezed the happiness of having found that man and compared those two days, that would never end, with those that she had spent with the Leopard and even before that.

In Milan, if necessary, she would practice even that profession! She turned around to get warmer and felt a touch of nostalgia for Oddo – how she had met him and got to know him the first day. Who knows if in Milan even he could always be kind and affectionate in that way. She heard the wind calm down, and it was for her a confirmation of that hope. Then she got up, partly because she would have been embarrassed to let Subissoni find her stretched out there by his bed. Downstairs it was dark, and she opened the window. The wind had cleared things up and a little sun lapped at the highest peaks of the snow drifts. The crows were back in action, screeching as they flew in flocks toward the direction of the sun. Dirce stood and watched them for a moment in their victorious manner, taking pleasure in the reflections that they sent sharply, toward the ground, because she had nothing against them.

When the wind died down, Oddo woke up too, still troubled with doubts – he had heard a little noise on the roof right over the ceiling of his room.

The crow of the Oddi-Semproni house had inspected the new surroundings with a few steps toward the gutters, and then, satisfied, he had thrown himself back in flight to join up with the front line of his companions above the Mercatale. In the arrogance of his thrust he had displaced an earthenware vase and produced the noise heard by Oddino. The latter had thought that it could have been the birds – the usual migratory ones that sheltered themselves in the garden. But they didn't need to see the rising sun to know that it was a good day to get back in flight, because, being perceptive and courageous, they anticipated the weather with certain organs and feelings, and by that time they were already on the first buttresses of the Apennines, already searching, during their first stop, for some remaining juniper berries and acorns, so that they would have greater strength and be able to climb up the Nerone through the Piobbico and Serravalle gorges.

Oddo did not leave his bed, searching there for another place where he could get rid of some of his doubts. He consumed the breakfast that his aunts brought him and meanwhile asked them for information about that portrait of

Origine. His aunts said that it must have been in the house for more than three centuries, having arrived as a gift to the poet Gian Leone from some Neapolitan academy, or perhaps from the Grand Duke of Tuscany. There should also have been, if Clelia's memory didn't fail her, a letter from the painter addressed to the poet Semproni. It was a rather impudent letter, in which this Salvator Rosa, after he learned of the destination of his work, asked for its restitution, adducing that he could not tolerate that a painting of his – all the more so in the case of a self-portrait – could stay there living beside a poet so whining and deprived of fancy and who would surely keep around books, things and persons equally whining and unsuitable, which would demoralize and discourage with their boredom the young and courageous Origine. That Salvator Rosa must have been half-crazy, and, in reality, no one for over a hundred years had ever wanted to buy that painting of his – not even the Parisian antique dealer and not even, a few years ago, that younger one from Bologna who continually closed his eyes. "Because of that look," said Clelia, "and because of that ferocious mouth, that scare you."

Oddino smiled in satisfaction at that story and as soon as he was alone got up to go and take another look at Origine. He once again was troubled by him. He thought that he wasn't yet ready to see Subissoni again and to call him the very next day would be putting himself too much in his hands.

At noon Giocondini arrived to ask if they had any need of him and also to say in a subdued tone that he had no news about the girl. Oddino got up and got dressed in his presence. Encouraged by this Giocondini told him how shortly before he had seen that crazy Subissoni in front of the bank, pale as a dead man, shaking more than a cane, not knowing whether to go in or come out, and who, upon encountering him, had jumped backward, but then gave a big sour smile, as if to excuse himself, and finally ran off in embarrassment.

Subissoni had already gotten home with all the money and was studying with Dirce the way to divide it up among the suitcases, the little trunk of books, and the handbags. He also had a list of the hotels in Milan, which he had secretly made from the telephone book in the phone-compnay office. And he had the telephone number for the taxis from Pesaro.

The telephone call to Pesaro was the thing that worried him more than anything else, as though it was the consummation of all their actions. Who would have responded from the horrible unitarian piazza of Terenzio Mamiani?

He calmed down when it became clear that another suitcase, in fact a big one, was needed for those of Vivés's things that Dirce could use. So he was able to go out and release more pressure and come back with a suitcase that had another one inside it, inside of which were hidden some food supplies and also the bottle of champagne for the end of the year.

With all these new things arranged one beside the other on the table, Subissoni didn't go out for the rest of the evening and for the whole next day. He spent the time between one room and the other, often in pensive silence in front of the ready and still-open suitcases. He ate and drank very little – just a few mouthfuls standing up. Every so often he went upstairs to cry, in Vivés's room. Dirce understood and avoided going upstairs so as not to surprise him.

At noon on the thirty-first it started snowing again, with the consequent passage of crows. From the window of his room Subissoni became indignant, and this time raised both his fists against those flocks. Even Dirce understood that they were not benevolent birds and that their way of flying, in addition to their call, was arrogant, and she understood that those flocks had a disorderly dimension, that they unexpectedly thinned out or thickened this way or that way as if to threaten.

"There is the majority," shouted Subissoni, "there are the phony beards, the sub-history, the militias, the magistrates!"

Toward evening, Dirce caught Subissoni by surprise crying on the stairs, because he hadn't been able to get to his room in time. She hugged him and held him up until he got over it. She did not start crying, sustained by an awareness that if she did they would together have thrown away forever any chance of attaining their goals, even if they had reached Milan and the factories.

Afterward Gaspare looked at her and saw that her cheeks were wet with tears and noticed that they were made of gold and of mortar, the kind that pottery makers use or what children play with along the river banks.

It stopped snowing again and cleared up, but by then the crows had taken up their places and were stuffing themselves and pushing each other to infiltrate still further. Some were already devouring the smallest pigeons and throwing the remains onto the city streets; others, attracted by the light, went to drop their dung from the height of the domes onto the altars, others on the vestments, and many others on the tribunal benches.

The Urbino night had a few stars above its towers, but the rest of the city was sunk in darkness. People said hello only if they knew each other and exchanged greetings with sighs of uncertainty. No one knew of any dancing anywhere and only some well-to-do people planned to get together at a villa in the country.

Several citizens had stopped in front of the brand-new announcement on the municipal building where it was written that the City Council and the Mayor wished to express their hope that the New Year would be the bearer of liberty and justice, as well as of prosperity. "Bearer, bearer?" they were grumbling. "What does that mean? They're talking like priests now too?"

The regulars were sitting in the wineshops, with their berets in hand in front of their glasses of wine selected from among the best for the occasion. They paid for each sip with a reflection and for the whole glass by bowing their heads and saying some serious word, any one at all. The older ones had more irony, they chanced a few farts in the face of the government and summed up the most recent death processions in Urbino and the ones that could have been theirs: they looked menacingly at death imprisoned in their glasses.

Subissoni had arrived at midnight getting increasingly pale and excited. After some difficulty in uncorking the bottle of champagne, he said victoriously, "Long live 1970... new... and material."

The word "material" – which who-knows-when-and-where she had heard for the first time – gave Dirce a sense of wealth and protection.

"Long live the material," she too proclaimed, and Gaspare accepted that interpretation as the happiest of New Year's wishes.

The clear night lowered the temperature a few degrees below freezing and formed ice throughout the countryside and on all the roads.

The dawn was so subtle and clear that the bells of the sisters at Santa Chiara were heard at great distances. Subissoni was already up, half-dressed, with the electric light turned on, and reading to himself one by one all the things he had to leave behind.

His emotions were at the point of turning into fear. The view through the window seemed to him like a painted glass suspended precariously on the story of a dream that he had not completed. He stepped back and saw the wardrobe at the other end hardly touched by the light and still cozy. He went and leaned on it, on one end, in such a way that the door opened: the smell of the air inside it would have made him even more vaguely emotional if the stub of a pencil had not rolled to his feet with the movement of the doors.

Vivés must have used it just to keep the doors closed – one of those inventions of hers that were as precarious as they were perfect. And she enjoyed seeing them work, and sometimes for longer than the very object that she had re-paired. With two hairpins in France she had regenerated the resistance of an electric stove and before, in Africa, she had lengthened the area of their barracks with the carcass of an auto, getting a wheel to stay right at the level of the window, in such a way that it could be turned according to the most disparate eventualities – she, who was also more secure and exact than an Arabic numeral.

Subissoni picked up the piece of pencil and saw that it was still usable. So on the wall between the wardrobe and the door he wrote "January 1, 1970. Once again I am departing to escape from the same plague. Here within it would never have arrived, but it is I who must go and cure it."

He had scratched his fingers to get to the end of the pencil, which after the first words was scraping more than writing. He stuffed what was left of the stub in his pocket and, feeling refreshed, he went to close the window. He gathered the things that he was taking with him and piled them on the window-sill. He turned off the light and with an embrace he closed the wardrobe as best he could. Then he started down the stairs, with the small suitcase banging on every step. He let it go before reaching the bottom. Downstairs he got busy making coffee.

A little later Dirce joined him, already dressed, even with her shoes on. They carried down all the suitcases and deposited them by the door. Then Subissoni finished dressing in front of Dirce as though she was supposed to make sure he wasn't forgetting anything. It was time to go and telephone. Finally he put on his felt pads so that he would not slip on the ice; when he was ready he raised one hand toward Dirce while with the other he felt his way outside.

The tenuous colors of the early morning made him lost in thought, and his determination met no obstacles. He didn't see anyone – a tiny necklace of ice and sun encircled every part of the city, which stood still so as not to break it.

Subissoni also proceeded with composure, turning just enough to look at the most beautiful spots.

On the slope of the Vigne there was nothing to write this time, nothing at all. In a moment he would use the telephone.

No one answered his first call at eight o'clock. He went from one cafe to the other holding in his hand, even when he was drinking, Vivés's pencil stub. He went to make the second call from the phone-company office, at half past eight, and this time someone answered. He said precipitously that he had to take a train from Pesaro at 11:50 and that all the taxis in Urbino were taken and would they please come and pick him up. The driver expressed some perplexity about the road conditions and asked if it was still snowing. Subissoni said that everything was normal and that, in any case, given the necessity of the situation, he was prepared to pay a supplement. He gave the easy address of the mill bar to avoid making the driver worry about having to drive all over Urbino.

Back home he lovingly carried each bag, one by one, to the corner of the street next to the bar without ever making Dirce come out. He would have her get in afterward, with the car right in front of the door, or he would walk her down wrapped in a blanket if the car couldn't make it up to the door of the house.

He stayed by the baggage for an hour, stomping his feet on the snow. He turned his back to Urbino and scrutinized the sky: there were no crows in flight, partly because once again the sun had disappeared behind a mass of black clouds, which closed off the entire view to the east. He had hoped that this storm, the same as so many others, would not get there in time to block his departure from Urbino! When he saw the taxi coming up he threw open his arms and shouted out his name several times so the taxi driver would recognize him. The driver complained about the ice he had encountered, so Subissoni went to get Dirce with the blanket. No one saw them go by and get into the car.

Before taking the road to Pesaro, the taxi driver wanted to stop at a gas station to check the air in his tires, since he thought that going downhill on the ice was even more dangerous. When he got out of the car he heard some rifle shots nearby that alarmed him: "What's that?" he asked. "Who are they shooting at?"

"They're old shots!" said Subissoni. "They're shooting around up in the hills, and even they don't know why. It's hunting. They go on shooting at random! Old shots at those who want to go away, at those who pass by, at those who don't want to die with them, at those who are alive and who, therefore, are a threat against their lives."

It was just a little after ten when Giocondini knocked at the Oddi's door. Oddino had had another bad night, with his limbs scattered all over the bed and with his head on top, torn by the idea of entrusting himself to Subissoni.

He was thinking about having him live in his house – in the attic or in the science room. But he was leaning toward those conclusions with a sense of dejection, as though he were about to give up the use of one of his legs, which was already sticking out of the bed. He got a hold of himself thinking that, at least, it would be a choice: find an administrator, take up a position in Urbino and, beyond, find Dirce... or even another one.

It was necessary, what's more, to fix up the library and the science room and to see to the management of his family's possessions, all the more so because within a few days it would be his twenty-first birthday. In reality poor Oddo needed somebody, as he began to realize how lacking he was in education and above all in goals. He wanted to begin looking for the letter of that painter, which he thought might contain some interesting point, when Giocondini came into the room. When he saw Giocondini he became gloomy, already weary of having to listen to some proposal on how to spend the holiday or to take another trip. Instead Giocondini drove his message home so strongly that he almost shook him out of the bed. "I found her!" he said. "I figured it out! I know where the girl is. She was kidnapped and I know that she is being carried off to Pesaro. Do you know by whom? By Professor Subissoni. By our anarchist professor! Tied up in a blanket and loaded into a taxi from Pesaro, twenty minutes ago. I just found out from the gas station attendant where the taxi stopped. How come, he said to me, a taxi came from Pesaro? And he told me who was there.

That's what the professor wanted! He wanted to steal everything from you and then turn you over to the anarchists and the communists. He kidnapped the girl to get money from you and to have you at his mercy."

Oddo found himself intact under the force of the blow and, more than amazement or anger, his whole body felt instantaneous shame for having had until shortly before doubts about his own legitimacy. He felt sorry for himself, partly for the complicated plot to which he had been subjected. And this self-pity quickly changed into a pride as powerful as his gesture of pulling himself together and pulling himself out of bed. The size of the offense and its subtle perversion were the measure of his stature and the moral rectitude of his destiny. Finally, he found that it was even right to have doubted, because in that way he himself had been the first to recognize the depth of the trap that had been set for him.

He got up and got dressed without pronouncing a word, but with a haste that made everything clear, even to Giocondini.

"I have the car right outside, with the motor running."

Oddo smiled and left the room. He hugged his aunts and ran behind Giocondini, while giving a victorious glance toward the picture of Origine. The house escorted him, stair by stair, corner by corner: visibility was still good in Urbino and the Mercedes sailed off securely.

Oddo sat in front, as he always did, and nodded condescendingly at the walls and the embankments in which he recognized his victory by the way they pulled aside. Giocondini pushed the speed to its maximum, because he too did not want to miss this opportunity of winning forever. Besides, he knew that the Pesaro driver was fearful, and he was driving a Fiat with a small engine.

At the intersection of the road to Pesaro the black cloud in the east was already low. A little further downhill it unraveled into a fog through which the road was still visible, but it hid its dangers by preventing the ice from shining and from being recognizable.

Every so often, through the fog from the hills farthest away and highest up, a house stuck clearly out, and Oddo acknowledged it in the luminous confirmation of his state and in the imminent fulfillment of his happy destiny.

Around a curve there suddenly appeared a horse, alone, with a red harness hanging like a noose. Giocondini was able to avoid him with a yank at the wheel, and he was electrified even more by his own ability and by the security of the big car.

"In a little while the fog will lift," he said, "even before the plain. Before Pesaro perhaps we'll be able to overtake them."

Oddo didn't answer. He didn't like the plain, and as soon as they found Dirce he would have to go right back home, without even looking around. He would have to get back to his own environment, free it from every doubt and reorganize the palace, even the external views.

The fog, in fact, shortly afterward, lifted, held up high by the peaks of the last two hills of the town of Trasanni. A stretch of countryside opened up on both sides of the road that was still slightly downhill and with a dusting of snow. At the bottom a row of willow trees marked the curve.

Giocondini was quick to accelerate, squeezing together in his greed the half moons of his thick neck, and he went into the curve at a speed of sixty-five miles-an-hour. In that spot the ice had stayed compact like silver, the way the clear night had put it there, not even grazed by the snow or by the gusts of the sirocco. To Oddino it seemed like the tiny lake of a common Nativity scene, like those of his companions whom he had abandoned along with school.

Giocondini tried to take the curve by simply throwing himself on the wheel, but it slid under him, into his jacket and out of control – as useless as any of his half moons and the rotund ideas that from his head slid unfailingly down along his vest... and beyond.

*This Book Was Completed on August 24, 1994 at
Italica Press, New York, New York and Was
Set in Galliard. It Was Printed on 50 lb
Natural Acid-Free Paper with
a Smyth-Sewn Binding by
McNaughton & Gunn,
Saline, MI
U. S. A.*

* *

*